The Legacy of Arniston House

By T. L. Huchu

Edinburgh Nights series
The Library of the Dead
Our Lady of Mysterious Ailments
The Mystery at Dunvegan Castle
The Legacy of Arniston House

EDINBURGH NIGHTS
Book Four

The Legacy of Arniston House

T. L. HUCHU

TOR

TOR PUBLISHING GROUP

NEW YORK

THE LEGACY OF ARNISTON HOUSE

A Tor Book
Published by Tom Doherty Associates / Tor Publishing Group
120 Broadway
New York, NY 10271

www.torpublishinggroup.com

Tor® is a registered trademark of Macmillan Publishing Group, LLC.

The Library of Congress Cataloging-in-Publication Data is available upon request.

ISBN 978-1-250-88309-4 (hardcover)
ISBN 978-1-250-88310-0 (ebook)

Our books may be purchased in bulk for promotional, educational, or business use. Please contact your local bookseller or the Macmillan Corporate and Premium Sales Department at 1-800-221-7945, extension 5442, or by email at MacmillanSpecialMarkets@macmillan.com.

First published in Great Britain by Tor, an imprint of Pan Macmillan

First U.S. Edition: 2024

Printed in the United States of America

0 9 8 7 6 5 4 3 2 1

For
Rujeko Huchu

Principal Magical Institutions

Calton Hill Library, incorporating the Library of the Dead: These are Scotland's premier magical libraries, both located under Calton Hill in Edinburgh's city centre. Together, they house an impressive collection of magical texts and books. There is an entrance by the pillars of the National Monument of Scotland, on the summit of the Hill. Alternatively, there's a further entrance via David Hume's mausoleum in the Old Calton Burial Ground. Those who don't practise magic are strongly advised against visiting as punishments for trespass are reportedly disproportionately severe.

Elgin (The): A term mostly used by the alumni of the Edinburgh School (see Calton Hill Library, incorporating the Library of the Dead).

Extraordinary Committee (The): An organ within the Society of Sceptical Enquirers charged with checking the powers of the Secretary. It consists of two heads of the four magic schools in Scotland, plus two board members of the Society, and one ordinary member drawn by lottery.

General Discoveries Directorate: An independent division within the Society of Sceptical Enquirers. It supports the secretary of the Society (currently Sir Ian Callander) in his role as Scotland's Discoverer General.

Our Lady of Mysterious Ailments: An exclusive holistic healing and therapy clinic on Colinton Road, Edinburgh. Clients include aristocrats, celebrities and the cream of Edinburgh society.

Royal Society of Sorcery and the Advancement of the Mystic Arts:
England's foremost magical society claims to trace its origins to the
mythical wizard Merlin, though contemporary scholars date its formal
establishment to the late seventeenth century.

Society of Sceptical Enquirers: Scotland's premier magical professional
body. It is headquartered in Dundas House on St Andrew Square in
Edinburgh's New Town.

Principal Places

Camelot: A notorious tent city atop Arthur's Seat. The population of
this place is difficult to estimate because of the transient tenure of
most residents. Due to concerns about crime from local residents in
the nearby neighbourhoods of Duddingston and Meadowbank, the
city council has made several attempts to clear Camelot – but with
limited success.

Dundas House: Designed by the architect Sir William Chambers and
completed in 1774, this neoclassical building located at 36 St Andrew
Square in the New Town was once the headquarters of the Royal Bank
of Scotland. It remains the bank's corporate address and simultaneously serves as the headquarters of the Society of Sceptical Enquirers.

everyThere (The): This realm is a nonplace beyond the ordinary world.
It is where deceased souls go before they can move on. Only a few
among the living can reach and navigate it safely.

His Majesty's Slum Hermiston: This slum is located on farmland in
the south-west of Edinburgh. It runs from the city bypass along the
M8. The dwellings are a higgledy-piggledy assortment of trailers,
caravans, shipping containers, garden sheds, etc.

Other Place (The): Little is known about this realm in the astral plane, but wayward spirits can be expelled there. It is believed there is no return for them from it.

Realms Beyond (The): Lying beyond the event horizon of the Astral Realms, these represent a higher dimension currently out of the reach of contemporary magical practice. Though much has been speculated about them, little empirical evidence exists to prove or disprove their existence.

Royal Bank of Scotland: Established in 1727, the RBS is a major retail and commercial bank.

RBS Archives: Located in South Gyle, the archives are responsible for collecting and preserving the records of both the Royal Bank of Scotland and the Society of Sceptical Enquirers. While the premises belong to the RBS, the archivists who work there are employed by the Calton Hill Library.

underHume: The basement area of Calton Hill Library. It houses practice rooms, laboratories and storage space.

Principal Characters

Briggs: Coachman and servant to England's Sorcerer Royal.

Callander, Ian (Sir): Scotland's leading magician. Secretary of the Society of Sceptical Enquirers. His role in the Society also makes him the Discoverer General in Scotland.

Cockburn, Frances: Director of Membership Services at the Society of Sceptical Enquirers.

Cruickshank: Ropa Moyo's magical scarf. A gift from her mentor, Sir Ian Callander.

Diderot, Octavius: Member of the Extraordinary Committee and the board of the Society of Sceptical Enquirers.

Featherstone, Calista: Head teacher at the Aberdeen School of Magic and Esoterica.

Guthrie, Irene: Head groundskeeper at the Edinburgh Ordinary School for Boys.

Hutchinson, Hamish: Principal at St Andrews College, Scotland's second oldest school of magic.

Kapoor, Priyanka: Healer at the Our Lady of Mysterious Ailments clinic on Colinton Road. She studied healing and herbology at the Lord Kelvin Institute in Glasgow.

Lebusa, Rethabile (Lady): Member of the Extraordinary Committee and the board of the Society of Sceptical Enquirers.

MacDonald, Avery: Second son of Dalziel MacDonald and a student of theoretical magicology at St Andrews College.

MacDonald, Dalziel: Clan chief of the MacDonalds of Sleat, one of the oldest and most powerful Scottish families.

MacLeod, Fenella: The only child of Clan chief Edmund MacLeod and a student of esoteric history at St Andrews College.

Maige, Jomo: Trainee librarian at Calton Hill Library and Ropa Moyo's best friend.

Maige, Pythagoras (Dr): Head librarian at the Calton Hill Library and Master of the Books for the Library of the Dead. He holds a doctorate in mathematics from the University of Edinburgh and is Jomo's father.

Mhondoro, Melsie: Ropa Moyo's grandmother.

Moyo, Izwi: Ropa Moyo's precocious younger sister.

Moyo, Ropa: A teenage ghostalker from HMS Hermiston in the south-west of Edinburgh. Ropa dropped out of school to support her little sister and grandmother by delivering messages on behalf of the city's dearly departed. Her activities secured her an internship with the Society of Sceptical Enquires, after which she resigned to find employment with Lord Samarasinghe, England's Sorcerer Royal.

O'Donohue, Gary: Resident of HMS Hermiston and Melsie Mhondoro's lover.

River: a vixen

Rooster Rob/Red Rob: Leader of the notorious street gang called the Clan. He governs Camelot atop Arthur's Seat in the centre of Edinburgh.

Samarasinghe, Lord Sashvindu: England's Sorcerer Royal.

Soltani, Esfandiar: Currently the Makar, the national poet laureate of Scotland, and an independent scholar best known for his biography of Robert Burns in verse. He is a non-practising magician married to Sir Ian Callander.

Walsh, Nathair: Deputy head boy and captain of the rugby team at the Edinburgh Ordinary School for Boys.

Wedderburn, Montgomery: Disgraced former rector of the Edinburgh Ordinary School for Boys.

Wharncliffe, Lewis: Student of sonicology at the Edinburgh Ordinary School for Boys.

The Somerville Equation

$$y = w(c+a-N)/t$$

y – yield
w – practitioner's potential
c – combustible material
a – agitative threshold
N – natural resistance
t – time

Discovered in 1797 by the polymath Mary Somerville, from Jedburgh, when she was only sixteen. This elegant equation was the first mathematical proof of the Promethean fire spell. Somerville's work is considered by most scholars to have been a key development in the shift towards magic becoming a true scientific discipline. Scotland's four schools of magic also use it to derive their pupils' potential by working out the 'w'.

The Four Magic Schools

These are the only accredited schools of magic in Scotland. They are highly selective and have very competitive admission standards. Qualification at one of these institutions is a requirement for professional registration with the Society of Sceptical Enquirers:

Aberdeen School of Magic and Esoterica, Aberdeen

Edinburgh Ordinary School for Boys, Edinburgh

Lord Kelvin Institute, Glasgow

St Andrews College, St Andrews

I

I work for English magic now. There's no way to sugar-coat it. Please, dinnae judge me like the horsehair-wigged folks who ply their lawyering trade on Chambers Street. It was a tough decision, true Scot that I am. But sometimes you gotta say fuck the flag, just show me the money. Can I get an amen? No? Whatever . . . Things are looking up since Lord Sashvindu Samarasinghe, England's Sorcerer Royal and head honcho at the Royal Society of Sorcery and the Advancement of the Mystic Arts, took a shine to me and became my patron. Forget that malarkey they always tell you about pulling up bootstraps; the only way up in the magicking game is who you know.

And so I currently find myself ensconced in the lush, velvet-upholstered interior of the Sorcerer Royal's coach. A cool white light brightens the interior, though there's no source of illumination for it. The clippity-clop of the horses on the tarmac outside is mixed in with the evening sounds of the city. Hawkers shouting out their wares, desperate for a sale before they head home; hustlers on the corners, enticing folks to shoot craps off their loaded dice – the general madness of the Edinburgh I love. Lord Samarasinghe has a perfumed handkerchief covering his snout. He hates the howling aroma, which hits you stronger than a teenager's oxters. And the smell's worse on days like this, when the haar drifts over from the sea, and the air's thick with that misty moisture. I don't mind it at all; it's an acquired taste.

'Out of the way, you wazzocks,' Briggs the coachman yells, cracking his whip.

Probably folks on the road, out of their heads on gear they take to numb whatever flames this tenth circle of hell throws their way. I wouldn't know, though. I'm sat with my back to the direction of travel, and I daren't stick my noggin out the window. It's much better being here, on the lush inside.

Lord Samarasinghe does look out, and grimaces.

'Peasants,' he exclaims. 'Keep them weak, makes them meek.'

'Is that what you think of me? A *peasant*?'

'I would be sorely disappointed if I'd given you the impression I thought otherwise,' he replies.

I frown, but bite my tongue. What an arrogant knob. Makes me miss my old gaffer Sir Ian Callander for a second or two. *Bollocks, don't be silly, Ropa.* He'd never have scored you a gig like the one Lord S has just set up for you today. Barely made a shilling when I was doing stuff for my previous boss. Still, I don't like people taking the piss, and I'm about to say something when Samarasinghe beats me to it.

'Don't be boring, Ropa. You can be anything with me except that.'

'I'll show you boring.'

'Thank goodness we're past those dreadful odours. I nearly brought up my supper.'

'I take it London smells of roses then?'

He grins. 'That's more like it, lassie.' He puts on an annoying fake Scottish accent. I swear he's only given me this gig so he can enjoy winding me up.

There's a naughty twinkle in Lord Samarasinghe's eyes. They are bright and intelligent, set beneath his impressive monobrow. He's dressed in a scarlet English court uniform with lavish gold embroidery across the torso, starting from the waist and broadening out towards the shoulders. There's gold detailing on his collar and the bottoms of his sleeves too. And the black trousers he's wearing have a red stripe running down the side seam. The only odd thing is his choice of military peaked cap, when you might have expected some kind of cocked hat from back in the day.

In lieu of a sword, the Sorcerer Royal has his cane, with the silver tiger's head on it. I've come to understand this sort of thing is the fashion for English magicians, who prefer wands for their accoutrements.

He looks into my eyes for an uncomfortable length of time and I'm loath to drop my gaze. Hanging out with the Sorcerer Royal is like walking on nine-inch rusted nails. You come out with stigmata or, in the best-case scenario, a dose of tetanus. I finally turn away and focus my attention on what's happening outside, as Nicolson Street gives way to Clerk Street, cutting through Newington. Even this late at night there's desperate folks lining the way, clutching cardboard signs.

'WILL WERK FOR FUD'

It's Beggars' Row out here, everyone crammed in 'cause the fuzz are kicking up a fuss and evicting them from the New Town. The Old Town's more the scene for down and outs anyway. Mingling amongst the tramps and vagrants are angry-looking men with plastic thistles pinned to the lapels of their coats, handing out leaflets of some sort. It's a powder keg out there.

'Tell me about your parents,' Lord Samarasinghe says.

I've been moving with him for a couple of weeks now, but this is the first time he's shown any sort of interest in my back-ground. I'm not sure why he'd be bringing it up now. Hmm.

'I live with my nan and my little sister. But she's away at boarding school,' I reply, still looking outside.

'That's not what I asked you.'

I bite my lower lip and taste my black lipstick. Then I invol-untarily grab a lock of my silver-dyed dreadlocks and tug it. I stop myself, but it's too late, I've given the game away. If the Sorcerer Royal had an ounce of decency, he'd apologize for asking about them and change the subject. Instead, he waits for a reply. Ironic, since he lied to me about his own upbringing when I first met him in the autumn, at the biennial conference of the Society of Sceptical Enquirers at Dunvegan Castle. Made out like he'd had a hard start in life, when in reality he's a rich kid from Edgbaston in Birmingham.

'Can we talk about something else?'

'No, we *may* not.'

I grit my teeth, but my obvious annoyance doesn't move Lord Samarasinghe one bit. He's a proper roaster, and now he's making me all nervous. Gotta be careful I don't have a wobble. Don't wanna embarrass myself any more than I have to. The coach rattles and shakes as we hit a particularly bad patch of road. My parents aren't something I like thinking about. Keep all that shut away in a vault at the back of my mind. What I have left of them anyways. I don't like folks feeling sorry for me, and I certainly don't need no one's charity. My name ain't Oliver Twist. I get by.

'They died when I was young and I've got gaps in my memory.'

'Go on,' he says patiently, in the demeanour of a rogue therapist. I would know, I'm seeing one at Our Lady of Mysterious Ailments, who my mate Priya linked me up with for my anxiety attacks and PTSD. You go in and, after gentle prompts, bare your soul, bleeding out onto her rug. Then you leave feeling lighter somehow.

'My father's name was Makomborero Moyo and my mother was Cora—' Frog in my throat. I can't . . .

'It's okay. Take your time,' Lord S says gently.

I shake my head. He's pushing me to talk about stuff I don't want to. Worse still, being in his forties, Lord Samarasinghe is round about what my father's age would've been had he lived.

'Cora is such a beautiful name,' he muses. 'I believe, and I might be wrong here, that it's derived from a Greek word which means maiden or heart.'

Sniffles. I want to cry, but I'm not going to. Not in front of Lord Samarasinghe. *Keep it together, Ropa.* It takes everything within me, every ounce of will to pull myself together. I don't much like thinking about my dead folks. Other dead people, no problem.

'My father was an academic. Gran told me he was the smartest person she knew. She also said he was bold, brash, and a wee bit arrogant, a regular know-it-all, who took himself too seriously. He loved my mother deeply. The two of them were inseparable.' I reach into my pocket to take out my phone, which has a picture Gran sent me ages ago of my parents together in the Meadows. But then I decide I don't want to show it after all and pull my hand back. Their faces are faded in my memory. Sometimes I fail to conjure them up altogether.

'And what did your mother do? She must have been a patient woman to put up with a man like your father,' he replies, leaning forward as though thoroughly engaged.

'She was a seamstress. The yang to his yin, my grandmother told me. If his head was in the clouds, she kept her feet firmly planted on the ground.'

'A perfect combination. Intellectuals sometimes become so caught up in their own abstractions they forget what's real. I've often had to teach young magicians that you can imbibe all the theory you want, but reality is far messier.' His tone is that of a mentor now. It kinda reminds me of Callander. 'In life, young lady, intelligence is overrated. Of course, it helps, and you can create or do amazing things with it, but if one isn't careful, it has a tendency to turn in on itself. I've seen many ruined by this. Those who go the furthest are not the ones with a high IQ, but a good EQ – emotional intelligence, the ability to have mastery over one's own self and to relate to others. But I interrupt and pontificate. You were saying?'

My own memories are so vague. I was young when they died. Thank Allah I have Gran to help fill in the gaps. Even then, the story I have of my parents is one dominated by the details of their passing. It's as if they were an old book, covers frayed, barely holding together, pages water damaged, sun bleached and faded. Only a few letters, perhaps the odd word, remains, and somehow the final chapter is the only thing left. All I have is the sound of my father's laughter, me flying into the blue sky, then falling until he catches me on the way back down, his strong hands gripping my armpits, before launching me back up again. My mother combing my hair, singing a song whose words are lost to me, but I remember the rise and fall of its melody clearly. Her gentle voice. I have memories of sinking into her bosom, listening to her heartbeat. Watching her crochet at night while my father was in his study. Glimpses. Little bits and pieces punctuated by blankness. What did my father's cologne smell like? Did he have a favourite food? Which of them gave me my sweet tooth? I remember bedtime stories read to me, but I can't recall which one of them read which story. Nuggets is all I have. But as much as I try to hold onto them, they burn like a bitch.

'My mother was the first to go. She died during childbirth, when my sister was born,' I say. 'She bled to death.'

'Oh dear. I am so sorry,' Lord Samarasinghe replies. He looks down at his lap as though searching for something to say. 'Womanhood—' He stops and shakes his head. 'These things are rather difficult.'

Which is why me and Gran haven't told my little sister Izwi what happened yet. She's too young to be able to handle that kind of weight. Whenever she asks, Gran just tells her mam fell sick and died. It's a half-truth. Back when I was ghostalkering, delivering messages between the living and the dead, it was always hard whenever I had a message to pass onto a child who'd been young when their parent died. I'd try to channel the whole equanimity shit each time, but it was tough dealing with that.

The funny thing is, through all my years of dealing with the dead, my parents have never come back to see me. They must have moved on already, beyond the everyThere. That gruesome realm, the first stop for the dead, which is glued to our world. I've hoped in the past I'd be able to speak with one of them, but it's never happened. I tried searching the infinite realms of the astral plane, until Gran had a quiet word and bade me stop. But every time I delivered a message from someone's loved one, I felt a tinge of envy it was for them, not me.

Yes, I was jealous, but happy for my customers too. I'm glad I do that less now, though, and am on my way to becoming a proper magician, thanks to Lord Samarasinghe. When he takes us to England, I'll have my pick of magic schools from the best in the world.

'How did your father cope with her death? It must have been quite a blow. Two children, all on his own. Never mind, I'm being silly, you were too young to know.'

'Gran said he was never the same after she was gone. Locked himself away in his study to grieve.'

'Who looked after you?'

'There was help. Childminders who came in when my father was working.' I suddenly remember that I didn't call him dad or papa or any of that. He was 'baba' to me. Gran told me it means father in Shona. It also has the same meaning in Swahili, Chinese, Urdu, Greek and a dozen other languages. But to me, it's a special word. Something personal, 'cause I've never heard no one else use it.

'But for as long as I can recall, I've been looking after Izwi, with my Gran. I kinda miss it now she's away.'

'These things are never easy,' Lord Samarasinghe says quietly. 'I want you to know, you'll always have an ally in me. I can't replace what you've lost, but I hope that's something, at least.'

I'm stunned. Is he actually being sincere? Don't even know how to say thank you. But it seems there could be something kind underneath the Sorcerer Royal's prickly exterior, after all. So I find myself opening up even more, and telling him the rest of it.

'Gran doesn't say it like this, but I've picked up bits and pieces. I think my father lost his mind after she died.'

'Grief does strange and horrible things to us.'

Lord Samarasinghe reaches out, maybe to touch my hand, but balls his fingers into a fist in the empty space between us. He pumps his hand up and down once or twice, then retracts it.

'He died in a car crash,' I say. 'Drove himself right over the cliff on the A1 to Berwick-upon-Tweed. Maybe he took his own—'

'No, don't say that,' Samarasinghe says urgently. He frowns. 'I know it's tempting, in the absence of fact, to speculate and fill things in. But that won't do you any good. Accidents happen. You can't know what was in his mind. And I'm sure he loved you girls very much and wouldn't have done such a dreadful thing.'

'Now you're the one speculating,' I reply, half in jest.

We can't help searching for answers. That's why ghostalkers, mediums, clairvoyants, priests and anyone with a hand in the extranatural will never run out of work. Samarasinghe is right, though. There's no use turning this over in my mind when there ain't no one else who can give me those answers.

The funny thing is I never told my old mentor Callander any of this. He didn't seem too interested in who I was as a person, or where I came from originally. We just stuck to work and not much else. I guess it's the dour Scots thing. Still, it's something to be able to tell my new patron all this. They're very different men. When I first met Lord Samarasinghe at Dunvegan Castle, I didn't much like him. But here in this carriage, I glimpse he has a beating heart and blood that runs red like the rest of us. Unless he's lying to me again . . .

'Ah, now we've left the ghastly odours of Auld Reekie behind, I believe it's safe for us to have a cup of Ceylon tea, wouldn't you agree?' Lord Samarasinghe says, mercifully changing the subject at last.

I grunt and remove my backpack, which is sat atop the picnic basket on my left. It's early days yet and I'm still study-ing the new boss man. Occasionally he gives a command dressed up as a throwaway remark or suggestion, and I need to be wise to it. Samarasinghe is a man of mercurial moods but I'm really starting to think I can work with him. Call it taming the tiger.

I reach into the basket and retrieve the cup and saucer, which are wrapped carefully in towels to prevent them cracking with each judder of the coach as it hits a pothole. This is expensive stuff, of the finest quality – bone china with a twenty-two-carat gold finish. It has decorated borders, finely detailed with roses, myrtle, rosemary and oak leaves. On the side of the cup is a fancy cypher with a crown atop it, surrounded by national emblems of the old United Kingdom – roses, shamrocks, thistles and daffodils. Reminds me that being with Lord S, I'm two degrees of separation from the king himself. Ain't that something to write home about?

There's a golden thermos, similarly engraved, inside the basket. I swear these rich folks flaunt it in your face. But no time to think like a bloody commie. I'm too busy balancing the cup and saucer in one hand, and pouring the Sorcerer Royal's tea with the other. It's a mission, given how juddery the inside of the carriage is. Once that's done, and I've sealed the thermos, I grab the small bottle of milk.

Lord Samarasinghe's face lights up. He's positively beaming.

'You've passed your first proper test.' He claps his hands with a childish delight. 'I was thinking, if she's one of those heathens who pours the milk in first I shall have to dispose of her in a shallow grave somewhere.'

'Phew,' I reply, unable to mask my sarcasm.

'Ah, don't get too cocky now. Your second test of the night awaits, and I for one am rather looking forward to it.'

He's still smiling as I hand the tea over, even as my stomach sinks. I have bad memories of the first time I was tested by my old gaffer at the Society of Sceptical Enquirers. It kinda scuttled my career in Scottish magic before it'd even launched. Let's hope tonight goes a wee bit better for me.

'Ah.' Lord Samarasinghe smacks his lips. 'A very fine brew. Aren't you having some?'

I pick up a cup for myself. 'So, who're these people who need my help?'

'We are going to visit a grand old place called Arniston House.'

II

We've journeyed past Cameron Toll, and through Liberton, where you can barely find a tree standing on the roadside, since they've all been chopped down for firewood. Once we're past the bypass, which arcs around the south of the city from Gogar to Old Craighall, we're safely away from the barren wastelands of Gilmerton, with Briggs still urging the horses on.

This is a dangerous route. It's best not to venture outside the city limits these days. Modern highwaymen ply their trade in the unlit wilds of Dalkeith. The news says they operate in gangs of five or more, some of them teenagers in hoodies, snoods covering their faces and budget Diadora sneakers on their feet. I feel a sense of panic as the carriage slows down, until Briggs halts it completely. I touch Cruickshank, my scarf, and then reach for my dagger.

'What are you doing?' Lord Samarasinghe asks, an amused expression on his face.

Before I can reply, Briggs calls in his broad Yorkshire accent from outside the carriage, 'Milord, it appears we've hit a roadblock.' The highwaymen often lay a log in the road to ambush their victims. 'Would you like me to deal with it?' The carriage sways and Briggs's boots make a loud noise as he lands on the tar.

'That's quite alright, Briggs. I need to stretch my legs a bit. Ropa, will you be a dear and take this from me.' Lord Samarasinghe hands me his cup and saucer, then winks.

The carriage door opens. Lord S never does this himself – not when he has us servants to hand. He takes his pocket watch out, checks the time, then puts it back, before stepping out with his cane.

'This shouldn't take long,' he says.

Briggs shuts the door. I'm about to peek outside when the curtains on the carriage windows draw themselves shut sharply.

I don't understand why we have to stop – this coach can fly. That's how we journeyed from the Isle of Skye back to Edinburgh a few weeks ago, and it seems like the Sorcerer Royal can do this when he's travelling long-distance. I'm sure tonight could have been an exception too. I try to open the door, only to find it's locked. Fucksake, I don't like being confined. I do the breathing exercises my psychomagician has taught me. In through the nose, out though the mouth. Repeat. Repeat. Until I start to calm down.

I hear the loud tapping of Lord Samarasinghe's cane on the road, indicating he's walking forward.

'God save the king,' the Sorcerer Royal says.

'Bollocks. The king is dead,' a man says, then he hocks loudly and spits. 'The new queen of Scots reigns in these parts and she's collecting tolls tonight.'

Coarse guffaws from his gang boost the highwayman's words.

'Gentlemen, you are blocking the king's road. Would you be so kind as to remove this obstacle impeding my progress?'

Lord Samarasinghe's voice is firm but cordial. 'I would be most grateful.'

Rough laughter responds to his request.

'You hear that, lads? This posh English wanker's come all the way over here to tell us what to do,' another man's voice says.

'Right, you better empty your pockets quick. And we'll be taking whatever's in that coach too. Come on, help them remove their stuff,' someone who sounds like their leader says. It's a female voice.

This isn't good. We should just give them what they want. From what I've heard, the highwaymen patrolling the A7 are real savages, given to bludgeoning, mauling, stabbing, scalping, impaling, and all sorts of unsavoury stuff. And if the leader's a woman, then it could only be Dirty Davina, the most notorious of the lot. Cruel fucker, who likes torturing her victims in the medieval style, so I've heard. Like, she apparently sucked the eyeballs out of one guy's head and left him to wander the countryside blind. 'Davina's kiss', they called it – I'll take the Glasgow kiss over that any given Sunday. There's a bounty on her head and all. But I thought she worked way out near the Borders. This is one of the rare moments in my life I find myself wishing the cops were here. There've been reports of cannibalism by her gang too . . . I really hope that was made up.

There's an awful quiet outside.

Someone tries to open the carriage door. They rattle it roughly and then tap on the window. 'Open up!' I grab my dagger tightly, ready to stab whoever comes in. One of the horses neighs.

'I don't think you understand the situation you're in. Shall we teach them a lesson, lads?' Dirty Davina says.

'We're trying to be reasonable, guv,' another replies. 'Maybe the big fella in the greatcoat can talk sense to his master. We're all working men here, after all.'

'No skin off my nose,' Briggs replies nonchalantly. He has that ex-military stoicism which can be intimidating to most, but probably means nothing to the highwaymen.

'Look at Mr Posh Twat taking out his pocket watch as if we're wasting his time,' says Dirty Davina. 'That's enough of that. Get 'em, lads!'

A disconcerting stillness follows, punctuated by boots walking towards a certain point. I'm proper bricking it now. No use playing cool when there's bampots ready to bash your noggin in. I feel the build-up of immense pressure, kinda like the weather changing. Then there's a terrible sound, like a drum beat perforating my entire being.

'What's he doing, guv?'

'I don't care, smash his brains in,' Davina orders.

The earth rumbles underneath the carriage. I sense an almighty entropic shift, as if the world is bending beneath the marching boots of an awesome army. And then it comes, the most horrendous cracking noise, like all the demons in hell chattering. I double over in my seat and cover my ears from this drilling, but I can't stop it coming through. My eardrums are going to burst.

Panicked voices coming from outside the carriage intermingle with the horrific sound.

The pressure builds up and I fall to my side in the seat, foetal-like.

The sound intensifies.

The horses stomp and snort like they might bolt.

And then the screams start. Terror. I've never heard anyone cry out like this.

'It's *eating* me!'

'Please help—'

'God, no, no, no, no.'

'It's inside me. Arrrrrrrrrrrrgh.'

'We're so-so-sorry.'

Their desperate pleas chill me to the bone. I find I'm trembling, goosebumps prickling up all over my skin. Sickening noises come through, like slabs of meat being torn apart. And still the horrible chattering continues, as if some incredible beast with multiple rows of teeth is setting upon them.

Then it all goes quiet again.

Very quiet.

I don't know which is more dreadful, but it doesn't last long before there's pitiful whimpering.

'Puh-puh-please. Not like this,' Dirty Davina begs, her voice quivering pathetically. Sounds to me like she's the last one standing.

'These are the king's motorways. It is he who guarantees safe passage,' Lord Samarasinghe says.

'I beg you.'

'I am not finished,' he replies harshly. Then more evenly, 'Madam, you have breached the king's peace. Or shall I address you as Queen of the Scotch? Answer me.'

'No, I'm no queen, sir. Please.' She's crying. 'We're just hungry. There's no honest work to be had anywhere.'

'Be that as it may, madam, you have challenged your sovereign, instead of seeking his mercy in the poorhouses provided for you. You've pitted your might against his divine right and struck the first cowardly blow. And so you will bear the brunt of his wrath. For only then can you, and any other brigands operating under the cover of darkness, understand that the king's laws are not a trifling inconvenience. It is your lot only to obey, and your life from birth till now, every second, every breath, has been the fruit of his kindness. Now you will learn the strength of his arm, the selfsame arm that cradled you from the instant of your conception.'

There's a shrill scream which threatens to shatter the windows on the carriage doors, accompanied by the sounds of many bones breaking, and then a body flopping to the ground.

Fuck me.

I cup my mouth with my hand and rise up to sit back in my seat. My ticker's pounding away like it's gonna burst out of my chest.

'I'll clear the log, milord. But first, let me escort you back to your carriage. It's nippy tonight, wouldn't want you to catch a cold,' says Briggs.

'You're very kind,' Lord Samarasinghe replies. 'I hope these criminals didn't startle your horses too badly.'

'My horses are good enough for the cavalry. Nothing scares them.'

I've still got my mouth cupped as their footsteps draw nearer to the coach, and I nearly jump out of my skin when the door's opened. Lord Samarasinghe steps up and into the carriage, rocking it a little as he does. He deposits himself on the seat opposite me, just as Briggs shuts the door. There're specks of blood on the golden embroidery of his uniform, almost like he was some sort of painter. The normally silver head of his cane is glowing red hot, so he's holding it by the wood instead.

I battle my nerves not to flinch when he turns his attention to me.

'My friend the Duke of Somerset throws the most impressive masquerade balls in the world. Have you ever been to one of those, Ropa?'

I shake my head 'cause I can't speak right now.

'Pity, I think you'd love it. It's only just occurred to me that he's having one tonight at Bradley House and I neglected to send my apologies. He has a fine estate. I will take you there one day . . .'

He's going on and on about the delights of aristocratic life, but I can't take any of it in. His voice and demeanour are too casual, a stark counterpoint to what I just heard happening outside. When he smiles, the carriage lights up, and it's a genuine smile too – I can see that by the creases at the corners of his eyes.

Briggs finally returns to the carriage. He cracks his whip and the coach lurches forward. After we've travelled for a while, a safe distance from the scene, the curtains retract by themselves. I see the clouds have broken, revealing the full moon smiling down.

Lord Samarasinghe is in a boisterous mood by the time we near our destination, out in the sticks near the old mining town of Gorebridge and the River South Esk. The town's become like something out of Zola's *Germinal*. The coal's running out now, meaning there's less work to be had. The air's fresher here than the reek of Edinburgh I'm used to, and neat hedges border the narrow lane we trundle along. Fallow fields lie within them, as do power lines which follow the line of the road. Briggs has been working his charges hard to make up for lost time, but the coach now moves much slower.

We pass a cottage on the left, a few lights shining through the windows. There's a healthy woodland with Scots pine, beech, hazel and ash. Under the bright moonlight it all looks so serene. I totally get why the super-rich prefer to have their estates out here. They've left the decay of the cities to the likes of . . .

I'm still nervous. Lord Samarasinghe arranged this gig for me out here. One that pays handsome like the frontman of a boy band. But it's going to be a test for me, as he said. All things working out as they should, once Lord S is done with his business in Scotland, we'll be moving down south with him. Reminds me, I still ain't asked Gran whether she wants to go. *Don't be silly, she can't say no.* And what'll Izwi think about it, since she's at boarding school all the way up in Aberdeen? There've been better opportunities for Scots down in England since way back when. We can't afford to mess this up, not when we're so close.

Can't wait for the day I get off this hamster wheel.

Somewhere in the night an owl hoots. A bit of drystone wall flickers past, running along the side of the road.

'This family we are visiting asked for you specifically,' Lord Samarasinghe says.

'Did they?'

'I found it somewhat satisfying that, since you're no longer in the employ of the Society of Sceptical Enquirers, they had to come to me.' His dark eyes twinkle with delight.

That's the thing about Lord S. He's thrilled to have one over on the Society, since I used to be intern to the secretary, Sir Ian Callander. I get the feeling he likes to parade me around as a trophy he stole from them. For a serious man he does play trivial games, toying with people. There's something feline about his personality, like the tiger on the head of his cane.

We follow a formidable stone wall until Briggs makes a right turn and the coach draws to a halt. I can't see what's up ahead. That's the weird thing about being a coach passenger – you can only see what's beside you. It might suit rich folks who don't have to care about much, but I like to know what's ahead, just in case.

'What's your business with Arniston House this late at night?' a guard asks.

'The Sorcerer Royal's paying you a visit,' Briggs replies.

'I wasn't told nothing about that.'

'Open the gate,' Briggs commands.

There's some hesitation until squeaky hinges announce the guard's compliance. Soon we're moving down a road lined by gigantic old lime trees standing like a guard of honour. When the carriage stops at last, Briggs opens the door.

'Youth before beauty,' Lord Samarasinghe says with a chuckle, gesturing I get out first.

I grab my backpack and exit the coach, then stand on the tar. My joints are achy. Horse-drawn carriages ain't too comfy, especially with the state of our roads. But now I'm outside, I notice a mist hovering over the ground. It wasn't there at the gate, I'm certain, but it seems to be hugging the massive mansion in front of me. It's an imposing Palladian-style building, with its straight lines and neoclassical vibe that was all the rage back when. Can't help but think of the tiny caravan I live in. There are a handful of lights on inside the first floor. The rest of the house is cloaked in darkness. I imagine our cara is much cosier anyways.

A thirty-somethingish man in a bulky, black fur coat stands at the top of the perron steps leading to the entrance. Must have slaughtered a fair few rabbits to create that. Suddenly makes me feel nippy in my hand-me-down. He has bushy eyebrows and thick curly hair matching his coat. There's a casual sophistication about his pose and he's very still, regarding me with haughty airs. But that changes to a more respectful demeanour when Lord Samarasinghe joins me.

The man descends the steps slowly and gracefully, almost as though he's gliding down them. He looks and moves like a model.

'My Lord Sorcerer, you do us a great honour by coming here,' the man says, charm oozing from his voice. 'Arniston House welcomes you.' He makes a slight bow.

'Viscount Mieville, it is a pleasure to finally come to your seat,' Lord Samarasinghe replies.

'I would show you in, but the matter for which I requested your aid is rather dire, and I would beg you to indulge me with haste.'

'Indeed, Scottish magic must be in a sorry state if, as it seems, you don't have qualified practitioners to deal with this sort of thing.'

The viscount casts down his gaze, embarrassed. He gestures for us to start walking. I follow behind him and Samarasinghe, while Briggs remains, tending to his horses. I catch the impression of Mieville's magic – it's something guarded, like a mask hidden behind silk, oud perfume in shifting clouds, all things to all people all the time. You can't help but be drawn to him, in the way beautiful people usually bend the light towards themselves.

We walk around the mansion, heading down a path which leads to the woods. We're in the shadow of the building cast by the brilliant moonlight. Somehow things feel even spookier still. I struggle to find my element when I'm outside of Edinburgh. Lately, my confidence's been shot a wee bit.

Mieville opens the palm of his hand and casts an orb of clear red fire to guide us through the dark. It hovers a little distance ahead, as stunning as the faded setting sun yet still illuminating enough.

'The problem we have is that over the past hundred years or so Scottish magic has neglected the extranatural. There were heady days of progress in the nineteenth century, but then it became caught up in the shenanigans of the table-rappers and unscrupulous spiritualists who were all the rage then. There were some unsavoury scandals involving members of the Society delving into the esoteric. And as scientific magic made great strides, our best minds turned to that instead, leaving our study of the extranatural to wither. This continues to be the case today. So we're forced to turn to more *primitive* practitioners.' Mieville glances at me over his shoulder. 'I apologize. Perhaps my phrasing was somewhat indelicate.'

I keep schtum and focus on silently practising my shanti. I'm already well aware ghostalking isn't considered real magic by the toffee-nosed. Recently picked up from the Library the book *The Theatre of Power* by Bryson Blackwood, a minor magician who rose to become Secretary of the Society of Sceptical Enquirers in the mid-twentieth century. Blackwood's first chapter, 'Everything is Performance', advises that you watch your mouth. 'As magicians we should understand that words have great power. Like when casting a spell, only speak when you are certain of the impact of your words, especially with your betters. Saying little gives away little.' He must have understood something about dealing with these aristo types. Their barbed comments coated in honey, the small traps they set in the most banal of conversations. It's exhausting stepping through this minefield. I had to quit my role as Sir Ian Callander's intern 'cause of that kind of malarkey, and then I might've been a wee bit more unguarded with my words. I won't make the same mistake again. Twice shy. Blackwood warns against trying too hard to get noticed or prove you're smart, 'cause it only ends up making you look like a knob. Not that I'm trying to impress the viscount; only Lord Samarasinghe's opinion matters to me. I'm done with Scottish practitioners. Will be gritting my teeth to sawdust just to get through this gig.

Mieville leads us to a cottage in the woods. Stone. A picture of Victorian prosperity, and from a time when they built with an eye to eternity. It must usually be peaceful out here on this estate, located as it is in the heart of woodland, surrounded on all sides by tall conifers. It's pretty dark out here, though, despite the viscount's orb, and I sense a powerful presence.

Normally ghosts feel like the subtle notes beneath the melody of a song. You'd have to pay attention to know they're there at all. This one feels like an almighty bassline – not something I've felt before. The landlord raps on the door and it's soon opened a fraction by a timid-looking old man in pyjamas and a nightcap. He's hunched and servile, regarding Mieville as a deity. Curiously, he holds up an Arabian-style oil lamp to illuminate the night.

'My lord, how may I serve you?' he asks, like this was the nineteenth century.

'We are here for your grand-niece.'

The servant opens the door fully and allows us inside. It's cold in the building, despite the dying embers of a fire still glowing in the fireplace. The furnishings look like cast-offs – a sofa with ripped upholstery, stuffing showing. There's a dining chair with a broken leg lying in one corner of the room. And the place has a peculiar odour to it, as often happens to family homes which take on a particular fragrance over time, which the inhabitants don't notice.

We're joined by a middle-aged woman with a white woollen bonnet on her head and a shawl wrapped around her shoulders. She curtseys and keeps her eyes cast to the ground.

'This is my brother's daughter, Una. She's the girl's mother,' the man says to Lord S and me.

'Wilfred here has been a loyal member of our family's staff since he was a lad, just like his father and his grandfather before him. And in that grand tradition, Una works in our kitchen. She makes the finest Cullen Skink in the country. I'll have you try it sometime. They have served us well, which is why I cannot stand for them to endure distress such as has brought us here tonight.' Mieville is the kind patriarch to his servants, it seems. In this age that's not a bad thing at all, I reckon. He turns back to Wilfred. 'And do you know who I've brought to help you with this bother?'

When the rich do you a favour, everyone has to know about it. Wilfred holds his lamp with both hands and inclines his head in a show of gratitude. Tears are already welling up in his eyes.

'The Sorcerer Royal himself, all the way from London,' Mieville announces.

'Bless you, sir, bless you.' Wilfred bows several times.

'No need for that, please,' Lord Samarasinghe says, waving his arm. 'I'm not doing anything. I've merely facilitated one of Scotland's finest practitioners in the supernatural coming to your aid, as requested.'

Wilfred looks confused. Una even more so as she regards me suspiciously. But if they harbour any reservations, they keep them to themselves.

'Show us to the girl,' Mieville says.

'Right this way, my lord,' Wilfred replies, leading us into a dark corridor. The lamplight casts strange shadows on the wall, flickering erratically.

The bassline I felt outside triples in volume as we walk in single file, me sandwiched between the two lords, as if there's no escape from what's to come. I battle not to reach for my dagger, senses going wild right now like I'm Matt Murdoch. The only thing helping me keep things together is the ashwa-gandha I've been prescribed by my shrink at Our Lady, alongside my breathing exercises, which I practise subtly so no one will notice. Can't afford to have a panic attack in front of my patron. Since I've been on the Indian herb, it's helped me a lot. Priya says it lowers the amount of cortisol flowing through my bloodstream. Makes me calmer and a hell of a lot less anxious.

Something scurries past in the dimness, making Mieville leap.

'Bloody rats,' he says.

'Apologies,' Wilfred says, stopping in front of a door and taking out a key from his side pocket. He slides it into the lock, then tries it a couple of times without success. I notice his hands are shaking, making the shadows on the walls tremble. The poor man's terrified by the looks of things.

When he finally gets the door open, a strange fog flows out, carrying with it the miasma of stale, rotting things which reminds me of the everyThere. Wilfred hesitates, glancing at his master before summoning the courage to enter the room. Even the viscount appears wary at the threshold. I turn to look at Lord Samarasinghe but can't see his expression in the dim light. I'm kicking myself I didn't ask for more details on what I was signing up for. All I knew was it'd be a test of my ghos-talking skills. And normally those jobs are about delivering messages between the living and the dead, so I just thought it'd be something similar.

It's ultra Baltic in the bedroom. The cottage is cold, but it's freezing right here. Our breath fogs, mingling with the miasma already in the air. The bedroom's a decent size. A rocking chair with a doll sits near the window, and there's a blanket box at the foot of the bed in the centre of the far wall. Someone very slight is in the bed, covered head to toe by a throw blanket, as though it were some kind of shroud.

'How interesting,' Lord Samarasinghe says with a quizzical smile on his face.

The figure under the throw sits up with such unbelievable speed and force the blanket is flung off, as though driven by gale force winds. Wilfred leaps back, crossing himself. But the throw then suddenly stops mid-flight, hovering in the air. Lord Samarasinghe waves his hand, annoyed, and it drops to the floor.

'Theatrics,' he says disdainfully.

'I think we should be careful,' I say. 'No taunting.'

He rolls his eyes as though I'm being ridiculous, but says nothing more. Thank goodness for that. Thin line between confidence and hubris.

The girl in the bed looks to be in her early twenties. Naked. Her skin's covered with horrible lesions, some of which seem infected, dripping pus. These scratches are in crossed-out lines, like someone's carved the tally method on her skin. She has her eyes closed and her long blonde hair floats unnaturally in the air, independent of gravity. Something else about her face bothers me.

'What's her name?' I ask.

Una comes into the room and begins to cry before anyone can reply.

'Get out of here,' I order the mother. She retreats outside the door, but remains in the corridor looking in. It's important in these kinds of situations to exude authority . . . At least that's what I think. No doubt can show. What would Gran have done?

'Sophie,' the girl's grand-uncle volunteers.

'How long has she been like this?' I ask.

'A week.'

'Ten days,' Una interjects.

'Sophie, can you hear me?' I say, testing the waters.

There's no response. She has her eyes closed still. Doesn't even look like she's conscious at all, more like a corpse come back to life. The only evidence of Sophie still being of this world are the wisps of fog leaving her mouth at irregular intervals, like she's forgetting to breathe at times.

'Do you see it?' I ask Lord Samarasinghe.

'See what?' Mieville replies, as though the question were meant for him.

The Sorcerer Royal gives me a look, but doesn't deign to answer my question.

It's what's around the girl that bothers me the most. A grey shadow clinging to her, boring down to the seat of her soul. Whatever its true form is, it's inside her. Even as her eyelids are closed, I see a second pair of black eyes looking out at me. The gaze repulses me, making me nauseous at how unnatural it is.

Gran told me about such things. But even when she was training me, when I followed her from place to place as she helped folks deal with poltergeists, not once did we encounter anything quite like this. I wish she was here now; she'd know what to do.

III

There are different types of ghosts. Fundamentally the same, but occupying different ecological niches, like Darwin's finches. With ghosts what differs is the way in which they manifest in our realm. The newbies are formless, as it takes a while for them to master the art of reforming their souls into something resembling the body they once occupied. Gran told me spirits don't have to do this, but the ones which fail to move on, and stay in the everyThere, are still so attached to this life that they can't help it. And the form they eventually take is pretty much the same as an adult wearing their old high school uniform. Creepy and a bit weird. These ghosts can't do much except hang about. They haven't yet learnt how to negate the pull of the everyThere, so they can only manifest for brief periods. So far, so good.

The next step up are the lingerers. Annoying buggers which can manifest so ordinary folks who have something of the gift can see them too, however briefly – maybe just as a shadow in the corner of their eye. That kind of thing. These tend to be a bit mischievous, though they're limited to only appearing at the place they died. You could have a thousand or more folks wandering about the same area at the same time, and only one or two of them would catch a glimpse of these lingerers.

Then you have the poltergeists. Them ones bring in the spondoolies for folks labouring in the extranatural trade, like I used to – a great little earner. 'Cause everyone's so desperate to get rid of them. Usually, they are tied to a house – intimate spaces where they torment and intimidate the residents for kicks and general maliciousness. These ghosts have mastered the art of touching the material world. They can't touch you, much less harm you, unless you consent to it. The human body is the most resistant thing there is to magic, 'cause it's a vessel of will. But the poltergeists will still drive you nuts stomping around the hallways at night, turning lights on and off, knocking and rattling, maybe even opening and shutting doors and windows, or doing the odd tugging of sheets while you're sleeping. I've cast a couple of these sorts back from whence they came by bargaining, or using my Authority. This is our world, not theirs.

The category the ghost in this room belongs to is the most heinous of the lot. Rarer than unicorn testicle soup. Most often, cases ascribed to them end up being simply a wee touch of schizophrenia in the supposed victim, or some other mental health condition. Very rarely does anyone from the other world genuinely acquire the ability to hijack a person. These ghosts are possessors. They are able, by suggestion or guile, to take over the body of someone else, someone living. Of all the transgressions the departed may engage in, these are the most egregious according to Gran. That's why I'm wishing she was here to deal with this herself. Most of what I do today, I learnt by seeing her do it first, though I never got to see her exorcise a possessor. Shona magic doesn't come as simply as Scottish magic, which you can read in a book and DIY, if you have the aptitude. The chivanhu craft is passed down by presence, voice and demonstration. I've had the two former, but not the crucial last piece in the jigsaw.

This will be like doing open heart surgery without ever having handled a cadaver, a scalpel, or even been in theatre before. As far as tests go, this sucks and I have a good mind to tell the Sorcerer Royal that.

I really shouldn't be doing this.

Turn and leave this place, Ropa.

'Are you ready, ghostalker?' Viscount Mieville asks.

'GGhhoossttaallkkeerr,' the ghost within Sophie echoes, using her mouth as a puppeteer pulls the strings of his toy.

Gran also told me that the longer these types of possessions go on, the more damaged the psyche of the victim becomes. Even if it's sorted later, they'll be all messed up. There's the rock. But if you attempt to excise the ghost and fail, it becomes even more deeply entrenched, so you end up making the problem worse. That's the hard place. And the worst-case scenario is you spook the ghost and end up excising both it and the victim's soul, in which case they die. That's the pit beneath your flailing feet when you're stuck between the rock and the hard place.

Decisions, decisions.

'WWee ssee yyoouu.' Sophie's words are hissed out, as though passing through a viper's jaws. 'TThhiiss bbooddyy iiss oouurrss. II ssnnuucckk iinn wwhhiillee nnoo oonnee wwaass wwaattcchhiinngg.'

'What gives you the right?' Screw this. I'm pissed off at the violation. I can't just leave it.

'TThhee TTaallll MMaann.'

The words strike me like a blow. My mind must be playing tricks on me 'cause the young woman in the bed resembles . . . no, it can't be, that's impossible. Been yonks since I last heard that name, and it's not one I much wanted to encounter again. What's going on here? Fuck it. We're in for a penny now. I unsling my backpack from my shoulders, bringing it in front of me, and open the zipper. I take out my mbira and toss the bag on the floor behind me.

Sophie, or whoever's inside of her, bares her teeth.

Snarl all you like, bitch.

Normally I use my mbira to synchronize the harmonics, enabling me to speak with visitors from the other side. Otherwise, all that comes out is gibberish, booga-woogaring, that kinda thing. But we can all hear this ghost, 'cause it's using a host who's tethered to this realm. Sophie's still in there somewhere, pressed down, squashed at the back, forced to watch in horror like a madzikirira, the nightmares of sleep paralysis.

'You le-leave her alone now,' Mieville says, but there's hesitancy in his voice.

'WWoorrmm.'

'I need you all to be very quiet,' I say. 'No one addresses it but me.'

'DDiiee. YYoouu aarree oonnee ooff uuss,' it hisses, 'aall-rreeaaddyy.'

Gran warned me they are quick to threaten you. And it doesn't get any bigger than death threats. Anything they can do to shake you, they will – to make you forget the rights you hold in this realm. A power forbidden to them.

'Tell me your name,' I say. *Don't ask them anything. Command.*

'TThhee NNeeww OOllyymmppuuss ssiittss aattoopp EEddiinnbbuurrgghh's SShhaammee.'

Don't let them distract you.

'I command you to tell me your name.'

Sophie hisses, covering her ears, swaying her head side to side. I walk towards the bed, but quickly duck as the retro wind-up alarm clock on the bedside cabinet flies at my head. It hits the wall and the alarm starts ringing, even though it's broken and the gears are scattered all over the floor. The little hammer goes nuts on the bells.

I'm hit by a wave of revulsion.

The eyes within Sophie follow my every movement. And behind us the door slams shut.

'This is not good,' Mieville says. 'That spirit isn't supposed to be here.'

'Shut up already,' I reply.

'You can't tell me what to—'

'She can,' Lord Samarasinghe says with a hint of annoyance. 'Go ahead, Ropa.'

Okay, concentrate.

'We can do this the easy way or the hard way,' I tell the violator.

'RReejjooiiccee. TTooggeetthheerr wwiitthh hhiiss ddiiss-cciipplleess hhee wwiillll ccllleeaannssee tthhee aaccrrooppoolliiss aanndd rreebbuuiilldd tthhee AAtthheennss ooff tthhee NNoorrtthh, ttoo lliigghhtt tthhee wwoorrlldd oonnccee mmoorree, aass iitt ddiidd bbeeffoorree. AAllll wwiillll bbeennndd bbeeffoorree tthhee oolldd nneeww ggooddss.'

And it goes on like its heid's full o' mince. In its drivel, it continues to evade my question and rejects my Authority. This has never happened to me before. Shouldn't happen. Not even with the worst poltergeist. What's keeping it tethered here? I wonder. Leaves me wading deeper into these uncharted waters.

Had I known, I'd have prepped better.

Shit.

'You have no business in this realm,' I say. 'But I'll bargain with you regardless. You can make any request, one within reason, and when it's done you must leave this place, never to return again.'

'TTrriinnkkeettss.'

'I can find your bones and bury them where you please, tell your family of your torment, or name your murderer if that's your grievance. I can ease your passage to the Land of the Tall Grass, where your ancestors wait to embrace you and tell you the truths of existence.'

'CCaann yyoouu oofffeerr mmee lliiffee?'

'Don't ask for the impossible. If you do not name a reasonable price, I'll take my gloves off and send you to the Other Place, the realm from which there is no return, only the gnashing of teeth for all eternity.'

'YYoouu aarree aallrreeaaddyy ddeeaadd.'

Screw this wanker, it's time to go old school. From someplace within Sophie's body, I can hear the wailing of her soul. It's as though every word this spirit speaks carves out a small piece of her eternal essence. It's using her as a battery.

I twang the first note on my mbira and Sophie's body flops

back in the bed, as though shot by a high calibre bullet. Doesn't last long, though, 'cause almost immediately she sits up again.

With my Authority undermined, there's a piece I can play for this particular situation. I start the 'Chaminuka Ndimambo', which invokes the divine authority of the mhondoro. This is a national spirit ancestor, son of the architect of the Mutapa Empire, and was a symbol of resistance in the wars of independence fought by my grandmother's people. Gran warned me that you don't invoke these powers lightly. As I strike my keys, calloused thumbs running over the metal, I go heavy on the bass to counter the possessor's resonance. Sophie screams even louder.

A tempest rises in the room, swirling around with her in its calm eye.

It blows out the lamp Wilfred is holding and I hear his body fall to the ground. He's sobbing, and we are in darkness, yet still I play on.

'Please stop, Sophie,' he cries.

A red light shines and I'm grateful to the viscount for conjuring this, though it now looks like the room is bathed in blood. There's tension in the keys of my mbira. The lords hold up their hands to shield us from the objects being thrown up in the whirlwind. I brace myself and inch forward, feet wide apart to stop myself falling over.

'By my Authority, I cast you into the depths of the Other Place, never to return,' I yell.

Sophie grimaces in pain. I see the foul spirit slowly being pulled out of her body. It desperately tries to cling on, but I battle it, pouring every ounce of my will into the melody. A plume of ectoplasm rises in the air. It forms strange shapes, foaming, boiling, roiling, stretched out.

We're winning . . .

But I feel . . .

My mbira, the keys . . .

They're growing firmer and I have to use more force with each strike. Still I fight, invoking something greater than a mere ghost. But it's getting harder. A sharp pain shoots up my left thumb, making me wince. I've misstruck a key, tearing off half my nail.

Pure agony.

Blood drips onto my instrument as I grit my teeth and keep playing. Something's very wrong, this isn't how it's supposed to go. I can't panic now, though. *Don't stop playing.* Until the keys are slick with my blood and the notes infused with my pain.

No, no, no.

The keys grow immoveable under my thumbs and my music finally stops. No matter how hard I strike the mbira, I can't draw any sound out of it. Not a peep. A flying pillow knocks me in the gut, almost winding me, and I'm driven back. The ectoplasm begins to shift back into the body of Sophie, swooping downward through her screaming mouth.

I'm stunned, don't know what to do. I could try another tune, but which one? *Think fast, Ropa.* What would be the point anyway, if I can't even play my mbira? I feel so exhausted, as if I've been drained. Cold sweat trickles down my forehead and my back.

Once settled back in its vessel, the spirit looks at me with malice, a satisfied smile cracking a fraction. The swirling wind eases too, becoming a subtle breeze.

'This doesn't seem to be going very well,' Mieville says.

'No shit, Sherlock,' I spit back.

I turn to Lord Samarasinghe for aid, but he merely folds his arms, as though none of this was any of his business. I drop my mbira to the floor and cradle my throbbing hand. I should . . . Maybe if . . . Perhaps . . . ? Bryson Blackwood teaches, 'when you make your move, be bold, do not hesitate', but I'm not sure what to do anymore. My previous encounters with ghosts, where I've always come out tops, have left me woefully unprepared for this.

'Is it over?' Wilfred whimpers.

'No, you imbecile,' his master replies.

I will have to admit to Lord Samarasinghe, to everyone here, that I'm a fraud. There's nothing more I can do; I can't save her.

'AAnn eeyyee ffoorr aann eeyyee,' the spirit says. Sophie's eyes open, bloodshot even in this red ambient light. Her right hand is forced to rise, brought up to her face, towards her left eye. I hear Sophie's soul wailing in despair. A squelch—

'It's taking her eye out!' Wilfred shouts. 'Stop!'

Mieville retches.

I jump onto the blanket box at the end of the bed, and, without thinking, leap at Sophie, smashing into her. We fall back onto the bed, me on top of her. Then I push my spirit out of my body into her, using the momentum of my leap. If I can just . . . push this spirit out into the everyThere. There's pressure on all sides of me. Pins and needles all over. I've never passed through anyone's body before, and I think for a moment I've come out the other side, till I realize the three of us are now tumbling into the swirling astral plane.

'I'm scared.'

'Trust me, Sophie,' I say, reaching for her hand, but grabbing her by the ankle instead. I haven't a bloody clue what I'm doing, 'cause instead of winding up in the bleak greyness of the everyThere, we're in a river of many colours. *Hold on.* I can't lose her here. The astral plane's infinite and if we separate, I might never find her again. And she wouldn't be able to make her way back, not without experience. I feel claws digging into my free hand and see the spirit holding onto me, trying to scramble past to get to Sophie.

'She's mine,' the spirit says.

We're dragged by the river's wild currents – up, down, sideways, through dimensions unknown, those beyond the three in our world. It's disorientating. I try to focus, and battle to fling this ghost off my foot. Here in the void, I see its true face: a balding man with thick sideburns running into his moustache, colonial style. He digs his claws even further into me.

'Curse you. I was promised life,' he shouts.

Still we fall, or rise, in the colourful void, until we crash into a realm I've never seen before, scattered like billiard balls. This place is a never-ending desert of hot white sand, a scorching sun above us. I barely have time to reorientate myself when a shadow passes over me. I look up and see only a speck against the brilliant emerald sky. Most realms are dead, but not all. Some have ancient things, much older than our kind. Beings beyond our comprehension. Lovecraft's wet dreams.

Sometimes they can be asleep for aeons, only to be awakened by an intrusion. They don't like to be disturbed – this is their realm, much as the Earth is ours – and I feel its menace upon my soul, like maggots on a wound. This is why astral projection is not for the uninitiated.

I get up and run towards Sophie, who's lying a hundred or so yards from me, though distance in other realms is an illusion. It doesn't work the same way it does in ours. A single step can take you nowhere or half a galaxy away, depending on the rules of that particular universe . . . This sand feels like broken glass under my feet. Her violator is up on his feet too. He must sense the entity swooping down from the sky above as he runs towards the girl.

Gotta get there first.

'Come to me, Sophie,' I call, but my voice comes out booming, like a megaphone, sending ripples across the sand.

'It hurts,' she says, disturbing the sand even more.

'You must. Now!' I don't want to shout, but I have to.

Wormlike creatures begin to burrow out, emerging from underneath the sand. They're buried things, unalive and thirsty in this desertscape, and unbridled menace is the only thing I sense from them. That and desperation for nourishment.

Nope. They won't be munching on me – I ain't no one's scran.

But Sophie's still frozen to the spot, poor lass. Doesn't help me that her violator's gaining ground much faster than I can. He's coming from the left, while I'm running into the sun towards her. If he takes her, he'll be able to use her to push back into our world, since her soul's entangled with her body. He's desperate, I can see, 'cause he knows he couldn't do this on his own. Ghosts which cross the threshold of the everyThere into the astral plane proper cannot go back ever. It's a one-way street.

Sophie looks at him, then to me. Seems she finally makes up her mind, 'cause she starts running towards me.

The worms and whatever horror's swooping down from the sky are also rushing towards us. Everybody in play, converging on the same point. Thank Odin Sophie's moving now, opening up the gap between her and the ghost, and narrowing it between the two of us. I concentrate, focused on the cracks within the astral plane, trying to find a gap. Not easy when you're running in this scorcher.

Nearly there.

Less than twenty yards to go, if distance here is the same as in our world. Time may also work differently. All this could be happening in the blink of an eye or till the death of the sun, and I can't tell which it is. The possessor ghost redoubles his efforts and begins to make up the lost ground.

Ten yards.

He's catching up to her, as are the worms, which make a high-pitched rattle as they go. Sound almost like cicadas. The sun's now blotted out by the ancient being swooping down for us. It's immense, creating something of an eclipse. But instead of the temperature going down, it intensifies, as though the creature's a magnifying glass. I dare not look up. I leap into the air, arms outstretched, flying towards Sophie, and grab her just before the ghost does.

Like thread through a needle, I channel us away from this world, just as the first worm reaches the ghost. As we slip through, the sound of its curses follows us. He's not going anywhere now – stuck there for the rest of eternity, with only those beings for company. But I have no time to gloat as I navigate the rapids of the astral plane, guiding Sophie's soul, holding her fast, close to my breast, as we make our way home.

'You're safe now,' I soothe her as best I can.

We're spat out somewhere in the sky above Arniston House, and fall like shooting stars through the tree canopy, through the roof of the servant's cottage, and back into the bedroom. Her soul passes through my body before sinking back into her own.

I'm still lying on top of Sophie when we come to.

She screams and shoves me hard off her, and I tumble onto the cold floor, landing on my back.

That was mental.

I lie there for a minute, contemplating my life choices. Wilfred's jabbering and I see Una has come back inside the room. She's at the bedside talking hysterically, bubbling, happy to have her daughter back.

Lord Samarasinghe walks up to where I'm lying and regards me from above. Then he offers me his hand.

'Bravo,' he says. 'I admire the improvisation.'

'How long was I gone?' I ask, looking up at him. My body feels okayish, so I haven't come back as an old person at least. That would suck.

'Long enough,' Lord Samarasinghe replies.

I take his hand and he pulls me up, showing minimal effort. No lie, it feels good to be back, and to have succeeded in freeing Sophie from torment. That would earn me brownie points on Gran's current rerun obsession *Touched by an Angel*. But I'm done with this ghostalking business. When Samarasinghe keeps his end of the bargain, I'm training as a scientific magician so I'll never have to do this sort of nonsense again.

'Well done, Ropa Moyo. This rogue spirit was going to ruin everything,' Viscount Mieville says.

'What do you mean by that?'

'Nothing at all. It's just dreadful that some random spirit can terrorize decent people. I knew you were the one to call on. I never doubted you for an instant.'

How they lie so easily. Don't care, I just want to get paid and go home.

The electrics must be back, 'cause the lights are on again. Yay. I still can't get over the fact Sophie reminds me so much of a man I knew once, from a spooky mansion in Edinburgh a while back. The butler, Wilson, who'd also talked of the Tall Man. The fog in the room draws back, but isn't lifted in a normal way – rather it's sucked in all directions, into another dimension altogether. Into the everyThere. Something's very wrong in all this hullabaloo. That world is glued to ours, but never before have I seen it exceed its limits like this.

I pick up my mbira and stuff it back inside my backpack.

'Are you okay, Sophie?' I ask.

She's smothered in her mother's embrace and has to wriggle out of it. It's only now Wilfred thinks to cover her with a blanket, 'cause she's still in her birthday suit, showing us all her bits.

'Get her some warm soup,' I say. It feels like something my grandmother would suggest. But when you've been to hell and back there's nothing a good Scotch broth can't make right.

'And teas all round, please, Wilfred. There's a good chap,' Mieville says.

'Very good, sir.'

I'm seething, thinking the good lord could have got it himself, to give the poor man a bit of time with his great-niece. But I know when not to meddle. I'm too exhausted to be getting into it with anyone right now.

'It felt like a horrible nightmare. I was there, seeing everything happen, but there was nothing I could do,' says Sophie, shuddering. 'Day after day stuck inside of myself, with that thing atop me. I couldn't breathe, I couldn't move. I wanted to cry out for someone to help me but I couldn't. Thank goodness you came.'

'Don't mention it. I'll always do right by you,' Mieville says, as he accepts the gratitude I'm certain was meant for me. Keeps the servants indebted.

'It had a complete hold over me; I was certain I'd die. Those vile things it said to you, Mama, that wasn't me. I would never say such things.'

'Where's your father? Is he somewhere around here too?' I ask Una. Poking my nose where it doesn't belong used to be my job when I was working with Sir Ian Callander. The habit hasn't brushed off yet.

'He said he was going to Edinburgh for work one morning, not long after Sophie was born, and never came back,' Una replies. 'Useless man he was. Hardly a father at all.'

'Abandoned his family and his job. What kind of man does that?' says Mieville.

'Do you have any photos of him?' I enquire, my mind

churning with possibilities. Grope in the dark and who knows what you'll turn up.

'Why, what good would that do?' Una replies. 'They were all burnt down in the Rowantree cottage we lived in, before we were given this place. We lost everything we had.'

'It was started for kicks by drunk teenagers from Gorebridge. It's dreadful when they wander out here. Used to be we didn't have guards keeping watch at night, but I sorted that out. These are dangerous times we live in.'

I drop it. There's not much else left for me here. My last job's done. I'm kind of numb from it, apart from the searing pain in my thumb where the nail came off. That's gonna be tender for a good while. I need some Savlon and a bandage, so I ask for the toilet and leave the room.

It's the next door down the hallway, so not far to go. I run the cold water tap and flinch, thinking about cleaning my thumb, but I just can't do it. Instead, I rummage through their cabinet and find a box of plasters, which look pretty dated, but beggars, choosers and all that. I open a fresh pack and wince as I apply it to my ruined thumb. It's still bleeding a fair bit, so I layer on a second and third to soak up the blood.

Then I put the toilet lid down and sit for a mo.

Just bow my head and let the adrenaline drain out of my system. Yep, I'm done with this life. Can't wait to go down south and start a new one. I rest for a bit, until there's a knock – Una checking on me.

'I'll be there in a minute,' I say. Can't a lassie have a moment?

I eventually return to the living area, where Lord S and the viscount are stood chatting about something. The furniture in this house is so messed up, they daren't dirty their fine clothes by sitting on it.

'This has been a fun night, wouldn't you say, Ropa?' the Sorcerer Royal says, positively beaming.

'Pay me. I wanna go home,' I say.

'It's rather late at night and my accountant is on holiday. You should invoice me. That's the *professional* way to do it,' Mieville says.

'Pay me now. Cash. I don't have a bank account.'

'That's hardly my fault, is it?' Mieville snaps at me.

'You will pay the girl what she's owed without delay,' Lord Samarasinghe says in a low voice. His mood has darkened in an instant.

Mieville opens his mouth, stammers, then thinks better of it. I'm grateful Lord Samarasinghe's picked my side in this. Our host fishes into his jacket pocket and produces a thick wad of notes. He starts to count, but Samarasinghe grabs the lot from him and hands it to me. It's a fair bit of money! There're benefits to working for English magic after all. Wait till Gran sees this. I try not to look too gleeful.

'I'd say she's earned her tip. Wouldn't you agree, sir?' he says and Mieville nods reluctantly. 'I trust you'll also remember to give His Majesty's Revenue and Customs their share. The black economy is killing this country. Right, that's all settled now and I'm rather famished after all this excitement. Perhaps the viscount would like to provide nourishment for us before we depart?'

'I want to go home. My grandmother's all on her own,' I say.

'Very well, Briggs will accompany you. And Ropa, I'm almost impressed by your extemporization. That doesn't happen often,' Lord Samarasinghe says. 'You'll go far in the magicking profession. I'll ensure nothing holds you back from now on.'

Those words stay with me all through the coach ride home.

IV

It's the witching hour when Briggs drops me off by the big roundabout near Hermiston Slum. The burly Yorkshireman in his greatcoat grunts – that's his way of saying goodbye or goodnight, I'm not sure which. Then he sets off back east on the bypass. Those poor horses pulling the carriage have put in a fair shift too. Serving Lord Samarasinghe isn't exactly a nine-to-five. But I'm just happy to be home. I've got a headache – those annoying ones which hit you on a temple, leaving the other side untouched.

Knackered, I drag my feet across the muddy field where rows of caravans, statics, containers and shacks have been set up. Brings it home stark when you've left a mansion in the woods, rubbed shoulders with nobles, and then come back to this. I love the place and adore the people who live here. I've made friends. It's been safe for us over the years too. On dark winter nights like this, though, I can't help but wish for something better. If I could take them all with me to England I would. But it's every man for himself and no god for any of us.

Lord Samarasinghe was impressed with me . . . Well, almost.

I wish all those bozos at the Society of Sceptical Enquirers could have seen me. My boots are caked in mud, but I'm too worn out to care. River pops out from her burrow underneath our small Rallyman caravan, and I kneel to kiss her.

'Hey girl, I've missed you too. Look what I've got for us.' I wave my bundle of cash at her, but she's not interested. Foxes don't care much for money. But she'll be loving it when I give her a juicy steak.

She whines as I open the door to leave her. 'I know I haven't spent much time with you lately,' I say. She looks at me with those large golden-orange eyes. 'Don't guilt trip me now, it's three in the morning, pal.' I step inside, leaving her be. I try to be as quiet as I can, not to wake Gran. It's just us two here now, since Izwi went to magic school. It's not the same without her.

Gotta remove my boots, 'cause I cleaned this whole caravan yesterday.

The brazier on the countertop's gone cold, the coal having burnt down. I take it outside and leave it next to the door. The window's slightly open, allowing a draught in. You've always got to do this, otherwise carbon monoxide poisoning will be the end of you. A couple of folks in this slum have gone that way – just drifted off in their sleep and never came to. I close the window, grab a spare duvet from the cupboard and throw it over Gran lying in her berth. Then I kiss her. Her lips are drawn, like she's smiling in her sleep.

I wonder what Gran dreams about.

Wait till I tell her about my exorcism tonight.

I ease myself onto my berth fully clothed. Too cold to do otherwise. Then I grab my duvet and shut my eyes.

* * *

I'm still half asleep as Gran's humming filters into my dream-
world, turning everything within it to wool and candyfloss.
Sometimes I make up my own lyrics to her tunes. This one's
filled with longing. I catch her zoned out a lot lately, as though
something's tugging at her heartstrings. Used to think it was
just a bit of fatigue, now I'm not too sure. Maybe she misses
Zimbabwe, or someone. And that someone is knocking on the
door right now.

'Come back later, Gary. My mzukuru's napping,' says Gran.

'I'm awake,' I mumble.

'No, you're not. You don't want to be like the princess from
Uzumba, who angered the king of dreams by refusing to dance
Jerusarema at his—'

'I know that one already, and the last time you told it, she'd
angered his wife by wearing a pangolin claw necklace.'

'Does this mean I can come in?' Gary says.

Gary O'Donohue is Gran's 'companion', 'cause old people
don't have boyfriends or girlfriends. They do keep each other
company an awful lot, so there's some truth in the label. I sit
up and wipe away the gunk from the corners of my eyes. I'm
still a bit worn out from last night's shenanigans, but I should
be making my next move. Hanging with these two for too
long's like watching the History Channel without the cutaways.
I'm sure Hugh Miller, the nineteenth-century fossil hunter,
would have learnt a thing or two from them . . . Cancel that,
he was a wee bit dodgy. Then again, they all were in them
days, weren't they?

'Blooming rats have raided my stores again. They snatched
a pound of my smoked haddock. I was looking forward to

having that. And can you believe they left me with droppings which I've had to clean up as well?' Gary moans as he strides over to Gran and gives her a peck.

'Gross, get a room, people,' I say.

'I've not been seeing much of yous about the estate, Ropa,' says Gary. 'Been up to your usual mischief then, have you?'

'Minding my own business. Keeps the rent paid and the belly fed.'

Gary hovers before deciding to sit next to me, 'cause Gran's berth is full up with material, extending over to the shorter berth used by Izwi when she's about. She's working on something a bit weird. Loads of synthetic material. Maybe it's a shell suit of some sort, though there's way too much material for that. Folks come here all the time leaving her with wool, to see if she can make them something cool. But this is proper nylon, which rustles as Gran hand sews different pieces together to form some kind of red and black mcthingy. Then she has all this kernmantle rope lying around too. Nothing like the usual jumpers and scarves she knits.

'What are you making?' I ask.

'A little present for one of your little friends,' Gran replies somewhat cryptically.

'We'd make a mint if you actually sold some of this stuff instead of giving it away for free.'

'Your nana's dressed half the estate. This is keeping my head warm and all.' Gary O'Donohue points to the black beanie hat on his head. It's got cute little hearts worked into the design too.

He's a great addition to our family, especially in the summer when his veg patch is brimming. I wish I had more time to hang with Gran, but Gary more than makes up for me. He's there when Gran's feeling iffy 'cause of her diabetes. Means I don't have to worry as much when I'm out and about. She's well taken care of. I'll be able to spend more time with her when we're in England, though. If I make anything close to the cash Lord Samarasinghe gave me last night, then we'll be well and truly sorted. Which brings me to the matter at hand.

'Gran, I need to talk to you about something important,' I say.

She slows her sewing and looks up, face puckered. Here goes.

'I've been offered a great opportunity in England by a top business out there. I'll be able to go back to school.' Can't say it's a gift from the Sorcerer Royal, 'cause Gary O'Donohue is here. Much as I love him, some things are for Gran's ears only. 'It's the full ride. And on top of all that, we'll have a small house, a proper one, where you and Izwi can stay. The people who're organizing this will also take care of your health. They have the best doctors and stuff down there. Our lives would change so much. Isn't that exciting?'

Gran sits there, impassive. Her cloudy eyes stare off into the far distance, some place none of us can reach. It's what we've always wanted, ever since Gramps, rest his silly soul, gambled the house away. No more drifting around. A house with running water and maybe power too. Someplace warm.

'What do you think?' I ask. 'Gran . . . Gran?' She then seems to snap up.

'It's a surprise,' she says.

That's it? I show her my winning lottery ticket and this is all I get in reply? I'd guessed she wouldn't be thrilled about leaving Scotland, but I didn't think it would make her pass up something like this.

Gary looks like he's in pain. I know it's a blow for him too, but what can I do? His bushy brows draw together, twitching. Then he nods very, very slowly.

'I think you should seize this with both hands, Melsie. Your granddaughter's done something truly special. Not many leave Hermiston Slum unless that be inside of a wooden box. I know your health isn't the best, but this gives you a fighting chance. There's no way you could spend another winter in this place.' There's sadness and resignation in his voice. Then he tries to sound more cheery. 'This is what I'd want for you. But before you go, we'll throw you the mother of all leaving parties.'

'And you could come visit,' I say, knowing full well Gary can't afford the shilly-shilly into town, let alone a ticket all the way down south. Maybe if I saved I could get him something. I'll make a plan. 'How about it, Gran?'

'I won't make it to London, Ropa,' she finally answers. There's a weariness in her tone which I find troubling.

'Of course you will, Gran. What're you talking about? We're gonna make it big, 'cause Lady Luck's smiling down on us now.'

Gran shakes her head, looking pained, and resumes her sewing. I'm seething. Gary gives me a subtle gesture of his hand to try to stop me speaking, but I can't keep quiet.

'No, Gary, she said she won't make it to London. Is there something you're not telling me, Gran?' I say. 'And what's all this rope for anyways?'

The big sycamores near the canal which runs through our slum have seen a few unfortunates swing from them lately. Hard times creating all sorts of issues. Nah. Not Gran. I just as quickly feel ashamed to be even thinking like this.

'Perhaps we could discuss it another time. My joints hurt.' She flexes her fingers before finishing one final stitch, and then starts rolling up this thing she was making.

I'm relieved on seeing it's actually a parachute, and the nylon kernmantle rope's attached to it. Still weird, though.

'I'll talk to your nana, Ropa,' Gary offers.

I'm thankful he's on board. He really does love her and wants what's best for her. Then I check the time on my phone. Shit. I've got an appointment at Our Lady of Mysterious Ailments this afternoon, and there's no time to wash or anything like that.

'I've gotta go,' I say, getting up.

'Please could you give this to Priya, if you see her later?' Gran says, offering me the rolled-up bundle of black and red she's just sewn together.

'What's she going to do with this?' I ask, but Gran doesn't answer.

Looks like she's in a bit of a mood with me now. I'm running late, though, and I don't wanna mess up the vibe, so I stuff it into my backpack. Can't even force it to fit, so I let huge chunks of it dangle outside the bag. No idea what Priya's gonna make of all this, but that's not my problem. I hop over Gary's leg and head for the door.

'Won't you kiss me before you go?' Gran says, her voice quivering.

'I'm running late as it is,' I reply shortly, turning the door handle.

But I stop before I open it. I remember something Gran told me when Izwi and me were bickering ages back: *'You're sisters. When you argue, do so with love.'* I guess the same applies to her, even when I think she's being a right old cow about this opportunity. Must be she's just scared about moving to a new country. She's already done so once in her life, and now she's put down roots in Scotland.

I go back, kiss her, and give her a great big hug.

She holds on when I try to pull back, and then she starts crying. I feel awful. I've never made my grandmother cry before. All of England ain't worth one drop of her tears, and so I tell her I'm sorry. Then she tells me she loves me, no matter what.

V

Reckon I'll ride my bike along the canal with River trotting by my side. Someone's trimmed the path running alongside it, just after Wester Hailes, so it's pretty clear for this time of year. The council doesn't bother with this kind of thing much anymore. There's the skeleton of a narrowboat docked near the Slateford Aqueduct, which carries the Union Canal over the Water of Leith. The railings on it haven't been painted in a while and the rust's eating into them.

I've got an earworm dangling down my auditory canal, reading Elizabeth Fulhame's work *Catalysts and Accelerants: A Guide to Refining Practical Magic* to me. She has subtle ways of helping the practitioner reduce the time it takes to create a spell. Marginal gains. But a fraction of a second here or there makes a huge difference. It was the last audiobook the late librarian Mr Sneddon ever recommended to me in the Calton Hill Library. I kinda miss him now he's gone.

C'est la vie and all that, I guess.

Below the canal, alongside the Water of Leith, is an old building yard, as well as the Slateford Bowling Club, and an abandoned supermarket which was stripped bare ages ago. The cold cuts into my face as I cycle, so I loop my scarf over my mouth one more time. River rushes into a thicket to sniff at something. The land along the canal's rich for foraging, even in a winter like this. Soon it'll be time for the acorns and chestnuts. Blackberries grow in abundance here too. The trick is to time it before anyone else gets to them, but not too soon 'cause you don't want to be harvesting unripe fruit. It's a fine balance.

Makes me wonder whether I'll be able to do the same in England. I mean, I know Edinburgh like the back of my hand. It won't be the same down south. I guess that's why Gran's so scared of moving. Leaving behind everything we know and everyone we care about.

'I wonder if the English like foxes,' I muse to River.

She's magnificent in her winter coat. In the summer she can be a wee bit revolting when she's moulting, but now it's lovely and thick. Makes her look like she's put on a few extra pounds.

'Come on, girl. We're taking the long way round today.'

I always dither before my appointments with the psycho-magician, and we just about have enough time. Takes the edge off, though I really have to resist the temptation to lie. Then afterwards, I'll head off into the city to see my wee pally Jomo at the Library. Oops, almost forgot, I'm meant to pick up the Sorcerer Royal to take him there too, for an appointment with Dr Maige.

In the distance I can make out grey figures, barely visible as they blend into the dull sky. It's a bit early for the dearly departed to be manifesting like this. Even in the dimness of the day, with the sun a mere shiny patch against the bleak blanket smothering the city, ghosts shouldn't be abroad just yet. Nah, I'm just mistaking wisps of smoke pouring out of the chimneys in the south for spectral activity. Must be losing my touch.

'Come on, River, over we go,' I say. 'Yeah, I know you've got other things you'd rather be doing with your time, but stick with me. I got paid well last night, and I think you're due some venison. I'm talking *real* game here. I'm not one of those arseholes who'll stiff you with a slab of beef and call it venison.'

We come up to the bridge after Meggetland and cross over onto Colinton Road. The area we're in now is too damned close to the Edinburgh Ordinary School for Boys for my liking. Me and them posh wankers don't get on one bit. Not after all the shenanigans that happened during the last Society Conference at Dunvegan Castle. Now why would I start thinking about that malarkey so close to the clinic?

Happy thoughts.

No remorse.

'Ground yourself in the present, Ropa,' I say.

'Easier said than done,' I reply.

Okay, I need to stop talking to myself. Must be 'cause I'm nervous. Finally we hit the gates of Our Lady of Mysterious Ailments, the exclusive magical clinic where my bestie works. I couldn't afford nothing here, despite my recent solvency, but Priya's pulled a few strings and so I'm allowed to use the facilities.

The gardens are still immaculate, despite the time of year. They've brought in some greenhouse structures to protect their precious herbs. Polytunnels of steel tubular frames covered with polythene sheets. Must be heated too. And the scents! When they hit you it feels like glorious spring. I almost forget the nip going through my boots.

'You can't bring that in here,' a new receptionist says to me.

'She's my emotional support animal,' I reply, pulling out my earworm and pocketing it.

'I've just done them floors,' the cleaner, armed with a mop bucket, complains.

'Touché,' I reply.

'I don't think that retort works in this particular instance, Ropa,' my psychomagician says, entering the reception area. 'You're late again. It eats into our sessions. I'm beginning to get the impression this is deliberate, so you'll be happy to know I rescheduled us to right about now.'

Dr Morven Checkland, hobbit-short, is wearing a cardigan which matches her auburn beard. And she has a ponytail, with numerous loose strands dangling out of place. She wears large oval glasses, sitting at the tip of her snub nose, and this looks very red, as though she's had a bad cold. Until you realize that's what it's like all the time. It doesn't help either that her voice is very nasal, so it took me a while to suss this out.

'I love the new earrings,' I schmooze.

'And you've dyed your hair silver,' she observes.

'It doesn't mean anything,' I say.

Checkland gives me a noncommittal shrug and I wanna protest. That's what meeting with her feels like. Every slight gesture, pause, phrase, seems as though it's undergoing some deep, profound analysis. Sometimes I tell her to chill, but then again, I know even that would mean something to her.

When I first met Checkland, she said she was heavily influenced by the work of the Glaswegian psychiatrist Ronald David Laing, who while not a magician worked closely with the healers at Our Lady.

I'd love to see what she scribbles in her notes on me . . . No. Not really. Never.

She leads me to her office on the ground floor, right at the back of the building. It has large windows looking out to the garden, where some patients are convalescing in the bitter cold.

Dr Checkland waves her hand and the curtains draw shut.

The room is still warmly lit by the Himalayan salt lamps, one behind her desk and the other on the wee table in the corner diagonally opposite. Though we're in a clinic, this space feels very much like a home office. There's a small bookshelf with various psychology tracts. It also has a few novels by Dostoevsky and Camus, whom Checkland says were virtually psychologists, before the term was invented.

There's a calming scent in the room. Lavender mainly, with hints of Roman chamomile and sweet basil, maybe even a touch of peppermint too. They waft out of the essential oil diffuser next to the lamp. Certainly works on me. I feel pretty mellow whenever I come in here. Like, I'm proper nervous out there, but once I'm in the office, and Dr Checkland has shut her door gently, everything kinda sloughs off.

I plonk myself on the couch and put my feet up on a pouffe. Contrary to what you see in films, you don't have to lie down when you talk to your psychomagician. I wouldn't want to either. That'd make me feel like there's a weight on my chest which I can't shift. No. I'd rather be sat up, so I can just breathe.

River settles down on the carpet near my feet. She's always mighty relaxed when we come to this office. Soon her head drops and her eyelids become heavy, and I wonder what foxes dream of during daylight hours.

Checkland's standing by a small cabinet, where she turns on the kettle for us. Must have very little water in it, because it doesn't take long at all to boil. She pops some teabags in plain white mugs and hands me one.

'Chamomile,' she says.

'You'll have me flat out horizontal at this rate,' I quip.

'Your legs are jiggling. Are you planning on running out again?'

I shake my head. I did bolt the first time I came here, when shit went too deep. Then ended up taking it out on Priya for bringing me here. Checkland walks around the room, setting up crystals in a pattern which seems random to me. Most of them are aquamarine and sodalite. The latter's supposed to be empowering, to help you speak your truth, that sort of thing. She places one azurite on either side of me, and then goes to take a seat in the wing chair at my right. It's set at an angle, so we don't face each other directly. When I look, I just see the side of her face, crow's feet by her eyes shifting whenever she squints.

'It's been a mad week,' I say at last. She nods, encouraging me to elaborate. 'I did an exorcism pulling a spirit from a person for the first time.' I show her my broken nail. 'It was a bit tougher than I expected, but I got the bastard.'

Dr Checkland tugs at her beard. It's kind of soothing seeing her do that. Like she's all there for you, listening to every word.

There's never any real pressure to punctuate the silences. Like right now, I know she's waiting for me to resume once I'm ready. Best of all, she never looks like she feels pity for me, or anything like that. Treats me like a grown-up, and that's the way I prefer it. I can take anything from anyone save for pity. Stuff that.

There's a weird clock on the wall. Three hands sit against a real yew tree base, with the tree's rings a stark reminder there are other ways of measuring time. Midnight is marked by a crack along the stump, and the central rings are much darker than the other ones. There are cracks along its edges too, not quite where the hour notches should be, 'cause these ones are natural. But the really crazy thing about it is, when you first enter the office, it's set at midnight, with all three hands pointing north. Then at the end of your session, the second hand may tick a bit, or it could be the hour hand pushing to tick off an hour or two. Sometimes nothing at all happens, and the time remains still. Or it might even retreat backwards. Checkland told me that the clock starts at midnight and every client's treatment ends when it finally touches midday.

I'm still only at four in the morning, with a few minutes to spare.

Used to be, I thought I could rush it, like cramming for a test, but you can't fool the clock. It reads your energy. That's why they call it the Psyche Timepiece, after the goddess of the soul who was born a mortal woman.

Checkland continues to tug gently at her beard, staring into the wall opposite as though she's in a sort of trance. We've never talked about my anxiety – not in any great detail. My psychomagician believes that discussing it directly would be to merely deal with the symptom, not the cause itself. Instead we go round in what feels like a circular path up a hilltop, hidden behind grim, grey clouds.

'I had a bust-up with my nan,' I volunteer, standing up.

'What happened?'

I don't much like sitting down for too long, would rather move around the office – it helps me think. And so I head towards the desk and walk around it, hands behind my back. There's my version and then there's the truth. I hesitate and decide to tell it like it happened. I see the second hand of the clock move a fraction out of the corner of my eye.

I leave Checkland's office somewhat lighter, but battered and bruised all the same. That's the hallmark of any good workout. Good thing I ain't paying her for this, 'cause unlike them rich folks, I'd be mighty sore if this was my gym subscription.

'There she is,' Priya shouts from reception, where she's been waiting for me.

'What happened to your hair?' I ask.

'You don't like it? I thought we could be twinnies?' She runs her hand through it. 'Doesn't go with my face, does it?'

'It's very manga,' I reply.

'Oh, you know how to make a lass feel great about herself,' Priya says with a laugh.

She's dyed her hair silver like mine, but with a pink fringe worked around it. Looks great, I love it. We could be the Corsican sisters, the way she looks.

'I've got a present for you,' I say.

'It's not even Valentine's, babe.'

'Not from me, silly sausage. This one's from Gran.' I'm relieved now I can take this damned load out of my bag. Priya opens out the parachute and inspects it, running her hands over the stitching. Now she's unravelled it, it covers a large area of the reception, and the staff don't look too pleased about that. Priya's eyes widen and then she grins. I wait for her to say something, but she doesn't. Merely folds the parachute up again and stuffs it in a pouch at the back of her wheelchair.

'It's the best present anyone's ever given me,' she says. 'Tell Gran I absolutely love it.'

'What on earth are you gonna do with it?'

'Damned if I know.' She shrugs.

There's weird, then there's . . . never mind.

Me, Priya and River make our way towards town, first to pick up Lord Samarasinghe. When we get to Morningside, there's angry-looking men and women in trench coats stood in the middle of the road holding placards. They don't obstruct the bicycles, carts and electric cars from going about their business. But they hold their position with determined looks on their faces.

Some of them are no older than I am. Their placards read: 'Bread and Work', 'Dignity', 'RIP 1707', 'Enough is Enough', 'Think of the Future Generations', 'Unite for a Better Life' and 'Every Man Dies, Not Every Man Really Lives'.

And loads of similar slogany sounding stuff. Bit ballsy of them to be out here in the cold, but I'm not too sure what Johnny Law'll make of all this. Me, I'd rather have gone around and avoided being spotted anywhere near them, but Priya seems to be cool wading through it, so I follow her lead. Even she's gone quiet, though, after being chatty moments ago. A man with a thistle in his flat cap is holding a megaphone, shouting some shit about the Seven Ill Years returning sevenfold this year. In the 1690s, Scotland had its coldest decade in a millennium. It was some Biblical-type shit that set off a famine, killing a ton of folks back then. Bodies on the roadside, and vagrants wandering the countryside desperate for food, begging for any bit of charity. Aye, those were lean times. Nearly broke the country and all.

I recognize the looks of some of the men watching from the sidelines. Their clothes are in better condition than the rags the protesters wear. Their hands are smooth from not doing any real labouring. Years working for the Clan mean I can spot informers a mile away.

'Come on, Priya. Let's get out of here,' I say, as a girl thrusts some kind of leaflet at me. Nope, I ain't touching that.

'I'm with you on that one,' she replies, speeding up.

We move well away from the Morningside racket, hastening our stride through Tollcross, and scurry further along until we're up the steep slope of Johnston Terrace, where I have to help Priya with her chair. It's tricky, wheeling my bike along too.

'I'm well knackered today. Lethington's working me to the bone lately. It's not easy given how demanding our clientele is. I don't get it. You eat like a slob all your life, and you don't bother exercising, then you expect someone to miraculously sort it out. Like, hello. Half the time they don't take the advice you give them, especially pertaining to lifestyle changes.

They all just want a magic pill to cure it. And to top it off, I have a disciplinary, because of some dobber who's made a complaint against me.'

'Ah, the stressful life of the gainfully employed,' Lord Samarasinghe says, appearing beside us as we hit the Royal Mile. 'That's what separates you from this lot.'

Bloody hell. Well, I guess it saves us picking him up from his place. Now to the Library.

There're the thistle-wearing types up on the high street too. A disparate band of the old and young, all genders, unified by their desperate circumstances. But to stand here, on these slippery setts, holding placards, is asking for it.

I'm kinda relieved we've got Lord S with us now, though I wish he'd stare a little less contemptuously at the mob. His tailored dress looks more than out of place, given the mended rags most of this lot are wearing.

There's the ill odour of metaphorical gas in the air.

One tiny spark and it'll hit the fan.

None of this means anything to the Sorcerer Royal as he walks through the crowded streets. And people make way for him. Even the buffest, most dangerous-looking types step away. He taps his cane on the setts as we walk past St Giles' Cathedral. On any other day of the week, he might be the gentleman flâneur taking in the marvels of the Old Town. I can sense the tension building around us.

'Good friends, brothers, sisters, will you not join our just cause?' a burly woman in an apron says, stepping in front of him.

Lord Samarasinghe places his cane gently on her left arm. I shudder thinking about those blood-curdling screams I heard last night. This woman doesn't seem like a bad person. Then I'm relieved when Lord Samarasinghe delicately moves her to the side, out of his path.

We proceed behind him, with me staring down, doing the best I can to ignore those Scottish glares. I remind myself I work for England now. Fuck them all.

The crowd clears a little as we cross over North Bridge and push past the struggling stores, former whisky shops and touristy haunts turned into charity shops and bargain bin outlets. The reek of piss and shit wafts potently from the wynds and closes dotted about. Broken windows. Burglar bars. Security men and members of the Clan smoking cigars, warding off would be shoplifters from the businesses that have paid protection fees. The rest are left to fend for themselves.

I'm turning to go towards Princes Street when Lord Samarasinghe stops suddenly, bows his head and then walks off the pavement into the road. He stands there for a moment in deep contemplation, before turning back to look at the junction. I point towards the Balmoral to let him know this is the fastest route to the Library, but he ignores me.

Then he snaps his fingers and a bouquet of delphiniums mixed in with roses appears. The blooms are gorgeous, vivid red against true blue, and lush despite the season, as though this was the height of summer. Priya gives me a look and I shrug. Lord Samarasinghe closes his eyes, holds the bouquet to his nose and inhales deeply, savouring the scents. He holds his breath for a while, before letting go with a sigh.

'So this is where it happened,' he says.

He turns and walks back into the middle of the junction,

where he then places the flowers, before coming back to us. His shoulders droop. There's a weariness to his gait, as though the weight of the world has come crashing down upon him. His face is contorted with grief. I've seen that look before, back when I was ghostalkering, delivering messages from the dead to those they left behind. Doesn't matter how long it's been since they passed, the histrionics might be gone, the drama of the wake long past, but like those underground coal fires which burn forever beneath our feet, you can be certain the hurt remains, right there. Lord Samarasinghe looks small and vulnerable suddenly, like an orphan. He clasps his hands together by his waist. It seems the might he wields has been overshadowed by something much more powerful. Who is it that he mourns?

'Our sovereign's parents were in a carriage coming back from the Royal Lyceum, where they'd been to watch the Scottish play.' He looks heavenward and then at me. 'It was then here, on this very crossroads, that the separatists and their sympathizers waylaid them, overpowering the men guarding them, who were loath to fire at their fellow countrymen. On this very spot, they reneged on their promise that, even should their vile goal of Scotland leaving the Union come to fruition, they would not see the crowns separated. It was to be like in the time of James the first, who is James the sixth to you. Fine words. But lies.'

Priya goes blank. I can tell she totally doesn't want to be here right now. Neither do I, to be honest, but what can I do? I know how this story goes. Lord Samarasinghe begins to walk and I can only follow.

'They forced the king onto his *knees*. On these dirty cobble-stones. And they put a collar around his neck, then dragged him on all fours, as though he were a dog. These streets rang out to their rendition of "Flower of Scotland". Can you hear it, Ropa, echoing through those dark alleyways?'

I judge that one to be rhetorical, so I stay schtum.

'Do you know the words?' he asks.

'I do,' I reply.

'Sing it. I want to hear them.'

I shake my head. This ain't in the job description. Priya's trembling in her chair and I wish we could swap 'cause my legs are jelly now too.

'Sing!' he shouts.

What can I do? It's not gonna win me a spot on any talent show, but . . . I mumble the 'hill and glen' part, definitely savaging any mention of 'Proud Edward's Army', and mangle anything about sending them 'homeward tae think again'. The second stanza's no better than the first. 'But we can still rise now / And be a nation again.' Who on earth thought it was a good idea to stick those lines in there?

I try to stop but Lord Samarasinghe says, 'Continue. I'll hear all of it.' Priya joins in and lifts her voice, proper belting it out now. Someone in an alleyway picks it up too. And then another, lying on the pavement, begins to sing. A baritone voice bellows, a shopkeeper stepping out to join in, as it travels the length of the pavement, climbing up the walls, out of windows flung open. And at the top of the Mile, the national anthem ignites the protesters somehow, spontaneously start-ing up a second time.

A lopsided smile appears on the Sorcerer Royal's face. He cocks his head, listening, scanning the faces around us, before continuing his walk. It seems he's taking us further down the Royal Mile, towards Holyroodhouse, instead of going straight to the Library.

'It would have sounded like that. Except the reports have people throwing excrement and tomatoes at the king and queen from the windows. Ah, the queen, you want to know what they did to her?'

I shake my head, and tighten my grip on the handlebars of my bike.

'They stripped her completely naked. Those vulgar eyes staring at her marks of motherhood. She who bore two sons to serve this nation. They laughed and sneered at her, even as she held her chin up, lofty despite the outrage she was suffering. Oh, I can understand why the Scotch and the French had their Auld Alliance back in the Dark Ages. Cut from the same cloth,' he spits.

Yeah, from the late thirteenth century onwards, we had a thing with France, teaming up when either party was at war with England, which happened often back in those days. This alliance endured the Hundred Years War, when Edward III set out to conquer Scotland. Then it cooled, but remained beyond the War of Roses, only becoming obsolete once the Scottish and English crowns united under James VI or I, depending on which side of the border you're from. The queen's ordeal had shades of Marie Antoinette, for it'd been a good while since a monarch was treated so roughly on this island.

There's raw emotion leaking from the Sorcerer Royal as we cross over Jeffrey Street to the bottom of the Mile, where setts have given way to tarmac, for they're too expensive to maintain. He stares at the ground ahead of him, as though tracing the old monarch's trail of blood from being dragged down this street on his hands and knees. This is a tale seldom retold in Edinburgh. On the rare occasions you hear it spoken of, whispered voices and nervous glances over the shoulder punctuate its rendition. The anguish is written on Lord Samarasinghe's visage. It's almost as though any moment now he'll get on his knees to wipe the ground. He then goes silent. Each step weighted with history, and at his age somewhere in the shadow of his living memory.

'I should probably go wait for you at the Library,' Priya whispers.

'Like hell you will,' I snap.

No chance I'm letting her bail, leaving me alone in this awkward situation. I guess we gotta play it cool, but I get nervous every time we pass someone with a thistle pinned to their dress.

'Ropa, do you see who I see?' she says, this time with more urgency.

'Son of a bitch,' I say, glimpsing a thin, pale lassie who, on spotting us, dives into Dunbar's Close. 'Quick, don't let her get away!'

Fenella MacLeod. Last I saw her was at the Society conference in Dunvegan Castle on the Isle of Skye. Her and a couple of lads from the Edinburgh School had killed Mr Sneddon and nicked the Fairy Flag. They went underground and vanished straight after that. Not a trace. Seeing her here, in the city of Edinburgh, sets my hunting instinct off, and I wanna dash after her. But I'm tied to Lord Samarasinghe right now. And catching them is a Society issue, not my business anymore. She's dyed her hair coal black, but it'd take more than that to make me forget her face. And I can guess she's not going into Dunbar's Close for the beautiful gardens hidden back there.

If Lord S minds Priya dashing away, he doesn't show it at all, and I'm really wishing I was right behind her. This is why I prefer being my own boss. I'll never get used to being on someone else's clock.

Be safe, Priya.

We pass the Canongate Kirk, in whose yard Adam Smith is buried, fittingly alongside a certain merchant called Ebenezer Lennox Scroggie. A man who inspired some English author going by the name of Dickens. If I'd hoped to entertain the Sorcerer Royal with such stories, the moment has gone. Maybe if we'd passed by on a different day, I could have shown him the city as I see it. It's my job, after all. Then we make our way past the ruins of the new parliament. That one's a story for another day too.

I can't stop thinking about Priya, though. Knapf. Sent her off without thinking. But again, Fenella MacLeod and that lot ain't my problem now. Stuff the Fairy Flag. I need to let go of things that don't concern me. I'm tired of making dumb moves and getting into scrapes where I ain't got no skin in the game, only to get my chebs pinched for it.

I send a quick message to Priya, calling her off and asking to meet at the Library instead. I hope she gets it.

The wrought-iron gates of Holyroodhouse swing open before us. Never in my life would I have thought I'd make it into this palace. I'm used to seeing it from behind the safety of its walls.

'They had to replace these, of course,' Lord Samarasinghe says.

The original gates were torn off by the mob who held the king and queen hostage. One of them was later discovered in the possession of an antiques dealer in Manchester and taken to the British Museum. What became of the dealer is anyone's guess.

The policemen guarding the palace today seem to be on edge as well. They can see what's going on inside the city. None of them engage the Sorcerer Royal as we enter, instead staying at their posts. Occasionally one might glance, but none dare look at him directly. It seems they too are afraid of him.

I've lived to see the man who scares even the pigs.

We are tiny beneath the grandeur of the palace. Bryson Blackwood teaches stuff about how power resides in whatever captures people's attention. Signs, symbols and spectacle. These grand old buildings do that to us, as we can't help but gawp at them, but this one is a grim, miserable place. It has a certain air of despair clinging onto it, and you can't help but feel it creeping through your pores. It's more like a giant mausoleum than a home. I have to do everything I can not to shrink before it. If I've learnt anything from my days with these folks, you've got to act as if you belong, though. Everyone's wearing a mask, even Lord S, and I need to become better at putting mine on if I'm to get ahead. That and minding my own business.

He stands in front of the entrance, before kneeling and placing one hand on the tarred driveway. And then Lord Samarasinghe heaves and begins to weep. Heavy tears dripping down his cheeks and splashing onto the ground. So deep, so genuine, so profound is his emotion, it's like those events decades ago only happened last night. He doesn't need to relay it, the last part of this story. How, on this very ground, the separatists finally bludgeoned the king and queen with boots, fists and clubs. They broke bones and tore flesh, taking more than their fair pound, spilling more than a single pint. Battered them beyond recognition. And when they were done, they entered the palace to loot and ransack.

I watch Lord S and wonder at this different side to him. Is this depth of emotion real? And all the while I can't help fidgeting with my phone – Priya's not messaged me back yet. I'll just have to hope I see her at the Library.

VI

River whimpers and pulls back when we come to the third pillar on the left of the unfinished Parthenon on Calton Hill. The hairline crack on the pillar is our way into the Library, and despite her being here with me plenty of times before, she still doesn't like it. Lord Samarasinghe waits silently while I try to coax her in. The sun's setting, painting the broken clouds on the horizon violet and indigo. I've still not heard from her and I'm becoming a bit worried.

Today River's making more of an almighty fuss than usual and the promise of treats doesn't seem to be working. I grow impatient, feeling the boss watching me.

'Be gentle, Ropa. Foxes are such sensitive creatures.' Lord Samarasinghe crouches, and, to my surprise, River allows him to pat her. 'There you go, little one. Portals are taxing to your acute senses, we know. But it'll be okay. Do as I do.' His voice is so gentle it could put a baby to sleep.

He steps into the fissure, and, lo, River follows him in.

Traitor.

I go through after them, stumbling with my bike, and we wind up in the familiar anteroom, in front of the steps that lead down into the Library proper. Maybe I should say *libraries*, because there's two of them combined into one under here: Calton Hill Library and the Library of the Dead. It's the same staff who run them both, though, and any differentiation is purely academic, of the splitting hairs variety.

I hand over my desiccated ear library card to the wee old man in bellhop attire who guards the entrance. His face is wrinkly, and he adds a few more on there as he frowns to inspect it. Once satisfied, he gives it back and turns to Lord S.

'Library card, sir?'

'This is Lord Samarasinghe, England's Sorcerer Royal. He's here at the invitation of Dr Pythagoras Maige, your head librarian.'

'I don't care if his name's Rasputin. No library card, no entry. Except for the fox – we only make exceptions for *Scottish* wildlife in this institution.'

Can't I catch a break? The last thing I need is pally here to be pissing off England's most powerful magician, triggering some kind of diplomatic incident in the process. I'm about to start negotiating when a pair of footsteps thud rapidly up the steps, along with the sound of keys or coins jangling too. Jomo Maige then bursts into the room, breathless, his acolyte's white robes flapping about as he almost collapses in front of the old man. A bunch of keys are dangling off a rope-like cincture around his waist.

'Mr Taskill, forgive me,' he says, struggling to catch his breath. He thrusts some papers at the old man who takes them with a sceptical look.

'It's Teàrlach. And if I read this date correctly, young Mr Maige, then it says I should have received this letter of introduction and temporary pass for Lord Samarasinghe last night.' He gives Jomo a withering look.

'Sorry, I is, was, tasks, yes, held up.'

'Talk sense.'

'I messed up, Mr Teàrlach. Please don't tell my fa— the head librarian. He'll kill me.' Jomo waves weakly at me. 'Ropademical.'

'It's Ms Moyo to you,' Mr Teàrlach says. 'The calibre of boys working in this institution leaves a lot to be desired. Lord Samarasinghe, you may enter our Library. Please ensure you deposit your wand at the reception downstairs. And you, Ms Moyo, I'm sure you know where to leave your bicycle too.'

'Follow me, my lord,' Jomo says, seemingly eager to leave Mr Teàrlach to his tasks.

We descend the steps hewn into the rock which makes up Calton Hill. Lord Samarasinghe is slow and deliberate, inspecting the art on the walls. In this section of the Library a lot of it is Christian iconography, because the Ethiopian craftsmen who worked on it were under the impression they were creating something akin to the monolithic churches at Lalibela. I learnt later that this wasn't the fault of dodgy trans-lation but a scheme to protect this secret place. Indeed, the builders, who thought they'd be going back to their country once it was finished, were enticed with homes and induced to stay. How could they leave, when some of them had already mingled with the locals and fallen in love by then? Their names remain etched upon moss-covered tombstones in the old grave-yards here. They're easy to find – just look for the ones with elaborate Coptic crosses.

'What do you think?' I venture to ask Lord S, recalling the awe I felt when I first came in here.

'Of what?'

'This place,' I say.

He doesn't reply, giving me nothing. I smile, knowing this is exactly what Blackwood meant when he argued you should never seem impressed by anything around you when performing in the theatre of power. 'Cultivate a certain appearance of having seen it all before, done much better elsewhere. That way even cultured people will defer to your superiority.' You might have been to the great palaces of the world – Versailles, Mysore, Topkapi – and attended the grand cathedrals, mosques, synagogues and temples – St Basil's, the Hagia Sophia, the Temple Mount, or even the Wat Chaiwatthanaram – but you'd still be moved by something when you come into this library. And even more so in the wide-open vault where the reception is, which we now enter.

Candles flicker in the dim recesses, like stars against the infinite black night. There's a vastness about Calton Hill Library and I haven't covered it all yet. No sooner do I discover one nook, than I find a cranny elsewhere.

Waiting at the reception in his scarlet robes is Dr Maige, Jomo's dad, and he remains impassive as we approach, until we're standing before him.

'My Lord Sorcerer, it is a great joy and privilege to welcome you to our humble library,' he says, bowing slightly, as does the receptionist Mr Evelyn next to him. 'It has been over a century since someone bearing your office has graced our sacred space.'

'My Lord Librarian,' Samarasinghe returns the courtesy.

I must seem flummoxed by this label because Dr Maige's eyes sparkle and I can see his lecture mode kick in before he speaks again.

'These young ones won't know that the keeper of this library is traditionally granted a peerage. A practice we are most pleased has been recently revived.'

'Yet you do not take your seat in the House of Lords,' the Sorcerer Royal observes.

'I've been reliably informed I'm better off associating with dead trees than I am politicking,' Dr Maige replies. 'Perhaps we could continue in my office before I give you a tour?'

Lord Samarasinghe consents and the two leave us, with Mr Evelyn swanning off to sit behind the reception desk. I can see the manoeuvring has started in earnest. The granting of Dr Maige's peerage will be sure to drive a wedge between the Library and the Society of Sceptical Enquirers. The Library contains Scottish magic's most precious treasures – works holding all its knowledge. But I'm not sure the Society could have done anything, since the Library is independent of it, something which used to cause a bit of friction with my old gaffer, Sir Ian Callander. I wonder what he makes of Dr Maige inviting the Sorcerer Royal to the Library.

Snatching this institution out of the grasp of the Society of Sceptical Enquirers would be a real coup for the leader of the Royal Society of Sorcery and the Advancement of the Mystic Arts. Would that even be possible? It's hard to know what the rules are anymore. The only thing which might help Scottish magic is the fact the head librarian is a stickler for those rules, whatever they are.

I stand in front of a white marble relief depicting Dolos, the Greek god of cunning and treachery, making a fraudulent sculpture of Aletheia, as his own master Prometheus watches on. The irony of the scene being, as Mr Sneddon once explained to me, that Aletheia was the goddess of truth and sincerity. I close my eyes, overwhelmed by a wave of emotion, and try not to miss him. But I can still hear his voice, asking what Prometheus's approval meant, since he'd been the creator of the original sculpture.

This place is packed with classical Greek statues, a collection greater than that at the British Museum.

'It's very apt you should admire this particular relief, since you too are a liar.' Frances Cockburn's voice interrupts my reverie. 'I was wondering when you'd show up here again. We half expected you to try breaking into Dundas House.'

'I'm sorry to disappoint you,' I reply, turning to walk away. She's one of the tossers who had me kicked out of the Society . . . well, almost, before I quit on them.

'I'm not through.'

'Go bother someone else, Frances. I work for the Sorcerer Royal now.'

'And how do you think that's going to go? What do you know of English magic? It's nothing like you'd expect.'

'Jealous doesn't suit you. Neither does that tacky two-piece suit.'

Cockburn purses her lips. 'Well, now you're here, Sir Ian Callander would like to have a word with you.'

I stop and look over my shoulder. I did leave the gaffer rather hastily, back at Dunvegan Castle. There was too much going on and I was done with the Society. Didn't want him trying to change my mind.

'He can arrange that with Lord Samarasinghe.'

'Word to the wise, Ropa Moyo. You'd do well to leave Scotland and never come back. No one wants you here.'

'Why, thanks for the advice, Frances. I fully intend to.' I give her a wink.

Cockburn's mouth is set in a hard line. It's gotta sting for them – an intern for the secretary of their organization choosing to jump ship and then work for English magic instead. I draw what satisfaction I can from it, 'cause they sure as hell didn't give a damn about me when I was busting my backside off for them.

Jomo and I move off, tracing our way around the balcony sculpted out of rock. The inside of the Library is a giant orb, ringed with balconies that lead to the bookshelves. Beyond those are a maze of rooms, alcoves and tunnels. And like a lab rat, you learn something new every time you explore it. Practitioners walk up and down the central staircases, shifting from one section to the next, while some are reading at desks below. Others browse the infinite shelves. We descend a series of steps set against the wall, until we reach the next tier.

'You sure it's a good idea to talk to her like that?' Jomo asks, once we're clear.

'She's a fuckwit.'

He flinches. '*Shh.* You can't say stuff like that in here.'

Dork. 'You seen Priya come in before us?' I ask.

'She came in ages ago looking hot and flustered. Something about seeing Fenella MacLeod?' Jomo grimaces, but quickly turns back to his jovial self. 'You want my advice, Ropa? Leave it well alone.'

'I agree.'

'It's not worth the risk . . . Huh? You agree with me?' He looks so relieved I could tug his cheeks.

'Naturally. Where's she now?'

'Somewhere in here.'

Which could mean anywhere. Given the size of this place, the quickest option might be to stick her face on a milk carton. I'm glad she's alright, though. I'll have to find a tactful way of telling her we're not to mess with Society business like that anymore. In the meantime, I intend to borrow a couple more titles from here. Maybe they have one on taming a Sorcerer Royal, or a travel guide on how to deal with the natives in England. I'm not liking the dodgy look on Jomo's face right now, though. I can read him like an open book, and he's got something to say, I know it.

'Out with it, then – you look bunged up.'

'Who? Me?'

'No, Mr Maige, I'm talking to this two-thousand-year-old sculpture in front of me.' I point at its lower torso and puny boaby. You couldn't even pee standing with that.

'I wanna take you somewhere,' he says hesitantly.

'If it's sunny and there's white sandy beaches, I'm game.'

He rolls his eyes.

'What? I thought that was pretty funny. Come on, man, you have to give me that one,' I say, punching him in the arm.

He lets out a half-arsed 'ouch' for my efforts. And anyway, since when did this dork start rocking sideburns like it was the olden days? Jomo sets off and I'm forced to follow him, wondering what the next surprise will be. His nervousness is setting me off too. He must be edgy working under his domineering dad like this, and I know Jomo's determined to succeed. Normally I'd be prodding him as we go, second guessing what he's about, but I'm too zen for that now. I doubt there'll be many other visits for me here either, the place where I first learnt scientific magic.

Still haven't told Jomo I'm planning on moving down south. Not sure how to break it to him. We've been pals forever, and I know how it'll go afterwards. Like, you call and text for a while, pretending you can keep the friendship going, but eventually the well dries up. Distance does that. You lose all the cool stuff in common that held you together. Then they make new friends, and so do you. Problem is, I really like the ones I've got now. They understand my accent.

He leads me down to the floor where David Hume's sarcophagus is kept. I have grim memories of that, but I figure he wants to carry on to the underHume, where there're cool labs and spaces where anyone can practise magic, which isn't allowed up here.

I look up and see the rounded splendour of the Library rising to its peak – on a busy day like this it's a hive. Hume and the magicians of old laid the eggs. Then somewhere up there are the drones and worker bees going about their lives. And everyone feeds off the honey that is the books and texts in this place. Despite the problems I've faced with folks like Cockburn, whenever I've come into this sacred space, I felt I was a part of something. It's the wisdom in the books which held us together, much as the pheromones in the hive do. We have all been shaped by it.

I don't know if I'll ever have that feeling in England.

'You coming or what?' Jomo urges, slipping into one of the arched exits leading away from the underHume. It's small and discreet and, unlike the others, not lit – so much so that it's noticeable. This leads into a sizeable room, with massive wooden crates stacked atop each other, all loaded with books. An old workbench sits in the middle, with several stools around it. Whereas most of the library is tidily kept, this space smells of glue and there's piles of texts, loose pages and torn covers scattered on various tables. I get it now. Jomo wants me to see the spot where they repair books. He's been in the doghouse with his dad for a while, so I can easily imagine him being set to this particular task.

'This is the infirmary where we treat sick books,' he says proudly.

'Look at you, Doctor Jomo.'

'Please, I'm a surgeon. That's why they call me mister.'

'Cheeseball.'

We laugh and I fall in love with the Library all over again, as I walk up to a table and pick up a book restoration manual by Alfred Wraxal. There's tools set out on the workspace too. Jomo points them out for me. Gummed linen book repair tape, which he says is good for spines and covers, self-adhesive mending tissue for 'acid-free' repair to pages (whatever that means), a bone folder, a scalpel for cutting, and a document cleaning pad for removing surface dirt on the pages. This is different to the gum eraser used for surface cleaning of the same. And then there's a neutral-pH adhesive, which does similar stuff to the repair tape. I'm happy for Jomo. There's pride and confidence in how he shows me these things. And it's a step up from the cleaning and scrounging his dad had him do in the past. Not that that wasn't important too, but it's only now he seems to be learning the trade properly.

'We also have the book-binding gear over there,' he points out.

It's a medieval-looking bit of kit, with tools my gran would have no trouble recognizing, like the waxed thread and large-eye needles.

'What's that?'

'Sewing awl tool, and another bone folder,' Jomo replies. 'Check this one out.'

'I guess books can be hurt, just like people. Crack open the spine and they let you into their pages, but with each touch, flick and dog-earing, they break down just as we do. That's why I'm never letting Callander and those Society arseholes back into my life.'

'Hey, forget about them. You've got your friends, and we're here for you.' Jomo puts his arm around my shoulder.

River, who was hovering by my side all this time, well behaved, takes off, sniffing about the room like she owns the place.

He lets go and picks up a book from the top of a pile on a metal book trolley. Must be the ones ready for discharge. He offers it to me, and I take the thick text with leather binding. Grenville's *Observations on Esoteric Phenomena in Ross & Cromarty*. It's a first edition and I open it very gently. The musty, earthy scent of old books hits me, merging with the sharper tones of glue. I flick through, hoping to spot where he's repaired it, and you wouldn't notice unless you were looking for it. There's hairline fissures where torn pages have been restored, and a kind of whiteness against the yellowy book where some cleaning's been done – subtle traces of fine workmanship.

I have one friend, Priya, a healer who fixes broken people, and the other, Jomo, who heals injured books.

'You received your shoe allowance yet?' A librarian I haven't met before is standing in the doorway.

'I didn't know we were given one,' Jomo replies.

'Of course we are. All this walking up and down the stairs on this rough rock puts serious wear on your soles. I'll be taking it up with the man himself then,' the librarian says, leaving.

'Who's that?' I ask.

'Mr Rotwein. He's normally on the team of proofers. You know, the mathy types whose job it is to deduce whether new spells are actually that, or just differently worded versions of old magic. He's been sour since Sneddon died, because he was pulled from the office where they normally work and made to grunt like the rest of us. They say you need one quality to be a proofer: an aptitude for maths. The problem is that for most of them this is balanced by a thorough disdain for the readers who librarians are supposed to help.' Jomo pauses, reaches out and takes the book from my hands. 'This isn't what I called you here for, though. Come with me.'

The far walls of the room have the stone-carved shelving, same as the rest of the Library, though these ones appear to have been hacked in hastily, without any polishing. They hold books, ledgers, lots of fragmented marble sculptures, and some other equipment, as well as broken tools of the library trade.

The back wall is full of the marble pieces in particular. Cracked gods and smashed heroes, fair maidens with missing limbs.

'Where do all these come from?'

'Greece, in the main. But we've got Roman and Persian pieces in our collection too. Mr Sneddon . . . well, he knew a lot about this kind of thing.'

'You know why some call this place "the Elgin"?' a crackly voice says from the corner, startling me, which in turn startles Jomo. I spot the same wee old geezer from upstairs, now sitting on an antique marble throne, which doesn't look at all comfortable. He's changed out of the bellhop outfit into an equally bizarre black frock coat, with a high-stand collar and high-peaked kepi hat.

'Mr Teàrlach, you nearly made me jump out of my skin,' I say, touching my heart.

'Torquil,' he replies.

'Oh, you know it's impossible. Torquil, Taskill, Teàrlach, no one can tell the difference,' Jomo moans.

'Your father certainly can, and for the firstborn and sole heir you act like the runt of the litter sometimes.'

'Yep, definitely Torquil. He's the sharp-tongued one.'

'Care to fill me in?' I say.

'They're triplets and work shifts on rotation. Haven't you noticed that every time you come in it's the same guy you see? Mr Teàrlach is the friendly one, and Taskill likes to keep to himself.'

'There's a fourth triplet, you numpty, and if you ever see him it'll be the last time, so be thankful you ain't.' I'm pretty sure this makes them quadruplets, but say nothing. 'You've interrupted my train of thought. Where was I? Ah yes, Thomas Bruce, the seventh earl of Elgin, Ms Moyo. The same man who brought us back these Parthenon marbles from Athens, nearly bankrupting himself in the process. That's why he had to sell some of them off to the British Museum. His contemporaries, who ought to have helped him and celebrated his triumph, instead smeared his name, calling his actions vandalism. Imagine that, young lady. A fine man such as he, a preserver of precious artefacts, equated to the barbarians who sacked Rome? But a strong man treats aspersions with the indifference they deserve, and so he carried on with his great work.'

Torquil turns his head sharply, as though a sound has caught his attention, and leaps off his chair with a haste that belies his old age. I've heard nothing but I sense growling. Not audibly, but the vibrations of it hit my chest as though Cerberus himself was in front of me. Makes me step back involuntarily.

'Is everything okay?' Jomo nervously asks.

Torquil stands there for a wee while, very still, as though relying on his senses for something. And then, just as suddenly as he rose, he flops back onto the uncushioned throne, panting as though the exertion was taxing.

He continues: 'There were plans for a Scottish National Monument in the early nineteenth century, you know. And it was here, atop Calton Hill, that Lord Elgin proposed building a replica of the Parthenon. After all, we have sea views from there, just as the original sits on the hill of the Acropolis. It

was a magnificent idea, which found favour with the enlight-
ened of the time. We were the Athens of the North, with a
brilliance to match that of the ancients in all their intellectual
endeavours.' His pride and enthusiasm are infectious. There's
a glimmer in his eyes, as though the events he speaks of are
unfolding before him. 'Two architects were assigned to it in
1822. Charles Cockerell, the English archaeologist who'd
studied the Parthenon, and the Scotsman William Henry
Playfair, recently returned from his travels to Egypt and
Abyssinia. They would be co-architects, like Ictinus and
Callicrates, the builders of the original temple. Some remarked
it was a strange decision that Cockerell should be given the
key responsibility of reconstructing the building, while Playfair
was to play second fiddle, tasked with constructing the cata-
combs below it, where a burial place was conceived for eminent
personages. Subscriptions were sought and the two architects
made a start, one above, the other below. Teams of horses and
men brought the stones from Craigleith Quarry – a compli-
cated, costly undertaking, which burnt a hole through the
budget straight away. Of the temple that was planned, all we
have to show for it are twelve columns, standing true as Jesus's
disciples, and the architrave. Further funds could not be raised.
Cockerell hung his head in shame and went back home across
the border, vowing never to return to the city in which his great
monument still stands as the ultimate testament to hubris.

'But even though construction had halted, the hill began to
enjoy a certain reputation. It was said knocking sounds could
be heard coming from within it. People claimed to see horses
laden with something at night, led by strange Moors. This went

on for years, a growing myth. But as you will have figured out, Lord Elgin had just diverted the funding, securing more from friends of Scottish magic. And it was in great secrecy that the Library was built. *This* is his lasting legacy. They didn't name it for him, but they ought to have done. Touch anything in this place, breathe the air inside it, every molecule, and the very floor you stand upon, it's all thanks to Lord Elgin.'

That was kinda wild.

Torquil looks expectant, like I might have something to say about all this, but I know when to haud my wheesht, so I keep quiet. Seems to me the Library, much like the Society itself, is the product of pilfered funds. That was the way they did things back in the eighteenth and nineteenth centuries. Still, we've got all this cool stuff, so . . .

'What really brings you down here, Mr Maige?' he asks.

Jomo kinda tweedles about.

'The prisoner asked to see Ms Moyo, so I've brought her here.'

'And this has been approved by the head librarian?'

'Yes,' Jomo says, a little too quickly. I know when he's lying. And all this shit about 'the prisoner'? Unless Patrick McGoohan is somewhere inside the Library, then I don't want to know nothing about it.

'Very well, you feed 'em, I guard 'em,' Torquil says.

Jomo steps forward to a bust of Hades, who's on a shelf along with the twelve other Olympic gods. You can tell it's Hades by his frown. Must be pissed off stuck down below where the sun don't shine, while his brother Poseidon's off surfing, and Zeus is gallivanting about, raping or doing some such villainous shit. Who am I to judge the gods? Jomo places his palm on Hades's face and there's a scraping noise, rock upon rock, as the shelf retreats, revealing a narrow passageway beyond.

'Take a torch with you,' Torquil says, and, as if on cue, one lights up on the left wall. 'Fifteen minutes is all I'm giving you.'

'Who's down there, Jomo?'

'Come on, we don't have a lot of time.'

The Library has many secrets, but not all of them are hidden in books, it seems.

VII

You can smell the stench of despair that's leached into the rocks below. That and sweat. The walls seem to close in on me, the very antithesis of the open spaces of the Library. I turn back to see the shelf shutting behind us. Makes me feel like I might never get out of this place. Give me a cemetery over this catacomb any day of the year, because that's what these bare walls represent: the death of freedom.

The ceiling above keeps dropping lower and lower, until it's just above our heads. A tall person would have to really stoop in here.

Whatever ventilation the other sections have must not be wired here, 'cause the air is hot and muggy, and, further in, the walls are sleek with moisture. Our footsteps make far too much noise down the corridor, echoing off metal doors on either side. Someone's banging on one of them as we pass. When we make it to the end, there's another door. Jomo stands aside and hands me the lamp, before opening the hatch on it.

'The Edinburgh Ordinary School for Boys was Lord Elgin's alma mater, in case you were wondering. That's why we still call this place the Elgin, while the others don't. I couldn't help overhearing your conversation,' a familiar voice says.

'Jomo, what the fuck? Why did you bring me here?' I yell. 'I told you I'm done with all of this. Come on, let's go.'

'You don't understand, Ropa. I had to, for your sake,' he replies.

The man behind the door laughs. I hope there's at least six inches of steel between him and us.

'You ought to listen to him, he cares for you deeply,' the man says. Fine words, treacherous like the gorgeous silk of a spider's web. If they touch you, they ensnare you.

'Montgomery Wedderburn, ex-rector of the Edinburgh School. The man who would be secretary of the Society,' I say. 'I hope you're not wasting my time.'

The last I saw of him was at the disastrous conference on the Isle of Skye. There he'd challenged Callander to a duel, trying to force his way into becoming the leader of Scottish magic. He put up a good show, but Callander defeated him in the end. Until it turned out that winning the duel would have been a secondary prize for Wedderburn. The whole thing had been set up as a distraction, to allow his students to steal Dunvegan Castle's most prized possession, the Fairy Flag. And something more is brewing now – their next move. There must be a reason Fenella MacLeod came to town. Who's she with – did Priya see? *No, Ropa, don't get sucked into this bullshit.*

'There it is,' Wedderburn says. 'I can see those tiny cogs in your head turning.'

I hold the lamp's flame nearer the open hatch so I can see his face. Just his eyes and nose are visible, though. His skin's pale from the lack of sunlight, but there's an angry red streak where my lightning struck him. Long story.

'Your scars are healing well.'

'Our Lady's finest healers cared for me. And I rather like my battle scars. They remind me that I stood for a cause, one I still believe in.'

'Yeah, well, you lost.'

'The battle or the war?'

'You and that so-called Fifth School of yours.'

'There are only four schools of magic in Scotland. You know that,' he replies dismissively.

Nope, I'm not doing this. I'm not gonna be dragged back in again. Scottish magic is full of backstabbing and conniving. It's a cesspit filled with poisonous vipers, who'll strike you with a smile. Seeing Wedderburn's made up my mind and settled any doubts I might've had. I'll go home and tell Gran we are moving to England, no discussion. I turn around and head for the exit. Jomo touches my shoulder and I brush his hand away. This is his life, him and his dad, I don't have to stick around for any of it.

'For a perceptive girl, it surprises me you are so blind as to your true origins,' Wedderburn calls. I keep walking briskly. 'Tell me, what do you truly know about your parents?' I slow down. 'Oops, it seems I might have let the cat out of the bag.'

My feet are now stuck, glued to the spider's web. I stop completely. Part of me knows I shouldn't believe a word coming out of his mouth. But I've known him to tell the truth before too. And he's mentioned my parents. He is slightly younger than my father would have been, but that doesn't mean he couldn't have known him. Nah. I can't let him get inside my head. I remember how he visited Jomo after he'd been attacked in Dunvegan Castle. Then he gave my friend more support than his own psycho dad had, which I'd thought was nice. But now I look back and see he was really grooming him. Making sure that in the eventuality he wound up in this hole he'd have a friendly face. The librarians aren't drawn from the schools of magic, so he couldn't count on one of them being an Edinburgh boy.

'I know everything I need to know about my parents,' I say.

'Do you believe the fairy tales your abductors told you?' Wedderburn leaves that dangling, a fat worm wriggling on a barbed hook.

My mouth feels dry. I swallow.

The other prisoner bangs louder on his door and begins yelling obscenities. How long have they been in there? This place could make you lose your mind. It's inhumane. But Wedderburn sounds as sharp as ever. I need to be careful.

'In case you haven't noticed, you're the one locked up in a cave and I'm free,' I say.

'The cruellest prisons are the ones without walls. They make you think you're free when you're but a puppet dangling on strings. I will be the one to set you free, Ms Moyo.'

'Ropa, I swear I wouldn't have brought you here if I didn't think he had something important to tell you,' Jomo says. 'I'm sorry, alright? Hear him out, please.'

Sweet Jomo. Always screws up with the best intentions in the world. Can't he make the link between Wedderburn and the death of Mr Sneddon, the librarian who was always so kind to him? With his father being so constantly severe, he'll fall for any older man who gives him a pat on the head and a few tender words. I feel my temper rising and close my eyes, then take a deep breath. The fire shines through my shut eyelids. Whatever happens, I mustn't take anything out on Jomo. He means well. The road to hell and all that.

But I've been holding Jomo's hand for far too long. He doesn't see obvious danger because he can always rely on me to get him out of a bind. It's been like that since school, when I used to fight the bullies picking on him. Nearly got expelled a couple of times.

'Sneddon's blood is on your hands,' I say, walking back to the door so I can stare him in the eyes.

'Funny you think I'm the only one with blood on my hands, yet you're happy to shake bloodier hands than mine. Even those who've wronged you. I guess you just don't know it yet. There was a song from back in the day that describes you perfectly: *young, gifted and ignorant*.'

'Talk straight,' I shout.

'That temper reminds me of your father. You should have seen him drunk on a night out.' He laughs, as though at a fond old memory. 'I remember when we went out slumming it in the White House in Niddrie and these guys tried it on with us . . . Well, let's say the bouncers ended up kicking us out. Those were the days.'

'I don't care if you knew my father. It means nothing to me.' But I do care; oh, how I do.

'He cried the day you were born. I was the one who took him there, on my Triumph Speed Twin, and we waited together until the nurses called him in. Before he left, he told me he was naming you for himself.'

My father's name was Makomborero Moyo and I am Ropafadzo Moyo. In his mother tongue Makomborero means 'blessing', exactly the same thing mine means in a different dialect. And our surname means 'heart', which is also the symbol of our totem. I don't understand how it all works, but according to Gran, these sacred things are passed down in the patrilineal line. What Wedderburn is saying is true.

'Blessings of the heart,' he says, as though echoing my thoughts. His eyes glint, reflecting the flame of the torch.

'Shut up,' I shout, staggering back, hot tears running down my face.

It's like a dam's burst and all the work Dr Checkland's done with me is swept away in the flood. Something flashes in my head: a picture of my father on the floor, his lifeless eyes staring at me. Heels tapping on parquet flooring. A voice, muffled, like it's coming from behind a storm, saying—

Jomo touches me and I shove him back.

It's the spider's venom. My mind's playing tricks on me. My father died in a car accident. There's no way I could remember seeing him like that.

'You're a fucking liar!' I say.

Wedderburn pushes the tips of his fingers out the slot, as though reaching for me, but his whole hand can't fit through.

'I was your father's closest friend, Ropa. The best man at his wedding. But I couldn't save him.' There's remorse in his voice. 'That is my greatest shame. For if he'd been here with us today, everything would have been so very different. It's my love for him which made it hard for me to bear the sight of your face. You remind me so much of him. The way you pout, ah, and now you frown, just as he did, with those feisty eyebrows. Every time I see you, it's as though I'm looking into the face of a ghost.'

Genuine or fake? I'm so confused right now. Gran told me I look more like my mother. I have the pictures, and she always emphasizes my eyes and nose, which I got from her.

Wedderburn pulls his fingers out of the grill and retreats back inside his cell. This man knew my father, was his best man even, yet he's said nothing all the times I've met him. Showed absolutely no sign of all he's saying now. If they went to school together, surely that must mean . . . Can't be. I was told my father was an academic, not a magician. Unless something was omitted, since magicians can also be scholars. Was this deliberate? Still, what is the point of all this? So what if he was?

It would mean I've walked past many people in this library, maybe even had conversations with them, who knew, but no one thought to mention. I consider all the people who've avoided me, and the ones who've tried to have me kicked out of the Society – was it because I'm poor and from Hermiston Slum, or for some other reason, one rooted in the past?

'Was my father a bad guy?' I ask. You wouldn't mention someone's dad in polite conversation if they'd turned out to be the Limbs in the Loch Killer, would you?

'Never. He was the greatest practitioner I ever had the privilege of knowing. And he wanted a better life for both you and your sister, your mother too. It's just that they wouldn't let him. You've had a hard time, but I thought you should know, it didn't need to be this way.'

'I don't understand what you mean.'

'We don't have much time. The visiting hours in this place are rather diabolical . . . I'm sorry to bring you so much distress, but look at your life, everyone around you. Do you honestly think all this is a coincidence? If you want to know the truth, you have to ask your *grandmother* Melsie Mhondoro what happened on that fateful Samhain night. She and your mentor, Callander, owe you an explanation.'

'What do you *mean?*' I ask again.

'I swore a vow and it's not my place to confess other people's sins. Jomo, we're done here. I've given her all the help I can. Now leave me in peace,' Wedderburn says.

'Hey, what does Gran have to do with any of this? Answer me, goddamn it. Wedderburn!'

'That's enough, young lady. You are disturbing the prisoners, and your fifteen minutes is up,' Torquil says firmly.

'No, please. I—'

'Mr Maige, kindly close that hatch right now.'

Jomo slams the hatch shut, as the world falls from beneath my feet. 'Sorry,' he seems to be saying, but I can't hear properly. The walls are closing in on me from all sides. Pins and needles. I can't breathe. Why is the room spinning? Make it. Stop. Oh no, it's happening to me again.

VIII

I'm reeling as I stagger out of the Library prison, with Jomo leading me like I'm an invalid. Torquil has a grim look on his face that brooks no discussion. Normally I don't like talking or even thinking about my parents. Let the dead worry about the dead. There's too much going on in my life to be bogged down with memories of them, and it won't ever bring them back. No one comes back. Not unless they're spooks, and what good are spectral parents anyways?

'Where are you two coming from?' Priya suddenly appears, wheeling herself past Hume's sarcophagus. 'Ropa, you look like you've seen a ghost.'

'Give her a minute. She's had some unexpected news,' Jomo says.

'Damn. Did someone die?'

'A long time ago,' I reply. 'A very long time ago.'

My noggin feels like it's been stomped on by an elephant. I check my phone to see the time. It's really late. I need to go see Gran and have this out with her, but I can't just now 'cause the Sorcerer Royal requires that you wait on him until dismissed. And I know what side my bread's buttered on.

I reach into my backpack for a bottle of water and take a swig.

'Did Wedderburn tell you anything else?' I ask Jomo.

'All I had was a leaner version of what he just told you.'

'They're holding him *here?*' Priya says, trying to keep up. 'I guess it makes sense. But given he's been neutered, shouldn't they put him in a regular jail? By the way, Fenella gave me the slip.'

'We need to forget about him, forget about Fenella, and anyone else. I'm sorry I sent you after her, Priya, but this isn't our problem anymore. None of it is. As far as I'm concerned, this is an issue for Scotland's Discoverer General. In the meantime, I suggest we go back upstairs, 'cause I need to wait for Lord Samarasinghe.'

Priya raises her eyebrows, shakes her head slowly, and then says nothing. She fiddles with the arms of her wheelchair.

My father was a practitioner. Why wouldn't Gran have told me that? He was her son-in-law. There must be a reason she isn't fond of the Society, and of me learning Scottish magic. That's why back in the day she tried to teach me Shona magic instead, but I was crap at it. Could it be she was jealous? No chance, that's not her style. I am so confused right now. Having the version of your life you hold dear thrown into question doesn't feel so great. I've always known who I am. Doesn't everyone? And there's always been Gran and Izwi there with me. Now I feel like them folks who wake up with no clue who, or where, they are. Only in my case it ain't amnesia.

Then there's the Callander angle. I've seen him with Gran before and the two of them know each other. There's a history there. But I've never felt the need to pry – it wasn't necessary. Like, who cares what old people did before the Big Bang anyways?

Wedderburn made it seem like there was more to it, though. Come to think of it, when I first sneaked into the Library and got into all sorts of trouble, Callander was there to bail me out. How convenient. Then he gave me my ninja scarf, Cruickshank, which Gran obviously knitted. And Esfandiar Soltani, Callander's husband, also gave me a bulletproof coat which had belonged to her . . .

No, I should stop. That way lies every conspiracy theory ever put on the net. Coincidences take on the form of cosmically ordained causality.

I pull out my phone and open messages from Gran. I start to type. . . but I can't find what to say and delete the few words I've written.

'Your hands are shaking,' Priya points out.

'It's cold down here,' Jomo replies. 'No chance the Library's getting central heating any time soon.'

'But you have so much excellent kindling for a bonfire.'

'Don't even joke about that,' Jomo says with mock outrage. 'If the other librarians hear you, you're toast.'

'Come on, let's go upstairs,' I say.

I'm still present, but desperately need to clear my head. Feels like I'm standing on quicksand instead of the solid rock this Library's sculpted from. Priya holds my hand, squeezing it gently, before letting go and heading for the stairs.

'Jomo, you guys could at least invest in a lift,' she says, before incanting an arachne spell, which allows the tyres of her wheelchair to adhere to any surface, setting her scurrying up the stairs in a jerky fashion. The spell's named after the daughter of Idmon of Colophon, who was a supremely gifted weaver, and was arrogant enough to challenge Athena at the craft. So the goddess wove an outstanding tapestry of the gods in their divine glory, while Arachne did a saucy one of them doing amorous stuff. Sex sells, even back in ancient Greece. It turned out Athena wasn't into porn, and she was pretty miffed about the whole thing. Though it was more likely she was using this puritan outrage as an excuse to cover up the fact she'd just had her arse handed to her by a mere mortal. But she had an excuse, so she shredded the offending work. Arachne was like, that's harsh, and hanged herself. Athena, being the goddess of wisdom, was then like, nah, that's a bit too much, you're not messing up my cred with the other gods, so she turned the rope into a cobweb and Arachne herself into a spider.

I think it's a much better origin story than saying a radioactive spider did it.

Anyways, that's the ambulatory magic Priya uses to go up and down stairs, ceilings and other awkward spots. It's pretty complex, though. Not the sort of thing someone like me, who's a self-trained novice at magicking, could ever pull off. I can manage simpler stuff, though. One day . . .

With Priya out of earshot, I put my hands on Jomo's cheeks and pull him to me.

'At least buy me dinner before you kiss me,' he says awkwardly.

'Listen to me very carefully,' I say. 'That man in there is not your friend. I don't care what you think you know, but I want you to stay away from him. Don't listen to anything he says. You hear me, Jomo?'

He scratches his head and kind of half grins like a moron.

'Promise me.'

'Geez, okay, I promise,' he replies. 'It's no big deal.'

I don't have a great feeling about this, but I let him scamper back to his duties. My mind ain't right at all – thoughts zipping along so fast I can't catch them. Questions upon questions. I'm itching to get on the phone with Gran but I can't. Not because there's no reception in this cave anyways, but this is a talk I need to have with her face to face. If there's stuff she knows about my parents which she hasn't yet told me, I have a right to know. Izwi too. An overwhelming weariness settles on me, like fog engulfing a hill. But I have to shake it off and carry on as though nothing's happened.

'Come on, River. Let's go.'

And so I wind up back at reception and hang out with Priya for a while, catching up, before Lord Samarasinghe returns, led by Dr Maige. The two of them are laughing like old pals. That's how it is when the Sorcerer Royal pours on the charm. He touches Dr Maige's elbow and shoulder. Apart from the odd handshake, this is the first time I've seen anyone enter the head librarian's personal space like that. He likes to be aloof. There's even an odd flirtatious note to Lord Samarasinghe's smile. That easy tilting of the head of someone who knows he's blessed with good looks. Makes me want to puke. River too by the looks of things.

'It's such a waste for a wonder of the world to be reserved exclusively for a provincial band of practitioners. Your institution should be a beacon, inviting magicians from everywhere. Think how that would stretch your influence across the globe,' Lord Samarasinghe says.

'There are rules,' Dr Maige replies, without much of his usual conviction.

'The world is divided between the rule takers and rule makers, my lord librarian.' I notice the way Samarasinghe uses Maige's new title as a lure.

'I meet with no proposition that is not connected with an ought, or an ought not.'

'Hume?' Lord Samarasinghe says, leaning over the balcony to gaze at the sarcophagus below. 'He seems so tiny and inconsequential from up here.'

Dr Maige frowns and recoils. The Sorcerer Royal has overstepped the mark.

'But he is the oak seed which has grown into this fine tree of knowledge that is the Library,' Lord S continues.

'Quite right.' Dr Maige's face softens a little, but the wariness doesn't quite leave. He's on his guard now. 'It has been an honour and privilege to show you our humble library. I hope you will favour us with another visit in the future.'

I notice he doesn't say 'soon' or 'near future' but points to a vague timeline. There's a flash of annoyance on the Sorcerer Royal's face, which passes so quickly you'd not even notice if you haven't spent time with him. Instead he smiles, baring immaculate white fangs.

'Shall I escort you to the top?' Dr Maige asks.

'That's quite alright. I have Ms Moyo here with me for that.'

'Yes, she knows the Library very well.' This comes out as a burn. 'Good day to you both.'

I sense a certain disapproval from Dr Maige of the path I've taken. It's easy enough for him to judge, with his cushy job and the privilege that comes with it. But I'm striking my own course. The Sorcerer Royal's cane taps against the old stone floor of Elgin's dream as I give Priya a quick wave goodbye, then lead him up the stairs to the exit.

Me and Lord Samarasinghe wind up outside in the cold evening air. It slaps my face, reviving me after the stuffiness of the Library. River brushes herself against my leg. I feel better with her beside me. At least I know she's not keeping any secrets from me. I can trust her with my life.

The Sorcerer Royal's in a wee bit of a sour mood. It's all there in his knitted brow. He clearly didn't get what he wanted from Dr Maige, and so he'll be plotting his next move. I was thinking I'd take him back to Holyroodhouse, but it seems he has other ideas. He walks with his hands clasped behind his back, head slightly bowed, following the tarred path that is Hume's Walk, leading towards the Dugald Stewart Monument. Somehow I don't think he's in the mood to discuss the virtues of Scottish philosophy.

It's when he's in these kinds of funk I'm most anxious. It's all so precarious. If things don't work out for me with Lord Samarasinghe, I'm fucked. There's nothing on paper agreed between us. All I have to go on is his word. But I'm also wary that things might not fall as I've planned. Huitzilopochtli knows, I'm trying to make sure the outcome's to my advantage, but it's hard to predict all the pitfalls that may scupper my plans. I wonder what Bryson Blackwood would do in such a situation.

Lord Samarasinghe comes to a stop just beyond the monument, taking in the view of the city. He closes his eyes and draws in a deep breath. When he exhales, he seems to become calmer.

'I'm going to have more work to do in this dastardly city than I imagined,' he says, cape fluttering in the wind.

I know well enough to leave him alone with his thoughts and keep schtum at times like this. With Callander it was . . . different. I stick my hands in my pockets and stare out at the city.

The haze of those yellow lights spreading out.

Smoke billowing from ten thousand chimneys.

The shapes of the old buildings lit up.

From above, it looks so beautiful.

Flashing red lights marking the bridges over the Forth.

You can just about hear the chanting of the protesters on the Royal Mile from here.

Something wells up inside of me. I'm going to miss Edinburgh. It's home and all I've ever known. I wipe away a tear forming in the corner of my eye, then take out my phone. The light nearly blinds me, given how dim it is up here. I message Gran and tell her I have some questions about my past which only she can answer. I hesitate for a bit, before pressing send.

'The Scotch are a stubborn people given to sharp vicissitudes of emotion, lacking even the most basic understanding of realpolitik,' Lord Samarasinghe opines. 'It falls on us to guide them. In the same way a parent must protect the child from their whims. Even when they don't understand what you're doing is for their own good.'

'Do you have such a low opinion of us?'

'I have a low opinion of everybody.' He sweeps his hand across the city. 'They've failed to contain the rat plague. At this rate it will no doubt reach the north of England by winter's end. This will exacerbate the problem of a poor harvest from last season. Soon the country will be starving, and guess who they'll blame for their own folly?'

I leave this hanging 'cause the answer is obvious.

'You wouldn't understand. I forget you're so young some-times,' he says softly.

'I need to go home now,' I reply.

'You may if you wish, but I have a small job for you.'

Umm. I really need to get back, so I can talk to Gran and find out what Wedderburn was talking about.

'Friends of mine on Danube Street in Stockbridge are having a bit of trouble with a pesky poltergeist and I told them I happened to know the right person to help them with it. You'll love Bartholomew and Cordelia Wainright. They manage assets my parents own up here in Scotland.'

'I can't. Not tonight. I've got something I need to be doing.'

'That's a pity. They are willing to pay over the odds for your services. I guess I'll simply have to tell them to find someone else then.'

I've already got a ton of cash from the last gig I did for Lord S. It's enough to pay rent this month, put food on the table, get Gran's meds, with plenty left over for a few luxuries like three-ply bog roll. More than I've made on any job I did back when I was ghostalkering proper, before I took on notions of becoming a magician. Still, can you ever have too much cash? Can a squirrel ever have enough nuts stashed? If what

Lord Samarasinghe's saying is correct, there's lean times ahead. Knapf.

'No, wait,' I say. 'I'll do the job.'

A slight smile creeps up on the Sorcerer Royal's lips. There's a ping and I get a message back from Gran: 'Ropa, my beating heart, I knew this day would come, but I never thought it would be so soon. Come back home and I'll tell you everything.' There's a little red heart punctuating the end.

Okay, this job should be a quick in and out, then I'll run home to her after. An hour or two won't make any difference.

IX

There's something strange going on in the everyThere. The way ghosts are tethered to that realm isn't normal at all. A job that was supposed to be a breeze just lasted a good few hours, and I'm knackered as I head out the Georgian terrace on Danube Street, clutching my dosh. Even River's a wee bit antsy. We've been at it all day now, and into the night. I stuff the cash in my bag and take out her can of Pedigree that I was meant to give her earlier. The way things are going, I can at least buy her good dog food. She likes it.

I open the can and pour its contents straight out onto the pavement.

A curtain in the house opens a fraction; the Wainwrights are watching. I give them a wee wave and they shut it again quick. They're a nice couple actually. Crazy how they live in that massive five-bed all alone like that, though. No wonder a ghost decided to squat with them. Wasn't anyone they knew, just some drifter unconnected to the building or its occupants in any way, which made for an odd haunting. Still, it was a good gig, but it's messed up my timings.

River is noisily gobbling up her scran like there's no tomorrow.

I check my phone. Voice note from Izwi, messages from Priya and Jomo. Nothing more from Gran. I message Izwi back first, 'cause I've neglected my little sis for a while. She's having a blast at boarding school it seems, and I enjoy hearing her reports about her little friends. Makes me feel bad for the ones she's left behind at Hermiston Slum, though. I swear her accent's changed a wee bit. Kinda posh-sounding now. Class traitor.

Gran will be asleep by the time I get home now. It's too late. I really, really want to talk to her, but I can't wake her, it wouldn't be fair. I won't be able to sleep either, though. My nerves are keeping me on the edge. Them herbs I'm taking don't seem to be helping. Not with this.

'Are you done having your late-night tea?' I ask.

River answers by taking one last lick of the pavement, then bounds off ahead of me. I wrap my scarf, Cruickshank, snug around my neck before unchaining my bike from the railing at the front of the building. Then I hop on and get to pedalling. If it was during the day, I'd follow the Water of Leith, but those paths ain't well lit at night. So I'm following River up onto Dean Terrace – she knows the way home – when I suddenly have second thoughts.

I won't be getting any sleep tonight. Not till I have answers. I could go to Priya's, but she has work in the morning and I wouldn't wanna disturb her.

'This way, girl . . . I know, there's been a change of plan,' I say, cycling down Carlton Street instead, and through the network of roads onto Orchard Brae.

This takes me past the Western General, a hospital that's seen better days, and onto Crewe Toll. I go through Muirhouse and onto Marine Drive, which leads down to Silverknowes Beach. River's kinda protesting, and I'm sure she'd rather be back in her burrow by now, but we can sleep it off in the morning.

The beach is deserted.

If it wasn't for Cruickshank, my dagger, my catapult, River and a handful of spells I know, I wouldn't be out here in this part of town at night. But the car park on this beach was the first place me, Gran and Izwi stayed nights after Gramps had lost our house in a gambling debt. God rest his soul. I remember being scared here, until Gran pointed out the great sea wall, which shields the city from the waves, and said it was there to protect us. It's concrete and rock, solid, and the sound of the waves crashing against it was the lullaby putting me to sleep all those years ago. It's good to hear them again.

There're a couple of lights at intervals along the dyke.

They say they put them up there so folks near the coast would forget they could no longer see the lights from Fife across the Forth. I don't know about that. It serves as a reminder to me, even though I wasn't here before the dyke was put up. That's the problem with grown-ups telling you about how things used to be. It makes you nostalgic for stuff you never saw.

What if my conversation with Gran changes everything?

I hope she doesn't tell me I was adopted. Not that there's anything wrong with that, but it'd open up a can of worms. Surely it can't be that. No one keeps that sort of stuff secret anyways. There's got to be something else to it.

I check my phone; the time's hardly moved.

Grabbing a BLT sarnie from my bag, I undo the clingfilm

and take a bite. River nuzzles my ankle, but I'm not falling for that.

'You've already had yours, greedy vixen.'

She gives me a plaintive look, but I'm not budging. Alright then, maybe just a little. I break off a morsel and hand it to her. Nearly bites my fingers off, she does. And then I stuff the rest down my throat before she can try that trick on me again.

Living in a caravan, back when we still had Gran's car, the whole city was our home. We were never stuck in one place for too long . . . Come to think of it, how had she still owned a petrol car long after most folks had been forced to give theirs up? Unless you were well connected, you couldn't get fuel for them anyways. I've never thought about it before, but it doesn't quite add up. We were poor and knew practically no one.

Who *is* my grandmother, and who was my father?

I shouldn't keep speculating on these things, I'll go mad. It's nearly morning anyways. No point freezing my tits off longer than I already have. I'm still a bit of a way from home and it's all uphill towards Corstorphine, which is a pain this time of night. I'm also starting to feel a bit drowsy. Should've gone home straight away.

'Sorry I kept you out this long, River,' I say. 'I needed to clear my head. Thanks for being there with me, though.'

This time of the year, dawn takes her sweet time. The goddess Demeter's still weeping for her daughter Persephone and taking it out on us, even though we had nothing to do with her abduction. But I'm sure Gran will be awake by now. She's not one to lie in like that, not when there's knitting or needlework to be done.

I'm going to make her a nice cup of tea and then we can chat properly.

There's a couple of carts on the road already, all headed for town. A few bikers too.

'God save the king,' I say to one.

He doesn't answer me. Grunts and carries on like I've farted or something. Screw him. I make my way down the Drum Brae, over the roundabout, and then past the police station opposite the big supermarket, where a nightwatchman patrols with his baton stick dangling at his side.

It doesn't take long before I'm cutting through Sighthill, then crossing over the bypass and back to HMS Hermiston, where a handful have their fires going in the morning already. The pirate power lines running down from the pylons sway in the gentle morning breeze. I climb off my bike and approach the caravan, while River rushes ahead, keen to get to her burrow. But then she stops abruptly, stands on her hind legs and starts pawing impatiently at the door. It's not like her to be so keen on getting inside.

'What is it, girl?'

I slow as I step closer.

Something's off.

In the dimness it takes me a while to register, but when I do, I can't unsee it. What's silver duct tape doing on all the frames around the windows of our caravan? I place my bike on the ground and circle it. Then I see there's duct tape every-where, not just on the windows, sealing the door too, and the air vents.

Who would have—

It can't be Gran, if she's inside – there's no way she could have done the door up too. My heart's thumping as I bang on the door. 'Gran, you in there?' I hear the faint sound of the TV. I reach for the strip on the door. My fingers are stiff 'cause of the cold and I find it hard to peel a section off.

My thumping heart goes up a gear.

Please.

'Gran, talk to me,' I say.

I slip a fingernail under the duct tape at last and peel an edge, working it off from the bottom, all the way to the top. Then I tear off the strip running along the top of the door, and the other at the bottom as swiftly as I can.

I turn the handle and pull it. The door's locked. Reaching into the pocket of my jeans, I take out the key, but my shaking hand misses the hole first time. I try again, until it slots in and I unlock it, then I throw open the door finally. River rushes in before I can.

A gust of warm air hits me.

'Come on, Gran, answer me,' I say, leaping inside.

The brazier on the countertop's still warm. Only just.

I freeze on the spot. Gran and Gary O'Donohue are both here. He doesn't normally sleep over – at least not when I'm around. Gran's got her head in his lap and she's fast asleep. Her face is serene, like she's at peace, a quilt thrown over her. Her knitting's on the floor – unfinished baby's booties. But where are her needles and ball of sky-blue yarn? Gary's sat upright, his left hand on her shoulder, and his head is bowed, chin to the chest, as if he'd nodded off in the middle of watching the telly, which as I could hear is still on. It's now tuned into the early morning news. River looks back at me, then walks over to Gran and nuzzles her, licking her face.

I bite the back of my hand hard.

This can't be.

I want to go to them as well, but my feet are rooted to the spot. Can't move. Only the pain in my hand tells me this isn't a dream. I try to speak but my throat's gone dry and I croak. Swallow. Try again. River's looking at me expectantly.

'Gran? Gary? It's me.'

It's okay, they're sleeping. They were just very tired and they fell asleep. All I have to do is shake them awake.

I inch forward cautiously. I put my hand on Gran's foot and gently push it.

'Wake up, Gran. This isn't funny, you know. We need to talk. And you should be back at your own place, Gary O'Donohue. No sleepovers until you put a ring on it,' I say with a feeble laugh. 'Guys?'

I reach over and touch Gran's shoulder, right where Gary's hand is. He's a bit clammy but warm. I give them both a good shake but neither stirs. *Please wake up.* I place my hand on Gran's neck and then all power leaves me and I slump onto my bunk.

The duct tape.

The brazier.

This can't be. I've always warned Gran to leave the window slightly open when she's got the coal fire going. She knows better than this. So does Gary. There's no way either of them could have thought it was a good idea to seal up all the ventilation coming into the caravan. But someone did. They must have sat there, chatting away, not smelling anything, not sensing the air turn to poison around them. Maybe they noticed the place was warmer than usual and they might have enjoyed that. They wouldn't have been able to think straight, as the carbon monoxide entered their lungs, building up in their blood, bit by bit, replacing the oxygen in the red blood cells.

'Gran, please wake up,' I beg, tears now streaming down my cheeks. 'You've got to wake up. Don't do this to me, Gran. Nah . . . not like this. Come on now, get up. Get up. Get up, Gran!'

They'd have felt weary. Maybe yawned a little and remarked how tired they got at their ages. And then they fell asleep. The world suddenly loses all colour and meaning. My heart . . . I've never felt anything like this. A knife cut through my very soul. Gran is a part of me. Was. What will I tell Izwi? Who else should I tell? Wake up, Gran, I need to see your eyes. We don't have to talk. You don't need to say anything to me. Let's just sit here like we used to. I'll put on *Hamish Macbeth* and watch him waltzing about Lochdubh with Wee Jock. Let's do that, shall we?

I grab the remote.

I'm going mad.

All these years of delivering messages from ghosts, seeing their families reeling, I thought I knew. But I didn't understand anything at all. I was young when my parents died and barely remember them. I was sad, that much I know, very sad. But I never felt this.

Grief.

With no idea what I'm doing anymore, I sit here on my bunk, staring at Gran and Gary. Their forms blur in my tears.

Was this my fault? I don't know what to do. I truly am lost. If this is a dream, I want to wake up now.

I reach forward and touch her again.

Gran.

My world, my reason for living, my love, my conscience, my teacher. I should have been here with her. If only I hadn't taken on that bloody job. Fuck the Wainrights and their fucking ghost. Fuck Samarasinghe. Fuck Callander. Fuck magicians everywhere in the world. None of that was worth a hair on Gran's head. And Gary, sweet Gary. Who'll do your allotment when spring comes, hey? That shack of yours won't last another winter. You were here with her when I was supposed to be. Oh, what a mess.

River places her head gently on my lap. She's warm, while Gran's cooling to the touch.

Call for an ambulance . . . They don't come out here, though, not to the slums. We've got to fend for ourselves.

My head's spinning.

I lean back and close my eyes. Want to scream but my voice has left me. I should have closed the door behind me again – that way I could go with her to the Land of the Tall Grass. No . . . I can't leave Izwi behind. Not with those magicians.

Every moment with her I took for granted.

Every tiff we had.

I take it all back. I'll love you better. Come back to me, Gran. Come. Back. The world closes in on me and I push out of my body, into the astral realm. If I can find them quickly, maybe I can save them. They haven't gone cold yet. Bring their souls back and take them to Our Lady. Then Priya will know what to do. I've got to try.

I'm hovering above, looking down at them, at our three bodies in the small caravan. Gran and Gary look like they're sleeping, just as I am. I push out of the cara into the night air. The slight tingle of the electric wires passes through me as I rise up, into the night, and the slum grows smaller, the city shrinks, and the world becomes tiny shapes of shadow and light. I find the point I'm looking for, with colours swirling round, and thread myself like a needle into the everyThere. That realm glued to our own, where death reigns as life does in this world. Our conjoined twin. At least I try to, but it's like I've hit a wall. I relax myself. I need to be calm, to concentrate, pour every ounce of my will into that grey splodge. I focus and try again, but it's like continuously smacking my head into a brick wall.

This has never happened to me before, or other astral travellers I've heard of. Is it something to do with the strange things I noticed going on with that realm recently? Ghosts turning up in the city at odd times when they shouldn't have. I dismissed them as smoke from chimneys, but they weren't. The exorcisms I've performed were harder than they ought to have been too, as though the boundary between worlds has been tampered with.

Going to the everyThere is as easy as stepping into the next room. At least it should be. But there's some barrier thing there now, and I'm like one of those birds flying into glass. I could keep trying until I snap my neck. In fury I bang my head against it once more. What would Gran do? She never mentioned the possibility of this realm being cut off from ours.

Yet when I was out before, I felt its presence stronger than ever. How then is it possible that its tide is more intense, yet it's more separate to us than it has ever been?

Think, Ropa.

No, no, no, no. If the everyThere's sealed off, that means Gran's and Gary's souls will pass beyond before I can stop them. When souls do that, they can't then come back to this realm. The everyThere's the anteroom to the point of no return. Who or what created this barrier, and why now? Could it have something to do with whoever's responsible for Gran's death?

I go around the grey, attacking it from all angles, looking for points of weakness, but it's all firmly cut off from my soul. There's no way in. Exhausted, I finally descend again, like one of the fallen, until I pass through the roof of the caravan and settle back inside my own body. When I open my eyes, I'm back in the same place. I then notice something scratched into the ceiling of the caravan: a great big letter 'I' and what appears to be a stick drawing of some kind. It's not very well done. A child's hand. Could have been Izwi back in the day. But every night I lie on this bunk, staring up at that ceiling, and I haven't seen it before. I think it's a puppet of some sort – the ones with a wooden stick stuck up their backside. Maybe something phallic.

Someone drew it there last night, but why? And they took Gran's knitting needles.

Have to call the police. The pigs and me ain't never been friends, but I need them today. Yeah, that's what I'll do. I take out my phone and dial, 9-9—. It starts ringing. Unknown number. Fucksake, now's not the time. I hang up, press 9, and it starts ringing again. I'm about to hang up a second time when a message from Rooster Rob, my old underworld boss, pings up: 'Dinnae dare hang up on me. PICK UP NOW.'

'Now's not a good time, Rob,' I say, trying to sound normal.

'Listen tae me very carefully, lassie. Grab your shit and run away from there, quick as you can. Come tae Camelot.'

'What—'

'No time. The polis's coming yer way and they'll arrest yous on sight.'

'How do you—'

'Stop wasting time. I've got a mole on the inside, says he's heard it on the radio and they've got a tip-off. They're doing yous fer murder. Open and shut. That mean's yer going doon.'

'But I didn't—'

'Dinnae argue, dinnae think. Get out.'

X

Someone's trying to set me up for the murder of my own grandmother? The Lothian and Borders Police are more crooked than curly fries, and if they want you done for something . . . Well, let's say they have a great track record of soliciting confessions using methods not seen since the eighteenth century. I hustle out of the caravan, grab my backpack and bike, rouse River and skedaddle down the canal path hidden by the dank winter's dawn. The poor vixen's reluctant to leave Gran. She knows something truly awful's happened.

Takes everything I have to drag her and me away from there.

I snatch one last look at the caravan that's been home all these years. It didn't keep us warm, but it was safe and dry. Even if I didn't have to run, I don't think I could ever live there again. Everything about it smells and feels like Gran. Now I've lost her, along with everything we have in the world. All of it. I glimpse a posse of pigs on horseback appearing at the big roundabout over the bypass. Even from afar, I can hear the clip-clop of hooves against the tar as they head towards the slum. They never come out here unless it's with a show of force. They call it 'policing by consent'.

My grief gives way to burning fury, brighter than anything

I've experienced before. Hand on the hilt of my dagger, I swear I'm going to find the person who did this and make them pay. I let go and start cycling hard, going so fast it's difficult for River to keep up. I know where to go for answers.

I think back to the business at Dunvegan Castle, when Sneddon was murdered and an Ethiopian scroll stolen as a bit of misdirection. What they'd really wanted then was the Fairy Flag – a magical relic taken from the Fae by the Clan MacLeod, who'd remained its guardians and used its power to rule over the Isle of Skye, besting their rivals the MacDonald Clan. The Fairy Flag has the power to open up portals between worlds, so it would make sense that, with enough skill, it could be used to seal up passageways too. Did someone use it to block off the ways to the everyThere? That which can be done can be undone. I suddenly feel sure – find them, and I find Gran's killer. Wedderburn might be locked up in a cell, but I have no doubt he knew something about this scheme. Maybe all the things he said to me earlier were a ruse to make me go home quickly. I should've been inside the caravan with Gran, so I'd be snuffed out too.

Who else but the former head of Edinburgh's school of magic has the sort of connections to make the police look the wrong way when he needs them to? And he's malicious enough to order this done to a poor old woman who's never harmed anyone. One way or the other, Wedderburn's meeting the pointy end of my dagger. They bound his will when he was taken prisoner, so I needn't fear his magic. He'll pay.

It won't bring Gran back, though. Gary neither. It was a long shot, trying to push through to them in the everyThere.

I just wish I'd had the chance to see them both again. That won't happen now. My rage burns so hot the cold morning air doesn't even touch me. The wisps from my breath floating away are the fumes of the fires deep inside of me. They can only be quenched by blood. I want to stop and cry, but I vow not to shed another tear until I've had my revenge.

The canal path is dead this early. A family of swans is already patrolling the waterway, though. I envy them 'cause mine's been stolen from me, all due to Scottish magic and Wedderburn, along with his brainwashed little followers. First it was my sister packed off to boarding school. Now it's my Gran's life. But I'll do whatever it takes to help Lord Samarasinghe bring these fuckers down. Every last one of these magicians can go to hell, starting with Wedderburn.

Cruickshank wraps itself tighter around me. My scarf is mourning the death of its maker too.

I see thick black smoke billowing in the distance when I hit the Tollcross end of the canal. Wisps of white smoke too. There I dump my bike into the brown waters of the canal. It's way too distinctive for me to be scuttling about on it. I'm gonna have to make other changes too, 'cause right now I stick out like a sore thumb. But first things first. I decide on taking the Meadows and using the pathways, instead of the roads which are more likely to have pigs on them. I'll cut through the university grounds, across Bristo Square, and from there work my way up to Calton Hill via the underpass to South College Street.

River's pensive. She senses something's wrong about where we're going.

'We're doing this for Gran,' I tell her.

The air's filled with a vague vinegary smell, which gets stronger and more acidic the closer we come to the city centre. There's figures running hither and thither. Someone cradling a broken arm, bone sticking out, passes me, wincing in pain. On South Bridge, a woman is washing a man's face with bottled water. As I cross the street, I see officers in riot gear clearing the Royal Mile. Definitely not going that way then. Young students pour out, battered and bruised. There's discarded placards. Thistles trampled upon. It's pure mayhem greeting the day in the city.

'All we're asking for's bread,' a middle-aged man says.

'The only thing they're giving out's rubber bullets,' replies one of the students.

'Our rights . . . '

What did they expect, singing banned anthems and protesting in front of the castle? Reminds me of Lord Samarasinghe's words about testing the might of the king. Not a good idea in this climate. Anyone can see the Magna Carta's expired, I think, as I move away from the crowds, River close behind. I have my own shit to worry about.

It's not long before we reach the dam made of rubble and debris from the old council offices. It holds this side of the New Loch, which is flooding the old Waverley Station and the Princes Street Gardens, all the way to the West End. Marking the limits of the dam is the small nook from the old Regents Road, and this leads to Jacob's Ladder, the hundred and forty steps which take you from the Old Town onto Calton Road.

I'm fortunate there's no police down here. They must be concentrating their forces on clearing the Royal Mile of protesters. The steps are steep, but I don't feel them, fuelled by rage as I am. I've got to start planning, though. The second exit from the Old Calton Burial Ground may prove necessary when I make my getaway. Jomo has a key. No, don't get him involved in this. He'll do anything for me, but if I'm a true friend I won't ask him for help. Same goes for Priya. She's always there when I need her, but I know she's also a wee bit sensible and will try to talk me out of anything too extra. They wouldn't understand. It's not one of their own who's been gassed.

After the steps we make it onto Calton Road. There's people running west on Princes Street, followed by more pigs in riot gear. It's pure bedlam out here. First thing in the morning too.

I jog on, eager to get off the main road. The last thing I need is to be nicked and sent to gaol. I take two steps at a time going up Calton Hill. From up here, I can now see more smoke coming from Leith and Niddrie. The whole city'll burn if they don't clamp down on this. That's why I wanted to take Gran away from it all. I falter, thinking of her. It breaks my stride and I clutch my heart. Courage. I put my other hand on the hilt of my dagger and make my way to Edinburgh's Shame. Then I take the third pillar and slip into the Library, with River in tow.

Strange, there's no one in the anteroom today.

Torquil did say they change over. This is great – means I can sneak in without being seen. I try to walk as silently as I can through the cavern, and down the steep steps leading to the main reception. A couple of young magicians scurry up the stairs past me. River pricks up.

'Wouldn't go down there if I were you,' one of them says without breaking stride.

I notice an acrid chemical scent coming from below. Some smoke too. There's no way they're having a riot down here as well, surely? But it dampens my haste.

'Here we go, River.'

There's a haze of smoke throughout reception, which is also unattended. A loud boom comes from a balcony above, and a shower of papers flies through the empty space in the middle of the Library. Voices shout in alarm. Folks are running between the shelves and alcoves of the Library, and I have to avoid another bunch desperate to flee. It's mayhem in here. I keep to the walls and move in the shadows, then kick something: it's the wee old man in his bellhop suit slumped against the wall, passed out. I don't know which of them is which. The bump on his forehead tells the story. He's been roughed up.

'Stand your ground. The Library is under attack. It's your duty as Scottish magicians to defend it,' Dr Maige's voice calls out. It echoes through the nooks and crannies, sounding as though there are hundreds of him.

'If you don't confront us, none of you will be harmed. Challenge us and face the consequences,' says a posh, familiar voice. Hamish Hutchinson, principal of St Andrews College, the second of the four schools of magic. 'Be reasonable and give him to us.'

'Never.'

'Then we'll take him by force.'

'You are sworn—'

'Those old vows mean nothing in the new order that is to come, sir. There will be new gods to watch over this city. It's to them you will swear new oaths.'

What's Hamish Hutchinson doing here?

I creep over to the balcony to see what's going on, passing by a magician hiding under the table. Our eyes meet and he puts his finger to his lips. I saw this cowardice before, on the Isle of Skye. Most Scottish magicians only care about their own wallets and hides. It's striking that in this whole library no one's standing up to fight Hutchinson. Then again, you'd need big cojones to challenge one of the four heads of Scottish magic. And then it hits me. Hutchinson was Wedderburn's friend. The Edinburgh School and St Andrews are rivals, but close. They think themselves superior to the Glasgwegian and Doric Schools. When Wedderburn challenged Callander to a duel and lost, it was Hutchinson who was his second, as I was Callander's. I'm going to lose my shot at Wedderburn if they set him free. I run to the stairs leading down, pulling out my dagger as I go. Ready to slash and stab at anyone who comes at me. I won't let them get away with this.

This one's for you, Gran.

Her life won't have ended in vain for their petty games. Fuck their new gods. I feel Cruickshank unfurl from around my neck, until both sides of the scarf hang down my torso. On the second from last section of the Library, I peer down once more to get a clearer view of who I'm taking on. Motherf— there's a whole bunch of them. Most I know, and a few others are unfamiliar to me. Hutchinson's assembled a right old gang. He's flanked by Lady Rethabile Lebusa and Octavius Diderot, who're both members of the Extraordinary Committee – the group charged with checking the powers of the Secretary of the Society of Sceptical Enquirers. Lady Rethabile is in a flowing scarlet robe, with an emerald choker on her neck, like she's going to a ball. She gives off the vibe of a viper: delicate, slender, deadly and poisonous. Diderot's in a grey suit and wears a bowler hat with an orange feather stuck in it. He has a nonchalant air, as though threatening the most important library in Scottish magic, the one every magician's sworn to protect, is a walk in the park for him.

There's a loud crack of lightning from up above, in the highest balcony. Brilliant sepia lights up the whole place for a millisecond. It's answered by the pneumatic pfft of a soliton, and burning pages of books float downwards. There's clearly a duel going on upstairs.

'Keep the quadruplets separate,' Hutchinson says. 'We can't let them form a choir. They are more dangerous that way.'

'Like a pack of wolves,' Lady Rethabile remarks.

'Against us they might as well be jackals. And we're only just gathering our strength,' says Diderot.

'There'll be time to congratulate one another later. Right now, we need the young ones to open the dungeon.'

'You shall not pass,' replies Torquil's voice, with all the menace of a hound of hell. A slight tremor passes through the Library.

But what chance does he stand against these practitioners, backed up as they are by Fenella MacLeod and those other students behind the heist at Dunvegan Castle? This undoubtedly means Lewis Wharncliffe and Nathair Walsh must be close by. Maybe upstairs causing the racket that's making paper rain down through the Library. I'm still assessing all the folks down below when I'm startled by footsteps behind me.

'Hello, sunshine. Have you missed me?' a familiar voice says.

I turn quickly and hold my dagger out in front of me. It's Wilson! The butler from the spooky Edinburgh mansion, Arthur Lodge. He has a demented look of glee in his eyes. His butler's suit and tails look worn, with holes in – surely the sign of a life on the streets. He still has his white gloves on too, whose digits flop about because his fingers were amputated at the first joint. He gives me a satisfied smile and I'm frozen, recovering from the shock of seeing him here. Then I notice something else about him. An uncanny resemblance to Sophie, and even Una to a lesser extent, written in his cheekbones, the mouth, nose and eyes – just as I had thought back at Arniston House. Wilfred, too – that dodgy accent you get when working-class folks hang about too much with the rich. Faux. Is there some connection to them? Either way, he shouldn't be here – the man isn't even a magician.

'What are you doing here?' I ask, desperate to draw out a connection.

'You cast me low indeed when you brought Arthur Lodge to the ground. But my true master, the Tall Man, never forgets his loyal servants. Rejoice, for his return is at hand and those who opposed it will burn.'

'—'

'In case it's not clear, I mean people like you, sunshine.' There's menace in his tone.

'Stay away from me,' I say, swishing my blade in the air.

'We gave you a chance to join us.' He rushes at me, faster than I imagined possible. As I stab at him, he steps away, chopping at my arm. I've overextended and the jarring impact makes me drop the blade. He hits me in the face and I stagger. The blow has cut my lip and I feel it sting. I've just been bested by a geriatric. Clearly I'm not at the top of my game.

'That's for the brounie you slaughtered,' he says, kicking my blade away.

'Wilson! Quit fooling around. We need you down here,' Hutchinson shouts up.

'Yes, master. I was just taking care of a little problem,' he replies. Then he turns to me, the smile still fixed on his face. 'I guess I'll see you later, sunshine.'

Wilson walks off with a surprising confidence. All the times I knew him, he was servile – except when he was being a dick to those under him, but that was always with an air of cowardice. Now he strides away as though he owns this place. I've seen that swagger before, in the pussies at school who were friends with bullies. In many ways they were worse than the bullies themselves.

That's when I notice Mr Evelyn in his magnificent robes, cowering behind a bookshelf. He shakes his head, as though afraid I might give his position away. Librarians aren't magicians, so I wouldn't expect anything more. But this place feels even more hollow than before, as though the very hearts of the people who use it are but empty shells.

A sudden boom and crash makes me flinch.

I retrieve my dagger and re-evaluate my options. This is a Society problem, not mine. But that's me being a chicken, like the rest here. I can't leave before my blade has tasted Wedderburn's blood. The smoke in the air gets thicker. I look across where lightning cast by some magician has caused a shelf of books to catch fire. A cloud spontaneously forms from the ether and floats over, settling atop the burning books until they're smothered. The Library has an effective fire suppression system, it seems.

A classical statue falls to the floor and shatters.

There's no turning back, so I head downstairs after Wilson, moving more stealthily than before. I'll be the assassin then. The way he left me so easily seems to indicate no one in this place has factored me in as a threat. The stone wall is cold and rough against my back as I creep further down. I don't care about the rest of them, I'm only here for one man. But even now I find myself wishing Priya was beside me. She can handle herself and knows better magic than I do.

I crawl around the dark edges and find a spot to hide behind Hume's sarcophagus. It's not easy being stealthy on a floor littered with paper and debris. I catch my breath and peer over the top of the tomb. Hutchinson has at least ten people with him. They're all magicians – I can sense their power. Dr Maige is standing with Torquil in front of the door leading into the workshop, which in turn leads to the dungeon. There's something dignified and firm about the head librarian. I remember he once said his red robes were made of a dye mixed in with a drop of his blood, for he was sworn to protect the Library. I don't think he ever envisaged the possibility that it might be against Scottish magicians he'd have to make this stand.

Someone flies down from a great height, nightclothes flailing amidst the shower of pages raining down. There's an entropic shift, and I see the cushion of an anemoic spell as the figure lands next to Dr Maige and Torquil. The man in the nightclothes is the spitting image of his brother beside him.

'I thought Walsh and Wharncliffe were supposed to take care of that one,' Lady Rethabile says. 'Never trust the Edinburgh Boys to do a job best suited for St Andrews.'

'Those divisions are irrelevant now,' Hutchinson replies.

'I must warn you Torquil and Teàrlach are formidable. You'd do well to reconsider your folly. The Library is willing to over-look the events of this morning, should you do so. You have my word,' Dr Maige says.

'Well, that is very reassuring, isn't it?' Hutchinson says. 'Bring the boy.'

There's movement in the shadows of the third entrance, the one leading down to the underHume. Then out steps Avery MacDonald, holding Jomo by the scruff of the neck. My blood boils. How dare he touch my best friend like that. I need to create some sort of diversion to free him. He can't handle this kind of heat, gentle soul that he is. There's fear written all over his face. I've seen it before many times, like at Dunvegan Castle when his dad was giving him an almighty rollicking for losing the Ethiopian scroll. He's shrunk in on himself, while Avery looks cool in a denim jacket and white T-shirt, hair gelled up as though he's just stepped out of an eighties movie.

'Give us what we want and you can have your son back,' Hutchinson offers.

Dr Maige looks Jomo in the eye, holds there briefly, then shakes his head.

'My duty is to this Library,' he says.

I swear even some of Hutchinson's own crew look gutted by that. Jomo most of all. He lowers his head, hands trembling, and removes his glasses.

'Father,' he says.

'Don't you dare, Mr Maige. Be a man,' his father replies coldly, curling his lips in disgust.

Avery shoves Jomo forward, forcing him beside Hutchinson. He stands very still, looking at the ground, his demeanour devastated. His shoulders move up and down as he takes deep breaths. Then I sense a change as he looks up at his father, because Dr Maige's own expression turns to confusion. I wish I could understand it, but Jomo and the others have their backs to me so I can't make it out. We're interrupted by the appearance of the old man in the bellhop gear who I saw passed out earlier. His forehead bump looks angry and red, but he stands at the entrance to the stairs looking furious.

'Taskill is here now,' Dr Maige declares with confidence. Addressing his colleagues, he then says, 'As head librarian, I command you to seal these intruders here.'

The three old men begin reciting a spell simultaneously, as though tied together by an invisible thread. I catch the invocation of Tartarus, the god who presides over the hell pit, where men and even gods are imprisoned to suffer for all eternity, without reprieve. I sense a drastic entropic shift. When magicians come together to weave a common spell it enhances their will – for magic is a product of human will, according to the

Somerville equation. And the more in sync they are, the more profound the magnification. The very walls of the Library grumble in response. These small old men seem to stretch up and become giants. The candles burn brighter, making their shadows longer. Fenella, who's closest to Taskill, is pushed by an invisible force and she slides inwards, against her will. Indeed, the same happens to Hamish Hutchinson and Lady Rethabile, and their group all begins to skid towards a common middle.

Louder and louder the three old men chant, their words weaving together as surely as a smith layers sheets of steel to create a stronger blade. Avery MacDonald is hit by the force too. He braces against it and tries to push, but it's too strong for him. There must be something intrinsic to the Library which magnifies the spell – one that's already made stronger by the choir of the trio. In desperation Fenella incants and fires a thermosphere at Taskill. But as the fireball hits their spell it dissipates, absorbed into the ether.

Jomo's trapped right there inside with them and I fear the worst.

'You cannot break this trap. It has served the Library well for centuries,' Dr Maige says. 'And know that you will be judged harshly in front of Hume before this day is done.'

'Conjuring the shackles of the Titans won't hold us,' Hutchinson says.

He reaches out to touch the barrier driving him back. Lady Rethabile and Octavius Diderot flank him on either side, placing their hands on his shoulders. Together they begin a counter-spell, using words of ancient Greek that can alter entropy dreadfully. The temperature in the cold Library rises.

Work's being done. I feel utterly inadequate with my simple dagger, scarf and catapult. Even my bulletproof jacket made of Ankara print, which used to be my gran's, doesn't give me enough of an advantage. I only know a handful of spells – what use can I be in this situation? A loud crack sounds, like glass shattering. Dr Maige's eyes widen in shock.

'Hold them here. We need the aid of the secretary,' he says in desperation.

But Callander's not here and the few magicians who might have tried to help have either fled or are hiding in the recesses of the Library. The atmosphere around Hutchinson and his team takes on an eerie glow, with hairline cracks appearing, as though the air itself were metal under stress. The three guardians of the Library desperately continue to work their spell, trying to repair the fissures. But these expand, growing ever larger, until there's an almighty supersonic boom and explosion. Huge quantities of air blow outward, knocking Dr Maige and his colleagues up in the air, and then against the Library walls.

Dr Maige is stunned by the blow.

Taskill, already weakened by an earlier assault, lies unmoving on the floor, blood trickling from the back of his head.

'Bind and neuter them,' Hutchinson says.

'There's a fourth who is far more powerful than these three,' Jomo says.

'We'll get to him later. You have the key?'

'Right here,' Jomo replies, taking the bunch of keys from his rope belt.

Jomo?

'Release Wedderburn.'

Dr Maige slowly rises to his feet. He's unsteady and shaking, but he fights to stand up, even as Torquil and Teàrlach are seized by Lady Rethabile and Octavius Diderot. Alarm is written over the head librarian's face – it's the first time I've seen him so completely rattled.

'Mr Maige, what do you think you're doing?' he says in a weak voice. 'Don't you dare.'

He slides back onto the floor, defeated, red robes flowing out on the hallowed stone like blood. And I'm just as shocked as Dr Maige when Jomo strides past him confidently. Even the way Jomo walks is suddenly different: chin up as though disdainful of his father, shoulders square as if he owned the place.

Oh, Jomo, what have you done?

Of course, you need a prison guard to help you escape. Even though he's only an acolyte, Jomo's been working here a while and has information that's useful for this prison break. It then dawns on me that Wedderburn has been working on him even more than I feared, feeding him lies and dreams. And I've worried for years about the way Dr Maige treats Jomo: belittling him, shaming him, finding fault in every little error, real or imagined. Seems like the camel's back broke and now everything's fucked.

Torquil screams as Lady Rethabile, helped by Fenella and Avery, begins to neuter him. I feel sick hearing it. The human body is the most resistant thing there is to magic, because it's the ultimate vessel of will – the place from which all magic proceeds. Magic done to someone else's body can either be accomplished by consent or by coercion, and this is why the procedure is the ultimate violation. Torquil's face is contorted, veins bulging, the sinews straining on his neck, as they raise him in the air, arms and legs splayed as though he's being drawn and quartered.

'This is your fault, Dr Maige. It didn't have to be this way,' Hutchinson says with practised remorse in his voice.

Torquil's body arches and something inside him breaks. A wave of terror rushes through me as he slumps and falls to the ground.

'It's done,' Lady Rethabile says matter-of-factly.

'This is what happens to the practitioners who dare stand against us.'

Something has died inside of Torquil. His eyes are open, staring out, but it's as though he sees nothing. Drool escapes from the left corner of his lips and rolls down to his chin. No one's home.

'Shall we do the others?'

'No, they can be thrown in the dungeon for now – I think we've made our point clear,' Hutchinson says.

There's a certain unease in the room, radiating out to all points of the Library. A line's been crossed. From this point on, nothing in Scottish magic will ever be the same again. A social contract's been torn, shredded like the pages from the books littering the floor of the Library. Even the younger magicians, Avery and Fenella, seem more uncertain than they were earlier, though they still carry out the orders given to them. Only Teàrlach remains sombre in the bearing of a captured enemy combatant. But there's something burning in his eyes. I know that look, I've seen it in the mirror: the desire for revenge. A spark that if not contained will rage until it swallows the world.

'My own son. He can't do this,' Dr Maige says, shaking his head.

'There's a new generation now, different from every other that's come before it. We have been their guardians for years, nurturing them, teaching them, preparing them for the great work to be done. The job of restoring Scotland to its rightful place as the beacon of enlightenment, and Edinburgh as the Athens of the North.' Wedderburn's voice carries forth from within the corridor leading to the dungeon. He emerges into the light, gaunt and pale, yet somehow still looking professorial, despite the poverty of his dress. 'Your son, Jomo, understands this, which is why he has joined us, as have these other young people I am delighted to see again.'

'My good friend, Montgomery,' Hutchinson says as Wedderburn approaches.

The two men grip each other in a forearm handshake as though they were ancient Romans or something.

'You've done sterling work, Hamish.'

'And now I unbind you, and restore to you the magic I took after your duel with Sir Ian Callander. It was your great sacrifice that set everything in motion.'

There's a cheer from the students and collaborators. Then I glimpse someone with a languid gait coming down the stairs. Bloody Lewis Wharncliffe looking like a wannabe glam rocker in a leather jacket.

Fuck this. I hold my dagger in a reverse hammer grip, spring up from my hiding spot, and jump onto the top of Hume's tomb. From there I leap at Wedderburn, aiming straight for his heart.

XI

There's a pneumatic hiss, a flash of golden light, and a soliton with the force of an HGV lorry hits me mid-flight, changing my trajectory and throwing me back on top of Hume's tomb. I hit the edge of the marble with a thud and tumble beside it, then roll to the ground. I would have stabbed myself or broken a rib too had it not been for Gran's coat I'm wearing.

Wedderburn is holding up his hand, having repelled me. He flexes his fingers as though testing out his recently returned powers, before looking at me with barely concealed condescension.

'It's Callander's little pug,' Hutchinson says.

'Shall I take care of her, master?' Wilson says, stepping towards me, the same fanatical grin as before on his mug.

'You are all traitors. Lewis, Jomo, the lot of you,' I say.

I feel blood trickling down the side of my temple. Must have hit my head on the way down too. That's gonna hurt come the morning. If I make it till then. Lewis grabs Wilson by the shoulder and stops him coming at me. There's pity written all over his face. I can take anything except that.

'I'm sorry it has to be this way, Ropa. But it's for the greater good. You won't understand it now, you're not a real magician with a true comprehension of why we must . . .' Lewis trails off. All I hear in his voice is Weddernburn's rationalizations. Some people still want you to think they're good, even when they knowingly commit evil acts.

'You promised not to hurt her,' Jomo says. 'Ropa, I'll explain everything one day. Trust me.'

'Look at yourselves. Murderers. Thieves. Oath breakers.'

I fold my legs under me and push myself back up using my left hand.

'Stay down,' Hutchinson commands.

I stand up anyway and change my grip to hold the dagger edge-forwards. But there's too many of them. It's like walking into a pack of hyenas. Fenella MacLeod takes a step towards me, malice in her eyes.

'Leave the girl be. She's not worth our efforts, and she belongs to Lord Samarasinghe now. We'd do well not to offend the English whose alliance we seek to renew,' Wedderburn says at last. 'I don't know what your problem is, but these matters concern Scottish magic, which has nothing to do with you anymore. But if you continue to harass us, Ms Moyo, I may well change my mind. Consider this an act of kindness.'

I desperately want to run at him again, but I've been driven only by my anger and grief. Getting myself killed right now won't bring Gran back. In *The Theatre of Power*, Blackwood cautions: 'Of all the emotions, anger carries the greatest cost, second only to love. If you let either of those overwhelm you, be prepared to fall.' I wanted instant gratification, but anger clouds judgement, and especially in tough situations, I need to be clear. If there's anything I've learnt in my time with these magicians, it's that this is all a game to them. People's lives are something they toy with to attain their goals. I'm going to have to be smarter from here on.

I look into Jomo's eyes as I sheath my dagger, returning it to my side. The only blood it's tasted is my own. I've nicked the palm of my hand with it. Jomo blinks a couple of times and turns away from me.

'I think she understands,' he says to them.

'Good, let us not waste any more time here. There's work to be done for our Black Lord,' Hutchinson says.

'Lock up the head librarian and his minions in the dungeon they so happily keep. The rest of us are to go to the Library of the Dead,' says Wedderburn, putting his hand on Jomo's shoulder with the tenderness of a loving father. He then leads them all towards the stairs. I watch, seething inside, wishing every one of them would die and be buried in a shallow ditch. Even Jomo, my once best friend.

I untuck my T-shirt from my jeans and wipe my face with it. I'm feeling so powerless. The worst part of all is knowing what they did to my grandmother, but not being able to prove it. They haven't even given me that. Which means I'm not off the hook, and I'm still gonna have the filth after me as soon as I leave this place. Wedderburn's *kindness* is the same as a hunter leaving a wounded animal instead of finishing it off.

I'm so very tired of all this.

Can I even walk away? It would be so easy. I curse the day I helped a ghost with a missing kid which led me down this path. All I've ever gotten out of meddling with the magicking world is misery and grief. I remember when I first started and

Gran tried to warn me away from it all. But I was naive, seeing the opportunity for cash which her kitchen table magic could never give me. *Self-pity ain't a good look either, Ropa.* I crack my knuckles, then follow Wedderburn and his crew upstairs.

This time I make sure to keep my distance.

I move subtly behind the shelves, tracing the opposite route to the far end of the Library. From there I can see them better as they approach the massive teak doors with their Arabic inscriptions in the Zanzibari style – Dr Maige's personal touch.

This place is two different institutions nestled in one location: Calton Hill Library and the Library of the Dead. It shares Edinburgh's dual nature of the Old Town and the New Town, those divided halves of a single self, just as much as Scotland itself is divided into the Lowlands and the Highlands, the Scots speakers and Gaelic speakers. A duality between reason and passion, order and chaos, which runs through every single facet of our being. We are the nation of Doctor Jekyll and Mr Hyde. It's written in our souls as much as it is in the landscape and architecture. This library is yet another manifestation of the same phenomenon. Calton Hill Library contains *texts*: orderly, scientific, sane. And the antithesis of it, the Library of the Dead, holds *books*, creations of flesh and bone taken from leading Scots through the ages: chaotic, whimsical, capricious – so much so that reading from them is undertaken with great care and training. I would know: I tried it once and wound up in hospital.

A rat scurries along the floor in front of me.

'Open it,' Hutchinson says.

Avery moves forward to push open the doors of the Library of the Dead, but finds them locked. He tries a couple of times, more for show than anything, before turning to his principal. Then he takes a step back and incants a Heraclean spell. Heracles was a demigod known for his strength, and this spell invokes the myth of him breaking down the doors of Hades to retrieve Cerberus in the last of his twelve labours. It creates a radical entropic shift, and a flash of light emanating from Avery hits the doors. They flex, bending inwards, with the creaking old wood impossibly stretched, like rubber, before they snap back again, hitting Avery and knocking him to the floor.

He scrambles back up and sets about trying once more.

'Move aside, MacDonald, I'll do it,' Wedderburn says, hand outstretched, palm facing the door.

'Are you sure you're strong enough yet? It will take time before you're fully recovered,' says Hutchinson.

'You underestimate the strength of his will,' Lady Rethabile chimes in.

Jomo steps forward. 'These doors are protected by Janus craft. The god of two faces, past and future, who protects doors, gates and boundaries. Whatever spell you set on them will only turn back on you twice as strongly. They're deadly. Only a librarian can open them when they're locked, as is the case now. Allow me,' he says confidently.

'I always knew you were underappreciated, young man,' Wedderburn replies, patting him on the back.

Jomo only has to turn the handles and pull, and the doors obey, throwing themselves open without complaint. A brilliant white light issues from within. Standing just inside the threshold is the fourth quadruplet, wearing black robes with silver stitching at the hems. He's identical to his three brothers in face and demeanour, but seems half a foot taller and more imposing than them. It's clear he's the alpha of the litter, and I'm not surprised it falls to him to guard the Library of the Dead.

'Tormod,' Jomo cries out in alarm.

'Who dares disturb the peace of this final resting place?' the guardian challenges. 'And where are my brothers?'

'We are true Scottish magicians whose birthright is the treasures of the Library,' Wedderburn responds.

'Where is the keeper of the books?'

'The head librarian is currently indisposed, but as you can see two heads of the schools of magic are here.'

'Curious, I heard one head had resigned his post and was being held prisoner in this here library. I will not allow you in today, tomorrow, or ever again, sir.'

Tormod holds out his hands on either side and commands the doors to close. That's when I feel an entropic shift, as Lady Rethabile Lebusa launches a thermosphere at him. But it flies in slow motion, as though time had slowed down. Tormod shifts aside and responds with a vicious soliton wave, whose fury I can feel from this far way. But even as he does so, Octavius Diderot, Wedderburn and Hutchinson are all hurling spells at him. The old man moves quickly, dodging their lightning strikes, creating heat sinks for their thermospheres, and retaliating with countermeasures. But they still drive him back, using sheer numbers as Fenella, Avery, Lewis and Nathair enter the fray too.

With the doors open, I feel the hum and pull of the books on the cushioned shelves. Those grotesque artefacts made of human flesh and bone. They have a draw about them, a sort of charm that invites you into their pages, and this spills out. But this time it feels magnified. I want to stand up and go inside, and it takes everything I have not to do so.

Suddenly Avery and Fenella stop dead in their tracks. Wilson greedily makes a beeline for the nearest bookshelf. Jomo steps backwards, as if fighting the force drawing him inside.

Even Octavius Diderot has given up the fight.

There are silver channels and runes set within the stones of the Library of the Dead, and they glow with an ethereal light. I realize that Tormod has amplified the *lure* – the quality of the books in the library that makes them as dangerous as the sirens of old.

'Resist it, God damn you,' Hutchinson tries to rally his enamoured co-conspirators.

An overwhelming rotting smell seeps out from the Library, yet somehow it attracts you too, and I realize this place is a Venus fly trap. I pray that the lure will capture these horrible folks and hold them in here for ever. Forcing their way in might have been easy, but leaving seems like it'll be much harder. Even Jomo, librarian though he is, desperately holds onto the stone balcony, using every ounce of will not to be dragged inside.

Wilson grabs one of the books from the shelf. The binding is made of skin, the spine of bone, and there're ribs running along the covers, holding it sturdy. It's like an ugly, tasty slab of meat. He inserts a hand into the pages, and it seems as though the book latches onto him. Then he begins to shake his hand, crying out, 'Get it off, it's eating me. My hand!'

He flings the book onto the ground at last, and it comes away with a spray of blood. His hand is amputated at the wrist and he wails, clutching the stump.

'No, please, not again. Let me go,' he cries.

The other books on the shelf call out to him. They call out to all of us. I'd been told only highly trained magicians can read them, and now I understand their true danger. But while the rest of us are enamoured, Wedderburn, Lebusa and Hutchinson are immune enough to continue their assault against Tormod. The air in the Library gradually takes on a grim, mistier tone, but it's not smoke. Rather it's as if the sea's dense haar has settled in. I notice that the areas near the bookshelves are clearer, and I can feel the moisture in the air as I breathe. It creates little droplets against my skin. This is the Library's fire suppression system, which is pretty cool. It's just their security that's a bit meh.

Fuck, the books keep calling me.

They tug harder at my entire being. Struggle as I may, I can't hold out against the lure much longer. My legs start moving against my will, going one way while my fingers peel off the pillar I'm holding onto. This is bullshit. I'm forced onto my hands and knees. It's not an external force battling me, but something coming from within. The same magic that leads birds home no matter where they might be. Except this time, it's to a bunch of books which will probably chew your hand off, as Wilson's desperate screams can attest to.

There's three young magicians, two lads and a lassie, must be in their late teens, heading towards the Library of the Dead. Their eyes are filled with a certain excitement, as if they're late, rushing to a party. And more folks appear from the places they were hiding all over the Library. Fucking cowards. This could all have been prevented if they'd stuck to their vows and protected the Library against this other lot. But now they're dragged out of their foxholes, the lure calling everyone to it. I finally understand the power of the Library under attack. The books it guards are simultaneously its security of last resort. Once unleashed, no one may leave. But the danger is for those like me and Wilson, untrained in reading them. That's what separates the truly great magicians from any would-be intruder. The young trio have reached the entrance, those wide-open wooden doors, and they walk straight in, oblivious to the thermospheres and solitons cast by the magicians duelling Tormod. The cracks of thunder are deafening, as though we are inside an almighty storm.

As soon as the trio reach the shelves, they reach desperately for books.

'Rethabile, grab the books we're after before this place is swamped with readers. Give Diderot a hard slap across the face. We'll handle Mr Tormod here,' Wedderburn says.

'You boys like to have fun all by yourselves,' she replies sharpish, peeling away from the battle and wandering off into the maze of shelves.

A few more, who've made their way from the section above, stream towards the Library of the Dead. I'm like, screw this, and desperately try to slow my progress towards it. River bites onto the hem of my jeans, trying to hold me back too. Better not poke a hole in them. Actually, do your thing, 'cause this is like being dragged by white-water rapids.

'Ropa, no, stay away,' Jomo yells.

'I can't,' I say.

'The books are out of control, they'll devour you. Only their master, the head librarian, can settle them once they're in a frenzy like this.'

'You should've thought about that before you signed up for some death cult, man.'

'It's not what you think. Our actions will speak for themselves.'

'Great job so far, ten out of ten,' I say.

I've made my way around the circular balcony now and am almost where Jomo is. Thought I was moving much slower than I actually was. Try as I may, I can't stay away, and judging by the screams in there, everyone who's not trained in reading the books is being chomped on. Seems I'm next on the menu. What a clusterfuck.

Jomo grabs my arm and pulls me over to where he's at, between the statues of Athena and Apollo, the goddess and god of knowledge, who stand guarding the entrance to the Library of the Dead. Keeping one hand on the balcony, he draws me nearer and I wrap both my arms around him, with my head against his chest. I feel his other arm tight against me.

'You're safe here with me. I've got you.'

'What have you done, Jomo?'

'You don't understand, Ropa. You know nothing about what it feels like to be me.'

'I've known you most of your life, you wee knob.'

'Man, you don't get it at all. Look at you – always off on adventures, doing magic, talking to ghosts, solving mysteries.

People might not like you, but they respect you. They know you're strong and smart, and you kick ass. Even my father says you're something special. He'd never tell you, but he does it all the time, comparing me to you. Tells me that I was given all the opportunities you never had and still I manage, somehow, to cock it all up. You should have heard him talk about you when you recovered the scroll at Dunvegan Castle – the scroll that I lost . . .'

My best mate, jealous of me, of all people? Then he truly is messed up in the head. I grip him tighter, wishing I could slap him. A tear slides down my forehead and runs across my cheek. Jomo's crying. I raise my left hand to his face, feeling the stubble on his jawline, and run it up to his afro. This used to be us in school, back before I gave the man the middle finger. I'd comfort him when the bampots and bullies were messing with him. I'd protect him. Now it seems I have to protect him from himself.

'You know what the worst part is?'

'Stop digging, Jomo. Sometimes you've got to stop. We can fix this, you and me.'

'It's not just you and me anymore, Ropa. That's just . . . aargh, I don't even know how to say this without seeming like a jackass . . . Before, yeah, it was us, you and me against the whole wide world. We were—'

'Storm and Gambit.'

'I was about to go with Steve Rogers and Sam Wilson, but I guess I'll take that. Then Priya came along and everything changed. Before I knew it, you were spending more time with her, and whenever there's action going on, it's her you turn to.

It's never me anymore. Sometimes when I'm with you guys, I feel like I'm a third wheel. She knows more about what's going on with you than I do.'

I place my hand on his cheek and squeeze.

With the thumping of his heart, I can just about forget the pull of the lure. I can ignore the raging inferno around us, how everything's going to shit. We're safe here, in our friendship. But Jomo doesn't see that. I thought the issues he had were only with his dad, but it seems that's made him paranoid about other relationships too. Now he thinks Priya's a threat. He doesn't understand that she complements us, and she's just as much his friend as he's mine. And if we don't do stuff as often as we did back in school, it's 'cause we've all got other things to do now. But it's not about what's true, it's about how he feels.

'I'm sorry if I haven't seemed as available to you as I should. We can change that, make more time for one another. But you've got to remember, Captain America and the Falcon also had the Avengers around them. Priya loves you very much, as do I. She'd be hurt if she thought you didn't value her friendship as much as she does yours.'

'That's not what I meant. Things aren't the same anymore.'

In the fifth chapter of *The Theatre of Power*, Bryson Blackwood warns: 'The greatest danger comes from family and friends, for your inner circle forms your blind spot. This is human nature.' He advises you become suspicious of the people closest to you, for they can do you the greatest harm. 'Be wary of them more than you would be with strangers.' But while Blackwood might have been speaking of the sharks around him, he doesn't know Jomo like I do. I'd take his advice on a lot of things, but on this he's just wrong. Jomo ain't doing an Anakin Skywalker anytime soon.

'Peter Pan and Wendy,' I say.

'Huh?'

'We have to grow up, Jomo. And it starts by us fixing this mess we've gotten ourselves into. Those Zanzibari doors are consecrated, aren't they? When they're closed, the lure of the books doesn't spill out into the rest of Calton Hill Library? All we need to do is shut and lock them again, with everyone inside. Wedderburn and them lot might resist a while longer, but they can't hold out against the pull of those books for ever. It'll give us enough time to free your dad and hopefully put a stop to this madness. We can do the right thing. It's not too late. You with me, man?'

Jomo holds still for a bit, then I feel him nodding, his chin brushing against my head.

'I need to hear you say it.'

'I'm with you, always.'

Phew – I'm glad he's seen sense. Jomo's always had his heart in the right place. He doesn't belong with Wedderburn and that murderous lot. Though he might be ditzy alright, he's fundamentally a good, sound lad. I give him one last squeeze and let go. Almost immediately I feel the seductive pull of the lure urging my limbs to move again. We're a few steps away from the doors, and if I don't line up my angles right, I'll be sucked inside. Good thing Jomo's a wee bit more resistant, being a trainee librarian and all.

'Help me to the left-hand door, then you can do the right, okay?' I say.

He puts his hand around my shoulder and guides me. Walking against the lure is like having a strong wind pushing from behind you, and so you have to arch backwards and make sure you step right. We make it to the left-hand door and Jomo shoves me behind it. Almost immediately, I feel a wee bit of relief from the lure. The wood seems to temper it somehow, so I keep a tight grip on the handle, ensuring the door's covering me at all times.

Being behind it like this, I can't see Jomo going over to the right-hand door. So I count the seconds between each breath, and when I think I've given him enough time, I begin to push the door, putting my shoulder into it. The bottom scrapes against the floor. Have to use all my might, because it feels as if some force is trying to keep the door open at all costs.

'Give us a hand, River,' I say.

She doesn't disappoint, though it's kind of like she's just nudging at the door instead of giving it any real muscle. No wonder foxes ain't beasts of burden.

There's a loud whistle from somewhere at the top of the Library. Sounds like code for something, and could only mean the cavalry are arriving. I intensify my efforts, grunting with the effort, the wood hard against my shoulder. Let's shut these bastards in. I've nearly done my side, but Jomo's taking longer. I miscalculated how long it would take him to reach his door. Factoring in the lure, I should've given him a few extra seconds.

I can't cross over to help him, though, 'cause I have to keep my side secure. And I doubt, this close to the Library of the Dead, I'd make it across the gap without being sucked inside.

'Come on, Jomo. You can do it,' I encourage him.

'It's. Pushing. Against. Me.'

'Don't be a softie.'

Jomo half laughs, half groans. Even the most difficult task can be okay when your mates are with you. Once we've sealed these folks in, we'll have taken control of the situation, since only a librarian can open the doors again. Hopefully it'll hold out against their magic. But with hungry zombie books inside, I'm sure they'll have their hands full . . . if they have any hands left.

I reach out to try to help Jomo with his side of the door, but it's frustratingly that bit too far. All the while I have to keep my focus on the left-hand door as well. Lady Rethabile slips past me and out, holding three gigantic books in her hands. So, this isn't just a jailbreak, they're also interested in nicking artefacts. Which books are those, and why are they so import-ant to them? Her face is slick with sweat as she observes me for a second before proceeding. There's a smirk on her face, and I want to punch those perfect cheekbones.

'Jomo, hurry,' I say.

But we're too late. Next it's Wilson who staggers out, wincing as he cradles his bad hand. Octavius Diderot shepherds the younger magicians after him. It seems that slap woke him out of the trance the books had placed him in. He moves with a grim determination, paying me no attention.

'We can still do this,' I say, desperately reaching for the other door which remains tantalizingly out of reach. Why's it taking Jomo so long?

If we can trap Wedderburn and Hutchinson in there, it's still a win. But I've spoken too soon, as both men walk out the door, Wedderburn firing one last thermosphere inside. He stops next to me, gently helps Jomo to move the door within my arm's reach, and I grasp it finally. Then he takes Jomo by the hand and pulls him away.

I can't let go of the doors because that'll only unleash further chaos, and the lure will get me too. The screams still coming from inside show the books continue to have an almighty feast on their would-be readers who're left in there.

'Jomo!' I shout.

But he avoids meeting my eye as he walks away with Wedderburn. At last, I realize what's going on. My pal's cheated me again. Jomo and me used to be thick as thieves, and this was supposed to be for ever, but now we're split for good. We've become different people, even though we started in the same place. In one night, I've lost my nan and my best friend. I'm losing everyone.

'Hurry, you heard the signal, Callander's coming,' Hutchinson says.

'We can take him,' Wedderburn replies.

'And risk the work in a duel with him? No, we've come too far.'

'You're right, open the pathways.'

I look over my shoulder, still focusing all my energies on pushing the doors, and see Hutchinson reach into his inside jacket pocket. There he retrieves a tattered, faded brown cloth made of silk. *The Fairy Flag.* I've half a mind to rush Hutchinson and snatch it, but with those magicians around I wouldn't even make it near. And I have to close these doors.

He holds the flag in his left hand and begins to incant something in Gaelic, the language of the Sidhe and their kin

155

in the Highlands. He waves his right hand over the flag as he recites. Blast these doors, I'm nearly there, almost got them shut. The misty air takes on a blue tinge, then there's the sound of heavy rocks shifting. I start to smell something ancient, like rotting leaves in an untouched forest. Roots and grubs. The scent of the world before it was spoiled by humankind. Suddenly that shimmering void is rent in two, and an old footpath appears, inside of a thick woodland.

That's what the Fairy Flag can do, open gateways between worlds, but which world is this? It's not one I've been to on the astral plane. The trees are gnarly and twisted far beyond any I've seen before. Though their needle-like leaves resemble pine, their orange colour's not something you'd expect on evergreens this time of year.

'There's our shortcut home, my friends. Stick with me and do not divert from the path under any circumstances. If you get lost, you'll never find your way out again. The occult roads of the Fairy King are not kind to those who stray, especially those of our kind, against whom the Fae hold a grudge,' Hutchinson says, stepping into the portal.

I have to go after them.

Using all my might, I finally heave the doors shut. I turn quickly, but as I do, I see Jomo's the last one through the portal. I run to the gap and leap, but it closes and I merely land on the floor, hard.

It's taken all my strength to close those damned doors and I'm knackered as hell, panting and all. River stands over me, probably wondering what all this is about. Not that I've got too many answers for her at the mo.

I don't have time to catch my breath before voices sound from the reception area of the Library.

Oh shit, I've got to hide.

'No one has dared attack the Library since the Second World War, when the Nazis sent an infiltration team who landed on the coast in Port Seton. But they were soon repulsed by our practitioners,' Callander's voice booms.

'That was then, sir. Now it seems from the reports no one stood up and fought to defend the Library,' Cockburn says. I'd know her voice anywhere.

'You can't compare the third-rate charlatans practising today to those men.'

'And women.'

'Quite right, of course.'

'Do you smell smoke?'

'My nose isn't quite what it used to be, but I do see signs of the Nephele cloud formation fire defence that's in effect,' Sir Ian Callander replies. 'Ready yourself, Frances, we don't know what awaits us within.'

So this is the cavalry arriving, Cockburn and Callander. I know Callander's formidable, like a great battleship whose guns could level a small city. There's no fear or alarm in his voice. I'm now on my knees, hiding behind a bookshelf, watching from a wee gap I've created. He looks furious in his tweed suit. Cockburn, in her grey attire, seems equally up to the task. Following timidly are Sinéad, Abdul and Carrie from the Hamster Squad. Though magically trained, them lot are more Society administrators and not the sort of warriors you need in a scrap.

They stand and inspect the chaos around. The torn books and pages. Broken statues. The signs that this sacred space has been violated.

Got here too late.

I resist the urge to rush out to Callander. Once I'd have told him everything, but I've left Scottish magic now. And if there's anything I remember from my short involvement with it, they always look for someone to blame for shit they've caused themselves. Cockburn doesn't much like me, and I'm sure she'd shank me at the first given opportunity. I broke one of the cardinal rules of *The Theatre of Power*: 'Never openly outshine your superiors for they will surely move against you.' That's why she's a prick to me, always trying to chop this tall poppy to size.

A faint call comes from inside the Library of the Dead proper.

Cockburn makes for the door.

'Don't,' Callander says, grabbing her arm. 'The books are in a frenzy and only their master can calm them now.'

'There are people inside there. Where is Dr Maige?'

'That's what we'll have to find out. But we mustn't be hasty. Since Dunvegan, I've had cause for great concern. It seems the events from there have spilt over into Edinburgh, our home of Scottish magic.'

Callander is the Discoverer General in Scotland, a modern version of the Witchfinder General of old. The last in the line of men like John Kincaid, the famous witch-pricker from Tranent in the seventeenth century, who made a fortune in his trade, leading to many executions until he was outed as a fraud. Not that Callander is anything but genuine in his affairs, as far as I know. And even though he's Secretary of the Society of Sceptical Enquirers, and the foremost magician in all of Scotland, I fear he might as well be herding cats with the way this lot go on.

Cockburn, the Director of Membership Services at the Society, for all her faults is unflinchingly loyal to him. Even she looks unnerved by all that's gone on here.

'Sir, if the reports are correct, you have Hutchinson, Wedderburn, Lebusa and Diderot, who form the majority on the Extraordinary Committee, moving against you. That gives them a degree of legitimacy.'

'The decisions of the Extraordinary Committee have to be unanimous if they are to challenge me. Where stands the fifth member, Mary Hanley?'

'Hanley was drawn by lottery from the general membership, but she enjoys a close relationship with Wedderburn. This isn't to say she's not independent, but I get the sense she'd rather be tending to her own business out in Stirling. She often just goes with the majority.'

'That leaves you as the only safety pin,' Callander says sourly.

'A precarious position to be in, given the circumstances,' Cockburn replies wearily.

Callander places his hands on the balcony and stares down into the depths of the Library, deep in contemplation. He looks older than I've ever seen him. The lines on his face, deep cracks, as though this betrayal has shattered him. Wedderburn was his close friend, after all.

'You three, find the head librarian,' Cockburn orders the Hamsters.

They don't seem too keen to be heading into the depths without having Callander alongside them, but they obey anyway, splitting up to cover different areas of the Library.

'Be careful,' Cockburn calls after them.

I sense even she understands the magnitude of the moment, and how they might be inadequate to it. But she stands with Callander, not rushing him, patiently waiting for a decision. Because turning it into action is her job.

'The police say Ropa Moyo murdered her grandmother. Detective Inspector Balfour called to tell me himself. He remembered her from an incident at the Advocates Library and, knowing she might be magically trained, has brought the issue to my office,' Callander says. 'That's what I should have been dealing with, but now this.'

'Melsie Mhondoro was your friend, wasn't she?'

Callander nods weakly, but when he raises his head, he appears angry and fierce. He doesn't really believe I'd do such a thing, does he? Surely not. But I left him and went off with Lord Samarasinghe. Callander doesn't owe me loyalty anymore. No, he's more honourable than that; I'm certain Callander's different from these others who change sides at a whim. If only I could . . .

'I need you to find Ropa Moyo and bring her to me. Use force if you must.'

'I think I know just the right person to track her down,' Cockburn says.

That's when I take my phone out of my pocket. I turn it off and slide it onto the bottom bookshelf, between Simon Laidlaw's *Reinterpretative Frameworks of Stochastic Magic* and

H. P. Laikie's *Option Valuation: Alternative Models to Examine Spellcraft Efficiency*. I figure, what are the odds of anyone picking this dry shit up, especially given the thick layer of dust on the shelf and on top of the books. They're not going to be able to use my phone to track me, that's for sure. Got most of the numbers I need memorized anyways. Still, breaks my heart to leave the device, 'cause it's got all my stuff saved on it: photos, messages, voice notes from Gran. I miss the sound of her already. . . *Don't*. The police are after me, and so is the Discoverer General. Whether they really believe I murdered Gran or not doesn't matter. I know how the law works in this city. They'll try to pin it on me anyway. I need to escape this place and plot my next move.

XII

There's only one place for me to go in this entire city right now. Funny how things work out. You promise never to be in a certain space, with certain folks, but it turns out they're your tribe and they've been there for you all along. Even when you'd turned away from them. There's smoke still rising from the city centre as I make my way past the Burns Monument at the foot of Calton Hill.

River's following, silent as a shadow.

Down below is the Canongate graveyard and a few ghosts are stirring in the middle of the day. Ill tides for all of us right now, I think, taking the footpath leading into the New Calton Burial Ground. This was built after the Old Calton got full up or something. The thing about the dead is there's always more of them. Doesn't matter how many graveyards you build; the bodies keep coming. Makes me wonder where they'll take my gran now she's passed. I stop in the middle of the cemetery, unable to move. My feet are heavy. I rest against a tombstone as the memory hits me hard. It's a strange feeling this. There's a few moments when I'm moving and it's like everything's okay, and then it hits me out of nowhere. Waves of it. Right when you feel you're coming up for air, it washes over you.

Drowning you.

There's ghosts here too, the old sort – misshapen beings unable to find their human forms fully because they've been gone for too long. My grandmother's spirit must be wandering in the wilderness, unable to rest in the everyThere before moving on, because it's been locked to her. I hope she's with Gary at least. I can't keep going and I find a gravestone to sit on, burying my head in my hands.

Don't cry.

I won't.

I remember when Gran told me what happens to the souls of people who lack clans, or those who've been so evil the necessary rites are denied them. Then there's the unfortunate ones: victims of murder or war, or just plain old misfortune, who pass far away from their loved ones. She called them 'those who are not in the light'. The wanderers unable to find their way to the Land of the Tall Grass, to the halls of their fore-fathers – punished to move through the wilderness until they find someone to guide them home. And when she taught me the ghostalking trade, after discovering my gift, she said there was a Greek word for people like me: *psychopomp*. I laugh thinking about how silly it sounded even then, like a made-up word. It means those who guide souls to the land of the dead. Who's going to guide Gran home?

Yes, she's strong. But I've seen what the violation of murder does to the spirit. Most people think it's just the body that dies, but the premature sundering of the soul from the vessel has diabolic consequences.

I used to call them 'deados'.

The word deadened my feelings so I could just do my job.

Now I can't, because whenever I see these wandering spirits, it makes me worry that my own grandmother is out there somewhere, trapped. These thoughts are killing me.

I always assumed we had more time.

Shouldn't have argued with her over nonsense. And all this time I spent chasing cheddar, I should have been home with her instead. My pockets are filled with cash, but it won't buy her life back.

Stop moping, Ropa, you have to keep moving.

River places her head in my lap and I stroke her fur.

'You miss her too, don't you, lass?'

I know she does. But we have to get out of town and out of sight. That's the best thing for us right now. It won't help Gran if I'm locked up in some gulag. I give River a pat on her shoulder and stand up. My backpack feels heavy and my limbs molten, but I know if I can just take the first step, I'll be able to take another. One foot in front of the other.

Reckon I'll avoid going past Holyrood and the Parliament for now. The place'll be heaving with pigs. I'll loop round onto Abbeyhill, through Spring Gardens, which should take me the back way until I get to Arthur's Seat. The neighbourhood's so quiet today. Curtains shut, like folks are hoping no one will see they're home. Word's gotten around there's trouble brewing in the city. The people who live this close to the centre don't want none of it 'cause this is home for them. Although maybe a handful are out on the streets, battling His Majesty's Constabulary. The more I think about this, the better it seems for me. If the cops' resources are all tied up, then they might have less invested in finding the murderer of a poor old woman from Hermiston Slum. Which means the General Discoveries Directorate is the one I have to worry more about. Either way, I'll need to stay on my toes like I'm the principal dancer in the Bolshoi Ballet.

It's a slow trudge up Queen's Drive. The slope feels steeper than it's ever been as I haul myself up it. Memories of when we . . . No, I don't want to think about that. Gran, me and Izwi.

I wipe my nose on the sleeve of my coat.

The one that used to be Gran's.

I won't see her tonight.

I spot a couple of sentries up the road. Lads hardly older than I am, watching smoke rise over the city. They look edgy, but one of them recognizes me and waves me through.

'Bit grim down there, innit?' he says.

I don't feel like answering him, so I keep walking. There's only one voice in this whole entire world I wanna hear right now.

'She's a bit rude an' all.'

'Leave her be, she's Rob's wee pal. Dinnae start nothing with him.'

'Fuck her.'

'Shut it.'

I listen to the wind to see if I can catch an echo of her breathing. Maybe hear the sound of her rasping in the leaves. Or the crackle of her laughter under my crunching boots. I've been hollowed out by her absence. Her and Izwi were the reason for my living. Each day I woke up and went out to work was for them two.

Camelot appears before me – the collection of tents sprawled out atop the hill. There's folks going to and fro with buckets, fetching water from Dunsapie Loch. A couple of wagons drawn by horses are parked on the verge of the road. Between the tents are a few slightly more permanent structures, such as a tin shack, just off the footpath leading to the top of the hill. Someone's also erected what appears to be a bothy with a grass thatch a little further up the way, though it doesn't have windows in it. The old double-decker bus is still there – no doubt with one or two new occupants in it. What's obvious to me is Camelot's grown in size for sure. It's not just itinerant men stopping by. There's a couple of families too with bairns running about. The population of this place changes as fortunes go, but it seems to have taken on a greater air of permanence. No one's going to erect a shack and then leave it. Too big an investment.

But some things don't change, like the big old circus tent set apart from everything else.

The Rooster himself opens the flap to the tent as I draw near and keeps it open for me.

'I was worried they'd nabbed you,' he says, allowing me inside.

'Smells different in here,' I reply.

It takes a wee while for my eyes to adjust to the low light in the tent. As usual it's packed with junk. He's still not sorted out the tiered seating on the right side. There seems to be a new stage at the front too. But he's got a few more tables and alongside them are metal cabinets with shiny new locks on them. Where there used to be pilfered electronics and gadgets for sale, the tables are now laden with food – a random mix of stuff. Canned veg, fruit, fish and meat. Oats. Rice. Bags of pasta. There's even some pet food thrown in the mix.

'You opening a corner shop, Rob?' I ask.

'Clown all yous want, Ropa Moyo, but I've seen what's going on doun there, mind. News is the Highlands are filled with starving gobs, all making their way south. There wasnae harvest to be had for the mould, and what little they gathered's been gobbled by them greedy rats. I ken what's coming an' it's biblical. Soon nae amount of cash or gold'll get yous an ounce of scran.'

'If that's the way it's going, then tell me, Rob, how long d'you think you can keep those hungry mouths out of this tent?'

He cracks his knuckles and grunts in acknowledgement.

'Aye, it's coming fer us all. Been harder than ever keeping order on this hill . . . I'm sorry for your loss, lassie,' Rob says, voice softening. 'Yer nana was one of the good ones.'

I want to respond to him, but it catches in my throat. He gives me a gentle nod and walks on by, to sit on his throne. The Rooster is the king of this hill. He rules over the whole domain. I remain where I am, not quite knowing what to do, until he points to the worn sofa on his right. Me and River go over to sit on it. There's a fire going in the brazier, a two-hundred-litre steel drum with holes poked in it. It's nice to be warm.

The fumes from a brazier killed my nan.

I look through the holes into the bright yellow fire dancing within. It can warm you, or it can kill you. I guess it all depends. What doesn't change is the true nature of the fire. Prometheus's cruel and horrible gift to us.

Rooster Rob's observing me keenly, but I pay him no mind. He reaches behind his throne and retrieves a bottle of moonshine. I notice his rainbow-coloured fingerless gloves knitted with what looks like Merino wool.

'Aye, she gifted me these, if you was wondering,' he says, gruffly. 'They're my favourite pair.'

Then he sniffles, opens the cork with his teeth, and spits it. He pours a drop to the floor and takes a hard swig, wincing after he does. Even though I'm caught up in my own grief, I notice he's taking it hard too. Gran had that effect on people. Marie from Hermiston used to say that once you knew her, it was almost like you became family.

I keep forgetting about Gary O'Donohue.

Am I selfish for mostly thinking about my grandmother? She loved him too. And he didn't deserve to die either. No one deserves to – not before their time.

'Sorry to disturb you, like, Rob, but we've got a problem with the fights tonight,' Cameron McQuarrie says, walking in with a loping gait. He notices me, stops, then pushes his curly hair back. 'I'm sorry for your—'

'Save it, Cam; she's nae wanting that the now.'

'Well, I . . . aye, cannae be easy.'

'There was a point you were making,' the Rooster says.

'Aye, we've got the fight pairings right enough and the bets are coming through, but Dovvy Grant's come doun with the skitters, an' half cannae get his fat arse off the lavvie. He's too ill to go on.'

'Who's he fighting?'

'Angus "Big Beef" Anderson.' Rob whistles long and loud,

scratching his mohawk as he does. Cameron continues, 'A lot of bets was laid on that fight. Fourteen-year-old lad's been KO-ing eighteen-year-olds like they wasn't in his league.'

'I'll take him,' I say. I need to punch someone, so it might as well be this slab of beef. 'What's the purse?'

Cameron chuckles awkwardly.

'Dinnae get me wrong or anything, I'm all for equality of the sexes an' all that bollocks, but they wouldnae've named him after a fucking cow if he was your size, Ropa. His dad says he's gonna be bigger than Ken Buchanan, and the city better be getting a statue ready for him an' all.'

'You gonna give me this fight or not?' I say, turning to Rob.

The Rooster scratches his chin, quietly considering. He exchanges a look with Cam, who's shaking his head, mouthing, 'No fucking way.' But I keep my eyes locked on Rob. This is his hill and the final decision's his. Used to be I would box a bit when I was with the Clan. They throw this fight sesh once a month, and I'm just in time for it. I really need something to take my mind off things, until I work out where I'm going next.

'On yer heid be it, Ropa Moyo. If this be what yous needing the now. But ken, there's better ways of taking yer mind off things,' Rob replies at last.

The footpaths lead to a clearing which is just below the peak of Arthur's Seat. There's no electricity tonight so the city's a bleak blackness below, punctuated by flames from a burning tower block in Peffermill. A few folks stand gawking at the inferno in the far-off distance. We have our own fires going atop the hill tonight too. There's a fiddler, supported by two lassies playing the bodhrán. These are wee drums of goatskin stretched over a circular frame, struck with wooden beaters. They thump like a heartbeat in time to the jig the fiddler's playing.

There's a carnivalesque atmosphere – almost as though the riots in the city have nothing to do with us up here. Maybe this is what it's like to be on the outside, to be free from it all.

I've still got my coat on, and jeans and boots. The first pair of fighters take to the centre of the ring, which is really the open space on the grass surrounded by spectators. There's an older fellow with a Don King hairstyle who's playing referee, yelling various commands as the crowd grows impatient. Cameron comes over to wrap my hands up. He starts with my left, going from my wrists, then the thumb, mid-hand and knuckles, before finally taping the gauze down. Can't help but notice he has a white towel dangling off his neck.

'What happened to the nail on yer thumb?' he asks.

'Long story,' I reply.

'This is stupid, Ropa. But if yer really doing it, then I might as well try tae school yer. The Big Beef's corrie-fisted, so he's coming at yer southpaw. Dinnae be deceived by his bulk, the lad's elusive like Muhammad Ali had a mutant bairn with Willie Pep. Hey, listen to me.' Cam gives me a couple of little slaps. 'This isnae a laugh, ken? Yer best chance is tae stay inside the pocket and clinch whenever yer can. Else his range alone's enough tae send yer doun napping.'

'Your confidence in me's heartwarming, Cameron,' I say.

'Fuck you,' he replies, finishing up taping my right hand. 'Come on then, it's showtime.'

I'm in a half-daze, walking past the crowd and entering the ring. *What am I doing?* Big Beef takes one look at me and starts laughing. The spectators soon join him, like it's all some kind of joke. Except for Rooster Rob, who's watching from the edge, sat on a chair, with two other shady-looking types on chairs either side of him. Must be the VIP section.

I shrug off my jacket and hand it to Cameron, before taking my place inside the ring. Then I loosen my shoulders and throw a few combinations in the air. My dreadlocks are tied back and I feel them swoosh against my back.

'Come here, both of yous,' the ref says with a faint Yardie accent.

'I'm not fighting a girl,' Big Beef protests, staying in his corner.

'What is this?' his dad shouts, which sets the crowd off laughing again.

'I take it you're happy tae forfeit the purse right enough?' Rob asks casually. He has that bored vibe cool people often wear in public.

Big Beef turns to his dad, shaking his head like he doesn't want any part of this. I pay them no mind, and continue shadow boxing, keeping myself warm and limber. The spectators look more confused than anything. I get the feeling quite a few of them are here for Big Beef, to suss out if he's the prospect they say he is. I don't care, I've been in scraps with big kids before. You hit them hard enough they squeal just the same. I'm gonna show him. Big Beef's still shaking his head, when his dad turns him round and pushes him roughly inside the ring.

The lad takes a step out again and is promptly shoved back inside.

'It's okay if you're scared. Just moo and I'll go easy on you,' I say.

A collective 'ooh' comes from the crowd and now they're laughing at *him*. Big Beef grins uneasy like. He shakes his head and glances at Rooster Rob, who gives him a nod. Either way, he still looks like he doesn't want to be in the ring with me.

The ref gives us the 'good, clean fight' spiel, then tells us to touch gloves, though we're not wearing any. Big Beef offers me a fist bump, and his is the size of a sledgehammer against my ball-peen. He backs away a few steps, with puzzlement still written all over his face, even as the ref compels us to fight. He has a scar on his top lip that pulls the left side up into a sort of permanent half-smile, but his eyes are intelligent and searching. His cheeks are ruddy, as is his nose. I keep my guard up and move towards him, taking the centre ring, while he circles away from me. He keeps his right hand low, and the left up near his cheek. I track his movement – a trained lightness on the balls of his feet, which are in canvas trainers. Makes me feel heavy and plodding in my boots. Every time I make it within range, he changes angle and circles away. The crowd boos in response.

'We came here to see a fight,' someone shouts.

'Take it to the nightclub if you wanna dance.'

'Gaun lassie, get him.'

I shut them out and lock my focus onto Big Beef, weaving as I go. It's been a while since I've been to one of Rob's shows and I don't move half as well as I used to. I finally work my way inside and land a shot on the body, following it with one aimed at his cheek, but he leaps out of the way just in time. That gets the crowd going, though. Half the win's in getting them on side. I taunt Big Beef to stand and fight, and the crowd roars even louder in my favour. In the corner of my eye, I see Cameron anxiously holding the towel around his neck.

Big Beef stops slipping and sliding long enough for me to land a couple more on his body. It feels good to punch something, but it's like hitting a brick wall, and he takes them well. And he still hasn't returned a single blow. The most he does is use his bound-up fists to shove me off, keeping me out of range, but well within reach of his long arms.

'Enough of that, Beefy,' his dad shouts.

I don't see it coming, maybe just a flash of starlight, but all I remember is suddenly lying on the cool grass with a dozen faces hovering over me. Cameron's one of them, so's Rob, and the ref's waving his arms over my face. I'm not in any pain, though. Can't quite remember what I'm doing here. Oh yeah, we were boxing and I was up on points . . . I think.

Reckon I've had my arse handed to me again.

I sit up.

'That's gonna hurt in the morn, Ropa,' Cameron says, touching my temple.

'How did I do?'

'You showed heart, sister,' Big Beef says, offering me a hand up. 'Those shots to the body were sweet. My poor liver.'

I'm a bit wobbly right now, but he puts his arm around my shoulders. I only just about come up to his chest. He's a big lad, alright. The ref comes between us and raises Big Beef's hand, as if the outcome wasn't obvious. I feel heat on my right temple where I was caught. Feels nice. It's taking away some of the numbness I've been feeling.

I was never going to win against a bigger lad who fancies himself the Fighting Carpenter, not unless I cheated. It reminds me, as I retrieve my jacket, scarf and weapons, that the real fights, out there in the world, don't have rules like this one. But tonight he's won it fair and square, and I shake Big Beef's hand, before walking off out of the crowd. I'm still a bit unsteady, but something in me feels lighter now. Nothing like a bit of shock therapy.

I head back alone across the hill. The heat's kicking in against the entire right side of my face. Yeah, that's gonna swell. Could do with a bag of frozen peas, but I figure those're in short supply in Camelot.

I make it back to Rob's tent and plonk myself down on the sofa, where River is waiting for me.

'You should see the other guy,' I tell her.

From the look she gives me, I don't think she quite believes me. Vixen.

I'm there a good while, slumped on the sofa, feeling the pain settle in on my face. The Rooster's left his moonshine, so I reach across and grab the bottle. I take a swig. It burns and I cough, splattering it out. Eww.

'Jet fuel,' says Rob, entering the tent.

He goes over to a cabinet and riffles inside it, then comes out with a cutthroat razor, which he flicks open and closed a couple of times.

'Good to see yer can still take a beating as well as the next man. Disnae matter how you win – it's what yer do when yer knocked doun that counts. Now, did yer ken when I told yous I had a mole inside of the polis? Well, they've got a good few rats out here too, an' you stick out like a sore thumb. Dinnae ken what you'll do about the fox, but the hair's got tae go. The man looking for you's Detective Inspector Balfour. Really nasty, like. Lockjaw and all. Once you're on his radar, he won't let up till the chains are on yer. And it's not fer the law he does that. He's a psychopath.'

'I don't care,' I say, attempting a shallower sip of his booze.

Rob picks up a small copper bowl filled with water, and he has a bar of Wright's soap, plus a wee towel draped over his arm. He places these on a table, before taking off his own coat and rolling up his sleeves. I notice he keeps the fingerless gloves on, though. There's a melancholy about him, a certain kind of slowness, which River imitates as she shadows his movement. Doesn't take her long to become bored, though, and soon she's off ferreting about underneath the broken circus stands.

The fire's dying and the chill cuts right through me. I'm numb all over when the Rooster approaches and crouches in front of me. He says something. I don't hear it, and maybe it's his voice or me, but I nod anyway. He puts the bowl of water on the sofa's flat armrest on my right. And then, metal-studded platform boots and all, he steps onto the sofa, turning to sit behind me on the backrest, so he's above me. I don't feel much like talking to him anymore. Or anyone for that matter. Everything about me's heavy, like my tears have soaked inside and messed up all my stuffing.

'Pass the bottle,' Rob says.

I do and he takes an almighty swig. Can smell it coming off his breath – that and maybe his tea too. He takes out his phone, punches at it, and a Bluetooth speaker somewhere behind me plays horns, conga drums, that guitar: 'Loaded' by Primal Scream. Takes me back to the days I was burglaring with the Clan. Rob used to play these old bangers before we went out on jobs, and say some epic shit like: 'Even if the pigs snatch us, we're going dancing through the night.' A load of tosh, but when you're a kid like I was then, it sounded pretty fucking rad. That was when . . . I bow my head, but Rob touches it gently, like I'm a bairn or something. He grabs a lock of my hair and I feel some tugging, then it falls onto my shoulder. Been growing that for years, but I don't feel nothing now it's gone. Rob hesitates, as if wondering whether I'm gonna flip. But I simply close my eyes as he takes hold of the next one.

'Nae justice fer the likes of you and me. That's why we've got each other.'

'Just shut up, Rob!' I scream at him, finally exploding. River pricks up and watches us from a distance. I feel the scarf stir in my pocket.

'Sorry, cannae do that the now. Words is all we've got, even when it's a lot o' mince.'

I sit there raging as he cuts off more of my hair. His voice becomes the thing I hate most in this world. I ball my hands into fists and place them on my lap. But Rob keeps on, saying he's not going anywhere just now, even though I'd rather be alone. I'm already all alone anyways. I don't want to listen to these vapid clichés and any of it, but then he starts talking about Tony 'Fin' Ballantine, his old boss. I know Rob was just a foot soldier in the early days, and worked his way up the ranks. Knew how to make himself useful, and could handle himself in tough situations. Most important of all, he was no clipe – never grassed up no one to the cops, not even when they sent him down for a five-year stretch.

'Came out into the blistering cold of April with nothing but the gear I went in with. Baltic that year it was, with snow and all. Nothing but the shirt on my back and a pair of trousers. Not one fucker came tae get me. There I was on Calder Road when a woman, wearing the same coat you have on, walked up to me and handed me these gloves, and gave me a bomber jacket. Made me look like a right jellyfish, but I was too cold tae care.'

He says that after five years inside, Gran's was the first kind face he saw. And she gave him a ride to Niddrie, where his old man lived on Friary Road (which is more Greendykes in my eyes, but whatever).

'Thought she was a copper wanting something on Old Fin, so I had my guard up . . . Kinda like you should've had at the fight tonight.'

The dig makes me smile. Me and Rob go ways back. He's alright. So, Gran apparently told him that Fin would come round that same night with the lads and ask Rob to go on a job. Easy cash, something to get him back on his feet, since he was skint. Made it sound like a favour.

'"How do yer ken all this?" I asked her, and she said she just did. Made her sound even more like polis tae me. That or a rat of some kind,' Rob says.

But Gran told him the job would go sideways harder than any crab had ever gone. She gave him some money and said she was paying him not to go. It was proper weird, but Rob was broke so he took it thinking he'd stiff her anyways. There's no way he'd have turned down a job Fin asked him to do. But when things went down that night, he got cold feet and made an excuse that the screws had bust his ribs when he was inside. The next morning, he heard the news. Turned out Fin and the gang had raided the house of an ex-para, who happened to be packing an SA80 and wasn't afraid to spray lead like it was going out of fashion. Fin's death, and the chaos which resulted, saw Rob rise to the top of the Clan.

'I owe everything tae that woman. Didnae see her again fer years, till she turns up here dragging a caravan with yous in tow. Then she asked me tae school yer in everything aboot survival in this town, as payback for her help back then.'

Wait a sec. I always thought I was disobeying Gran when I went out stealing with the Clan, and now Rob's saying she asked him to have me join? The penalty for leaving the gang can be ruthless, but I can see now why the Rooster went easy on me. Why would Gran have wanted me to be involved with a gang in the first place, though? Doesn't make any sense to me . . . I would suspect he's fucking with me, but that's not Rob's style. He may be many things, but a liar ain't one of them. The man has a code he lives by, and that's what makes him leader on this hill, because his word's sounder than a shilling.

'Forgot something,' Rob says, when the last of my locks falls to the floor.

He steps off the couch and rushes to a dresser near his bed, which is on the wee stage. My fingers twitch, missing my phone, and I stare into the dying embers glowing within the brazier. Rob rummages about and then returns, pausing briefly to toss a couple of logs in to get the fire going again. The sofa groans when he steps back on it and sits beside me, a wee bowl in hand and shaving brush. He stirs up the bowl's contents and the scent of oranges and spices hits me. Then he sets about lathering my head. It's kinda irritating when he gets me behind the ears and on my nape.

'Haven't been to the salon in a while. You missed your true calling, pal,' I say.

'Didn't we all? In another life.'

'Some other world.'

'Same difference. Dinnae move or I'll scalp yer like this is the Wild West.'

It is. I stay very still as he guides the razor from my fore-head, over my crown, and to the back. He wipes the residue off using the towel then continues, working from the middle of my head down to the left. The razor makes a scratchy noise against my scalp.

It doesn't take long before I'm bald as a Malteser. And when he's done, the Rooster tosses the blade in the water and wipes my head clean with his towel.

'How do I look?' I ask.

'Like my butt cheek,' he replies.

'Your one's hairy,' I say and he laughs.

We carry on having a good laugh on that couch. Feels like the world's been put to rights somehow – just a little. I'm actually okay . . . I am. I . . . She's not here. Will never be here, not like it was in those old days. Like yesterday. It's not fair how I'm still here and she's not. I should have been in that caravan with her last night. I should have saved her, or gone with her. I'd give anything to make her one last cup of tea . . . to hear her voice. And when Primal Scream's 'Sad and Blue' starts playing, I lose it and start fucking crying into the notes of that harmonica. Stupid song.

Rob places his paw on my shoulder. 'That's right, Ropa Moyo. Let it go. Give out but dinnae give up.'

XIII

I don't know when I fell asleep, but I wake up slumped across the sofa with a sleeping bag thrown over me. My shaved noggin feels frozen like it's never done before. There's a warm furry body on the couch with me at least. Smells like River alright. And the Rooster – he's red-eyed, bags and all, sat upon his throne, watching me like he's been up all night. He's holding a steaming enamel mug in his hand, and the coffee's so strong I can smell it from here.

'What time is it?' I ask.

'Whatever it needs to be,' he says. 'You have to rest.'

I put my arm on River, feeling her body rise and fall with her breathing. We stayed up most of the night – me bawling my eyes out and the Rooster telling me stories about Gran. I never really appreciated how close the two of them became. Seems like he warmed to her and considered her a friend of sorts. He told me that there were many nights, when me and Izwi were asleep, that she'd come over to have a drink and a blether. They both shared a love of the hill and the wandering folks who pitched tents here for a season or two, before they moved on. He also said she was a no-good stinking cheat when it came to cards. Swore he'd lost quite a bit before he took to checking her sleeves whenever they played a hand. And he misses her laughter, much as I do.

I didn't mean to sleep – it's taken me one day further from her. I can't explain it, but I somehow thought that if I just stayed awake I'd be able, by some sleight of hand, to hold her in this realm. Now I worry that each night I sleep I'll start forgetting her, the same way my parents became blurs in my memory.

'Next time yer in a scrap, remember, there's nae rules in the real world. And the playing field's tilted against the likes of us. So think outside the box. That's the only way the underdog wins, not by playing their way.' Rob places his index finger on his temple, reminding me to use my head. Used to do this to me all the time, when I was rocking with the Clan. 'I'm relieved you remembered my lesson and got rid of your mobile. There's a new one on the chair for yous. Much as I love your company, Ropa, yous cannae stay here any longer, it isnae safe. Even after the chop.' He waves his hand over his hair.

'Ta.'

'Dinnae. I've got you a new backpack, and taken the liberty tae move your gear into it.'

I notice the vintage canvas rucksack on the floor. It's army green – decent. There's a new black jacket beside it. No, that's actually Gran's coat, turned inside out. The inside pockets work just as well when it's flipped – thoughtful craft went into its making. I didn't realize it could do that, but it seems to've happened when I took it off to snooze. Saves me from having to get a new one. The Ankara print on the other side was way too conspicuous anyways, so this is a much better look for me.

River gets up, gives me a lick, and steps off the sofa. She stretches on the ground, arching her back, making me yawn. Rob stands up and walks over to where I'm lying down. He's holding the coffee in one hand and a key in the other.

'I've got a squat sorted for you in Bonnington. Some place tae lay low till the dust blows over,' he says, giving me the key. It has a little cardboard tag with an address on it.

'Why do you live here if you can have a house?'

'Up here on Camelot's the only place I'm a free man,' he replies.

I sit up and put on my boots. These might be worn and patched up, but they're the only pair I'll wear. My heart's still heavy, and if I stay like this I'll sink. I need to keep moving, and find help to bail me out of this hole. Then I'll be able to get to the bottom of whatever Wedderburn and them have planned, and blow it up. Feels like I'm missing something, though. A piece to a much larger puzzle. I pick up the phone and use the front camera to take a look at myself. Bloody hell – nearly get a scare. I run my hand over my head, just to make sure I'm really me. They'll be looking for some lassie with dreads, not Ripley from *Alien*. Rob's not done a bad job at all.

'Beanie hat?' he asks.

'Nah, I'm good, but a bit of oil or lotion would help,' I reply.

'Anything for you, baldie. And be careful out there. Amidst all this rioting and chaos, I've heard the Travelling Folk are about in town.'

He gives me some kind of beard oil, which I guess should work as well. It's all skin at the end of the day. I kit up with the rest of it, finally throwing the rucksack on my back. Yep, it's time to move. I hold out my hand to shake Rob's, but he pulls me in for a godawful bear hug, like he's gonna squeeze the life out of me. Then he lets go and steps back, sniffs, his lower lip trembling. He turns and walks towards his throne.

'You're a good one, Rob,' I say.

He doesn't turn back, but just gives me the finger. That's my cue to get going. I knee River gently and we head out of the tent. My noggin's instantly bloody freezing and I'm regretting not taking Rob up on that offer of a beanie hat. I reach into my jacket pocket for my scarf, but the first thing that comes out is a green and black beanie with a dreadful pom pom on top of it. Sly bugger slipped it in with the dodgy hug. Beggars, choosers and all that. I put the damned thing on and my hairless scalp thanks me for it. Next, I wrap the scarf round my neck, making sure it covers my mouth and nose, before I make my way down the hill.

There's still smoke on the skyline as I descend. Must be pure mayhem down there, but I'll keep using that to my advantage. Sleep has cleared the fog in my head somewhat and I'm making a plan. The first thing I need to do, though, is find Lord Samarasinghe. If anyone can help me, he can. I'm sure it'll have strings attached in the shape of a net, but I'm desperate. I need him to keep Johnny Law off my back, and also to warn him Wedderburn's plotting something in the city. Hopefully he can keep Callander, the Discoverer General, at bay too, since I work for English magic now. Reckon with his aid, I may get some form of justice for Gran and Gary O'Donohue. But I'll have to be wary, 'cause as Blackwood warns, asking for help exposes you to the whims of your saviour and they may choose to extract a disproportionate price. After all, 'it's the helping hand that has the upper hand.' I'll have to make it clear to the Sorcerer Royal there's something at stake in all this for him too. Find a way to convince him I'm not just asking for aid but helping him protect an investment, so it seems as though his actions will be in his own interest.

I'm down by St Margaret's Well when I realize I won't be swanning into Holyroodhouse that easily. There's still loads of police around it – Scottish coppers. Even though I've had my hair cut, they'll know who I am as soon as I ask for Lord Samarasinghe. And if they nab me before I see him, well, that one phone call thing only works on old TV shows.

It's nearly ten o'clock. What I do know of Lord Samarasinghe's routine is that he walks between Edinburgh Castle and Holyroodhouse most mornings. So I could catch him some-where off the Royal Mile. The downside is that, after the riots, there'll be plenty of bobbies in the city centre too, so I gotta be careful not to get nabbed there either.

The city's wynds and closes will work to my advantage, especially in the morning gloom. I shove my freezing fingers deep in my pockets as I make my way off the roundabout and past Dynamic Earth. From there I get to Crichton Close, which takes me past the old Poetry Library, whose wooden cladding's been stripped off for firewood, exposing the bare concrete underneath. Someone's at least taken the care to scribble graf-fiti in verse on it, but it still looks minging.

I push on up, into the alleyway that joins the close onto the Royal Mile, and stop there. I brave a look up and down the Mile. A few wary pedestrians are wandering about amidst the street sweepers and business owners rectifying the carnage of last night, taking stock of what they've lost.

Here's hoping Lord S comes along soon. While I hang about, I think of whom Cockburn's probably sending after me. It's undoubtedly going to be someone vicious, and I've already lost a duel to a trained magician. The couple of spells I have up my sleeve will just have to cut it. I should have learnt more when I had the chance.

'I've got you, though, River. You're more loyal than these two-legged wankers.' That's how it is for me now. This fox is the only person I can really trust. I rue the day I ever got caught up in all this magicking bollocks anyways. Best I lean against the wall and try not to work myself up. I need a clear head. I pull off my backpack and reach into it, having to rummage a bit, before opening the front pocket where Rob's placed my pack of ashwagandha. I take two capsules and chill.

Fortunately, I'm not waiting that long before a familiar figure lazily strides past. I peel off the wall and shadow Lord Samarasinghe, who's casually strolling through the wreckage like the gentleman flâneur, with his hands behind his back. His shoes crunch against some broken glass on the pavement, and the cape he wears flutters in a light breeze. He stops to help an elderly shopkeeper with a heaving black bag, meant for the bin in her alleyway, and I halt to watch discreetly.

'Dreadful, isn't it just?' he says.

'I've put my life into this and they've just wrecked it, like it's nothing.' She sniffles, and Lord Samarasinghe takes out a silk handkerchief and kindly offers it to her. 'At my age, how do I start over? They took everything.'

'Don't give in to despair, dear lady. 'Tis always darkest before the dawn.'

'Fine words. I know you mean well, but that won't fix my shop, will it?'

Lord Samarasinghe nods, and then he lifts his left hand and takes a brief look at it, before using his right to pull off the chunky gold ring he has on. He casually hands this to the shopkeeper, then resumes his walk before she can thank him. By the time I go past her, she's still standing there in disbelief, inspecting the diamond at its centre. Have to say, I'm as surprised as she is.

I tail him till he makes it to the corner with St Mary's Street and decide it's finally safe enough to approach him.

'You didn't come in for work this morning. I assume that's the Calvinist work ethic you Scotch are known for? I spent most of last night reading up on John Knox because I couldn't sleep. Not with the racket that was going on outside. Oh, the *stench* of this place. Careful you don't step on any blood there.' He takes me by the elbow and guides me away from a slumped body on the street. It's that of a man with a thistle pinned to his lapel. Skull smashed in by a baton stick, no doubt.

I feel weak and almost swoon, but the Sorcerer Royal's grip is firm.

'Steady,' he says. 'Remember to breathe. Though it can't be easy with that scarf covering your mouth and nose.'

Don't know what's wrong with me. I guess I'm just tired of seeing dead bodies. That man lying on the pavement is some-one's son. A brother. Friend. Something. All that reduced to a pile of flesh.

'This morning I received a rather curious invite to number 36 St Andrew Square, from none other than Sir Ian Callander himself. How wonderful is that, Ropa?' He's gleeful and excited and still hasn't let go of my elbow. 'It's taken a while, as he's so far avoided me since I came into the city, but I'm certain he's begun to see sense at last. Everyone kisses the ring in the end. That's what puts the Great in Britain.'

'I need to talk to you,' I say.

'Imagine the look on his face when he sees us walking in together. *The stone the builders rejected* – that's you, Ropa Moyo, and I want all those hoity-toity practitioners of Scottish magic to see we do things differently down south. They were still burning witches when we were admitting ladies of refinement into the Royal Society of Sorcery and the Advancement of the Mystic Arts. I'm exaggerating, of course, but you get the gist.'

'It's important,' I say.

He stops and looks at me, all concerned.

'Whatever is the matter, my dear girl?' Policemen are coming down the street and I hesitate. 'You have nothing to fear when you're with me. I know your life's been hard, but believe me when I say everything's about to change.'

He checks his pocket watch and begins to walk faster, taking us down North Bridge. I may have misread Lord Samarasinghe; the more I get to know him, the more I can see his heart's in the right place. I'm starting to feel safe with him. Well, the same kind of safe you might feel if you had a pet tiger. It's still a carnivore and could eat you at any time, but beneath the killer's a cuddly cat who purrs. The Sorcerer Royal will be my salvation.

And so I vomit everything out, leaving nothing inside my gut. The breakout of Wedderburn and robbery at the Library. The Fairy Flag, the Black Lord. Wilson's reappearance, and his likeness to Sophie. Things that have happened to me in the past when I worked for Scottish magic. I even tell a few secrets I'd sworn were only for Sir Ian Callander's ears. The One Above All and the Tall Man. Siobhan Kavanagh and the Missing Children. The Midnight Milkman, who once chased me on these very setts. When we reach St Andrew Square, he pauses, takes out his watch again, and then says: 'Callander can wait. You are so much more important.' He leads me right into the square so we're standing on the footpaths, in the shadow of the statue on the big plinth. From there we can see the head-quarters of the Society of Sceptical Enquirers – that grand old building which hides secrets and corruption. I finally tell him what they did to Gran and how the police are after me. And that I don't feel safe from the Society of Sceptical Enquirers anymore either.

'I need your help and your protection,' I say.

Lord Samarasinghe furrows his brow, mighty concerned as he takes in everything I've told him, while I look on hopeful.

'Well, isn't this such a pity,' he says. It's as though a shadow flashes across his face as he lets go of my elbow, and his entire demeanour changes. 'I was beginning to really like you. But surely you don't expect me to walk into the home of the Society with an accused murderer wanted by the authorities, do you? You were meant to be a sort of bridge between Scottish and English magic, a child of both. I ignored everyone who tried to warn me you were nothing but a common criminal. I suppose

I've always been rather progressive. But no, this will not do. It's not proper at all.' Lord Samarasinghe pauses, looking at two police officers in riot gear coming from North St David Street, diagonal from where we are, near the centre of the square. Then he smiles, vicious-like, and winks at me before waving his arms to attract the filth. 'Let's see if you sink or swim this time, Ropa. Officers! I say, officers, this one's a member of those dreadful Thistle people!'

XIV

I put on my shades and walk away quickly from Lord Samarasinghe. He's chuckling after me as if my life's a game to him. It was never my talent he was interested in. I was just a prize – the intern of the Secretary of the Society of Sceptical Enquirers defected to English magic. Now at the slightest hint of scandal he's shoved me under the bus. I'm seething, but it's not his fault. Dealing with him was always going to be the scorpion on the toad's back. He can't help what he is. More than anything, I'm bricking it 'cause I've given up a fair few secrets and been shafted in recompense. That leaves me with ZERO pals in this city – the sort of thing that's likely to bite me in the arse in due course. Dumb, dumb, dumb.

'Run, River,' I say. And she scampers across the road, leaving me.

I'm heading diagonally past the sooty statue on the tall plinth, across from the windows staring down from the head-quarters of the Society, when in the corner of my eye I notice the two pigs walking briskly to intercept me. I try to appear casual, though I've got my shoulders hunched. If I run, I'll only bump into loads more of them in town. I'm weighing my options. If this was the Old Town, with its wynds, closes and courtyards, it would be so much easier to slip away. The New Town's grid construction makes it way harder. This is why most thieves prefer the Old Town to working here. My only chance is to make it to the old bus station over the road, I reckon, as I exit the square, crossing the old tram lines.

'Excuse me, young man,' one of the officers shouts.

Fantastic, I look like a boy, which means Rob's handiwork has helped. Though that makes it more likely I'll be associated with the rioters now. It's a Catch-22 situation.

'Stop right there,' the officer commands.

I ain't doing that. I hasten my stride across the road, going past Multrees Walk. The traffic light on that side of the road's been smashed and dangles off the pole. *Don't turn back.* Pounding boots on the pavements mean the two officers are running towards me now. I go past an old poster for one of the designer shops selling fakes on Multrees Walk, and then arrive at the entrance to the bus station.

Slip through the door with cracked glass.

There's a strong scent of decay and body odour: some of the homeless folks use this place as a base, since there's no buses running anywhere anymore. If those cops catch up to me, I'm in for another arse-whopping and I've had enough of that. I'm incanting a new spell by the time I make it to the broken escalator.

'Vulcan, father of the angry roiling molten rocks beneath, breathe your sulphur and ash upon this room, as you once did in Santorini.'

There's an entropic shift, a reordering of particles in the air around me, then a blast of intense heat like a wave. I focus my will on the gritty and harsh particles I've read up on volcanic ash. A smell of sulphur pervades the air, growing ever more unbearable by the time I reach the bottom of the escalator. On all sides of me is a rising plume of smoke, gathering in thickness and density. I work hard to concentrate and hold the spell together, since it's one I've only ever read about and never actually used before.

'Fire!' one of the occupants of the bus station shouts.

And then the pandemonium starts. Folks who were sleeping on the ground leap up, collecting their possessions, and begin to scatter, trampling over one another. Some are coughing because of the thick smoke spreading through the station. *I'm so sorry.* When I turn back, the air behind me is so thick, I can't see the police anymore, so I break into a run, finding myself in the mass of bodies headed for the exit.

'Everyone stop,' I hear the officer's voice call out, and it's immediately punctuated by a coughing fit.

I'm almost crushed in the mad rush, but I make sure I move with the wave, and, most importantly, don't trip up. We go past the shells of old National Express and Megabus buses, parked on the other side of the glass windows, and their occupants gawk at our mayhem.

I burst out of the bus station and into the fresh air.

From here I could go up Elder Street, which will take me back to Princes Street, or I could duck into the St James Quarter and seek shelter there. The alternative is to head down the way, onto York Place, and try to escape from there. Thing is, when you're being chased, the worst thing you can do is head anywhere in the line of sight, and so I quickly cross the road and duck into the disused St James Shopping Centre Car Park.

I can see what's going on from this old brutalist multistorey, and I have multiple exit routes in case I'm spotted. I might have been a dick using the smoke in a packed place, but if I know anything about Edinburgh's vagrants, they'll never rat out anyone to the police. However good my hideout is, it's also pretty clear they've taken to using this adjacent car park as a toilet, and I have to watch my step as the place is littered with jobbies. But I'm not one to have a delicate disposition, so scrunch up my nose and bear it.

The two officers emerge onto Elder Street coughing and spluttering so badly one of them removes her helmet and hunches over. Her chestnut brown hair spills all over her face as she does this. Her partner scans around, turning three-sixty, unable to figure out which way to go. Some of the homeless folk watch them warily. I can sense the hostility from here and the cop pulls her partner up, seemingly saying, 'We've got to go.'

They pick the easiest option, which is to go down onto York Place.

I stay put for a wee while, and then when I feel the coast is kosher, I bail, taking the lane leading to St Mary's. I try to appear calm, even as my ticker's still going wild. Reckon I'll be the least of the problems the Lothian and Borders Police have going on tonight. But it's still daylight and I have to get off the streets. Will be better for me to move about at night in the city centre.

I just want to go home.

To our caravan.

The thought alone roots me to the spot for a wee while, until I force myself to move again. I need a safe house – somewhere to hide. I finger the key Rob gave me in my pocket. I feel as though I'm walking through treacle as I go down Broughton Street, whose shops seem unaffected by last night's events. They're open but the shopkeepers stand outside chatting nervously, since business seems light. I go past the roundabout and the four-storey tenements that dot the place. I'm wishing I still had my bike with me when River pops up beside me.

'Thanks for all your help,' I say.

She has a way of moving in the shadows in the city centre, staying out of sight, taking routes with the fewest people. Foxes have this gift, which is why it's rare to see them most of the time, even though there are so many of them about. I guess that's why her and me are family – she knows how to survive, how to be invisible. The trick is to know when to spring out.

'They killed Gran, River, and we're going to get them all. Wedderburn first, 'cause he's giving the orders. Fenella next, since she's a proven murderer. Wilson. Avery. Nathair. Lewis. Diderot. Lebusa.' *And Jomo?*

As I walk, the hate in my heart sparks and glows like hot coals being blown on, dark energy burning. Gran used to say some Dalai Lama shit about hate. How it eats you up inside and all that. But the universe is a scale which needs to be balanced out. Eyes and teeth. I won't ever have her back, but I'll make sure the ledger's even in the final accounting of what's happening here. I'm always just reacting, though. Since the events at Dunvegan Castle, I've been several steps behind

Wedderburn and his lot. I need to get better at figuring out their moves before they make them. Easier said than done, that – especially now, when my noggin feels like mulch and my heart's hurting.

That's my only reason for being. For now, I'll worship at the altar of Nemesis, the Greek goddess of retribution, who wields her whip and knife as I do my scarf and dagger.

Me and River wind up going through Cannon Mills on Claremont Street. I swear I spot a couple of ghouls milling about in broad daylight – make sure I don't look at them direct, because I don't wish to attract their attention. A fair few of them must be from Rosebank Cemetery down the road. That place dates back to Victorian times, though, so the ghosts there have no business with the living anymore. At least they shouldn't. Yet here they are, beyond the boundaries of their internment, roaming about the streets as though this realm belongs to . . . Hang on a minute. Have they been stranded from the everyThere when it was blocked off, or is it now back and its influence in our world has intensified?

Spectral activity waxes and wanes with the seasons, peaking in winter and easing off in summer. But this is beyond the range of what it normally is. Almost as though the separation between our two realms isn't quite as it should be.

Think, Ropa.

I'm approaching the intersection of Broughton Road and Pilrig Street when I'm stunned by a mass of ghosts. They're all young men donning helmets and wearing rifles, wandering out of the cemetery with dazed looks upon their faces. There's at least a hundred of them, maybe more. Some are shaped more grotesquely than others, with hideous wounds upon their bodies. Still they shuffle and it's proper Baltic as I walk through them. They line up as though waiting to board a train, then step on and vanish out of sight. I remember reading that in 1915 soldiers from the 1/7th Royal Scots battalion mobilized in Leith, and were gathered to go out to Gallipoli to fight in the First World War. But there was a rail disaster in Gretna – many of them never made it to the front.

These are the types of souls Gran was good at helping. Now she can't even help herself.

I kick myself for thinking this. For being angry she's not here waiting for me. And my anger makes me pick up pace. To hell with these ghosts. Screw the first one I ever saw. I'd give this gift back and everything I own just to hear her voice one last time. To touch her. She's never going to embrace me again.

What will I tell Izwi?

I turn away from painful thoughts of that, instead focusing on my anger as I go past the steel-frame industrial units on Bonnington Road. They're disused now, with some of their cladding stripped, as well as doors, windows and roofing sheets all gone. What's left behind is a misshapen eyesore. I turn onto Tinto Place, relieved to be leaving the main road, and head towards the brick-cladded six-storey flats, whose square geometry clashes with the older tenement flats built from local quarried stone. I suspect there would have been more industry here once upon a time, since we're near the Water of Leith. The river which powered the industrial age, when mills dotting its banks produced paper, snuff and linen. It was polluted as much then as it is now that the city discharges raw sewage into it daily from our failing system. And so these flats on Haig Lane, which might have once been desirable, are now a bit iffy. There's broken windows everywhere. Those on the lower floors have installed burglar bars and notices about guard dogs to deter criminals.

The place looks grim and miserable. A couple of children play football in the empty courtyard, making noises that echo off the walls. Someone else is blasting loud music from an adjacent flat. I reach the address on the tag and turn the key Rob gave me. There's no lighting in the stairwell, and I'm greeted by the scent of piss. The walls are covered in graffiti. I slowly make my way up to the fifth floor. No point in even looking for a lift.

I check behind me one last time, making sure I wasn't followed, before I let myself into the flat. Have to make sure the door's locked and the chain's in place before anything else.

The smell of weed hits me hard. I go through the hallway, check the first bedroom, and see row upon row of plants set up in some hydroponic system. Looks like the Rooster uses this place as a grow house. I should be worried, but in for a penny and all that. Compared to being accused of the murder of my own grandmother, this isn't a biggie. There's empty packets of crisps, plastic bottles of Frosty Jack's cider, and plenty of cigarette butts lining the floor. The soles of my boots stick to a dark substance I have no desire to check out. Yeah, this'll have to do.

I place my bag on the floor of the living room. It's dark 'cause the curtains are drawn, so I open them a fraction to let some light in. At least there's a crusty couch. Plus a small twenty-six-inch telly with an old games console attached – the type that uses cartridges. They built them to last back in those days. I check out the cartridges on the TV stand.

I feel hungry, but I don't want anything. Tears me up inside to think I could eat while Gran's body lies somewhere growing cold. I sink into the sofa and lie down to consider my next move.

When Wedderburn's lot broke him out, they nicked some books from the Library too. And before that they'd pinched *The Book of the Shaded Mysteries of Solomon*, which isn't a real book, but a scroll owned by the Ethiopians. This must mean they're doing some dodgy shit with realms outside of ours, including the everyThere, our closest neighbour. And what was Fenella doing in the Old Town when me and Priya spotted her? Preparing for their attack on the Library from some kind of base? I wonder what Wilson's doing with them too – how does he tie into this madness?

They are definitely up to something big, but what?

They're working for a Black Lord, but where is he? Was he trapped inside the realm of the Fae? I rack my brain, trying to think of old stories or myths about people who became lost in Fairyland. But how would that be possible if the MacLeods had kept the Fairy Flag for centuries, meaning the Fae couldn't operate in our world with impunity? Or perhaps they're looking for someone from before that period. But how would they have survived this long? The Fae themselves are immortal, but I don't think there's any mention of such immortality being passed on to others who go into their world— hang on, Ropa.

Time passes differently in the realm of the fae. Kinda like when Thomas the Rhymer crossed over and found days out there were years in our realm. So you don't have to be immortal, you just have to tinker with time.

Then who *is* the Black Lord? And the Tall Man?

What does Wedderburn want at the end of all this?

More than anything, I know he wishes to restore Scottish magic to its former glory. This Black Lord character is supposed to help with that somehow. Why murder Gran, though? Payback for me bringing him down at the conference at Dunvegan Castle? That would be super harsh. Or was it something to do with what Wedderburn told me to ask Gran, about my father – that 'fateful Samhain night'? The pieces aren't adding up neatly and it's making my head spin. Whatever this project is, it must be huge, because Wedderburn has sucked in key members of the Extraordinary Committee, thereby compromising the Society. What's in it for them?

They've already caused so much chaos that Callander's been forced to seek the aid of the Sorcerer Royal, going against his oft stated wish of avoiding the attention of London and keeping Scottish magic independent.

Hmm.

Tonight I need to go on the hunt. Find out where Fenella, Lewis, Avery and Nathair were staying, in case I can scrape any clues from there. I'll also have to go to Wedderburn's, see if I find anything. There's no way he'd be dumb enough to go home, though. Not after he's just broken out of prison like that – Callander will be after him. And if I go there, I also risk being caught by whatever trap the Society might have set for him . . . or for me, seeing as Callander's after me too.

Been in many a bind in the past, but this is the first time I've been taken to the end of my tether like this. I'm on my own and I have to act. Lying low and hoping shit blows over ain't an option. Tonight, I'll get started – there'll be time to mourn later.

I'm half dozing in a funk when I hear rattling at the front door. Someone's trying the knob. Sounds like they're doing it gently, in the hope of not attracting attention. I jump up from the sofa and grab my gear, checking my new phone on the off chance it's Rob, but there's no messages from him. That door is the only way in or out of here. It's a long way down onto a tar pavement or brick-lined courtyard, and there's no pipes or anything, so getting out via the window's not an option.

Why did I take this place? Always have an exit strategy – that was the cardinal rule back when I was burglaring with the Clan. Should've taken my chances on the streets instead. But when your back's against the wall, you've gotta fight. This time I'm ready to cheat, to do whatever it takes to win.

'Get ready, River,' I say.

She arches her back in response and I'm glad to have her at my side. I adjust my scarf Cruickshank around my neck and ready my dagger. There's the police and Society both after me. I'm hoping it's the former, 'cause with the magic I know, I reckon I can take them – unless they're packing, in which case I'm screwed. I do the breathing exercises Dr Checkland taught me to stop myself going mental right now. But I sense an entropic shift and the barrel lock on the door pops in, dropping onto the floor.

Definitely not the police, they'd have used a battering ram.

The door swings open slightly and is kept in place by the chain. I'll attack when the hand reaches in to open it. I'm waiting for my opportunity to strike when one of the links in the chain glows red hot and snaps open as the person on the other side shoves the door in.

I'm incanting a pre-emptive soliton when I see who it is at the threshold. The wheelchair, the girl: my friend Priyanka Kapoor. Fuck me, is this who Cockburn chose to send? My doubts seem confirmed by how Priya observes me coolly, without moving inside. I realize now that I've truly lost all my friends, and I was right not to trust her. If she really was a mate, she'd never have tried to find me for them. Wonder what they promised her. Doesn't matter, it's her or me and I ain't planning on losing another fight. But how did she know I was here? Has she been following me? Maybe I was spotted on St Andrew Square as I fled the police and she's been waiting for the opportunity to corner me.

'Aren't you going to ask me in?' she says.

'You're on your own?' I ask, checking what the odds are against me.

'I didn't think I'd need anyone else, to be honest. Not when it's you.'

'So, Frances Cockburn sent you after me,' I reply.

Priya shrugs and moves into the flat. I step back. Gotta be careful, she's a classically trained magician and I've seen her duel before. She's a demon at it. Casts spells faster than the blink of an eye. As she comes further in, I keep backing away. There's confidence and shrewdness in her eyes – that look of someone who knows they can handle themselves. Everything inside me says I should make the first move to gain an advantage, but I hesitate.

How can I fight Priya? *To hell.*

I quickly incant a Promethean fire spell and hurl a sparkling hot thermosphere the size of a football at her. But in the blink of an eye, she's set up a heat sink, and I see the flames stream around her, dissipating, with the remnants flowing out the open door.

She's come out of it without a singe. There's a maniacal look in Priya's eye now and she grins. That's the psycho inside her. I always thought she enjoyed our adventures a bit too much. I've just cast a blazing fireball at her and she's smiling.

'So you really think you can take me on?' she asks, in a half mocking tone.

'I'll go through you if I have to.'

This makes her smile even wider.

'Seems to me this is a proper nippler we've gotten ourselves into then, Ropa. You know, back in the day the navy used to force people to join them. It was called impressment. You'd be drinking in a pub in some gutter, and a guy would offer to buy you a drink, then slip the king's shilling in your pocket. After that they either knocked you on the head or got you so hammered you woke up on a ship somewhere. The Secretary of the Society of Sceptical Enquirers has the power to impress any magician in Scotland, since he is the Discoverer General. It seems a cruel irony that I've wound up with your old job.

So yes, I work for Callander now and you can thank Frances Cockburn for that.'

I knew it. 'How's the pay?' I ask.

She laughs. 'I'm not an intern, Ropa. PS, I love the new look. It really suits you.'

I've backed away into the furthest corner of the living room, while Priya's still between me and the doorway – the only exit leading to freedom. I take a look out the window. Maybe I could bust out and do an anemoic wind spell, creating an air cushion which would break my fall. It could work.

'From this height you're likely to miscalculate the density and break your neck,' Priya says, as if reading my thoughts. 'If I recall correctly, the only time you ever did that spell was over a body of water in Dunvegan, so you were safe either way. It's up to you. Oh, hi there, River. I almost didn't see you with all the fire going on.'

Priya holds out her hand and a treat has magically appeared in it. River walks towards her. I try calling the fox back but she's having none of it and goes over to eat the biscuit in Priya's hand. I would call her a traitor, but she knows Priya, so it's a huge ask for her to understand that Priya's now the enemy. I sense Priya's magic, like a narrow burn that's bubbling white water, deep and with jagged rocks underneath the surface. That's kind of my thing, being able to sense a magician's potential. For now, I wonder if I could make it across the burn without drowning in it or being caught amongst the reeds.

'How did you find me?' I ask, buying time.

'You're not that naive, Ropa.'

'Rob ratted me out then.'

'You're an even bigger dafty than I realized,' Priya says, shaking her head. 'Of course he fucking told me. Rob knows I'm your friend, though you seem to have completely forgotten that. He knows I'm all you've got right now. Come here.'

She opens her arms wide, holding them out for a hug. When I hesitate, she cocks her head to one side, like, *really?* I slowly walk over to where she is, feeling conflicted, like a proper eejit, then I fall into her chair and hug her, holding tight. Priya's strong arms are like armour around me. I rest my head on her shoulder and let her take the weight. It was dumb of me not to trust her. But after Jomo, I've been so scared. I've known him longer than I have Priya and he just walked off with the people who killed Sneddon, Gary and Gran, as if it meant nothing. Then Lord Samarasinghe bailing on me was the final straw. I couldn't take another hit. So I chose to believe the worst of Priya, even pushed her away, but here she is for me all the same. And I'm so grateful she is, as my world is falling apart.

'You threw a fireball at me,' she says, laughing. 'It was kinda hot.'

'That's a shit pun,' I reply.

'Only because you wish you'd thought of it first.'

I keep my head on her shoulder, not wanting to let go. She rubs her hand against my back. Memories surface of the first time I met her in the Library, her dangling upside down from the ceiling, reading. The things we've done together, battling the Midnight Milkman, raiding Bo Bumblebeam's place, going toe-to-toe with Wedderburn in Dunvegan Castle. Milkshakes at Jaspers. My one remaining bestie.

'I'm so sorry about Gran. She was a really special woman. I know anything I say right now is a cliché, but that's because the enormity of what's happened is so overwhelming that nothing in any language known to us can capture it, let alone soothe it. They brought her body to Our Lady. Lethington and I looked after her personally. We examined her, and when we were done, we washed her, prepared her and dressed her in a white shroud.'

I begin to cry, thinking of Gran in a shroud.

'When we deal with a body, we treat it as we would the person. The entire time I was with her, I talked to her. Mostly I was gossiping about you.' Priya shudders and starts to cry. 'I told her everything we'd done and how much I know you fucking loved her. Then I kissed her for you and told her I'd take care of you, because you're my best friend.'

I have no words. When I try to speak it's all caught up in my throat. In this moment Priya and Izwi are all I have left. We sit there silently for a long while, holding one another. Priya's coat is soaked in my tears and I can hear her heart thumping away. The warmth of her skin. Her perfume smells like lavender and sunshine.

I only let go when my arms start cramping.

'Sit down and I'll make us a cuppa,' Priya says. 'This place is a dump, but they've got a kettle, and I imagine there's a couple of mugs in those cupboards.'

She's still holding my hand by the time I sit down again. Then she lets go and moves into the open-plan kitchen.

'Sorry I bust your door like that, but I'm sure we can replace the lock. Rob's going to be fuming. His fault really, though – he should have given me a spare key. Did you see all those cannabis plants in the bedroom? That's wild, like. Between you and me, the Clan provides Our Lady with all the medicinal marijuana we use. Their quality's consistent, unlike the other gangs which specialize in skunk. Random, I know.'

I can tell Priya's making conversation. The silence I was stewing in was oppressive and hearing her talk like this is a respite from what I know is to come. My hands are trembling. I put my feet up on the sofa and hug my knees, rocking back and forth. It's been a shit life this, but I never even knew it could descend to these depths.

Priya hands me a warm mug of tea and our fingers touch.

I take a sip and tell her it's pretty good.

'No idea how they have Fortnum and Mason's Royal Blend in this dump. Clearly Rooster Rob takes his brew seriously.' She has a sip from her own cup and raises her eyebrows, impressed. 'I hear Jomo's gone rogue – hard to believe. And apparently three recently qualified magicians were killed by the books and seven others injured. It's insane.' Priya shakes her head slowly, eyes closed, and I guess I'm not crazy. I'm not the only one Jomo's vexed.

'Do you know which titles they stole from the Library of the Dead?'

'Dr Maige and Callander are still assessing the full extent of the damage. It'll be a day or two before we hear something. It was total chaos when I went down there. Don't know how the Library will recover from this.'

I stop rocking myself and gaze upwards, thinking.

'I know that look on your face, Ropa. What are you cooking up now?'

XV

We're back in the Canongate, around where Priya lost Fenella MacLeod, somewhere on Dunbar's Close. Couldn't take the Royal Mile proper since there's a second night of riots and looting going on in the city. The noise is intense. Drumming and voices singing. The occasional report goes off, from guns firing teargas canisters or rubber bullets. My eyes sting and my throat itches. Priya's made us wear wet pieces of cloth covering our mouths and noses to ease the itch, but it still gets to me.

'It's all kicking off tonight,' she says.

'We need to be extra careful,' I reply.

'As far as statements of the bleeding obvious go . . . Anyways, I lost sight of Fenella as soon as I came into the garden.'

Even in winter, the garden of Dunbar's Close maintains its quaint charm, surrounded by low walls and tenements whose occupants have their windows shut tonight. The only hint they're within are flickers of light escaping through gaps here and there. The garden itself consists of neat, trimmed hedges, small box squares, and the occasional tree growing within. It's all very pristine – a counterpoint to the chaos of the Old Town in which it's set. The smart topiary collections amidst gravel pathways offer a serenity the upheaval in the city couldn't ever hope to break. It's a little pocket of tranquillity, whose very presence signals a sort of defiance, and, dare I say it, hope. I attempt a basic fire spell and with little effort a solitary spark lights up the air in front of me.

'What's that for?' Priya asks.

'This feels like an area of lower natural resistance to magic. It reminds me of the gardens at Dunvegan Castle, which had a similar feature. According to the Somerville equation—'

'Yes, yes, I know that already. Then the question is, why would Fenella be out here? It's a little too convenient, don't you think?'

From what I've studied, the world is resistant to magic, since shifting entropy means doing work. There are certain special areas, though, for example where ley lines meet, or areas where magic has been practised for centuries, where the resistance has been diminished. And in rare instances, where it's been inverted altogether. So practitioners come to these spaces in order to perform difficult spells, which might otherwise prove unwieldy in normal parts of the world.

'The tenements on either side were owned by David Dunbar in the eighteenth century,' Priya says.

'The writer?' I ask. Figures from the Scottish Enlightenment have always been of interest to me. These are the folks who built this city and made modern Scotland what it is today, for good or ill. Flawed geniuses, the lot of them.

'It's what David Dunbar's mostly remembered for these days, since he was a third-rate magician at best. However, he was a generous patron to starving artists and the new crop of scientific magicians, offering accommodations at a modest rate to practitioners in his circle. They formed a sort of lesser circle to the Humeans – Megadeth to Metallica, that kind of thing.'

'Must have made him a popular guy. And I love Megadeth, I'll have you know.'

'Easy, I wasn't dissing them, but I wouldn't take *Rust in Peace* over *Master of Puppets*. No sane person would.'

I'm not being dragged into that, there's work to be done. The link to David Dunbar explains why the natural resistance in these gardens is diminished. I can picture magicians in there on summer nights, practising magic and discussing the latest theories. It also means it's very likely Fenella was performing some kind of experiment in this area. But to what end? Again, I think back to Wedderburn's desire to recreate the past glories of Scottish magic. That's his appeal to his students, I believe. If someone dangled the opportunity to emulate the titans of the Enlightenment, it might be as though they'd offered you the key to immortality.

'You remember Siobhan Kavanagh?' Priya asks.

'How could I forget that sick celebrity who was sucking the youth out of kids. We dealt with her. May her soul rot in hell.'

'Amen to that, and I was thinking what you said at the time, about her having some kind of lab going – like her work was part of an experiment.'

'I don't see how it ties in with Fenella being here.'

'Stealing the kids' essence kept Siobhan youthful. There could be a connection somewhere.'

That's when I notice the one tenement flat whose row of windows have all the curtains open, unlike the rest. It's on the second floor, meaning whoever's in there doesn't need to fear anyone peering in. And it seems the riots haven't fazed the occupants either, which may well be the case if they're a capable practitioner.

'We need to look in that flat over there,' I say.

'Let's do it then.'

We exit the gardens and promptly find the main entrance to the tenements. The door's locked, naturally, but it doesn't take Priya long to break us in. The residents will be miffed they have to fix it, but that's their problem, not mine right now. The steps just inside are worn, especially in the middle, and the corridors don't appear to be well looked after. Used to be fairly affluent out here, this close to the Parliament and all, but most of Edinburgh's moneyed have moved out to East Lothian, so you're caught between renters and a fair few squatters in this area nowadays. I can imagine that whichever magicians were here might have still kept second homes in the area, but it's not anywhere near as desirable as it used to be. The last remaining homeowners occasionally moan, but Dunbar's Close and the Royal Mile won't be regaining their old status any time soon.

Priya's moving super cautious when we make it to the landing of the second floor. We scan the three doors there and settle on the blue one in the middle. That's the only flat which'll overlook the gardens, so it must be the one we're after. I tell Priya to wait a sec while I listen for any noises coming from within. You have to use all five senses when breaking and entering. Sight, naturally, checking to see if anyone's in, through the window if that's possible. Then you should also sniff things out. The scent of cooking may indicate the home-owner's there. Touch – the vibrations of someone walking inside might ripple through the door and walls. I know I said all five senses, but I haven't a damned clue how taste would help, short of inadvertently kissing whoever's inside.

Four senses it is then.

There's a knack to this, and you don't rush a job – that's the fastest way to become a guest of His Majesty's free accommodations in Saughton.

I decide there's enough silence within to indicate we can take a chance and enter. There's a slight entropic shift and the sharp sound of metal snapping, then Priya reaches for the brass doorknob and pushes the door open. Rob was going to teach me lockpicking, but I bailed from the Clan before he could. Knapf. Cruickshank slithers across my neck, readying for battle. We're greeted by stillness and I'm kind of relieved. I'm not feeling as confident as I used to about going into situations like this.

You'll be fine, you've got Priya with you.

River boldly walks in first, then Priya, and I make up the rear. There's a pair of dirty trainers on the hallway's cream carpet, and a coat on the rack. But in contrast to the main stairwell, this flat seems well kept inside – at least around the entrance. Someone's taken the care to maintain it, which makes me wonder who it belongs to. Maybe I've spoken too soon, because I then catch hints of an overpowering chemical scent, kinda like formaldehyde. It's mixed in with hints of iodoform, with the tone of something saline underlying all that. It reminds me of the smell of hospitals – the normal ones, rather than

Our Lady's aroma, which is always nice. But I can tell this isn't from actual chemicals but the remnants of an entropic shift lingering in the air, long after the spell's been done.

I spot some letters in a basket near the cupboard by the door. Final payment demands in brown envelopes with red lettering. A couple from the Royal Bank of Scotland, more than a few advertising leaflets, council tax notices. And they're addressed to Siobhan Kavanagh. I freeze, rooted to the spot. The world falls in on me, everything narrowing to a point. Pins and needles in my limbs. I know what's happening to me, again, but when I try to do the breathing exercises, it feels like my chest is clamped shut. I'm having a panic attack. It feels like I'm drowning, can't find the surface to break out, and all around me are the faces of the little children Siobhan hurt. Ollie, Grace, Mark, Katie, and so many more, all of them crushing down on me. I can barely stand, and have to lean against the wall, until I slide down it and find myself on the floor.

I'm in a tunnel in which there's no light. Only an oppressing, overwhelming depression, pushing in from all sides. It's like a hand's reached through my chest and is squeezing my heart.

Siobhan laughing, her shrill voice telling me, 'You think you've won? I've glimpsed your death in my own. You'll die at the hands of the Tall Man. He will get you and I shall live again.' She comes at me from everywhere, the faces of the children blurring until they merge into hers. The only thing I can hear is her warning over and over. The glee in her voice. The malice and menace. No. This can't be. I fought and beat her. I saved those kids from her, so why do I feel like I'm fighting a ghost? I want my mbira but my hands won't move. I'm locked inside my body, petrified. A cold sweat breaks out on my brow. This is all wrong.

I desperately need Dr Checkland but she's not here.

'It's okay,' says Priya. Her voice sounds so far away, like she's at the surface and it's travelling through a million gallons of water down to me.

I use every ounce of my will to look up and reach for the bright light. Her hands wave about me as she rebalances my aura. I slip and return. Have to fight to make it back. *No*. That's exactly what Dr Checkland warned me against. I have to stop fighting and let this flow through me, like a tree bending in the gale so its trunk doesn't break. *Be. Let go.* Then there's a lightness, a sudden unshackling, my chest opens up, and I gasp for air. The letters are scattered on the floor near me and I grab my chest. Eyes wide open. I can breathe again. The air feels sweet.

'Take your time,' Priya says.

'I've. Had. A. Wee wobble,' I manage.

'That's fine, these things happen. You're doing great.'

'But the medicine—'

'It's not a miracle cure, Ropa. You'll have good days and bad days, same as the rest of us. But lately you've been doing great. The panic attacks aren't as frequent, are they?'

That's the thing, though. When I have a good run, I feel I'm over it at last. And then, bam, when you least expect it, it hits you. Before I would've been embarrassed about it – try to tough it out and all that bollocks. Doesn't work, though. I have to live with it.

Priya picks up one of the envelopes and reads it, raising her eyebrows.

'No rush, hen, but this explains a lot. When you're good and ready, you'll want to see what's in the living room too.' She touches me on the shoulder.

I nod, though I'm barely able to get up. There's a phantom echo left in my nerves, and it takes a while for my body to feel right again. But finally, I manage to shift onto my knees and pull myself back up. I adjust my coat and hat, then give Priya the signal I'm ready for whatever she wants to show me. Though my mind's foggy, a thousand questions are swirling around it. It's too much of a coincidence that the flat owned by the celebrity busigician, who was abducting kids, bottling and peddling their essence as the elixir of youth, should be in the same place where Fenella disappeared. Priya's hunch was right. But how does this all tie together?

The presence of the old letters suggests Siobhan had no relatives to put her affairs in order. Seems like she's been forgotten about already. It's not like there was ever a body identified as her. For months the papers speculated on her disappearance, and then they stopped talking about her. Occasionally she's still mentioned on the net alongside Lord Lucan, Amelia Earhart, and, bizarrely, Elvis. But this is Edinburgh, people go missing all the time. Some of them don't want to be found. There're rumours Siobhan Kavanagh was fleeing tax evasion charges. Some say it was a botched life insurance job, though no one knows who exactly benefited from her disappearance. A few insist it's a stunt. But I know what she really was beneath the glitz and glamour, and I was there when she died.

'This place has a weird qi,' Priya says.

'I'm getting bad vibes off it too. Makes my skin crawl, like maggots are squirming on it.'

'Giving me goosebumps and the hairs on my nape are wilding.'

We move into the living room and see what looks like a makeshift lab, with a long worktop dominating the centre of the room. It's packed with beakers, jars, pipettes and other equipment, alongside a working Bunsen burner and some scales. There's a host of substances I've never come across before, as well as some magical texts. *Voodoo Diagrams* by Milo Rigaud and a copy of *In Search of the Zombie: Haitian Reanimation Facts and Myth* by Jonathan Laveaux. *Island Possessed* by Katherine Dunham. And then there's printed pages bound together of *The Book of the Shaded Mysteries of Solomon as Recounted by the Queen of Sheba* – the scroll Wedderburn's students stole from the Ethiopian wizards, and which we managed to recover at Dunvegan Castle. Seems to be a photographed copy of it. Which means Fenella and the others from the Edinburgh Ordinary School for Boys were undoubtedly here, using this place for their work.

'These aren't the standard texts they teach in the four schools of magic,' Priya opines.

'Lewis Wharncliffe was always a student of the esoteric,' I say.

Another book catches my attention. 'And here's something by a famous English natural philosopher and magician, one of the most prominent members of the English Royal Society: Robert Boyle.'

'*Some Physico-Theological Considerations about the Possibility of the Resurrection,*' Priya reads. 'This isn't something I've seen before either.'

216

'These arse-wipes are trying to play God,' I say.

'Or Victor Frankenstein,' Priya replies.

I kinda wish I'd gone with that one. The tall sash windows look out past the gardens, up to Calton Hill in the far distance. The buildings atop it are clearly visible, with the cylindrical Nelson's Monument forever standing in for an upturned telescope. This would be a great location to scheme about raiding the Library of the Dead.

The students clearly had no respect for Siobhan's property, because the walls are covered with mathematical equations and weird formulae. Most of it is in what I recognize as Lewis Wharncliffe's handwriting, but other styles are scribbled there too, indicating they were all working on it. Then there's strange drawings and glyphs which aren't from any standard alphabet I know. Perhaps that's why they had the Vodou books? I notice something that looks like an emphasis on circles. Not zeroes, like, but the circle of life, maybe. An ouroboros is included there. The rest of the markings all fly over my head without so much as shitting on it.

'Can you understand any of this, Priya?' I ask.

'I'm a healer and this stuff is well out of my area of expertise. If I was a generalist, I'd maybe find a way in, but this is advanced shit. There's no way the students could have come up with this themselves, surely.'

'Give me your phone,' I say.

'What happened to yours?' She takes it out anyway, unlocks it and hands it to me.

I take pictures of the walls, making sure I move around the room in sequence. There's one man I know whose job it is to turn magic into mathematics and I reckon he can work the reverse just as well. I start with the top near the door, then move to the bottom of each wall, going clockwise until I arrive back where I started. Once finished, I send them all over to Jomo's dad, pretending to be Priya, and ask him to decipher the magic. A crucial aspect of the librarian's role is proofing magic, so I'm certain he'll be able to handle this for us. I also tell him it's super urgent.

'There's something else we missed,' Priya says, pointing up.

The room has a high ceiling and I have no idea how anyone reached up there, but someone's drawn the symbol of a big letter 'I' with a stick man astride it over and over again, like this was the Sistine Chapel. But they ain't no Michelangelo that's for sure.

'I've seen that image before.'

'A guy with a spear up his backside, or some weird phallic thing? Yep, that's definitely a dick.'

'Could be a puppet on a stick.'

It means something, for sure. And I'll have to find out what. But for now, I need Dr Maige to crack that code we sent him.

XVI

This wet and windy Wednesday's the worst day of my life. It's the day of my grandmother's funeral and I'm not even invited. Priya broke it to me in the late night as we scurried through Edinburgh's streets, evading protesters and police alike. Last night was the most intense of the riots. The protesters built French-style barricades, sealing off the Cowgate and Grassmarket, after the police once again pushed them off the Royal Mile. The city was as noisy as Hogmanay as they shot fireworks and threw Molotov cocktails at the officers.

The air's still thick with gunpowder and teargas smoke.

In the daylight, both sides usually retreat to rest and wait for the night's escalations. They've been keeping the bobbies busy, which is exactly what I need to happen until all this is over.

Me and Izwi are Gran's only living relations. She's outlived three husbands and a daughter, my mother. Everyone else bound to her by blood is in Zimbabwe, which might as well be a world away. And since Izwi and me are minors, they can bury Gran as they choose – more so, now I'm on the run. The whole thing's a kick in the teeth and it feels like my soul's come loose.

We're in the flat Rob set up for me, lying on the sofa, my head on Priya's lap. Priya'd suggested going back to her place in Morningside, but that would have meant running the gauntlet through the thickest of the riots. So we came back here, to be among the weed plants. Played a couple of games on the ancient console earlier, which was a great distraction while we waited for news from Dr Maige. I'm really counting on him and just hope he won't be suspicious of Priya, knowing how close we are. It should be his son I'm relying on, but everything's changed now. Up is down and it's all gone sideways.

'I'll go and stand in on your behalf,' Priya says.

'I won't even get to kiss her goodbye,' I say, sadness hollowing out my words. 'And I don't even know where her soul is – if she's okay or stuck somewhere, since she couldn't enter the everyThere.'

'I'm sure she's found a way. She taught you how to navigate the astral plane, so if there's anyone who can handle that, it's her.'

'Her spirit is Shona, Priya. If the funeral rites aren't properly performed, she won't be accepted into the Land of the Tall Grass. She'll be condemned to wander for all eternity, cut off from her ancestors in the Shumba clan.' Priya nods but I can tell she doesn't understand. 'Shumba is the lion, and that's the totem of her clan. They produced some of the most important spirit mediums in the Shona world. Even her name, Mhondoro, means lion spirit, for their powers extended beyond their clan.'

'So you're of the *Mydoro* clan too. You'll carry on her legacy,' Priya says, butchering the pronunciation.

'It's passed down from your dad's side, so I'm something else altogether,' I reply.

'It's freezing in here,' Priya remarks, shivering for effect.

There's no gas flowing, though we have radiators on the walls, so I go to fetch a fan heater I spotted in the grow rooms. When it kicks in, the warm air circulating makes me think how heartbreakingly needless it was for my gran to have died just because we didn't have one in our caravan. If only I'd known.

'Calista Featherstone's bringing your sister to the funeral,' Priya said.

'I don't want Wedderburn and his lot anywhere near her. Please make sure they protect her. I know I can't stop the lies they'll tell about me, but Izwi knows I'd never do anything to hurt Gran.'

'Ms Featherstone wouldn't let them dare. She's not a woman to be trifled with. The care she shows for her pupils is legendary, and I believe she's taken a shine to Izwi. At least that's what I've been told.'

'Where will they bury her?'

It's lucky the Library's in a bit of a state at the moment. The last thing I need is for resurrection men to steal her body and have it turned into a book. Nah, that wouldn't happen, 'cause they only do that for the cream of Scottish society and Gran was a nobody. To them, not me and Izwi. To us she was everything. Priya tells me she'll be laid to rest at the Morningside Cemetery.

'But she should be taken to Corstorphine Hill on Drum Brae, that's the one closest to our neighbourhood.' I like that cemetery – it's tucked away, hidden inside a park surrounded by trees a hundred years old. Even the ghosts there are peaceful like. Perfect neighbours for my gentle gran.

'I'm sorry, Callander really did try, but the authorities wouldn't budge. They said folks from the slums don't pay council tax and so they aren't entitled to burial in their local area.'

'At least they didn't ship her off to South Queensferry.' I find the silver lining.

Our lives have been filled with moments like these, when we're reminded that those of us in Hermiston Slum, and other places like it, don't belong in the real Edinburgh. It always happened whenever we tried to see a doctor for Gran, to get her prescription. And it happened when we fought to enrol my little sister in the local primary. We hit that big old sign saying you're not wanted here. That's why I fought so hard to lift us out of that, so we could have a better life in a place where folks wouldn't thumb their noses at us. And we were *so* close. A ticket to England. Yet so far. *Oh Gran, your heart's too warm for that icy ground they want to put you in.*

'I will go for you,' Priya says once more.

'When you do, please tell her I love her always, until the end of all worlds.'

'Come on, I need to get ready,' Priya says, nudging me off her lap. 'I can't be late for this.'

She pulls her wheelchair closer so she can move into it. There's something else bulging underneath it, where she keeps her medkit in case of emergencies. I figure it's some sort of healer stuff and don't bother asking her. Not being there for Gran's send-off doesn't sit well with me. I *have* to go.

'Actually, I'm coming with you.'

'Look, Ropa, I know you're hurting, but you can't risk your freedom like that. It's too dangerous. Anyone looking for you will find you at the funeral,' Priya replies, brow furrowed. 'Tell you what – why don't I video call you on your new number, so you can see and hear everything going on? My phone's going to be sticking out of my jacket pocket, right here, near my heart.' She places her finger on her chest and taps it a couple of times. 'Deal?'

'Both your parents are alive, Priya. All four of your grandparents are still here too. Hell, one of your great-grandparents is still kicking about for fuck knows why. Good for you!'

I leap up off the couch and grab my gear. Priya looks deflated. I've landed a low blow. But I need to go – and I have a plan. She's still getting ready by the time I'm out the flat, rushing down the stairs two at a time. I burst out of the main door and feel the rain hit my face. It's well dreich and heaven's weeping today. Normally I move around the city quickly on my bike, but since I ditched it, everything takes twice as long.

River's at my heels – I didn't even see her follow me.

'Come on, girl. We're not missing Gran's funeral for anything.'

I half trot, half walk through the wet and miserable streets. The rain soon soaks into my woolly hat so my noggin's freezing and all, but I don't care. My breath mists up ahead of me as I go through Canonmills, headed for the New Town. From there I'll go around the loch, then onto Lothian Road.

I had to leave Priya, I needed some space. Felt like I was going to start yelling at her earlier. Not like she's at fault, none of this has anything to do with her, but I wanted to take it out on her anyway. I'm angry at her perfect life. Great family, right school, great job. And god, isn't she annoyingly beautiful?

I slow to a halt on Queen Street, near the red sandstone Portrait Gallery. It has a gothic vibe but is much younger than some of its neoclassical neighbours. I grab hold of a pike atop the metal fence closing off the adjacent gardens from the public. They belong to the residents of Poshville nearby.

'What am I doing lashing out at Priya for, River?'

She doesn't answer, just gives me a curious look.

'I know, I acted like a dick. I'm hurting and I want someone else to carry the pain with me.'

Can't hold it in any longer.

I grab my phone and nearly message Priya with an apology, but then don't. There's something holding me back. Gran once told me that sometimes when we're hurting, angry or confused, we take it out on the people we love. The key's to know you're doing it and then to stop. Easier said than done, though. Gran had that Gandhi thing going on which I don't.

My hand stings from holding the metal railing, so I let go at last. I stick my hands in my pockets, but not before checking my hat and scarf are covering my face properly. I'm now seeing the world through a small slit, like one of them medieval knights in armour.

They're going to give Gran a Christian service, which even though she wasn't one, she won't mind at all. They'll play the organ today, when she should have listened to the mbira sending her off. That or the sound of bagpipes, which she loved dearly. Melsie Mhondoro, you've broken my heart.

That poor woman.

By the time I arrive at the West End, there's tons of police patrolling the streets.

'God save the king,' I say to an officer who takes an interest in me.

'Long may he reign,' he replies, waving me past.

No true member of the protesting Thistlers would use that greeting without choking. Last night they nailed a list of demands onto the door of St Giles' Cathedral, and one of them was the right not to have to say those words, God save the king. It was Martin Luther hardcore, pics floating about on the net and all. But I'll say what I have to if it gets me where I want to go.

Just off Rutland Square, a footbridge takes me over the Western Approach without me getting my feet wet. From here I can then go back onto Lothian Road, headed through Tollcross. I check the time on my phone and hasten my pace. There's debris in the middle of the road: rocks and blackened glass from spent Molotov cocktails. Water bottles. A crowbar. Flyers advocating independence from London. A fair few rubber bullets. Someone's pair of spectacles. One shoe, the left foot. Plenty of broken windows, with shops looted and ransacked. It was a busy night alright.

I walk past two police on horseback, trotting towards the centre of Edinburgh. One of the things missing is traffic into town from the outlying neighbourhoods.

This city looks all the more beautiful in the rain, I think, bringing my arms closer to my body to stave off the chill. Morningside, and a good deal of Tollcross, seem to have come out of the riots fairly unscathed. Some businesses are defiantly open still, like the chiropodist and chocolate shop. Newsagents too. The city's bookstores remain untouched, so the one on

Bruntsfield Place is okay. The shelves in the food shops look ominously empty, though.

I leave the main road and go right onto Morningside Drive, where I head to a familiar, semi-detached property. The house has a well-trimmed hedge and a set of steps splitting the garden in half, leading to a red door. Have to make sure I've got the right number here. I could swear this door was blue the last time I came. It's the right place, though, and as I knock on the door I just hope my clients haven't moved. And that I can still trust them.

'Coming,' a man shouts from within.

River and me wait patiently in the rain, which is still pouring down. I'm soaked to the bone, but I don't care.

The door opens a fraction and a man wearing a black suit is startled to see me at the threshold.

'Who are you? How can I help you?' Bing Wu says curtly.

I remove my hat and loosen my scarf from around my face. It takes a second or two before he recognizes me.

'Ropa Moyo? Of course it's you! What on earth brings you here?' he says, poking his head out and checking the street left and right to make sure no one's seen me arrive. Then he beckons me inside, before shutting the door quickly.

'Who is it?' Connie calls from upstairs.

'You'd better come down, dear,' Bing shouts back up. 'And bring some warm, dry clothes . . . Christ, Ropa, you must be freezing. Go in the bathroom and take a hot shower.'

I'm surprised by his immediate kindness. He's asked why I'm here, but hasn't even waited for a proper reply before making sure I'm okay. I did a solid favour for the Wus a wee while back, so I reckon the scales are balancing themselves out. We go up the stairs and along the landing, its walls hung with vintage movie posters in frames. The bathroom's next to their son Max's bedroom and the place feels like a warm spring day, with their electric heaters on. The bathroom's massive. A cute picture of an elephant in a tub is stuck on the door, and a replica of van Gogh's sunflowers brightens up the room.

I don't linger and as soon as I'm alone, I'm out of my clothes and hopping into the tub, treating myself to a nice hot shower.

Reckon I could stay in here all day – it's so utterly refreshing.

Someone knocks on the door.

'It's me, Connie. Can I come in?'

'This is your house. Door's unlocked,' I reply.

She still thanks me like I've done her a favour, and I hear her scooping up my clothes from the other side of the white plastic shower curtain. Connie announces there's a new tooth-brush in the cupboard, before heading out again. The water washes away all the dirt on me, but no matter how much soap I use, I can't get to the sorrow inside. The barbs of it stay, stabbing inside me sharper than ever.

There's a fresh towel on the white storage trolley underneath the bathroom cabinet, so I dry myself, then put on the mustard-coloured pyjamas Connie's laid out for me. She's taken away my clothes. I put on the white robe and slippers too, and exit the bathroom. I really should have cleaned up after myself, but I can't be arsed. Not being rude or nothing, but I simply don't have the strength for it. The last thing I do is pick up my phone, which she's left on top of a bunch of pink face towels.

When I come back downstairs, I find River gnawing on a
bone. Bing and Connie are sat side by side on the big sofa,
and I take the armchair. Connie is also in a black dress. It's as
though they're both dressed for the funeral. There's a tray with
tea and biscuits on the coffee table.

'Sorry, that's all we have at the moment,' Bing says.

'We need to be careful. There's been an announcement on
the radio that they're starting food rationing with immediate
effect,' Connie replies. 'It's like we're in the Catastrophe all
over again.'

'Or the Second World War.'

'Still, we'll get by. It'll be alright,' Connie says. 'I'm so sorry
for your loss, Ropa. I never knew Melsie Mhondoro, but I hear
she was one of the good ones.'

'It's sent a shock through the magical community,' Bing
adds.

Their words pass me like a faint echo. I can't even touch
the tea and biscuits, 'cause my stomach's vanished somewhere.
All I know is they've mentioned Gran in the past tense. The
one place time will not allow us to go as it hurtles forward
relentlessly. Bing is an effectician – magicians who work in
the film industry creating special effects – and Connie is a
corporate lawyer, so I reckon they're better insulated from
events than my friends out on the streets. Though there are
circumstances in which even that's no protection.

'I can't go to the funeral,' I say. 'Can I watch it from here?'

Their house looks over the wall around Morningside Cemetery.

'I know what they've said about you isn't at all true, Ropa. We'll
help you in any way we can,' Bing says, taking his wife's hand.

'We owe you that much at least.'

A while back, their son Max Wu was in Our Lady of Mysterious Ailments with a fever that had resisted both medicine and magic. It was up to me to find out what had happened to him so he could be treated. Tough job that one. I'd just become Callander's intern at the time, didn't know what I was doing, but I muddled through and we were able to save Max's life.

I nod gratefully, and take the tea, not to drink it, but to use the warmth of the cup to soothe my hands. We sit there in an awkward silence. I don't much feel like talking anyway. What's the point of wasting words? Nothing will bring Gran back. I've worked with the dead long enough to know that.

'Hang on,' I say, sitting up and placing the cup back down. 'Why are you going to my grandmother's funeral?'

Bing frowns and looks confused, but Connie squeezes his hand. Not so subtle, since I see it.

'This can be a confusing time,' Connie says.

'I mean, we weren't close or anything,' Bing stammers. 'I personally never had any contact. Her contributions were immense.'

'What are you talking about?'

'We should show you upstairs, otherwise we'll be late for the service,' Connie says.

I guess Gran did help a lot of people who had dead relatives haunting them and stuff. It's an embarrassing subject for many. In this age of science, folks still find it hard to admit when they've gone to a medium or clairvoyant. That's from decades of suppression by the kirk, which was actually working hand in hand with the Society to clamp down on dabblers in the esoteric. So the work has to be confidential, and if Gran helped this couple, or one of them, then that's not something I should try to get out of them. The way the furniture in this room is oriented shows the Wus don't mess about with their feng shui. Reckon there might be a few others like them at the funeral who Gran assisted in some way.

It's scary that. Knowing she had a life outside the one she shared with us. Gran was active for a while with me, until her health forced her to stop doing house visits. I hope some of her old clients remember her. It'll make it easier for me, knowing they do. That way it's not just Izwi and me carrying her inside our hearts.

Connie rises and leads me back up the stairs.

'The best view is from Max's room,' she says, knocking on the door before opening it.

Max is in a black Kaneda T-shirt, featuring the hero from the *Akira* film wearing a red jacket with a blue/red pill emblazoned on it. Max's got jobby catchers on too, and is reclining on his single bed, holding up an accounting textbook. A notepad and pen lie on the floor. He finishes his passage and then smiles wildly when he sees me.

'Yay, my hero,' he says and throws the book down.

'This room's a pigsty. Thank goodness it doesn't smell,' Connie says. She picks up some clothes lying on the floor and throws the heap at Max, pointing to the basket next to the door. 'Laundry goes in there. How hard is that to remember?'

'I can't wait to leave this dump as soon as I finish uni.'

'Try completing your Highers first.' Connie may be snapping

at him, but it makes me think how awesome it must be to have a mum. 'Ropa needs to use your room. Leave her in peace. And if she needs anything, you're to help her out. Understood? Now go downstairs, young man!'

'Stop shouting at me, I haven't done anything. Sorry, Ropa. Old people,' he says, getting up all the same and walking out in a huff.

Connie leads me to the window overlooking the cemetery. Her and Bing were right, this is a perfect view over the ivy-topped wall, into the expanse of the graveyard. Across the road from the house is the stone wall surrounding the cemetery. There's trees which would normally be blocking my view, but as it's winter they've shed their foliage, making it easier to see through them. Already there's a funeral party in there, doing their thing in the corner. Some council workers, about six of them, are digging two more graves. I'm amazed they do it on the day. Looks like hard work, the ground being soggy as it is.

Fallen tombstones, rows upon rows of them, mark resting places. Not that they matter. Subsidence means the coffins travel underground, gradually migrating from where they first started – the earth is always shifting. Those who've left flowers on graves, and there's a fair few of them, have no real idea if their loved one is directly underneath anymore.

Connie drags over an armchair and places it in front of the window.

'Make yourself comfy, and give Max a shout if you need anything.'

She then goes out and shuts the door, leaving me to myself. I chill, holding the back of the chair, watching the gravediggers at work with their picks and shovels. Feel like running out and telling them to stop. Gran is okay, she doesn't need a grave. The doctors made a mistake. It happens sometimes, right? I've read stories about it: people waking up at their funeral, spooking everyone out. That's why the Victorians took to being buried with little bells, so they could ring for help in the worst-case scenario. Imagine that, waking up in the dark unable to get out. Must be awful. Gran's okay.

No she's not.

She's.

Not.

There's no hope. Still the rain falls. It's relentless, like the tears I should be shedding if I wasn't holding everything in. My phone rings. I let it for a while, and then fish into my pocket. Priya. My hand's trembling when I answer. Her face pops up on the screen and she looks at me briefly, before turning the camera.

For a moment I'm looking at a wall and half the profile of a pillar of some sort. She moves it about, and it changes to a light-coloured laminate floor, then freezes for a bit. There's a rustling sound coming from her pocket, and when it's finally well positioned, I can see the nave of the church. There's people taking their seats, while others are already in place. They're all dressed in a solemn black. The room buzzes with voices and I can't quite catch what anyone's saying. A stained-glass window is right at the front of the building, its arch symmetrical to the wood beams in the ceiling. And a simple pine coffin sits near the altar, as the organ starts playing at the Morningside Parish Church.

* * *

I stare down at the grey ghosts wandering Morningside Cemetery, listening to the powerful eulogy of the preacher, who never met Gran when she was alive, but seems to have woven a tapestry of things from what others have said about her. I recall a memory from when I was young, when Gran took me and Izwi to Oxgangs. We went via the Neighbourhood Centre on Firrhill Drive, which then had a cafe and a sensory garden outside. It was a haven of community near the flats, bringing lonely people together, because its walls weren't built to keep people out, but rather to keep them warm and safe inside.

The roof had a skylight which allowed the sunshine to stream in. Must have been autumn when we were there, but I'm not sure. I do know it was after Gramps had passed and Gran was in a funk, though she tried to keep cheery for our sakes. Even as a child, I could see the strain she was under. I'd given her my Barbie doll, hoping it would help. At that age it seemed like a huge sacrifice to make, but I see now not even Barbie could have lessened the pain she was in. Gran and Gramps had been separated for a year or two before he kicked it. That was after he gambled away the house we lived in. Outwardly, she'd been angry at him, but there were nights I heard her weeping. Though I couldn't understand it then, this was somehow also around the time I started seeing dead people in random places.

I was scared of them.

The cafe had lights dangling off the rafters. Noticeboards and chalkboards announced events and advertised places to help those struggling with rent or facing eviction. A group of elderly ladies was in one corner knitting. There were noisy young people running about. Community organizers greeted everyone with a smile and chatted with all, while volunteers manned the counters.

It was great to be out of our caravan and back in the world.

Gran didn't have a lot of money then. I know now a cheap place like that was the best she could take us to at the time. It was a luxury and I wish I'd appreciated it more. While we were there, random people stopped by at our table. They seemed forlorn, as though carrying an immense weight. Most of these folks were middle-aged, some in their sixties, and a handful much older.

I lost count of how many people came over to Gran.

Each one would show her a photo of someone, mostly young men, but some women too and older guys. Gran would ask them to tell her a story about the person in the picture. Mundane details, such as the foods they liked, a favourite football team. The school they went to. Their work, sometimes their passions. I remember hearing about one guy named Gavin who liked trainspotting. Made me wonder what that was.

'Real trains, not the novel,' Gavin's mum said.

'I thought it was a film,' Gran replied. 'What did he do for that?'

'Went out with his friends on a rowing boat to the flooded Waverley station, taking snorkelling gear. Then they'd check out the engines and rolling stock under water. Sometimes they went to old railyards too, to see the rusting locomotives. And he'd write it all down in his book.'

Gran thanked her for the information and the next person came to the table. She also collected a token from each: a toy, a watch, DVD, favourite jacket, the pile beside her growing ever larger. This went on until the light waned and darkness fell upon the city.

I was drowsy and dozing by the time she gently nudged me. Izwi had fallen asleep in the arms of one of the community organizers. I squinted and told her I wanted to go back to the caravan.

'We will later, child. Tonight, we have to help those who are not in the light to find their way to the Land of the Tall Grass.'

'But I'm sleepy.'

'I know you are. But what if I told you that losing a few hours of sleep will save someone from an eternity of wandering in darkness?' She held her hand out and I took it. 'Thank you, Ropa. Remember, you and I are psychopomps.'

'I'm not a psycho.'

She laughed and admitted I wasn't. We gathered the tokens the families had left at the table and placed them inside a box, with Gran mentioning the name of everyone associated with each object. Then she led us out into the chilly night. Most of the families had gone home already by then. She took me into a woodland nearby, a small, unremarkable parcel of land with a few paths leading into it and some benches. A young man who was already there, wearing a red cap and holding some rope, was startled to see us enter. He mumbled something and started to walk away. I could sense his anger and shame.

Gran sighed.

'Tomorrow morning, go to Fountain Park. You'll inadvertently bump into Kayla near Boroughmuir High. And you'll find she's already forgiven you,' she called out after him.

The young man turned back, perplexed. He stared at Gran
for a bit, dropped the rope he was carrying, and fled the park.
Now I'm older, I understand the moment. But then I thought
nothing of it, for soon we were wandering the woods, which
were filled with ghosts roaming aimlessly about. There were
so many of them, drawn from throughout the ages. Gran wasn't
scared, though, and neither was I, even though I could sense
the overwhelming despair. She would meet each one, talk to
it, and leave a token on the ground, or hang it off the branch
of a tree. We did this till the wee hours, right up until the
golden dawn broke over the horizon and the cloud of angst
had lifted from the park. The ghosts were gone – it was just
me and my gran.

Folks coming out of the service trickle along Morningside Drive.
They walk sombrely, slow gaits, gazes down towards the
rainswept tar. It's a mass of men and women in black far
exceeding anything I would have expected. Who was Gran that
all these people should come out in the dreariest dreich and
walk her body home?

Behind the first wave is a hearse, drawn by two black horses
wearing ostrich-feather plumes atop their heads. The horses
are driven by a female funeral director in a black top hat and
tails. She keeps her chin up in a dignified way, holding the
reins in one hand and whip in the other, though she doesn't
use it on the horses. It seems to be symbolic. The horse on
the left has a red cloth with golden tassels draped over its
hindquarters, while the other's swathed in black, though similarly tasselled. I've not seen this before on any funeral horses.

Normally they're draped in one colour, which may be black, white or velvet. Gran once told me the spirit mediums of the Shona culture only wore red and black, so someone's obviously taken the care to arrange this for her. I feel so grateful, since I would never have thought of that.

The carriage's back wheels are a bit larger than the front ones. It's a shiny black vehicle with a curved roof. The four sides of it are covered in glass panes allowing onlookers to see the pine coffin within. My heart aches to think she's lying in there all by herself. I used to lie with her in the caravan, which never went anywhere. Now she's going without me.

Something in my heart swells up and I fight back the tears. It feels like a wave gushing from inside me.

Gran.

And behind the carriage is Izwi, walking with her head bowed. She wears a black pleated skirt that reaches her ankles, buckled shoes, and a coat with a cape. Her hair's done in a bun on either side, parting in the middle. I cup my mouth and finally start crying. My sister is here. It's been so long since I've seen her, since she went away to board at the Aberdeen School of Magic and Esoterica. How tiny she seems. Oh God, she needs me with her. Does she understand what's going on and why I had to disappear? Why I can't be with her? What have they told her about me? I hope she doesn't believe I . . . No, she can't.

I place my hand on the glass pane, wishing I could touch Izwi as she walks past me. I can't bear her to think I've abandoned her, of her unanswered text messages on the phone I had to ditch.

Next to her is Calista Featherstone, the head teacher at her school, who looks like the woman from Scottish Widows in her hooded black robe. The red lining of it is visible from here. And slightly behind her, Sir Ian Callander and his husband Esfandiar Soltani walk arm in arm, Callander holding an umbrella over them. I remember Esfandiar saying he was Gran's friend, and his face is red from weeping. I wish I'd asked him more then. He gave me this coat I'm wearing; it belonged to her, once. He pulls out a black handkerchief from his pocket and dabs his eyes. Callander, on the other hand, is grim and stoic, though he seems shaken. There's a frailty about him, almost as though he's suddenly aged. There was a time, just after I'd become his intern, when I found him at our caravan, talking to Gran. It's clear to me now the two had a history.

Dr Maige is wearing a black cassock, holding to his chest a black book in a transparent plastic bag. I wonder if he's replied to Priya's messages about those strange formulae from Dunbar's Close. Mr Evelyn is there with him, holding up a black umbrella too.

There are so many magicians here. Some of them random faces I've crossed paths with in the Library. Others I met at the conference in Dunvegan. There's Bing and Connie. Priya's in between her mum and dad, who seem to have come all the way from Glasgow. Even Dalziel MacDonald from the Isle of Skye is attending in his black kilt. How can this be? Gran was just an ordinary ghostalker, practising a craft that's not even considered real magic by the Society of Sceptical Enquirers. Yet they've all turned out for her. The ones who're not with Wedderburn, that is.

What is water? Am I that young fish who missed it was immersed in water because the extraordinary was normal to it? I took Gran for granted. Yeah, we did some cool stuff together, but she was my nan. Old and safely boring. She had great stories, but I was so busy hustling, trying to keep a roof over our heads and our bellies fed, that I didn't *see* her.

The hearse turns into the cemetery.

Behind the magicians comes the sum total of His Majesty's Slum Hermiston, marching the streets of Morningside. You can tell by their poor dress. A lot of them aren't even in black, but they're wearing the finest they have, even if it be trackie bottoms or skinny jeans. They are the ones who don't have umbrellas and take the rain as nature intended. There's Marie and her wee boy Eddie, my sister's wee pally. Our landlord Farmer McAlister's walking among the crowd. Henry the coal seller seems distraught. They're all here in the unrelenting rain. Many of the folks from Hermiston have a piece of knitwear on them. It could be gloves, and there's beanie hats, of course. Others have insisted on wearing their cardigans and jerseys – they must be soaked to the bone right now. Loads of scarves. A child holds a knitted doll too. Gran used to knit for the community and she gave away her handiwork freely. As they trundle past, I see memories, because I was there when most of these pieces were knitted. When my grandmother was still alive. In our caravan.

These are all the people she touched.

Small acts of kindness and love.

There's even more folks too. Some I remember from my childhood. Gran's clients from when she was practising the chivanhu craft. But the vast majority of them are unknown to me. I wasn't around for the first seven decades of her life. I understand now why she could never distil all she wanted into my little head. And what more was she going to tell me, the night she died?

Rooster Rob and a fair few members of the Clan hold the rear. Tough-looking men and women in leather jackets with metal studs or exuberant fringes. Some of them look sloshed.

Everyone's there except me.

The guests take their spots around the freshly dug grave in the far-left corner of the cemetery. I can't see what's happening at the front, through the throng of mourners. I look at Priya's video call. Some of the people are cut off, so I can only make out legs and torsos, since the camera in her jacket pocket's pretty low down. Little Izwi is visible, though. Wet tear streaks run down her face.

There's a prayer from the minister. The audio isn't great, to be honest – could be the rain – but I hear when they announce the Makar. Esfandiar Soltani will read Burns's funeral poem. His voice is strong and distinct as he recites:

An honest woman here lies at rest,
As e'er God with His image blest:
The friend of all, the friend of truth;
The friend of age, and guide of youth:
Few hearts like hers, with virtue warm'd,
Few heads with knowledge so inform'd:
If there's another world, she lives in bliss;
If there is none, she made the best of this.

Esfandiar falters at the last line and his voice cracks. It sends shivers down my spine, seeing them all there with their heads bowed. She had love for each and every one of us. The sort that makes you feel you were special and unique in her eyes.

And then Sir Ian Callander begins to speak:

'The Second Science in Scotland has lost an outstanding practitioner. Melsie Mhondoro was a dear friend of mine. I first met her in . . .'

Some of his phrasing deliberately obscures things. You'd have to know what the second science is to realize Gran *was* a magician. And all this time I thought she was just doing kitchen table stuff. Once again, I realize I never truly knew my grandmother. What was going on with her, and with my father? Their connection to Scottish magic was kept from me deliberately. The sound of rain and the occasional cough means I miss parts of the speech, but the fondness Callander had for Gran resonates, as his voice cracks now and again. He's forced to pause at one point, and it seems quite a while before he can continue with his speech.

Callander is in the middle of his eulogy when the bleak sky is blackened by an incredible flock of fieldfares and redwings, flying over the rooftops. They circle the cemetery once, twice, thrice, several hundred of them descending upon the bare trees. The air's alive with their chirping calls. It distracts the people in the cemetery for a while and Callander has to pause again. But soon enough everything settles and he continues.

I'm watching through the window, as well as listening on my phone, when I see River leaving the house. How on earth did she break out? She trots across the road, heading for the cemetery. It's almost as though she knows Gran's there. It was

Gran who hand-fed her when I found her as a pup. I watch with envy as she disappears into the cemetery and, though I look out for her, I don't see her again once she's inside.

When they are done with their prayers and speeches, I collapse onto my chair as the undertakers lower Gran's coffin into the grave they dug for her. Something inside me had still thought this was all some kind of mistake. That someone might come and say, 'Stop, you got it all wrong.' That's not her in there, she's fine and at the hospital. Then we'd be annoyed, but afterwards we'd laugh at how ridiculous the whole thing had been.

Despite all the ghosts I've spoken to, the families I've helped, I don't think I've ever truly understood the meaning of grief. Not until now. There's nothing else like it.

And just like that, the mourners begin to disperse. How long has the whole thing been? A couple of hours at most. They walk off, going back to their lives. A couple stops to console Izwi and shake her hand.

I'm proud of how my sister handles the moment. *I'm here for you Izwi. We're all we have left now. And I'm going to make it back to you.*

XVII

As I watch the events coming to a close in the cemetery, I notice Priya and Dr Maige peeling off to a quiet spot near the wall. There are some who linger but the place is clearing at a moderate pace. The street below already has people headed to the main road. Priya's video call is still live and I can see Dr Maige's midriff, and the wall behind him. He holds his hands, fingers locked, by his waist, golden wedding band standing out.

'Have you managed to decipher the equations and formulae I sent you last night?' Priya enquires.

'Where did you find this extraordinary material? I could hardly believe my eyes. That I have lived to witness the birth of a new theorem was not something I could have anticipated. You don't understand, Ms Kapoor, but I've been proofing magic for over twenty years and never encountered something as elegant and beautiful as the work you sent me. I abandoned everything I was doing and have spent all my time since then studying the pictures. It took a while, because you messed up the order. Not your fault, this is advanced mathematics.'

'To what end – what's it all for?'

'There's not enough for me to go on,' says Dr Maige, scratching his chin. 'It's like looking at a room through a tiny gap in the curtain, not able to see the whole. However, there was enough for me to link it to a sophisticated manuscript I've been trying to unknot for years.'

Dr Maige starts to walk and Priya follows, moving away from the last few people left in the cemetery. The head librarian remains silent for a good while, evidently making sure they are completely out of earshot.

'Whoever's this is, the work they are doing is tied into some experiments Makomborero Moyo was conducting before he died.' I gasp, and it must be audible through Priya's phone because Dr Maige stops and looks around.

Priya touches her throat, pretending it was her. I put my phone on mute, so I can still listen in, but they can't hear anything from my end.

'Sorry,' she says. 'Ropa's father?'

The head librarian relaxes once more.

'He left behind three thousand handwritten pages titled *Beyond Life and Death*. It is a work so dense and complex I no longer concern myself with proofing anything else. I doubt I'll be able to complete my analysis of it in this lifetime. It's a task on a par with solving Fermat's Last Theorem, and my skills, while considerable, pale in comparison to those of a giant like Wiles. But even he would find this very challenging.'

'Yet I discovered all this in a place where a bunch of school kids were working. Wedderburn's disciples. Are you saying they've made headway?'

Dr Maige stiffens, and even from this far off, I notice his irritation, perhaps even a flash of anger.

'If that's so, what bothers me more is how they got hold of Makomborero's documents in the first place,' he says, evading. 'The papers were supposed to be solely in the safe keeping of the Library. Those were the orders Sir Ian Callander gave and I agreed, because it is a very powerful piece of magic he was working on. One which could cause disaster if it fell into the wrong hands. Who gave it to them?'

I know the answer to that one. My best friend Jomo. Anything to shaft his dad. Now it seems the revenge has gone too far, and I'm desperate to speak out of the phone, ask Dr Maige questions myself. This confirms my father wasn't some academic, he really was a magician of considerable powers tied to the Society, as Wedderburn said. Both him and Gran it seems. But why did she leave? And why did she keep these facts hidden from me, as did everyone else? Was it something to do with that Samhain night Wedderburn mentioned? A night known to be when the barriers between the living and the dead become thin?

'What would Wedderburn and his people have to do with Makomborero Moyo, though?' Priya asks.

'I've already said too much. Moyo's name is not to be spoken of. The things he— no, no. You must speak to Sir Ian. I've given you all the help I can,' Dr Maige says, turning abruptly and walking away. Then he turns back: 'You asked earlier about the missing books from the Library of the Dead. Unfortunately, there was an orgy of devouring which occurred and I've as yet been unable to calm all the books. I've had to seal the Library off to prevent anyone from being hurt while I work out a plan. Once I sort it out, I'll be sure to let you know.'

Like, what the actual? It's beginning to feel as though a huge chunk of my life was a lie. There's crucial information about my origins that seem to have been hidden from me. Things erased. Lies of omission. My noggin's nearly popping from all the gears cranking. Right now, it's important I don't get side-tracked, though. I need to join up all the dots and then move quickly to stop whatever Wedderburn's up to with his lot. They will never profit from murdering my grandmother, I'll make sure of that.

I had wanted to go and stand over Gran's grave and say goodbye. I was just waiting for everyone to go. Even the fieldfares and redwings have taken to the sky, returning to their business. But Priya and Dr Maige aren't the last ones to leave. From my vantage point, I notice two men milling about. They were there, attempting to blend in, when the next funeral party, the ones for the other freshly dug grave, came in.

And when that funeral party left, they stayed. They move from grave to grave, pretending to be mourners. I know their alert body language, the bulges in their jackets, tell-tale signs of hidden equipment. They're too prim and proper, but not outright posh like the majority of magicians who were there. It's a working-class vibe that disdains the working class. The air of those who serve power and the rich. I can smell a police officer from a mile away.

Which means I was right not to attend the funeral. Even if Callander could be swayed, these guys would have nabbed me. I'm in the armchair, still sat at the window, when there's a timid knock on the door.

'What?' I say.

'I'm just checking up on you, love. Would you like something to eat?' Connie asks as she steps into the room.

'No.'

'I've brought you some chicken soup and a roll anyway. It's what my mum used to make for me when I was sick. Mine's not half as good as hers, but I think you should try it.'

I thank her and try to ignore the steaming plate she's left on the windowsill. I've a slight headache coming on. Fuck it. I take the plate and have three spoonfuls of soup, before putting it back down again. It's actually pretty good. Then I go to lie down on Max Wu's bed. I cross my legs and place my hands over my chest. My head is pointing to where they buried Gran. Even if her soul isn't here, I've got some thinking to do.

Elementary.

Nothing comes to me. Then my phone starts ringing – it's Priya. I message her, asking to meet later. For now, I need to chill and figure shit out – too many pieces to this jigsaw which don't seem to fit. Priya lives in this neighbourhood too, up the way on Pitsligo Road, which is nearer the Bruntsfield end.

Motive.

There's a reason Gran used to make me watch detective shows all the time. Teaches you how to think. My heart's in pieces, but I have to set all of that aside and look at what's right in front of me. *Gran's knitting needles were gone.* Why would the killer take those? I message Priya and tell her to ask Callander questions about my Gran, and about my father too. Like, what exactly did Gran do in Scottish magic? Seems odd to me that she was hobnobbing with them and well regarded but broke. For all the time I knew her, she really didn't seem to care about money and liked living with our neighbours in the slum.

What was she running away from?

It can't have been enemies, since she was so easy to find. Must have been a deeper philosophical point she was trying to make. Like, fuck the Society and its wealth. Now, she was no Che Guevara, but she was always on the side of the down and out. A bit too much for my liking. As though she wanted to make amends for something. I remember a time she urged me to help the ghost of Nicola Stuart. I didn't want to, but then she said to me, 'Don't make the same mistake I did a long time ago and lose yourself in the soulless pursuit of money, child.' Didn't seem to matter at the time, but she still convinced me to help a spook who couldn't pay for my services. What's this past she never told me about, when she was chasing cheddar like that? Something major would have had to happen to pull her out of it. Something that separated her from Sir Ian Callander too.

Did she just want me to help Nicola, or she was nudging me down a path? Into a future where I inadvertently met Callander?

Hmm.

I should have asked her more questions about herself while I had the chance. Old people seem slow and boring, but I'm pretty sure at some point she'd have been as young and exciting as I am. Now that's a huge leap to make. Back in her day there was nothing going on, not like in our age. The only thing worth salvaging from back then was good TV shows. *Stop it, Ropa, you're getting distracted.*

I know we don't have much in our caravan, but why nick her needles? The whole taping of doors and windows is such a cowardly way to kill someone too. Almost as if they were too scared to go toe-to-toe with Gran. Once upon a time she had a bulletproof jacket. Insane. Then they waited until after she was asphyxiated to lift the bunch of needles, before they promptly sealed her back in again to make sure? That's proper fucked up.

It was arrogant of me earlier to think her murder had anything to do with me. Like, that they might have wanted to kill me. But Wedderburn just kinda shrugged me aside at the Library.

I go over to the door, open it, and yell out, 'Bing, can you come up here? I need you for something.'

Connie left my dry, pressed clothes on the chest of drawers near the door. Bless her, she's even cleaned my boots too. Gratitude don't cost nothing. I'll have to thank her later. Now I'm up, I pace around the room, my hands behind my back. Could do with a pipe but I'm hungry, and so I stop near the window and take another spoonful of soup. It's even better now it's cooled, like the flavours have settled.

Bing appears in the doorway, one hand resting on the frame. He seems exhausted. Funerals do that to you. And he's taken off his jacket and tie, the top button on his white shirt open.

'Everything okay?' he asks.

'You're a magician, right? I need you to tell me everything you know about my grandmother.'

'She's from before my generation,' he says, already making excuses, so I eyeball him. 'Okay, so I'm an effectician, a completely

249

different speciality to hers. But when I was studying, we borrowed and modified some of her spells for our work. It was tricky, because Melsie Mhondoro wasn't Scottish trained and her technique was not strictly scientific, but it worked.'

'Example.'

'Dreamworking. That's something she could do – sending messages in the form of dreams to people. We adapted it and used it for nightmare sequences in films. When you get the hang of Napier's transformations, you can—'

'But what was her job in the Society?' I cut him off. I don't want to become bogged down in the minutiae of film production methods. Bing appears disappointed, like this is a subject he happily converses in at dinner parties.

'That's the thing. From what I know of her bio – I didn't know her personally – your grandmother worked for the Royal Bank of Scotland as an actuary, not the Society.'

An actuary for RBS? Doesn't sound like Gran . . . 'Did she have a degree?'

'You tell me.'

I shrug. To be an actuary, you have to be really good at maths. I never heard Gran express a passion for numbers. Even when I was a kid, she didn't help me much with my maths homework, while she was kosher with all the other subjects. And wouldn't her magic be more scientific if she was an actuary? Even her career choice is somewhat strange. So Gran was working with big bucks and then chose to take the Franciscan vow of poverty? I'm crinkling my nose at the smell of fish in all this.

'If you really want to know about your grandmother, you need to talk to some of the higher-ups in the Society,' Bing says.

'Like I said, I was only into her work because of a technique I use for my special effects. It won me a BAFTA.'

The last time I was here he mentioned that award too. Reckon it's something he wants people to know about. Bing knocks on the door frame twice and leaves the room.

I hope Priya draws something out of Callander. No point in me even trying, 'cause he seems to want me in a hole, whether he believes the lies about me or not. Callander may be a powerful magician, but he lacks street smarts. When we were at Dunvegan Castle, I noticed that he doesn't much care for the politics of the Society, which is how people like Wedderburn leave him flat-footed. He's too decent for the chair he sits in. The reason Bryson Blackwood was a controversial secretary is he argued that power had nothing to do with good or evil, or morality, rather it was acquired to further one's own agenda. Of course, Blackwood left office under a cloud of scandal, but he still managed the second longest tenure in his office, which I see now is quite an achievement. Callander is blind to my circumstances, though. To him what matters more is bringing me to justice in the eyes of the law.

I close the bedroom door and strip off the clothes Connie gave me. They ain't my style anyways, though I'll admit they are super comfy. Then I grab my gear and dress up. She must have used posh people fabric conditioner because my clothes feel softer than they've ever been. And they smell well nice too. Her machine beats the handwashing I've always had to do in a bucket at our cara.

So, thinking back, it was when Gran sent me off on the quest to find a missing kid that I heard about the Tall Man for the first time. But who was he? There's a web around me, different strands that have woven themselves or been attached to me. It's now up to me to straighten them out – kind of like how I'd spend hours sorting out Gran's wool whenever Izwi had messed with her kit. The Tall Man had been interested in Siobhan's experiments with children, in stealing their vital essence – why? And how might they connect to Wedderburn and what he's doing? Wilson is the bridge between them that I can see.

There's frantic scratching on the door. I try to ignore it, but it only continues more ferocious-like. I open it and see my backpack in the corridor, with River beside it. She nudges me frantically.

'What is it, girl?'

She barks.

I rush over to the window and see another man in the cemetery with the two plainclothes cops. He looks up, right at me – I've been spotted by DI Balfour. He's in a grey trench coat, smoking a fag, and uses two fingers to point at me. Stupid of me to be pacing about like this, muttering to myself, when I should have been lying low. Balfour throws the cigarette down and breaks into a sprint, his colleagues following closely. Despite the riots going on in the city, he's still diverted resources to find me. I guess I don't have the cover I thought I did. Wonder who he's working for. Callander? Nah. It's bound to be Wedderburn. That's why the police were already onto me as a suspect. And if the Rooster is right, I'm a loose end that needs tying up.

I run out the room and grab my backpack, slinging it on as I go.

'Come on, River!'

I reach the stairs, sliding down the banister, and the front door crashes open as I land on the floor. Connie screams. Balfour lunges at me, but trips on the shoes near the door and stumbles. I'm running already, headed for the kitchen.

'Excuse me, this is a private residence,' Bing says, standing at the door to the dining room.

'Police. Out of the way,' Balfour shouts.

I'm already busting the kitchen door wide open, shooting through the conservatory at the back, but I lose crucial milliseconds unlocking the garden door. I get it open just in time, and am soon running over the wooden decking outside. I bump into a garden chair and it falls to the ground. River surges ahead of me, like she's the one facing jail time. This is a big fucking yard, and I'm startled by one of the cops running from the side garden towards me. Fucking semi-detached houses. He's young and fit, in his twenties, and he leaps to rugby tackle me. I barely manage an anemoic spell, hurling a wave of air at him, which knocks him off course and to the side. He rolls a couple of times and looks at me startled. Gotta be careful, I don't want to hurt them. The fuzz are the biggest, most ruthless and powerful gang in Edinburgh. Touch one of them and there's no coming back from that.

'Stop right there,' Balfour orders, but this restaurant ain't delivering.

I'm already running for the fence at the back. It's one of them tongue and groove wood-panelled fences, and River's over it in a flash. It's each vixen for herself it seems. I jump up and grab the top of the fence, where the creepers are growing. The wet leaves make it slippery, but I still manage to hoist myself up, using all my strength, and throw myself over it.

'Get her, you imbeciles!' shouts Balfour.

But I'm already up after my jarring landing, and running past the side of the neighbour's house, my backpack swishing behind me as I end up on Comiston Gardens. The odds of outsprinting the smoker Balfour are okayish, but the two fit lads he's with will catch me eventually. Fuck, I wish I had my bike. I run back onto the main road, and while they're still tailing me, I've gained a bit.

It's not enough, though.

I have no choice but to incant a powerful Promethean spell, set up behind me, and it explodes like a glitter bomb of white sparks – hope the brilliance will blind them for a bit.

'Don't fall for her little tricks. Keep going,' says Balfour, covering his eyes with one hand and running on. He's game like a pit bull, oozing raw aggression. That's why Rob warned me he was relentless. There's only one place I can think of in Morningside where I stand a chance of escaping them. I need to make it to Millar Crescent up the way.

Busting a gut, pretty much all my entrails, I run in the middle of the road, with flats on either side of me. Being chased by the law's not as fun as it used to be, when all you were looking at was a slap on the cheek. A wall's ahead of me, and I take a left, then have to jump over a back metal gate with a white plaque on it, reading 'Henderson Research Centre' in blue. I could go forward through the grounds, with lawn and trees up ahead. But instead I take the path to my right, which runs between the wall on one side and a brown brick building to the right. I swear there's people looking at me through the windows as I go. This is me at the Royal Edinburgh Hospital, the city's most important psychiatric hospital. I figure the sheer size of this place, with its many buildings, will work nicely as the haystack I want to hide in.

'There he is,' one of the cops shouts.

'She's a girl. Come on,' Balfour says. They are some way behind me as I make it to the car park.

To my right's the main exit leading back to Morningside. Another road leads up, around the back of the hospital complex. Or I could take a chance in one of the buildings nearby. Pot luck and all that. There's a tall, government office-looking building in front of me, with a sign saying it's the Kennedy Tower. I sprint across the road and go through its glass doors. There's a corridor to my left which joins the tower to the other buildings, so I run there instead of going up. The downside is it has windows, so Balfour and his lot spot me running and immediately come after me there.

I go past a porter wheeling a patient.

'Hey, you're not allowed to run in here,' he says.

'Sorry!'

Can't stop now. The next thing I hear is a crash, as the policemen bundle over him to get to me, but I'm already gone. I shove past two nurses coming down the corridor, take a left and then an immediate right. I pass by signs pointing to different wards and investigation rooms. X-ray, phlebotomy, that sort of thing. 'No smoking' signs. There's so many rats wandering the corridors. The types which have stopped fearing people, so you have to step out of the way for them. Mental health crisis posters. I run past it all without a clue where I'm going, until I notice a different car park outside by a roundabout. I take the door leading out there and find two dumpsters. I flip open the lid of the brown one and jump inside. They can comb the whole hospital if they fancy, while I wait it out here. I hope that bowfin smell doesn't ruin my clean clothes.

XVIII

There's great mobile reception in the bin, so I've managed to explain my plight to Priya. She seems to be finding the whole thing hilarious and has promised me a hot shower when this all blows over. I ask her to arrange transport and send her a location for us to meet. Then I hear footsteps outside and my heart leaps into my mouth.

'She could be anywhere, guv,' the cop says.

'We need backup. I want this entire place combed from top to bottom,' Balfour says.

'Everyone else is tied up with the riots.'

'This is a murder investigation,' Balfour complains. 'Let's check these bins.'

I sit very still, careful not to make a sound. Easier said than done the way my hands are shaking, and given the plastic bags in here. I hold my breath.

'Over there. The damned fox,' one of the cops says.

I hear the sound of boots pounding on the tar as they run after the fox, wherever she is. I wait a couple of seconds till they're out of earshot, then open the lid ever so slightly. I can see them rounding the three-storey building. This is my chance. I climb out of the bin and land quietly on the ground.

There's patients looking out the many windows on either side and I give them a wave. A couple of them wave back. Then I turn and go back into the building.

That was close. I move briskly and carefully, listening for any sign the cops might have spotted me again. Soon enough, I'm back out onto the streets, headed for my rendezvous with Priya.

After I learnt about the Tall Man, I heard there was someone else with the same MO. A fella going by the moniker 'The One Above All'. Pretty arrogant. In the Marvelverse, that's the nameless entity responsible for all life across the multiverse. But real life isn't some comic book malarkey. This figure was so dreadful that the ghost of Sir George MacKenzie of Rosehaugh warned me of its return, just before I cast his soul into the Other Place. He was the reason behind some students from the Edinburgh Ordinary School for Boys becoming sick.

If I knew then what I know now, I'd not have stopped him . . . well, I'd still have saved Max Wu, but not all the others. I feel so tiny in the face of someone named The One Above All, but I've dealt with bullies before. The question is why Sir George MacKenzie felt the need to prevent his supposed return to this realm. Nothing fits together. Whoever sold me this puzzle's mixed up the wrong pieces in the wrong box.

All rivers run to the sea.

Everything comes to a point.

I'm turning it all over in my head still when I meet up with Priya near the Carlton Cricket Club, whose grounds are eerily quiet in the dark. The grass there's overgrown, not having been tended to in a long time. But you can still make out the empty patch in the middle, where the flat pitch resists invasion. The clouds above are breaking, streaks of moonlight pouring through the rents. It's a full moon tonight. My boots splash a puddle of water. The wall on the other side of the road has an old parking meter – a box waiting for payment from traffic which never comes.

Priya's waiting by the corner of the West Grange Gardens, the flats in the area. It's been a while since I did a job out here. Ghostalking, not burglaring. She's with an older woman, who's wearing a straw hat and overalls. She also has an old donkey and a two-wheeled wooden cart that looks like it's seen better days.

'This the girl you're helping, Priya?' the woman asks as I approach. 'I'll take half now and the other half when you get back. If anything happens to my Benjamin, then you're paying for him too. Deal?'

'Benjamin's the donkey,' Priya says, filling me in.

'I don't like the way certain people have been eyeing him lately. Like he's meant for the pot, not labouring. That doesn't sit well with me at all. Ben's a much loved and respected member of staff in the Groundskeepers' Department at the Edinburgh School. Him and me have been working together for . . . how long now? Near enough twenty years, and I've never heard him take a sick day once. Oops, I've just told a lie there. May Jehovah strike me down. He did fall sick once, when he heard Hearts had won the league. Since then, I've stopped playing him football on the radio. Now *The Archers*, he never misses an episode.'

'Ropa, you've met Mrs Guthrie before, haven't you?'

I nod and greet her. We first met when she saved us from death by topiary plant, when I'd gone to the Edinburgh School for the first time. She's the school's groundskeeper and I'm surprised Priya would call on her like this for a favour. Then again, in this day and age it pays to be in the good books of a healer, in case you need their services down the line. Even in this cold weather Mrs Guthrie has her sleeves rolled up, revealing well-toned arms.

'I've heard you're in a spot of bother,' she says in her husky voice.

'Something like that,' I reply.

'Well, stop gawking and hop on board. What are you waiting for – a red carpet? I hope you know where we're going. And Priyanka Kapoor, you rouse a lady your mother's age out of bed this late at night and take her gallivanting, the least you can do is bring her a drink.'

'You're more my grandmother's age, but I've got your cider, so stop nagging me.' Priya pretends to be annoyed as she brings out a bottle of Old Rosie. It's one of those old-fashioned types of bottles, which have a tiny handle on the neck. Mrs Guthrie spits a wad of chewing tobacco onto the ground.

'Now you're talking,' she says. 'Warm up my old bones, because my husband's cooler than a popsicle on a February morning.'

'That's because he's dead.'

'Doesn't make it any less true, hen. Rest his soul, he was too good for this world.'

I go round the back of the cart, which is open without any sort of gate – seatbelts and airbags, anyone? It's better than I could have hoped for, since I don't fancy walking anywhere else tonight. My feet already hurt after all that running. There's a couple of sacks back there and some produce – the sort of thing people are rioting for in the streets. Curiously, she also has several potted plants at the front of the cart, including a rather large century plant – the broad succulent with a hell of a lot of thorns. Then hawthorn and firethorn. Holly too. I wonder if she was gardening at night, or she had the cart loaded for a run tomorrow and couldn't be arsed with emptying it. Still, beggars can't be choosers.

They took Gran's knitting needles.

For some reason that's suddenly pissing me off more than the fact they took her life. This isn't logical, but something from my gut. Feels like a right violation they should have done it.

I need to work out the piece holding everything together . . .

'Did you talk to Callander about Gran and my father?' I check with Priya.

'I think he's suspicious, since he cautioned me against helping you. He said the road we're on is paved with good intentions.'

'But what did he tell you?'

'That I must capture you with haste and take you to the Library dungeon.'

So, she didn't get anything useful out of Callander. Just more silence, more secrets. What is it, then? The Tall Man. The Fairy Flag – its power on the full moon. Gran's knitting needles. The night is coalescing into something new and sinister.

There's one other figure lurking in the shadows. The quietest voice in the room. Born with an innate understanding of power and able to pull strings from the shadows. I first heard the name on the roof of Dunvegan Castle, when I was pursuing the person who murdered Sneddon. True power doesn't announce itself with pomp and ceremony. It sits in the background. Self-made. Silently taking stock of events and shifting them to its own advantage.

This is the menacing figure of the Black Lord.

There's a certain kind of loyalty which can't be bought. That's why Wedderburn will stop at nothing to win his master's approval. I hit yet another brick wall when I asked people who they thought the Black Lord was. He had a minion with a Yorkshire accent going about the country buying magical manuscripts, clearly searching for something. He is the puppeteer and the rest of us are mere playthings – at best we might be promoted to pawns in his service. But who could this person be who has such great ability to bend people to his will? Not by force but by something more dangerous: hope. That, or the idea that any evil committed in his service is for the greater good. This was the special ability Alexander the Great had too, or, say, the Prophet Muhammad, peace and blessings be upon him, or Napoleon, or Martin Luther King. Any of these great men from the past who managed to bring people together, persuading them to sacrifice their own puny lives towards the goal of something more important.

For a brief time, I thought Lord Samarasinghe might be the Black Lord, but he laughed at me for making these assumptions. What the Sorcerer Royal knows, he keeps close to his chest. And he's proven he's no friend of mine.

But I realize now, behind all the trouble I've encountered

with regards to Scottish magic, there's been this constant, invisible hand pushing us all towards certain conclusions.

Priya pulls herself up onto the cart, then leans down to pick up her wheelchair. She turns round and folds it, before laying it flat atop the sacks in the back of the wagon. Then she shifts her bum a bit to make herself comfortable on the edge.

'Are you going to tell us where we're going, lassie?' Mrs Guthrie asks, sounding somewhat impatient. 'I've got work to do in the morning.'

'Gorebridge,' I reply absent-mindedly, 'cause an idea is growing inside of my head. I have to follow the threads to a nexus point. *The spirit who possessed Sophie. Wilson.*

The Tall Man.

The One Above All.

The Black Lord.

'All this is with one goal in mind, Priya,' I say, letting the words linger in the air a while. 'It's clear Wedderburn and his lot intend to bring someone back into this world. That's why they were studying Vodou, and my father's papers. And could be why they need the Fairy Flag. The question is who, and why.'

'No sane Scottish magician would mess with those sorts of powers,' Mrs Guthrie chimes in. 'There's a reason scientific magic limits itself to the explainable and knowable, unlike other practices around the world. Magic is supposed to be boring. The step by step gathering of evidence and formulation of spells with firm scientific backing.'

'You sound like an Edinburgh boy,' Priya jibes.

'I should. Been there long enough, haven't I?' Mrs Guthrie replies.

'And who is your new headteacher?' I ask.

She turns back and laughs, showing her tobacco-stained teeth. Then she looks forward, urging Benjamin on.

'Wait just a minute,' I say.

'Whatever for?'

'Just wait.'

We're there for another five minutes before spotting a dark object running through the street. It looks like a small dog, panting as it nears us, but it's actually River, coming back after evading the police. She stops in front of me, tongue sticking out – it could almost be a silly smile she's wearing.

'Well done, girl. Come on up, we've got to go.' I hold my arms out and she leaps into my lap. From there, I guide her into the cart. 'Stay away from Mrs Guthrie's prickly plants.'

'How did she know to find you here?' Priya says.

'She followed my scent.'

'It is rather strong tonight, you having been in a bin and all.' Priya and Mrs Guthrie laugh while I just kiss my teeth.

'Right, all aboard the Benjamin Express then. Ladies and foxes, buckle up your seatbelts, this is going to be a bumpy ride,' Mrs Guthrie announces.

We drive through the empty streets, heading up on Blackford Avenue. Mrs Guthrie has to guide one wheel onto the pavement where a wall has collapsed, leaving debris in the road. The houses here used to be posh back in the day. Now they're poorly maintained shadows of their former affluence. Hedges overgrown, potholes and leaves littering the way.

'The Edinburgh School has been placed under special measures, given the situation with Wedderburn. We're dealing with a lot of angry parents at the moment. A few donors have withdrawn funding.'

'They must be outraged by what he did,' Priya replies.

'Oh no, not at all. They're angry he's no longer at the school. The rector was very popular with parents, patrons, pupils and alumni alike. There's a lot of sentiment that he was treated unfairly. The head of the Edinburgh School placed in jail like a common criminal? They say the very worst they should have done was put him under house arrest and taken his word as bond. He is a gentleman, after all. Admittedly, the school's not the same without him. Standards are already slipping, despite the staff rallying and doing the best they can. He was a brilliant educator; you can't take that away from him.'

I'm stunned that, after everything, there's still people who'd want special treatment for Montgomery Wedderburn. It's jarring moments like these when you realize that however you might view a situation, there's always someone else who sees the opposite. Wedderburn did cause a scandal, though, and that's not good for the school's standing. They would rather have the affair just swept under the rug, like they do for all posh folks. Nothing to see here.

The cart hits a rough patch on the road, sending shock waves up my tailbone.

There's bright flashes of light coming from the city. Me and Priya see them because we're facing away from the direction of travel. Gets me wondering why Priya trusts Mrs Guthrie at a time like this.

'So how do you two know each other?' I ask.

'Conferences. Mrs Guthrie has an encyclopaedic knowledge of indigenous herbs and natural supplements. She occasionally supplies produce to Our Lady of Mysterious Ailments too, especially in the winter. The heated greenhouses at the school are far superior to the ones we've got at the clinic.'

'Nothing I learnt from no books either,' Mrs Guthrie says loudly from the front. 'I did attend the Doric School, but everything I know about plants was passed down to me from my own grandmother, at her kitchen table in Drumnadrochit. And in case you were wondering, yes, I have seen Nessie, and, no, I didn't photograph her. It was none of my business.'

Don't know if it's the cider, but Mrs Guthrie does ramble on a wee bit. It seems she's enjoying our company, though, despite her occasional grumbling. I'm surprised by how fast we're moving too. Benjamin the donkey doesn't appear all that strong, but right now he's moving at a fair clip. Faster than any donkey has the right to. I keep my left hand on the side of the cart, just so I don't fall out. It's not the most comfortable ride.

'What about the staff – what do they think of Wedderburn?'

'They mostly fear him. He can make or break your career if you cross him. He might be sweet as blueberry pie to the parents, but trust me, if you heard him berating the staff in his office, you wouldn't like it.'

These magicians are so two-faced. They smile at you, while hiding a dagger behind their backs. That's why I appreciate Cockburn, despite her hating me. At least she's honest. We pass by the University of Edinburgh's King's Buildings, just off the West Mains Road. It's the campus where they do science and engineering. They also have the Royal Observatory nearby, where I once helped an astronomer. He believed that by making observations of the sky, we could inadvertently draw beings from a different part of the universe, and that an alien ghost had entered the telescope. It was wreaking havoc with their finely tuned experiments and they wanted a stop to it. It turned out there *was* a ghost messing about, but it wasn't from outer space. Rather, the now deceased amateur astronomer Susan Ehrman was angry with the fellows of the Royal Observatory for allegedly stealing her discovery of a planet-killer-sized asteroid, which was crossing Earth's orbit. I managed to bargain with her and a correction was made, acknowledging her as the discoverer of 134396, which no one else seems to know or care about anyway.

We pass some looters pushing wheelbarrows as we turn onto Mayfield Road. There's a man carrying a sixty-inch flat-screen TV on his head. Another with a fully loaded beer fridge on his back. Several have bags of rice, potatoes, boxes of canned food. Seems like a free-for-all in town.

'I'll swap you this laptop for your donkey,' a man shouts.

'All you'll get off me is a boot up the alimentary canal,' Mrs Guthrie replies.

'Give us a lift, darling.'

A couple try to chase after our cart, hoping to divert us, but Benjamin's much too fast for them. Things are really getting ugly in the city. I confess, part of me wishes I was in there for the jamboree. Reckon members of the Clan will be out and about, getting their hands on whatever they can. When civilization burns, the least you can do is warm your hands off the fire.

Mrs Guthrie keeps her donkey at a fair trot, taking us through Cameron Toll.

'Are you okay, Ropa?' Priya asks.

'I'm fine.'

She takes my hand. Stars sparkle brightly where the clouds have broken. Moonbeams and cosmic dust. The cart bumps along with each step Benjamin takes, and Priya doesn't say anything for a while. The tar glistens, reflecting the lights. I've been a wee bit of a dick to Priya many times, but she's still here. Still my best friend. Travelling backwards, we see the city recede from view gradually and gently. Tree stumps and broken windows. It's different from going forwards, where everything seems to leap towards you.

Because of Lord Samarasinghe's intervention, the A7's pretty peaceful, even this late at night. There have been no new reported highway robberies or kidnappings from here in a while. It's as though the highwaymen decided this patch of road wasn't worth the risk. I shudder at the memory of their screams.

'Come over,' Priya says.

I shuffle carefully to the right side of the cart where she is. She puts her arm around me and I rest my head on her shoulder. *Let me close my eyes.* I feel safe with her – she's won my trust completely. Gran once told me the universe has a way of balancing things out. That it behaves in ways alien to us, because we are tiny insects trapped in amber, unable to experience the richness of the ultimate reality. Our bodies and our senses can't really make out what truly is. Our ways of understanding the world are crude at best. But the universe is like those old-fashioned balancing scales. I joked that it was because she was a Libra. 'It gives with one hand and takes away with the other. The problem is not with the balance, it's that our minds aren't trained to be grateful for what we're given. Instead, we obsess about what's been taken away.' Those were her words to me. And I feel grateful now that Priya was given to me.

'You remember the first words you said to me when we met in the Library?' I ask. 'You were hanging upside down on the ceiling, reading.'

'I saw you walk right underneath me. Grim-faced lassie with green dreadlocks and black lipstick.'

'The hair's all gone now.'

'The lipstick's still there.'

'You said to me, "You're Melsie Mhondoro's grandkid, aren't you?"'

'So I did. What an odd way to start a conversation,' Priya replies, rubbing my back. 'I'll tell you why. Your grandmother was a good friend of my mother's. Mum was going to a retreat on the Isle of Iona on the day you and I met, and we were having a chat because I wouldn't see her for a couple of weeks. I was having boyfriend trouble – you know, the usual – and generally bollocksing up my housemanship. But it was kind of strange, because my mum listened to my moaning, then before she left, she said, "If you meet a weird girl today, that's my friend Melsie Mhondoro's granddaughter. Look after her." And then I bumped into you.'

'Hey, I'm not weird.' I laugh and nudge her head with mine.

'I knew it was you. And good thing I liked you too, because I wouldn't have bothered if you were a bawbag.'

Another thread leading to my grandmother, in a universe of infinite chance. How many trillions of things had to happen for this moment to be? Priya is my gift from Gran, it seems. Just as she asked Rob to look out for me too. She didn't leave me by myself. But does that mean she knew she was going, even as I shouted at her in the morning? It seems she didn't love me any less for my flaws.

'Thank you for being my friend,' I say to Priya.

'Don't be silly,' she replies, rubbing her head against mine. Her hair feels nice and soft.

We're about to go the lion's den, and there's no one I'd trust more to have by my side.

XIX

It feels like all of Gorebridge is asleep tonight as we pass through the village at a trot. The madness and orgy of violence in Edinburgh doesn't seem to have reached here yet. I wonder how long that will remain the case. But for now, I have to focus on the job at hand. I tell Priya we're going to a place called Arniston House, to stop Wedderburn doing whatever it is he's planning, and to retrieve the Fairy Flag. It's being used to create an imbalance in the harmony between our world and the everyThere. The two realms are like conjoined twins, distinct yet separate. There can be no life without death. And without life, death is meaningless. A yang without a yin is nothing.

'Are you sure they'll be here?' Priya asks.

'The Tall Man, the One Above All, the Black Lord – it all leads to this place. I was here a few days ago and I had to perform an exorcism on a ghost who seemed more tethered to this world than any I've ever seen before. Something very wrong is happening here, and I've only just twigged how it connects to Wedderburn and the others,' I reply.

'Lassies, we've made it to Gorebridge, as requested. This is as far as me and Benjamin go,' Mrs Guthrie announces, drawing the cart to a halt at the crossroads. 'Whatever you do from here on is up to you.'

'We may need you,' I say.

'I'm not messing with any of this, lassie. You asked me to drive you about like a taxi and I've done that. But you can't ask any more of me. I have a donkey and a cat to think about.' Mrs Guthrie takes a glug of cider and wipes her mouth with the back of her hand.

'Will you wait for us at least?' Priya asks.

'Aye, till the first sign of dawn and no longer, and only because I still want paying.'

I jump off the back of the cart and land on the tarred road. Craven they are, these Scottish magicians. I wouldn't expect anything more anyway. That's how it's always been since I first started fooling with them. Priya is an exception, Callander another. The rest seem to prefer comfort over all else. They've traded purpose and honour for convenience. I'm glad I'm not one of them. River's got more balls than the lot of them at the Society and she's a vixen.

She jumps down too and runs off into a hedge to explore.

Priya's fiddling with her wheelchair, popping it open again. She places it on the ground, perpendicular to the cart. 'Hold it steady,' she says, and I place my hand on the chair. She reaches out with her right hand, places it on my shoulder, and using the left, lifts herself off the cart, then swings over, plonking herself in the chair with a wee grunt. She removes the brake on it and rides over my foot.

'Feel free to break my toes anytime,' I say.

'Sorry, biped,' she replies.

We set off down the dark road. A cloud has covered the moon, which suits me nicely. On this quiet night, my footsteps seem to make too much noise, try as I may to tread lightly. We go past a solitary little cottage on the left, whose lights are turned off. Hedges run either side of us and I'm startled by the sound of a cow mooing. No idea where it's coming from. Otherwise, the night is silent. No crickets or insects making noise. Nor owls hooting in the trees abounding.

'I don't get it; they took Gran's knitting needles and nothing else.'

'That's so odd, why would they do that?' Priya muses. 'Unless the needles are an artefact. No. Maybe. Hmm. That would be a first.'

I touch the scarf around my neck and Priya sees it.

'Magical knitwear!' she exclaims. 'Fucking fabulous.'

'Callander gave me this one of the first times I met him. I thought it was just a stupid hand-me-down. Sorry, Cruickshank.' The scarf doesn't stir. It's immune to pettiness like that. 'What I didn't realize at the time is that this was my grandmother's handiwork. The scarf's saved me from a few hairy situations.'

'I would know, I was there for half of them.'

'So Callander was merely returning something that had been given, or loaned, to him.'

'Or passing on something that had once been made for him, now he doesn't need it anymore. You've seen how powerful he is. He doesn't need a magic scarf protecting him.'

I wonder what spells or charms are in the knitted items Gran gave away so freely to our neighbours in Hermiston Slum. It's not like they've all got ninja scarves, but if she could insert magic into their knitwear, what powers did she give them? I know Rob's never been to gaol since he met Gran. Did he just become a savvier crook, or does some of his success have to do with those gloves he loves so much? Whatever those knitting needles can create, they were worth killing for.

'If we find those needles with Wedderburn's people, it places them without doubt at the caravan. That and the drawing of what I thought was an "I" and a stick man on the ceiling of it. It was similar to what we saw in Siobhan Kavanagh's flat too in the Old Town. The person who drew those markings was also at my caravan.'

'I'll be glad when all this is done and you can take your old job back.'

I tell Priya we need to be quiet now and leave the main road. Don't know if anyone's guarding the house's main gate, but it would be dumb going through there. My burglar instincts kick in. Yet another gift from Gran via Rob. Only now I'm not using them to steal people's shit, but hopefully to take back what belongs to me, and what belongs to Scottish magic. Those knitting needles are my inheritance as much as the Fairy Flag is Scotland's.

'Let's cut through the woods,' I say, spotting a gap leading into a field.

River catches up with us as we enter. The grass is rather long and I'm struggling tramping through it. I notice Priya's having a shit time with it too, so I go back and help her out. It's hard work pushing the chair on this uneven grass, which is also boggy. We soldier on, headed for the tree line. There's a strange mist sitting low on the ground and this thickens the further in we go. I could swear it makes pushing Priya's chair that much harder.

'This is definitely giving me weird vibes,' she says.

'Glad I'm not the only one.'

River's sticking close to us and not wandering off as she tends to do sometimes. I can sense her unease, walking through the mist which comes up to her chest. It's not a steady mist, rather it roils and churns, almost like boiling water.

The further in we go, the higher it becomes, first swallowing up River, then Priya, and finally me, until we're all fully immersed.

'I swear you look like a ghost,' Priya says when she turns to check me out. She lifts her hands up and swishes them through the foggy air. Her arms appear to be covered in ash. Even the clothes she's wearing have lost colour, kinda like it seeped out during the wash. I'm getting the vibe of the everyThere again, but it's not supposed to be visible in our world like this.

The air smells like compost too. Dead things which have been rotting for ages seem to have come up again. I feel a heaviness in my limbs. This oppressive atmosphere lends itself to a certain melancholy, a lethargy that infects every fibre of my being.

'I'm not feeling too good right now,' says Priya.

'That's because the living aren't supposed to visit the everyThere.'

'It's like I want to stop breathing. I have to remind myself to inhale and exhale.'

'You've hit the wall. Keep on doing that – eventually it will pass.'

I check out River, who's still moving cautiously, but seems to be coping with it better than Priya, which is strange, since entering the Library of the Dead causes her issues. It's not quite the same thing, though. The Library entrance is a portal. This is entering an existential dread and encountering your own mortality – the certainty that one day you will die.

The three of us make it to the trees undetected, which is great.

Unfortunately, the fog works both ways – they can't see us but we can't see them neither, so we've got to be careful.

I slap Priya on the cheek hard and she gasps, taking in a huge breath of air.

'Don't. Forget. To. Breathe. The dead don't need oxygen, but you do.'

'You didn't have to hit me that hard,' she complains.

'You're welcome,' I reply.

It's difficult to get my bearings in here, but I reckon Arniston House is far off somewhere to the right. There's a bright red glow coming from there, and it doesn't look like a fire, the way it paints the fog. But there's one stop we need to make before that. How to find the little cottage in the woods is the tricky part.

'If we come to the main drive to the house then I hope I can guide us from there.'

It's slow progress through this woodland, where the trees pop up in front of us from nowhere. I can only hope I'm not taking us in circles. I stop, spotting someone carrying a lamp up ahead. They are going right, which is where Arniston House should be. I place my fingers on Priya's lips. At least now I have a better idea of where the bloody road is. Once the person is gone, we move past the grand lime trees and go across, finding another wee gap that takes us deeper into the woodlands which make up most of this estate.

I have to risk it, so I pull out my phone and open the compass app. It's not working. The electronic needle goes round in circles, unable to find true north – must be the everyThere affecting it. The house and Edinburgh are north of us, so Gorebridge is east. The road we've come off south. Okay, I can work with that. It means to get to the cottage, I have to go west-northish.

'You sure you know where we're going?' Priya asks.

'Without a fucking doubt.'

It's fifty-fifty, which is good odds in my life. *Keep going.* Checking the compass, which is still not working, I nearly walk into a ditch, but Priya stops me sharpish and saves the day. Where the hell is River? I look around and can't see anything. Oh, there she is, right beside me. Bloody hell, I can't even see my own boots. *Keep going.* There's an old fence post, yeah, I saw that last time. And then we're deep inside the woods, where the stone cottage with the slate roof is. The candlelight through the windows guides us there.

We wait a bit. I think I can hear Una weeping, a soft help-less cry, and wonder what's going on here. I bang on the door fierce, like I was a bobby.

'Coming, my lord,' Wilfred says from within.

He opens the door and looks startled to see me and Priya there.

'No, please, you're not meant to be here,' he says. 'I have to tell the viscount. No one's allowed except for the others.'

'Which others? Who else is here?' Priya asks.

Wilfred tries to close the door on us, but Priya holds it just in time. He pushes hard, but he's no match for the strength in her arm. Finally, she flings it open and the old man staggers back. We push inside and shut the door after River, then I lock it just in case. Wilfred has fear written all over his face. That and a guilty expression. He wrings his hands and curses.

Una's sat in their broken chair, weeping.

There's a roaring fire going in the fireplace, but the room's freezing cold still. It's as if the everyThere's vapour devours the heat before it has the chance to warm up the place. The windows have a film of ice on them.

I look around and immediately know what's missing, panic rising up inside of me.

'Una, where's Sophie?'

'Who's Sophie?' Priya asks.

'He said she'll be okay. We've got to have faith,' Wilfred says. 'They've looked after our family for six generations and they've never once let us down.'

'I don't want to give that man my daughter. I've seen the way he looks at her, like a lamb at market.' Una sobs and then blows her nose using the hem of her T-shirt.

'Her grandfather wouldn't let anyone harm a hair on her wee head,' Wilfred says.

'Who do you mean?' I ask, seeking confirmation.

'Wilson isn't my father. Can't you see he's not even your brother anymore? I don't know what he's become.'

'I won't hear those words under my roof. My brother is back, and we should be thankful for it. The master brought him home.'

'Look at what they did to him. You saw it with your own eyes. They told him he was going to Edinburgh for a new job as a butler to a wealthy family, and he comes back twenty years later with bits missing off him. That's not right at all.'

'Nonsense.'

'I want my little girl back.'

I first met Wilson, who, as I'd begun to suspect, is Wilfred's brother and Sophie's grandfather, in a house of horrors called Arthur Lodge in Edinburgh. Back then he was prisoner to a brounie that was tied to the house. A wicked spirit which took delight in torturing him. I'd always assumed he was enticed into the house, but it sounds like Viscount Mieville actually took him there. And now they've brought him back, with his first act being to kidnap his granddaughter. Just like the children who used to be lured into the house and abducted, before being sold on to the Midnight Milkman.

'Ropa, what's going on? Who's Sophie?'

'We need to go right now, Priya. I'll explain on the way,' I say. 'Una, come with us. I'm going to need you if you want your daughter back safely.'

'She's not going anywhere,' Wilfred says, holding her down.

I pull out my dagger and flash steel in the candlelight.

'If you stop her, or leave this cottage for any reason at all, I'm going to stick this through your ribcage right into that rotten heart of yours.' I bloody well mean it too.

Wilfred's eyes widen. He seems to be weighing his options – a knife through the heart or the wrath of his master. But I know cowards like him. He's no different to his brother Wilson. Slowly he walks over to the chair and sits down, and I sheathe my dagger. Una's hesitant. She takes a look at Wilfred, his furious eyes boring into her.

'Don't look at him, look at me. Take us to Arniston House.'

We step back outside, Una with us, and she locks her uncle inside, taking the key. Despite the fog, she then walks with the confidence of someone who knows every inch of this place like the back of her hand. She moves so briskly I have to ask her to slow down.

'The experiments with children Siobhan Kavanagh was doing were all leading to this,' I start explaining to Priya, but she cuts me off.

'If you're going to bring someone back, you need a vital essence and that's strongest and most unadulterated in children. And like doing an organ transplant, it requires someone close to that person,' Priya says. 'But Sophie is just the servant's kid. Surely using her won't work? I mean, you could use the energy, but at best you could only create a temporary bond. That's why Gray's experiments with his intromissioner during the Great War failed. It can't be done like that.'

'Una, who's the girl's father?' I ask.

She draws to a halt, stopping dead in the middle of the path. Her head's hung down, almost as though she's ashamed. She puts both hands to her heart, the strain evident in her bearing.

'I might be plain, but the viscount has needs, like all men do,' she replies, rushing her words. 'Started on me when I was a little girl, and my father would take me to him. It didn't use to happen all the time, mind. Things got out of hand. Anyway, she's my daughter, not his.'

It's a story as old as time. The lords who can't keep their hands off the staff. But this time it's worse, knowing Wilson offered his own daughter up for the viscount to have his way. Maybe he hoped that somehow he could use that relationship to gain a foothold in the master's house. But no servant like him could ever become father-in-law to his master. These aristocrats take their bloodlines pretty damn serious, because it's how they transmit land and wealth. Yes, they may have the occasional bastard, but they're heartless enough not to care. After all, he was happy enough to have her live in this run-down cottage while he enjoyed the luxury of a grand country house. Wanker.

'The same energy runs in families. It's in the blood,' Priya says. 'Your daughter could be in grave danger, Una, depending on who they want to bring back.'

'That's why I need you to get us inside the mansion,' I add. 'It's nearly three in the morning. That's the witching hour, when the dead are at their most powerful in this realm. And under the full moon, these lunatics will run their experiment. We've got to stop them.'

'I'll do anything to help.'

We push forward through the woods with an increased sense of urgency. I won't fail Sophie like I failed my gran, and Gary, and Sneddon. I swear on my life.

'I'm calling in Callander. Sorry, Ropa, I should have done this ages ago. There's no way the two of us can pull this off,' Priya says, whipping out her phone. 'The lassie's life is at stake.'

If Callander comes and things go south, I might end up in jail anyways, especially if I can't prove Wedderburn's lot were in the caravan. My freedom isn't worth Sophie's life, though. This is bigger than me now.

'Call him already,' I say.

'Fuck,' Priya replies.

'What?'

'I've got no signal.'

I check my phone too and see there's zero bars, so wave it about in the sky. Still nothing.

'You need to go to Gorebridge for a signal,' Una says.

'Is there a landline?' I ask.

'Does this look like Edinburgh to you?' she asks with a mocking laugh. 'We have to go to town for post too. When the power lines are down, we can go months before they fix them.'

The joys of the countryside. We don't have time to go there, and we can't get through to Callander, which means we have to stick with the plan. Arniston House looms large in the fog as we approach, still hidden behind the trees. We can't see the building proper, some black mist has shrouded it, following the contours of the building. It's as though darkness has been drawn to the place. The imposing main structure, with its large windows looking out over the countryside, has corridors leading to outbuildings in a sort of U-shape. Kinda like a cow with huge horns. But the house is the focal point, where the blackness is concentrated.

'From what you've seen, which part of the building are they using?'

'The old library upstairs, not the new one,' Una says. 'There're hidden passageways, I can tell you where to find them. They were built by James Dundas. He liked to move around unseen and spy on the family, as well as check out the young maids bathing. All you need to do is make it to the first floor and they'll take you to the top.'

'Okay then, that's where we'll go. But first, we have to take care of something,' I say. 'Where's the car park?'

'Which one?'

'Wherever their vehicles are.'

Sticking to the tree line, Una leads us to some old stables and outbuildings on the east wing, where four electric vehicles are parked outside. Two of them are sedans, one's a minivan, and the other is one of those tiny smart cars. I crouch and observe, and am nearly about to go over to them when a hooded figure emerges, carrying a bright burning lamp. It's hard to make out a face, but they look like a monk or something in their hood. It's downright weird, like this lot have stopped being scientific magicians and are now definitely a cult.

The hooded figure raises the lamp high and looks around. I'm frozen in place. We're less likely to be spotted if we appear to be part of the shadowy landscape. When the figure is satisfied all's clear, they open the boot of one of the sedans and lift something out – I can't see what. Then they shut it again and start walking away, feet crunching on the gravel.

'Stay here,' I say.

I move as silent as I can, keeping low and in the shadows. It's a short way to the first electric sedan. I pull out my dagger and slash the front tyre. It hisses as it deflates, and I'm wishing it could be quieter, but there's not much I can do about that. The sooner this is done, the better. Question is, do I do them one at a time, which'll take longer, or all at once, noise be damned? I pick the latter. I do the back tyre next, then move to the left-hand side of the car. No lie, it's pretty damned satisfying. Nothing like a bit of property damage to set the pulse racing. Part of me wishes I could nick the batteries too. They're worth a fortune on the black market. Old habits die hard. I crouch-walk around all the cars, making sure every single tyre has been bust, before I make a wee retreat back to Priya and Una.

'Great thinking,' Priya says. 'The next part's yours, Una. Find us a way in without us getting caught.'

'Promise me you'll take Sophie away with you when this is done,' Una says.

'We're not leaving you behind either. Come with us to Edinburgh. There's nothing for you here,' Priya replies.

'I can't leave. This place is all I know. I've hardly ever been to Gorebridge even, let alone Edinburgh. I just see the city lights from afar and wonder. I don't have no book learning or anything like that.'

'They'll bloody murder you if you stay. These are serious bastards and there's no limit to what they're prepared to do. You've got to come with us, understand?' I say.

She nods hesitantly and I'm relieved. An entire life lived here, in this prison, with her uncle and parts of it with her father. It's like one of them crazy stories you hear about men who abduct and hide kids in their basements till they're all grown up. Only here, the six thousand acres of this estate are that basement. I've had to learn to survive in Edinburgh. What can Una do when she's lived her whole life in service here? She might not have gone to school, but neither have I, so she'll be in good company.

Una leads us around the back of the building. It looks like there's renovations being done on this wing. We enter the dreadful black fog. If the winter's night was cold before, this is an ice bucket over the head – it takes your breath away. From there we carry on, keeping tight to the building so we pass underneath the windows. There's steps leading up into what looks like a living room, which would fit a hundred of my caravans in it I imagine. We can barely see the lawns beyond for the thickness of the fog. An ominous gong chimes from inside.

'We need to hurry,' I hiss.

'Incredible thermophasic shifts,' Priya says. 'There's some kind of increase in the agitative threshold round about here, and it's all flowing towards the house. Almost as if ley lines from the surrounding countryside have been bent by some brute force into this artificial nexus point.'

When we reach a side entrance to the newer part of the mansion, Una takes out a bunch of keys and tries them one after the other.

'Once we're inside, we'll need a massive diversion. Una, how much wood panelling is there?' I ask.

'It's everywhere,' she replies.

'Priya, you're on arson duty. I want you to torch everything from the ground floor up,' I say. 'Once we make it to the first floor through the hidden passageway, set the main staircase on fire too, so they can't get down to the ground floor. Tonight we're going in with flamethrowers, like Johnny Storm's throwing a rave.'

'Are you sure? This place is over three hundred years old . . . And Jomo should be somewhere about, too.'

I shrug. 'I'm counting on that. Jomo's made his bed and I hope he wets himself.'

Short of a blazing fire, I don't see any other way of stalling the madness happening inside. These occultists can burn for all I care. Every single one of them. But if that doesn't work, then I imagine they'll have to focus on trying to save the precious building. Which means we won't have a swarm of magicians coming after us.

We come into a small room filled with old furniture and some sculptures.

'That corridor leads to the new library on the ground floor. From there you can go to any part of the building,' Una says in a shaky voice. She's scared. I should be too, but I'm too miffed and the blood's pumping through my veins. She tells us where to find the entrance to the secret passageway on the first floor.

'Wait for us by the lime trees on the drive,' I say. 'We'll come find you once we've picked up Sophie.'

'We're so fucked,' Priya mumbles, then she looks at me and gives a mad grin. 'I love it.'

I swear she's proper mad. She seems to enjoy these situations a bit too much for my liking. We go down the bare corridor and open the door into the library. The carpet on the floor in there dampens our footsteps. Shelves are stacked with leather-bound books from floor to ceiling. It's pretty impressive to look at. These aristocrats have amassed a large private collection of first edition magical texts. Priya's looking as if she has doubts about burning them, and so I start it for her.

'Spark of Prometheus,' I incant, and a fizzing white spark darts across the room towards the far shelf.

'Someone's not messing about,' Priya whispers. 'I really do

think we should begin with the first floor, though, seeing as we're meant to come out this way.'

'Your heat sink will form a bubble around you. We burn everything as we go,' I say. 'And I'm not coming out this way.'

She grabs my arm, nails digging into the skin.

'Don't turn this into a suicide mission.'

'Oh, I leave martyrdom well alone. The pendulum will swing our way.'

'What the fuck does that even mean?'

I don't answer and walk out into the immense arcaded entrance hall of Arniston House. It's stunningly beautiful in the lamplight. An open space rising all the way up to the ceiling two floors above, with a gallery above and baroque plasterwork everywhere. Intricate designs of ivy and fruit, motifs of abundance, cover the bannisters and ceiling. There's a large antique mechanical clock, and two massive fireplaces blazing to keep the house warm, the smoke entering columns, for there isn't a direct chimney. Portraits of the Dundas family hang on every wall, generations of them spread across three hundred years. Me and Priya make our way across the parquet flooring, past the busts of eminent personages, towards an open door.

There's voices coming from upstairs.

We find a dining room and the aftermath of a dinner done. The carcass of a whole roasted hog sits in the centre of the table, rib bones exposed, along with the remains of side dishes such as buttered potatoes with chives, sage and onion stuffing, apple sauce, grilled vegetables and a massive bowl of coleslaw. Tonnes of gravy too. Clearly the starvation in town means nothing in this place of abundance. Montgomery Wedderburn,

Hamish Hutchinson, Rethabile Lebusa, Octavius Diderot, Viscount Mieville, Nathair Walsh, Lewis Wharncliffe, Fenella MacLeod, Avery MacDonald and Jomo Maige all sat around this table, drinking German Riesling and toasting to their success, surrounded by paintings by Raeburn and Ramsey. Wilson serving them, like the loyal oaf he is.

'Burn it all down.'

Priya flicks her fingers and incandescent green sparks fill the room. Wherever they touch, beautiful luminescent flames begin to crawl. Next, we hit the living room. The broad windows which should look out to the fields and the rest of the estate only reveal darkness now. We soon discover how well the couches and carpets burn.

I grab my katty and load the first stone as we take the main stairs up. The smoke rises and will soon start seeping through to the next floor. That'll be my moment. At the top of the staircase, I leave Priya to hold the first floor – she can exit once the flames start proper raging. I go to the bathroom where Una indicated there's a passageway. I try to open the door, but it doesn't work. Try once again. Oh shit.

'I'm coming already,' Avery MacDonald says grumpily. 'Can't even take a dump in peace . . . Hey, is that smoke I smell?'

I stand to the side of the door, putting my katty back in my pocket, and remove Cruickshank instead. I hold the middle bit, my arms a foot or so apart, and wait. The fire must be blazing downstairs, 'cause I feel the heat in the air. Avery flushes the toilet, then I hear him unlock the door, obviously not having washed his hands. He steps out, right past me, and I slip behind him, throwing Cruickshank over his face. He struggles and gags, trying to shake me off. He's taller and much larger than me, so it's like bull riding. I cling on, even as he grabs at my arms, and then I wrap my legs around his stomach and squeeze. He moves backwards and bangs me against the wall, but I hold fast. Cruickshank helps, tightening around Avery's mouth. This is what Rob meant when he told me to cheat. I can feel Avery try to expand his chest and take a breath of air, but every time he does, I squeeze my legs tighter around him. He stumbles and lands on one knee, his arms growing weaker, yet still he tries to throw me off. His hand reaches back to grab at my hair, but all he catches is my beanie hat, pulling it off. Eventually he becomes woozy, swaying side to side before toppling over onto his face. I pull out my legs just in time so as not to be squashed. Then I hold on for a bit longer, just to make sure he's not pretending, before finally letting go.

I don't know if he's dead or just passed out. No time to check. Cruickshank unwinds, moving like a python, and slithers up my arm before settling around my neck again. I give Avery a quick kick in the nuts just because, then walk over into the bathroom. The smoke's getting worse. I shut the door and lock it.

It's a pretty big bathroom, with white tiles from the floor to halfway up the wall. White bathtub in the middle, perpendicular to the door. Behind that's a toilet near the window. White cabinets and wood panelling run from wall to wall on that side too, and white towels are neatly arranged. It looks like a sensory deprivation chamber more than anything. No time to appreciate the decor, though. I go on my knees and turn the towel ring between the bathtub and the sink. There's an audible click, and a panel swings open towards me. I pull it fully open, then crawl inside – there's barely any room in it. I shut the panel behind me, and stand.

Ick factor when my hand brushes against cobwebs. I incant a single spark to life and this illuminates the passageway in front of me. Proper dodgy this whole business. It's completely bare here – unplastered walls and rough stone floor. There's a spiral staircase on my right and I ascend it. Someone's scratched the words 'Nemo me impune lacessit' into the wall. That's so bloody weird, because it's the Scottish motto 'No one assaults me with impunity'. But I guess it makes sense, given whose place I'm raiding.

Works both ways, motherfuckers.

I make it to the top of the stairs, where there's no landing or anything like that. They finish directly behind a solid oak panel. I note the catch on the left side, about half a foot above my head, and extinguish my spark.

'—to this great day, our great work is near an end,' Wedderburn's voice comes in, brimming with confidence and pride. There's religious fervour in it. 'Those who do not understand the values of the Enlightenment, these postmodern magicians led by Ian Callander, who poison our once great Society with their ridiculous progressivism, they shall be swept aside. Oh, we have endured ostracism, and for me imprisonment, but we know our cause is just. And the work we undertake is to restore Scottish magic to its place at the pinnacle of the sciences.'

'Hear, hear,' Hamish Hutchinson exclaims. 'We shall be great again.'

'And so, I have assembled you all here because you were

hand-picked as the finest practitioners, scions of our four schools of magic. Lady Rethabile of the Aberdeen School of Magic and Esoterica, Octavius Diderot, representing the best of the Lord Kelvin Institute, my dear friend Hamish Hutchinson, head of the St Andrews College, along with myself, standing in for the Edinburgh Ordinary School for Boys. Together with you bright young students, we have formed the Fifth School, joining all our talents in the service of our precious nation. And so tonight we will form a choir, channelling our will into a new theorem which will create a magic hitherto unseen on these isles.

'We will bring back the first secretary of the Society of Sceptical Enquirers, to lead us once again in these difficult times.'

XX

My whole life I'd been walking past the first secretary and never realized it. His influence has loomed large over the entire world, though he was but a man from a small town in a small country. But his reach grew beyond the shores of Leith and the Clyde. An influence that hasn't been dampened by time, it seems. The smoke isn't working fast enough, if they're already about to start this mad ritual. I see a pinprick of light filtering into this dark space and place my eye there. It's so bright, I see nothing for a second, but then I adapt and part of the room becomes clear to me. I am looking at what used to be the library in Arniston House, though now it appears to be where they keep an interesting collection of antique tapestries. Directly in front of me, at the far end of the room, is Wedderburn. He's decked out in a hooded black robe with an azure strip, the same shade of blue as on the flag of Scotland. The symbol of plinth and man is emblazoned above his heart. Opposite him, nearer my end with his back to me, is Hamish Hutchinson. His robes have a white strip. On equidistant opposite sides stand Rethabile Lebusa, who has a navy blue strip on her robes, and Octavius Diderot, who sports a red-coloured strip. Theirs are the hues taken from the Union Jack.

292

Why's the smoke not flooding into the room by now? I need to create a distraction. *Come on Priya – stoke the fires.*

In the middle is a great oaken table upon which Sophie lies bound, next to a large book, one of those stolen from the Library of the Dead. So, this must be why Viscount Mieville called me in to get rid of the 'rogue spirit' possessing her before. They had other plans for Sophie, and needed me to take care of the problem for them. It sucks to know they played me to further their designs. The book next to her is an impressive artefact, ribs and spine visible. The cover has a stretched-out face on it, and its binding is made from the hair of the person whose story is written within its pages. The book is both grotesque and beautiful to behold. Even from where I'm spying, behind the wooden panel, I can feel something of its lure. How it calls to everyone nearby. Around the edge of the table are milk bottles filled with an effervescent white fluid, which looks like starlight captured in glass. I recognize this as the product of Siobhan Kavanagh's experiments. A nectar taken from children which can be used as a drug called yang-yang by the frivolous, but also used by rogue practitioners to enhance spells. She was definitely working with this lot, then. I destroyed a lot of the stock she had on Gorgie Farm, but she'd been at it for a while, so they must have had a supply stashed before I got to her.

'Wilson, come beside me. You have been a faithful servant to Arniston House's heirs,' says Wedderburn. 'There will be a great reward for the sacrifices you've made over the years.'

Wilson hobbles towards Wedderburn, head bowed. He holds his arms out as though in prayer, and his bandaged stump shows where his robe's sleeve has slid back. There's a beatific

293

expression on his face as he nears Wedderburn and kneels before the book and his granddaughter.

'Viscount Mieville, take your place beside me,' Hamish Hutchinson says. 'And you, our students, draw nearer to complete the circle of our choir.'

Come on, Ropa, think. You've got to take them on before it's too late. But how? I could never hope to win against all of them. There should be a raging inferno below us right now, instead I'm here in the dark waiting, clueless. Should I go back down to check on Priya? The students move inwards from the corners of the room, which I can't see because the peephole's a right blinker. They take their places around the table. Wedderburn pushes his hood back and the rest do the same.

'Where is Avery MacDonald?' he asks.

'He went off to the toilet,' Nathair Walsh replies.

'What's taking him so long?' Hutchinson says.

'Never mind. The hour draws near and the *work* cannot be halted for stragglers. Jomo Maige, it seems the honour falls to you to complete the circle,' says Wedderburn, pointing to a spot for Jomo.

'But I – I'm not a magician,' Jomo stammers.

'Tonight, we abolish the separation between librarians and practitioners. This was accomplished when you aided us, for you broke the librarian vow of neutrality to serve the side of good. You've aligned yourself with the future and in so doing, have already surpassed anything your father ever accomplished.'

Folks need validation and this is an easy way for them to get exploited. We're all looking for someone to pat us on the head and tell us we've done good. No one's immune. And so

Jomo's achieved the acceptance he's always craved, from his new father figure. What a web of lies Wedderburn draws. My best friend walks round the table to stand beside Octavius Diderot. There's an air of pride about him now, dressed in those awful black robes. It's a sinful kind of pride. But he does look like he's found himself a new family, a place he feels valued. I want to shout out that it's all fake – Wedderburn's using him and will discard him. That's what these powerful magicians do. He's just a plaything to them.

'I will now give each of you your piece of the spell we will weave tonight,' Wedderburn says, and they hold their hands out, palms turned up. He clicks his fingers and sheets of paper appear out of nowhere, landing in those upturned hands. 'Remember, precision is key. Know where you stand in the tune. Everything must be incanted at exactly the right moment. There's no room for error or deviation. Jomo, your sheet will tell you exactly where you come in. Good boy.'

'Let us begin,' Hamish Hutchinson says, and the clock in the hall below strikes thrice.

The sound gives me shivers, and it feels like a wave has travelled through my body, as it has through the very fabric of Arniston House.

'Sprung from the silver egg which was the seed of creation, the order that began time, setting the universe in motion, humble beings of dust we may be, mortal we call upon the Protogonos Phanes, god of creation, for this plane we're in has an ever-flowing energy, the fruit of your rib . . .'

As Wedderburn sets the spell in motion, space seems to bend and everything becomes warped – a cosmic entropic rearrangement of fundamental forces, the building blocks of this realm. I feel queasy, almost as if the floor's opened up and I'm falling down an endless pit. There's a wrongness to this type of magic. The scent of burning flesh hits my nostrils and Sophie begins to writhe on the table, but she's bound and cannot escape. The bottles containing the stolen essence of other children pop open, and the fluids fizz out into the air. It's powerful stuff, likely multiplying the effect of Wedderburn's spellcraft.

Hutchinson enters with an incantation from his spell sheet whose mathematical formulation is anchored in Ananke, the Protogenoi of inevitability, compulsion and necessity. She who was the mate of Chronos, the father of time. It seems as though the two magicians are speaking over one another, but carefully listening to the timing, the cadence of their words, I decipher the coupling effect, gluing the spell together.

Fenella pulls two knitting needles from her sleeves and gives one to Hutchinson, before offering Wedderburn the other. Gran's needles! Although it could have been any of them who stole them, I'm suddenly sure she's the one who was at the caravan. Fenella is the murderer once again. My rage bubbles up and I have to clench my fists. Wedderburn and Hutchinson approach the table, then bring down the needles at the same time – one into the book and the other into Sophie's thigh. The girl screams and struggles to get away, but the cord binding her is too strong.

I move my hand towards the latch, then freeze. I can't take them all.

Lady Rethabile Lebusa begins another incantation layered atop the two already being spun. Hers is aligned to Thesis, the great matriarch, the goddess of creation from whom all life flowed. It is then all locked when Octavius Diderot inserts the Gaia block, invoking the goddess of the Earth, thereby giving the spell the ability to overturn natural law. I've learned about choirs and the power they hold, but this is beyond the perform-ance the triplets attempted in defence of the Library. This is a long spell. Taken together, it sounds like the ecstatic speaking in tongues of a Pentecostal congregation, but the words join the magicians' wills in a powerful way.

Next the students and Jomo join in to create struts and counter-points, further layers of magical glue enhancing the spell. This prevents its dissolution, where stress fractures may emerge from the inherent contradictions that mirror the counter-balancing forces of the universe. It's called *balancing*. The more complex a spell, the greater likelihood of it toppling over or collapsing within the weight of its own gravity.

'I feel something wonderful,' Viscount Mieville says ecstatically.

Sophie screams again as a silver essence begins to issue from the knitting needle embedded in her flesh, spooling and spiralling as it flows towards the other needle stuck in the book. It's like seeing a positive charge flow to a negative pole. And the side the book is on is insatiable, suckling greedily like a starving infant. Tears flow from Sophie's one good eye – the other is hidden by a black eyepatch.

Then the book does something I've never seen a book do before: it expands, almost as though it's taken a big breath in. This is followed by a noise like a sigh, which is weirdly as loud as Sophie's screaming. Wedderburn sweeps his right hand over the table thrice and the Fairy Flag appears, hovering over the young woman and the book. It remains suspended in thin air as the spell grows more frantic. The book comes undone, the ribs peeling off the human flesh of the cover, the spine reconfiguring itself. The face on the cover contorts into a strange expression. I have no choice now; I'll have to jump in and just hope. I'm lifting the latch on the panel when there's a loud explosion from below, shaking the very foundations of Arniston House like a 9.5-magnitude megaquake. Some of the students fall to the floor. The windows shatter, and a fine spray of plaster from the ceiling showers the occultists.

Thank you, Priya. About bloody time.

Thick smoke pours into the room, sowing chaos. The chanting stops.

'We're under attack!' Hamish Hutchinson says in panic.

'No, we're so close,' Wedderburn says.

'My house is burning,' the viscount shouts.

'Everyone, off you go and put the fire out. And find out who's doing this and kill them. Show no mercy. I will stay here and hold this spell together. Hurry,' Wedderburn says.

Hutchinson turns immediately, going for the door. He's followed by this flock, plunging into the deadly smoke. They are committed, I'll give them that. Wedderburn winces. He is one man holding together the most complex theorem ever devised. He holds both hands up, a superhuman effort as sure as Heracles held the sky up for Atlas. A drop of blood falls from his nose.

I open the latch and step out from my hiding place, with River right behind me. Wedderburn's eyes widen, surprised to see me.

'How?' The word seems to escape from his mouth.

'In the middle of St Andrew Square, visible from Dundas House, the headquarters of the Society of Sceptical Enquirers, lies the origins of your symbol. I thought it was an "I" and a stick-man drawing, but it's more than that. It is *the* Tall Man, a statue on a plinth a hundred and fifty feet high. The figure on it is the One Above All, looking down at this modern world he created, for he is also the Black Lord, the statue blackened by soot over the years. An excessive monument to a great man. The first secretary of the Society, the most powerful politician in Scotland in his time, the First Lord of Admiralty, Henry Dundas. I realize now that statue was placed there for a reason, so members of his cult like you would never forget their duty to him, wasn't it? You cannot visit the Society or the Bank without going past it. He will never be erased from memory. And if you want a spirit to return, you call it back home. That's what Arniston House was to him.'

Wedderburn grimaces.

The book squirms, unravelling its contents, spilling its guts as the protective cover peels off. Its movements are like death spasms in reverse. It's repulsive, but you can't tear your eyes away from it, as the old bones creak and crack. The scent of putrefaction mixes in with something akin to wet beef jerky, which cuts through the smoky air. Sophie coughs. The air's becoming harder to breathe and there's shouting from downstairs. I need to hurry. I load up my katty and aim at Wedderburn.

He could let go of the spell and confront me, but he holds on regardless. I see now how precious this thing is to him.

'You don't understand, Ms Moyo.' He's out of breath. A vein bulges across his forehead, which is slick with sweat. 'This is for Scot—'

Fine words, trying to weave a web around me, as he has with the others. I fire off my katty and nail the tosser in between the eyes. Wedderburn's eyes roll up and his hands flail, then he flops to the floor like a sack of tatties. Bullseye. The air becomes filled with a cracking sound, as though a fissure is running through a delicate porcelain artefact. I pop my katty in my pocket and walk up to the oak table.

I use my dagger to cut the rope binding Sophie's hands and legs. She cries out in pain.

'Shhh. I'm getting you out,' I say. 'Be brave for me, okay? Your mum's waiting for you. She's going to take you away from this horrible place.'

She looks pale and frightened, like a little girl younger than her years, the lines on her face telling the story of her ordeal. I've seen this look before on the kids I rescued from Siobhan. It damn well breaks my heart. I put my hand on her leg and carefully pull out my grandmother's knitting needle. She winces but holds on. I'm trying to be gentle but the needle's deep inside the flesh and has gone through to the other side.

Something makes the hairs on the back of my neck stand up.

A dubious grey presence pouring out of the Fairy Flag has settled upon the writhing book. No time. I yank the knitting needle out and Sophie shrieks in agony. The needle's in my hand now, slick with blood, and I drop it to the floor. But the essence is still leaving her body, so I reach over and grab the needle in the book – I need to take that out too. As I pull, a hand attached to a strip of flesh flies out from the foul lump of flesh and grabs my wrist. Its touch burns my skin like stinging nettles, and I grit my teeth to stop myself from shouting.

I fight against the hand, but it's strong, and since I'm leaning over Sophie on the table, I don't have much leverage. Knapfery.

'*Release me,*' the book says.

'Screw you, Thing T,' I reply.

It pulls harder, yanking me towards it. I fumble with my left hand, trying to reach my dagger, which is on my right side. We struggle, but I finally manage to draw the dagger out and stab at the hand. What comes from the book is more caterwaul than scream, an unnatural sound which feels like hot nails in my ears. The hand lets go, though, and I yank the needle out so forcefully I fall back onto the floor.

The fracturing spell reaches a crescendo, as if a million glasses are breaking all at once, and there's an incredible entropic realignment, resulting in an explosion. It sends a wave of air to all sides of the room, dropping the tapestries on the walls, knocking shelving down and busting all the windows open. Poor River yelps as she's flung through the air, landing against a wall.

My wrist's burning and welted where the hand touched me, and it's itching like a motherfucker.

Wedderburn begins to stir. He's still in la-la land, with a bloody red mark on his forehead. I need to get out of this house. I get up, grab the needles and stick them in my jacket pocket. Then I go up to Sophie, lift her off the table and onto my right shoulder, which is my stronger side, fireman-style. Good thing she's been on the Exorcist diet 'cause she hardly weighs anything.

I make sure she's secure, then walk round the table, out of reach of the book's demented hand.

'No, Ropa, you're ruining everything,' Jomo says, walking into the room.

His afro's a wee bit singed on one side and he coughs from all the smoke he's been inhaling.

'You can't win, soon we'll have the fires out.'

'Is this what you're about, Jomo? Hurting lassies? You're such a tough guy now, aren't you? Bravo,' I say.

The book wriggles. It's been spread out into something resembling a small man who's missing most of his luggage. It's breathing, dust pouring out of the orifice that was once lips. I reach for the Fairy Flag, which is the portal through which Dundas's spirit is reanimating those bits of his body that have become the book. As I yank a corner of the flag, Jomo runs swiftly across the room and grabs the other corner. It's a fragile piece of silk.

'Let go, Jomo. You don't know what you're doing. These people are using you.'

'I'm going to show my father I can be better than him.'

'This is not about him, you numpty.'

'*Everything* is about him. You don't know what it's like, Ropa. Your parents are dead, and that's a blessing. You have no idea.'

Wedderburn groans, struggling to his feet, wobbly and dazed. He's holding his head in one hand and shakes it, but he's still out of it.

'Jomo, you sweet fool. River, get him.'

She leaps onto the table, then lunges for his hand. Jomo pulls the Fairy Flag and I'm pulling at the other end. There's a loud rip and it splits in two, leaving me holding one half and Jomo the other. But he's not celebrating 'cause he's too busy bawling about the nip River's given him on his arm. Blood drips down and Jomo looks at me in disbelief.

'No, you imbeciles,' Wedderburn cries out. 'That is a priceless relic.'

He turns his wrath towards me, and I sense a radical entropic shift. So I'm like, nope, sayonara baby. 'Come on, River.' I run towards the window, Sophie still over my shoulder, and leap out, all the way from the top floor. A golden thermosphere shoots over my head, flying out into the night like a comet bearing ill omens. I quickly incant an anemoic cushion, not quite knowing where it will be, but I sense the air rushing down and I hit it before I'm ready. Then I feel River land somewhere beside me, before the air cushion bursts like a balloon and we're thrown to the ground.

River lands on her feet like she's a gymnast, while me and Sophie have a rough time of it on the gravel. The fog's now turned into a sinister red, bathing Arniston House and its estate, as though something has bled into our world. But we've stopped it. Bless Yahweh. The bust windows on the bottom two floors of the great country house have green and white flames blazing out of them. I glimpse the magicians within fighting to put them out.

I stagger to my feet, pick up Sophie, and start to limp away. My left ankle doesn't feel great 'cause I landed wrong. No time for that, though. I'm going as fast as I can when I turn to see Wedderburn standing at the window, starting up a new thermosphere. Oh fuckety fuck. He hurls it at us and I hunch over, shielding Sophie. But the fireball explodes just before it hits me, its fury radiating away harmlessly.

'Give her to me,' Priya says, appearing just ahead. 'I can't hold him off for ever, he's too powerful.'

I limp-run to her and deposit Sophie on her lap.

'I can't carry both of you,' she says.

'I'll be fine, let's go,' I say.

'Don't let them get away,' Wedderburn calls furiously from above.

We run towards the driveway. Priya's leading 'cause of her ambulatory magic and I'm just about keeping up. The tall lime trees will offer some cover, if we can just get to them. I turn again to look and the front door's burst open, Hutchinson, Fenella MacLeod and Avery MacDonald stepping out.

'You two, get to the cars. They won't escape so easily,' Hutchinson says. He starts to come after us, walking briskly, as though running was too undignified for the head of St Andrews College.

A soliton hits me in the back, throwing me forward, but I keep going. Then in front of us, in the middle of the road, is Wilfred with an axe. He's fuming, and I'm worried we'll be cut off, but Una rushes out of the woods and tackles him. They both tumble onto the road, rolling several times. Wilfred gets the better of her, pinning her down underneath him, then stands up, keeping one foot on her chest, and raises his axe.

I incant a sonic blast, sending a wave rippling through the fog, but it misses him 'cause I'm wobbly and tired.

'Sophie, I love you,' Una says, just as Wilfred brings the axe down onto her head. There's a sickening crack and a squelch. Sophie cries out for her mother, her voice breaking with shock and disbelief.

I promised to save her.

'You won't escape,' Hutchinson says. 'Surrender to us and we will spare your lives. There's nowhere for you to go.'

We are trapped between him and an axe-wielding geriatric killer. Priya's stopped just ahead of me, and I know that's because I was doing a shit job of keeping up with her. If we didn't have Sophie, and I'd ridden with Priya, we'd have been out of here in her wheelchair. There's no way we're going to make it to Gorebridge now, though. Already Fenella MacLeod and Avery MacDonald are running towards us. Even without the cars, they'll still be able to outrun me with my dodgy ankle. There's no wynds or closes to duck into like I'd have in Edinburgh. This is the countryside. I've messed this whole thing up. River's looking back and forth between Hutchinson and Wilfred. I put a hand on her head to calm her. When I see the blood and brains from Una's head on the road, I decide there's no way I'm sacrificing River tonight. 'Medals after death are a trivial thing. Live to fight another day,' Blackwood teaches. There's no other option.

'Priya, you have to go,' I say.

'I'm not leaving you with them,' she answers.

'Don't be a hero, man. This mission's a dud. *Go*,' I scream at her.

'I'm not leaving you,' she repeats through clenched teeth.

Stupid, boneheaded loyalty, Priya. But to be a leader, I have to put them ahead of me. If Priya and Sophie make it out of this at least, I can count it as a win.

'I've got the knitting needles and half the fairy flag. You let them go and I'll surrender to you,' I say. Even in defeat, sue for better terms.

Hutchinson laughs and claps his hands. Avery and Fenella flank him – their soot-stained faces have the look of hungry wolves. Fenella's especially. She's vicious and ruthless. Funny how I used to think she was soft, given her pale, anaemic look. When Hutchinson stops laughing, the atmosphere turns even chillier.

'I think if you look at your situation objectively, you will come to the conclusion you have no chips with which to bargain, young lady.' His voice has an incredible menace, heightened by his posh tone. 'There's a world of pain that awaits you. When I am done, you will wish you'd never been born.'

A weird rustling starts coming from the darkness beyond the lime trees. Like something small and feral is running in there. Makes me afeard hearing it. Like critters cutting through the grass. The great lime trees rustle about, their branches creaking and groaning from the effort. Their trunks then begin to twirl around like hula-hoopers. The entire avenue seems to have become agitated. Fenella yells out as a small bushy plant leaps from the fog onto her face.

Avery fires off a thermosphere but is soon attacked by another topiary creature set loose from Mrs Guthrie's pots. One goes straight for Hutchinson, but the head teacher wards it off with a timely soliton, blowing it and its leaves back as though it were tumbleweed. He doesn't see the one behind him, though. It leaps onto his head, covering his face entirely. He tears at it but it's glued onto him. A donkey brays and Mrs Guthrie's cart breaks through the fog, smashing into Wilfred and throwing him high in the air.

The cart brakes just in front of Priya.

'Are you coming or what?' Mrs Guthrie shouts.

Don't need to ask me twice. I'm bolting at the cart and stop to help Priya load Sophie in the back, before hopping on myself. River leaps in all by herself and settles near the front. Hutchinson and his students, distracted by the plants, fire off random thermospheres and solitons, none of which hit the mark. Mrs Guthrie's pot plants, freed from their containers, throw up soil and leaves in the air. They are ferocious, with multiple limbs or branches attacking faces, hands and torsos, thorns pricking into flesh.

'Let's go, Priya,' I say, offering her a hand.

She gives me a mad grin. 'I've got my own wheels.'

'Suit yourself,' Mrs Guthrie yells. 'Hold tight, Ropa Moyo. Come on, Ben, show me what you've got or it's the seaside for you.'

The cart kicks off with a sudden acceleration, and I have to clutch the side with one hand, keeping hold of Sophie with the other. I swear I've never seen a donkey run like Benjamin does. He canters along the drive as fast as a Roman chariot, ears flopping about. Priya's right by our side, rushing along the grass verge, before speeding up and moving in front of us. Mrs Guthrie keeps one hand on the reins and the other on her bottle of cider, which is nearly done. She takes a last swing and tosses it behind. Wedderburn and a few others have arrived to help Hutchinson, but before they can cast their wicked spells at us, the giant lime trees on either side of the road begin to bow. There's incredible popping noises as the wood, which has stood erect for centuries, bends like fresh saplings, the trees arching in pairs one after the other. And where they touch, they form a barrier.

The once-open drive is now completely impassable, covered by a dense thicket of branch and trunk. We ride on, leaving Arniston House behind, breaking out of the fog, and head for the safety of Edinburgh.

XXI

Poor Benjamin's soaked in sweat and breathing hard by the time we trundle to a halt in front of the gates of Our Lady of Mysterious Ailments. The sweet unseasonal scent of herbs makes this place feel safe compared to where we've just come from. The cart finally slowed after we crossed the bypass, Mrs Guthrie deeming it safe enough for us to move at a steady canter, though she kept us off the main roads, sneaking through neighbourhoods where we were unlikely to be caught.

Sophie's head is on my lap and I stroke her hair. She's breathing lightly. The important thing is she's breathing at all. Her eye is open, but all I'm getting is a blank stare. Hasn't blinked in a minute or two. So I gently close her good eye.

'I know what you're going through. It's tough, but you'll make it. I pro—' Better stop myself. Shit tends to go wrong when I promise stuff. And so instead I say, 'I hope.'

Although she's much older, Sophie makes me think of my little sister. When I saw Izwi at the funeral, all I wanted to do was go and give her a great big hug. Tore me into a thousand pieces seeing her watch Gran's box lowered. I wasn't there for her. Will she hate me for it for the rest of her life? I've been trying to balance the ledger, but the losses on my side are of priceless things. How do I make sense of that?

'You've earned your carrots tonight, Ben, my good friend,' Mrs Guthrie says, leaping down and giving the breathless donkey a hug. He brays in appreciation, before she turns to me: 'Let me help you with the poor girl.'

I gently lift Sophie up and deposit her in Mrs Guthrie's strong arms. I leap off the side of the cart and River does the same. Priya's already at the door, talking to someone via intercom. Our Lady shuts her doors at night. She doesn't have an A&E as such, the vast majority of her patients being wealthy toffs coming in for a retreat or lifestyle therapies. She does have a few beds for patients who are worse off, though. This is where I first met Max Wu when he was unwell. If they could bring him back from that, they can help Sophie.

A bleary-eyed helper opens the doors and lets us in. He's dressed in white and his name tag says Kieran Bell. In a normal hospital, he'd be called a carer or orderly, but here, where there are healers, they prefer the term 'helper'.

'I need a treatment room and a consultant,' Priya says.

'Mr Fulford is on duty tonight,' he replies. 'Let's take her to treatment room four. I have to log her in, though, and take a payment before admission.'

'There's no time for that,' Priya says.

'I'm sorry, we're not allowed to—'

'Kieran, move out of my way, right now,' Priya says firmly.

He blinks a couple of times, before begrudgingly stepping out of the way. It's money that gets you through these doors and Sophie doesn't exactly come from the de la crème. Priya tries to keep her soul intact by doing free work at Camelot and in the slums during her spare time. She's that hummingbird with a drop of water in its beak trying to put out a veld fire. I'm glad she's forced our way in now, though. The fortune I've made doing gigs for Samarasinghe's people would burn out in under a week in this place. All because Hippocrates didn't have nothing to say about healthcare for the poor in the oath named for him.

We move briskly through the calm ambience of the clinic. The walls have soothing artworks with water features or lush rainforests, and there's a scent of jasmine and rosemary lingering in the air. At night this place is an oasis of peace, and when we pass an occupied room, the patient is knocking them zeds out. They don't have wards in here. Every patient gets their own room, complete with an individualized meal plan set out by the naturopathic nutritionists, whom I've seen wandering about in the daytime. This is the stuff money buys you, while the other half sleep on mattresses in the corridors of the understaffed and overcrowded Royal Infirmary.

I wince 'cause my wrist's still burning, as if someone's put a whole bunch of cigs out on it. The welts have blistered and contain massive pockets of water, all in the shape of a palm and five fingers. The pain's worse than losing a fingernail. It's constant and intensifying, and feels like Death himself's touched me. But I'll ask for help later. Priya needs to focus all her attention on Sophie right now.

We enter the treatment room via a set of white folding doors with glass panes in them. There's an electric plinth in the middle of the room, and Mrs Guthrie gently deposits Sophie on it. She lays her on her back, facing the soft ceiling lights, before stepping back. The room has a long sideboard, with multiple drawers on one side, and a smaller unit in the corner behind the plinth.

'I'll need to stabilize her, since they've syphoned her qi,' Priya says. 'She's still haemorrhaging.'

'Is there anything I can do to help?' says Mrs Guthrie.

'I need a Beaton tourniquet and an Egyptian lapadian set,' she says.

Mrs Guthrie and me are blank 'cause we've never seen none of that, but Priya must be thinking out loud, since she goes over to the sideboard herself and opens one of the bottom drawers. From there she retrieves a plastic box containing several large crystals. And then she takes a cloth that looks like a tallit prayer shawl to me and lays it on top of Sophie, covering her from head to toe.

A short skinny man with a sharp beak nose and round spectacles walks in, Kieran in tow. This must be the consultant Mr Fulford whom Priya had asked for.

'You and you, out,' he says to me and Mrs Guthrie. 'Kapoor, what have we got?'

I don't want to leave Sophie, but Mrs Guthrie touches my shoulder and firmly leads me out of the room. We stand in the corridor for a bit, watching through the glass of the door. Mrs Guthrie has her arms folded. There's a zen quality to her, as though she's a linden blossom tree upon a gently sloping hill.

'Let the healers work their magic, we're no help to them here.'

'I wish there was something I could do.'

'You've already played your part, lassie. The art of being a useful human being is knowing which role you should perform in any type of situation. That's very important. Otherwise you'll be knocking heads with everyone everywhere you go. It's been an exciting night and I see no reason why you and I shouldn't sit down for a cup of tea, or cider if they have any. Maybe not that, but I've heard they use rum for certain treatments here.'

'I know a staff room that's got Jammie Dodgers,' I volunteer.

I guess all the running about's finally made me hungry. We wander through the clinic and wind up in a staff room upstairs. I turn the kettle on and sit down, waiting for it to boil. I pull a face involuntarily and cradle my burning arm. The fire's shooting up my forearm now, all the way to my elbow. It's so intense I want to puke. My lips are dry and I feel weird all over. Heart palpitations. I must be tired after everything. Haven't had much sleep either. I'm suddenly so exhausted, my limbs are too heavy.

'You alright, love?' Mrs Guthrie asks, and then her eyes grow to the size of saucers checking out my arm.

'It's just a scratch,' I say.

'I'm going to get you help.'

She stands up, but the door swings open and Cornelius Lethington strolls in, with a newspaper folded under his arm. He sees me with his favourite biscuits on the table, ready to be devoured, and his expression changes instantly to a look of concern. The consultant healer drops his newspaper and strides over to me quickly. Then he takes my arm and starts to inspect it before I've even said a word to him.

'Hades' markings. Were you touched corporeally by some-thing not of this world?' he enquires with grave concern. 'Why wasn't I informed immediately? Ms Moyo, I need you to consent to treatment right now.'

I try to reply but my lips don't seem to want to move.

XXII

Waking up to the song of thrushes, I try to open my eyes but there's gunk sealing them shut. I'm lying on something soft and spongy, it's almost as if I'm floating, and there's water running. Takes a while to unglue my eyes, then I'm greeted by a green blur. I have to blink a couple of times to focus, and when I do, I see I'm outside. No, that can't be, it would be freezing this time of the year.

I try to lift up my head, but it's heavy and takes some effort. I appear to be trapped inside a mound of earth. I hope I haven't slipped out into the astral plane, or have inadvertently found myself deceased, 'cause that would really suck. But I'm not outside. When I look up, there's a slanted glass ceiling and the sun's directly overhead. Or at least I can see its halo through the clouds. The walls of the room I'm in are constructed of wooden logs almost entirely covered in climbers and vines, except for the wall near my buried feet, where an artificial waterfall runs down into a small pool.

'Hello?'

There's no one here. I try to wriggle free but the earth has me bound tight. It's warm, though. There's grass growing on the sides of the mound, and I notice some of it near where my arm is buried has withered and died.

'Anybody there?'

The only one who answers me is the singing thrush in the vines. We're deep in winter but this room feels like Beltane, the rites of May, a celebration of spring, when nature rebounds. I feel refreshed, like I've slept off the shittiest day of my life. I'm usually on the go, so it feels nice to be still like a plant for once. My mind's not even racing like it always does. I could be here for ever, growing a hair's width a year, my toenails becoming strong roots.

A bunch of vines move out of the way, revealing a door which opens, swinging outwards. Priya and Lethington come in. The rings round Priya's eyes show she hasn't had much sleep.

'I could stay like this for ever,' I say. 'I feel *amazing*.'

'Root envy,' Lethington says to Priya. 'Drastic improvement, though.'

'Thanks to you. I don't know how I missed it. I was so focused on Sophie that I didn't see it right there in front of me.'

'You're a good healer, Priya, just not infallible. None of us is. Although when you find time, I strongly recommend you acquaint yourself with Scrymgeour's *Codex of Unfamiliar and Exotic Maladies*. I honestly don't know why it stopped being a standard text,' says Lethington. 'And you, Ms Moyo. I'm delighted to see you are nearly cured in my specialist healing mound. I believe this is the second time I've had the pleasure of treating you. At this rate, next time they'll be asking me to resurrect a corpse.'

Sarcasm is still the lowest form of humour – zero stars for bedside manner. Lethington wanders over to me and places the back of his hand on my forehead. I'd recommend he use a thermometer, but I'm not going to tell him how to do his job just yet. Then he places his index finger on my neck, below my right jaw, to check my pulse. He does this while looking at his wristwatch. Then, when he's done, he steps aside and asks Priya to do the same. When she's done, she gives him a silent nod and I figure I'm going to live.

'I dare say we've succeeded in drawing out the contagion.' He touches the mound lightly and the earth crumbles on either side, leaving me lying there with all this dirt on my body.

'When your flesh is touched by a being who's crossed the limits of the separation between worlds, your body undergoes a toxic shock, like with a snakebite. This is different from normal ghosts, the sort you deal with,' Priya says. 'Reinserting you into the earth binds you to this realm, and allows the earth to absorb the foul effects of it from your body.'

I lift my hand and flex it. It's still pretty sore, but the pain is manageable now. Priya takes it in her own and examines the less angry welts.

'What will you dress it with, Ms Kapoor?' Lethington asks, and I realize he's treating her like a student.

'An aloe vera and dock leaf dressing should do the job,' she replies.

'Go ahead then,' Lethington says.

Priya seems pleased to have got it right, geek that she is. She's still beaming when there's a knock on the door and Frances Cockburn walks into the room. If there was ever a skinny face I never wanted to see again, it's this one. Cockburn's been on my case ever since I first met her. This time, though, she regards me with a certain coolness, which is different from her usual contempt.

'Well done, Priyanka. I knew you could do this. I'm certain the Discoverer General will want you to make this a more permanent job.' She turns to me and adds with satisfaction, 'You will be in the prison under the Library for a very long time.'

'I need to see Callander first,' I say.

Priya washes down my arm and bandages it. I thought I was going to see her chop up plants but it seems nowadays the healers have no time for that. There's a supplier who provides bandages infused with the various plant essences they need for dressings. It's so soothing when it touches my skin, I almost coo. Once that's done, I'm up and getting dressed into my gear, Cockburn not letting me out of her sight. She insists she'll take me and Priya to Callander herself.

The ride there, in her Neale electric car, is excruciating. The factory which assembled it in Glasgow closed down long before the Catastrophe. But it's a fine car, with a sturdy battery that can take thousands of cycles of charge. Don't know if Cockburn's watching the road ahead, though. The whole way there, I catch her eyeing me through the rear-view mirror.

Sir Ian Callander lives with his husband at Innerwick House on Ellersly Road in Murrayfield. This is where some of the remaining rich live, behind ten-foot-tall walls with barbed-wire fences on top. You can see the line where the original stone wall was enhanced by three extra feet of brick walling. A neighbourhood-watch patrol team coming up the road stares at our vehicle with interest. The men are wearing stab-proof vests and carrying baton sticks and cans of mace. They begin to approach but the electric gate slides open and Cockburn drives in before they make it over to us.

I'm super nervous, sat in the back of the car twiddling my thumbs. It's been a while since I've spoken to my old gaffer. The last time was after his duel with Wedderburn at Dunvegan Castle. I slipped out and left, before being given an offer I couldn't refuse by Lord Samarasinghe. You could say I ditched Callander, and by extension Scottish magic, but shit wasn't working out for me with them. Overworked and not paid at all, like Queen Victoria was still on the throne. Nah, it wasn't for me. Still, I kinda like Callander. He was okay actually, and I picked up quite a bit from him. It's just we're from different sides of the train tracks, and his office makes certain demands of him.

Innerwick House is walled off like the rest on the street, though it would be a poor life choice for any burglar to attempt a job around here. Too many CCTVs and security features. The pickings might be rich, but the cops take crime here seriously. It's impossible to get close anyway, with the neighbourhood watch challenging any of the 'wrong sort' of people, from the 'wrong end of town', who might be walking around the area. Even if you're just minding your own business. I've heard of people who they couldn't pin anything legit on still being slammed with a loitering charge, just for strolling on these pavements.

Even the Clan stays away from this lot. The wealthy are the savagest bampots on the streets of Edinburgh and they have the law to back them up every time. Best to take your chances with the middle classes, who are, in the main, sheep. Rob once told me this was a game of risk we played, and knowing who not to mess about with was the most important thing any self-respecting burglar could learn.

Callander's house has about an acre, give or take a few square metres. Pristine chequerboard lawn and immaculate flower beds with mahonia, clematis and daphne, whose winter blooms push away the gloom. Callander's vintage two-seater red Bentley is parked near the main entrance, meaning Cockburn can't follow the drive round to the back of the building. She stops the car and I try to get out, but discover I've been child-locked in.

'You really don't trust me, do you?' I say.

'You can now return my purse you lifted when you came into this car,' Cockburn replies.

Well, I had to try. I fish about in my jacket pocket, then hand it back to her.

'Thank you,' she says, and opens her door to step out.

Priya undoes her seatbelt and turns back. She gives me the *really?* look and I shrug. Old habits. In any case, the city and its people are a resource. Make the most of every opportunity, otherwise they'll say you hang about waiting for handouts. Still, I'm seething 'cause Cockburn's got the better of me. She opens the back door on her side, meaning I have to slide across the seat to get out. Petty for a woman her age.

'Leave your fox inside the car,' Cockburn says.

'Animal cruelty.'

'It's winter, she won't roast to death. You can fetch her later.'

I step onto the gravel and check out the stone-built Georgian palace Callander calls home. It has two storeys and two chimneys, both spewing smoke. There're creepers growing across the face of the front wall, so it's all green, save for the windows and doorway they've left free. And then you have some wee shrubbery around the front of the house. I don't know if this is purely aesthetic or more defensive gardening. Their presence makes it hard for any burglar to get at the windows, which on a listed building can't be adapted to a more secure contemporary type.

Cockburn's at the boot lifting Priya's wheelchair out when Esfandiar Soltani opens the front door. He's in a mid-thigh-length velvet smoking jacket with a quilted satin shawl collar, and wearing slippers on his feet. He stands there for a second with his right hand in the jacket pocket, almost as though he cannot believe his eyes. Two white Jack Russells dash out, barking excitedly and wagging their tails. I now understand why Cockburn asked me to leave River in the car. Dogs and foxes don't much like one another, and if I had to make a choice, I'd fuck these little dogs up before they hurt River. They both circle my legs, pawing at me, and I bend to pat them before straightening up again.

'They adore you. Pudgy and Pattie are very good judges of character. They growl whenever our solicitor comes by. Ropa, darling, I'm so happy to see you,' Esfandiar says, sweeping across, throwing his arms open and embracing me.

He holds onto me for a good while, and I can smell his spicy aftershave. Then he lets go and cups my face in both hands. He has rouge on his cheeks, and is wearing red eyeliner – the mascara he's used also makes his eyelashes appear divine.

'You remind me so much of her.' There's a thin film of tears in his eyes. 'Oh, this is such a dreadful business. Come here.'

He embraces me again and weeps for a wee while. Esfandiar's a poet, a man of deep feeling and emotion. I warmed to him from the first time I met him. There's something about him that draws you in and, despite my not liking most toffs, he's one of a few exceptions I make. A non-practising magician too, Esfandiar's genuine and authentic, which is a rare thing among his peers in the Society. He lets go of me and dabs his eyes with a brightly coloured silk handkerchief.

'I'm being silly. Please come on in, let's get out of the cold,' he says, leading us into his house. Cockburn makes sure I go first, so she's behind me. 'I am so happy to see you too, Frances, and you as well, Priyanka. We seldom have visitors from the Society at the house anymore.' Esfandiar lowers his voice to a pretend whisper. 'And that's a good thing in the main. I told Ian to keep his business at Dundas House. Oh, that man and his organizing. He's gone off to a meeting at the Murrayfield Golf Club. You'd think it was St Andrews or Loch Lomond, but he simply cannot stay away from there.'

I don't know nothing about golfing, but it strikes me as a wee bit out of touch that folks in these parts should be having meetings about golf when the city's burning. It's almost as though we're in another country, and the Edinburgh I know is foreign news out here. Still, I'm relieved Callander's not home just now.

Esfandiar stops in front of the door to the drawing room and asks for our coats. You kind of half expect folks living in posh houses like this to have a butler at hand, but things don't work out like that. They have to do it themselves, like when Jonathan Harker visited Count Dracula in his castle in the Carpathian Mountains. There's a mirror above a bureau on the left and his image reflects okay, so I figure Esfandiar's not about to do any bloodsucking. I take out Gran's needles and my half of the Fairy Flag from my pocket, before removing my jacket and handing it to Esfandiar. Priya and Cockburn give theirs up too.

'Through there,' Esfandiar says. 'I'll take these to the cloak-room.'

In the drawing room there's a well-worn salmon carpet that's probably been in here for generations. You can see the flattened bit following the arc of the door. The furniture in here is all antique. I wonder if it's been handed down, or this is how they chose to outfit the room. A chest of drawers is against the left wall, with a lamp on it and a Shona soapstone sculpture. There's a couple of two-seater fabric sofas facing one another in the middle of the room, on either side of the roaring fireplace. A couple of tables and wooden chairs at the side of the room offer extra seating.

I choose the sofa facing the door and sit near the fireplace. The wood crackles and hisses. It could only have been Esfandiar who picked the art hanging on the walls. Pop art pieces by Eduardo Paolozzi from Leith and John McHale from Glasgow sit either side of a drab portrait of some old nineteenth-century geezer who must be a Callander ancestor.

Esfandiar returns carrying a silver tray with a pot of tea, cups and some biscuits. He places it on the oval coffee table in the middle of the room.

'Give it a few minutes to infuse,' he says.

'Where did you get the sculpture?' I ask.

'Oh, that. Do you like it?' he replies, standing upright and drifting towards it. He runs his hand against the smooth soapstone. '*The Mermaid and the Maiden*, it's called. At least in translation. I can't pronounce the name in the original language. It was a wedding present from your grandmother.'

More signs of their closeness.

'Why don't you guys like talking about her?'

Esfandiar stiffens and begins to rub his hands. He retrieves a clay pipe from his pocket and sticks it in his mouth, then promptly returns it again.

'Perhaps you should speak with Ian about that, darling.'

'I'm talking to you, aren't I? You were her friend. I deserve to know the truth about my own grandmother. It's strange, usually when most people die, all everyone wants to do is to talk about them, but with Gran the magicians don't seem to want to say anything about her.'

'Oh, yes, well . . . Cup of tea, anyone?'

'Tell her,' Cockburn says. 'It can't hurt, given where we are now.'

Since no one else asks for one, Esfandiar pours himself a cup of black tea. He claims sugar is the worst drug invented and no one should ever drink tea with it, before taking a sip. He then places it down and returns to the chest of drawers, from which he takes out a large, thick book with a zebra print cover.

Priya wheels herself over to one of the substantial windows, underneath which is an old radiator. She stares out into the night, then says, 'You make me think of my own grandparents, Ropa. I know them alright, but I don't really *know* them. They're labels, like a role an actor plays in a film, or even me in my own job, where I play the healer and behave in a certain way. But my patients don't know me as a person. You get what I'm saying?'

Priya scratches her nose and resumes her seagulling, looking outside. Or maybe she's checking out her reflection. When Esfandiar returns, he takes the seat beside me and opens the cover of the zebra print book, placing half the cover on my lap.

'It's been a while since I've cracked open the photo albums,' he says.

I've heard of these. It's a thing people did in the olden days, when they printed out all their photos for some reason and kept them in a big book. This was before touchscreen phones, so maybe the ones they had at the time didn't take very good pics.

The initial page has four black and white photos arranged against a paper sheet, covered by a thin plastic film. The first is a picture of two young men in front of a wooden tuck shop. The tall photogenic one is in jeans and a T-shirt, has slicked-back hair and a cigarette dangling from his mouth. It's impossible to imagine the colours on these types of photographs. The quality's alright enough for me to see that Callander may have been a heartthrob back in his day. He's muscular but not too beefed up, retaining something of a boyish quality. Beside him, Esfandiar is more awkward-looking, with curly hair and an artist's faraway stare.

'Your grandmother took that photo with my Yashica Mat 124G. I was worried she'd break it because she was always goofing around and pranking people. Back then, I thought I was going to be a photographer,' Esfandiar says. 'I was very shy and didn't have a lot of confidence. I struggled to find the right words to say. But with a camera, you can capture a truth and show it to the world with just the click of a button. It's very powerful.'

Beside that picture, and slightly below it, is one of a young woman in a miniskirt and knee-high boots. She has one hand on her waist and the other Egyptian style. Gran used to tell me Zimbabwe was shaped like a teapot, and here she is, a slender little teapot. She can't have been long out of her teens in this picture – her face burns with a kind of daring bravado and her skin is smooth. It's probably long before she got her gorgeous liver spots. She's standing in front of a construction site, with diggers in the background and a couple of steel frames erected.

'I used a print of that one in a series I exhibited at a small gallery in Dundee. I titled it *Incongruent Things*. I'd take my female friends to what were then male-dominated places and photograph them there. Working men's clubs. Football stadiums. Even Bruntsfield Links, which didn't allow female members at that time.' He giggles. 'We thought we were being radical. And we were almost beaten up on a couple of shoots, but it was great fun.'

The next photo is of Gran and Esfandiar, heads poking out of a tent – this one isn't really as well composed and Esfandiar warns that, as a rule of thumb, the awful photos were likely taken by Callander. 'He doesn't have the knack for it.' The final one on the page shows Gran and Callander leaning back-to-back with fingers pointed up like guns.

'Sean Connery was James Bond back then,' Esfandiar says enthusiastically by way of explanation. 'I haven't looked at this in years. Look how *young* we were.' His voice cracks. 'Oh, Melsie, we were supposed to do this for ever. The summers were long. We had all the time in the world. It goes so quickly.'

It feels like revisiting this friendship is opening up a scab for Esfandiar. I never saw them all together, ever since I first moved in with Gran, and she certainly never mentioned them. I could only judge from what I saw once I was in her life. Everything before that's hidden behind an impenetrable fog – things that you don't even know exist until you bump into them. Callander only dropped by the caravan once, and it wasn't exactly a joyful encounter between him and Gran. I wonder if this is how me and Jomo are going to be. Broken up for ever. I need to bring him back to himself.

'Esfandiar, what exactly did Gran do for the Royal Bank of Scotland? Bing Wu told me she worked for them, but it doesn't sound like her. The Gran I knew didn't much fancy these big corporations.'

'Melsie Mhondoro was the most remarkable woman I've had the pleasure of befriending. I'm not just saying this because you're here, Ropa. Being with her was like going on an acid trip – don't ever try that stuff, it's bad for you, but we were hanging with hippies at the time. Anyway . . . her personality, her way of seeing the world turned your reality inside out. And if you'd been around the dour magicians I was raised with, it felt like we could create something new. I wish I could see the world as she did, but I only caught the glimpses she offered.'

Esfandiar picks up the knitting needles I've placed on the table in front of me and holds them with a certain reverence reserved for religious relics. He tells me that Gran was a highly gifted seer in her youth.

'Time is an elusive concept. We speak of it, we experience it, and we apply arbitrary measures to it. Seconds, minutes, hours – everything stretching out from the Big Bang to the very end. You understand why being a seer is so incredible? They are the very few magicians who may play with time.'

Cockburn inserts herself into the conversation. 'Think back to everything you've learnt about scientific magic. In our tradition, we value manipulatory magic, which is mostly playing around with matter and energy. But there isn't much we can do with time, apart from measuring it. We know it slows down near large objects with huge gravitational pulls, or really slows as you approach the speed of light, but we have no practical ways of manipulating it. The dimensions of space too we can splice, we can move through them in all directions. But not with time. To be a seer is the closest any of us ever comes to playing with its threads, and even then, ours is merely to feel the vibrations running through.'

'Can you see why she would be so valuable to the Royal Bank of Scotland?'

'I don't get it,' I say.

'Ms Moyo, magic gravitates towards money because of the laws Mary Somerville discovered in her famous equation,'

Callander says, suddenly appearing in front of the fireplace, where he stands with his back to me, warming his hands. It's a habit of his, popping up out of thin air. He wears tangerine tartan golf trousers, a white polo shirt and a matching flat cap. I catch the whiff of tobacco coming off him. But where his pictures in the album depict a vigorous young man, the deterioration is evident. The golf clothes he has on were bought for a fuller frame and seem to hang off him. He has lost an incredible amount of weight in a short time.

Yet Callander retains his gravitas. In fact, it's undiminished. His presence in the room changes the entire dynamic of our conversation, as if the communal energy shifts towards him.

'You should stop creeping up on people like that,' Esfandiar protests.

'I'm too old to change certain bad habits,' Callander replies. 'You know that already. I am sorry to have interrupted your riveting conversation, I will go and change first, then we can talk. Priya, your text updates on Arniston House have been enlightening.'

Callander turns and walks out of the room without once looking at me. There's something in his expression – a disappointment he's trying to mask. My mind's churning with questions, having just learnt of the affection once shared between Callander, Esfandiar and Gran. Was I wrong to bail on him and join Lord Samarasinghe, a bad decision either way? Callander saved me in the Library of the Dead, when Dr Maige was about to hang me by the neck 'til I expired. He then brought me into the Society, and though any plans to pay me were thwarted by Cockburn, he did give me books to aid my education. And he wasn't there for me all the time, he's a busy man, but I did have access to him whenever I needed it.

Most of my life I've thought I was good at reading people. I've always relied on having this particular gift. But if I was wrong about my best friend, then how could I have been right about Callander, who I've only known for like five minutes? The question is, is he going to turn me in or not?

XXIII

Esfandiar turns the pages of the photo album while we wait for Sir Ian to return. I see more pictures of the trio at swanky parties, on holidays in the Highlands, some at work dos, and others in a sort of domestic bliss. They seem young, happy and inseparable in their pictures. I stop in the middle where there's a picture of Callander, now in his forties, next to a serious-looking young student in the Edinburgh School uniform. The photos in this section are in colour. The young man next to Callander is none other than Montgomery Wedderburn.

'Oh, Monty,' Esfandiar sighs. 'He was the apple of Ian's eye, the first mentee he ever took on. They first met when Montgomery was still in school. Edinburgh makes sure its alumni support current students – that, and endlessly extorting them for donations. Montgomery impressed Ian with his keen acumen and appreciation for the great traditions of Scottish magic. He was a driven young man . . . But I guess Ian's never had much luck with his protégés. It's his curse.'

I feel the burn. Not that I think Esfandiar's being intentionally pointed, only saying it as he sees it. And as if sensing my distress, he pats my arm. The grandfather clock at the wall chimes.

'So, Gran was a seer and worked for RBS?' I say, desperate to uncover more.

'At the time, the Society of Sceptical Enquirers and the Royal Bank of Scotland were bonded so closely together they were two sides of the same coin,' Cockburn says. 'This is why we share the same offices, and have done so for two and a half centuries.'

'The Bank is always looking for talent, more so back then, and your grandmother's skill came to their attention. We were there celebrating when she was headhunted,' says Esfandiar. 'She went to the Bank, Callander apprenticed at the Society, while I went on to have a less illustrious career.' He laughs.

I don't know a lot about nothing but a banking job seems pretty solid. And Bing also said Gran worked there as an actuary, so there's nothing to explain how we wound up in a slum on the outskirts of the city. Esfandiar seems more comfortable dragging on about their bond in the good times than the reason behind their schism. He takes a sip of his tea.

'I think I'll have one as well,' Cockburn says.

'Me too,' Priya says.

'Ropa?'

'I'll drink the damned tea,' I reply.

The pot has cooled, but Cockburn places her hand on it and mumbles an incantation. A few seconds later it starts steaming. Esfandiar pours a little into our cups, not quite filling them up, but making sure we all get something. Pudgy and Pattie run into the room and spin around, all hyper. He shushes them and orders them to sit in the dog basket in the corner. I go for the sugar cubes in the stainless-steel holder and pick one out with my fingers, before Esfandiar points to the tongs next to it. I should use them, but now I'm too embarrassed to take another cube, so just leave it.

'It's really nice,' says Priya, raising her cup.

Here we are, calmly sipping tea after averting disaster and saving a young woman from having the life force sucked out of her. And now I'm finding out my grandmother, who was already super-duper awesome in my eyes, had some spectacular hustle back when she was young. The force is strong in my family . . . But what did Wedderburn mean when he said all that stuff about my father too? And what was Gran going to tell me about him before she died? I'll never forgive Wedderburn for what he did to her. Once we're done here, we need to focus on rounding him and his team up. They will face justice at the end of the day. Especially Fenella.

'Melsie worked in a secret department of the Royal Bank of Scotland that gave it an edge over all its competitors. It was called the Pythia Project at the time.'

Callander once told me that if you wish to understand the history of modern Scotland, you have to understand the history of the RBS. This was when I was chasing the Paterson fortune for the English spy Tom Mousey. I visited the archives of the Bank in the Gyle, and they had everything on their history, from the time it conceived the Company of Scotland Trading to Africa and the Indies, to the Darien Scheme and beyond. All this sprung forth from the schemes of William Paterson, a promoter of speculative money-making schemes. Incidentally, he was also instrumental in the founding of the Bank of England in 1694. Three hundred years later my grandmother was working for the same bloodsucking entity in its latest incarnation. Immortal Dracula may have been defeated and killed but the Bank is near invincible, rolling through the ages and wreaking havoc on lives with sub-prime mortgages, derivatives, credit cards, overdrafts and respectable usury.

'Banks at the time were on their way to becoming untethered from the real economy. They were morphing into sophisticated casinos, trading unfathomable stock market instruments. Some used supercomputers, running trading algorithms to some success. But what if you could cheat?'

'What if you could see the future?' Cockburn clarifies.

She explains the novelty of the Royal Bank of Scotland's project. Before this, seers practised in non-financial settings – at least those who claimed to have the gift, and their ranks were riddled with charlatans and chancers. Most of them worked informally, writing up horoscopes, doing palm readings at fairs, occasionally predicting sporting events or political fortunes. Some gained a reputation, like the Brahan Seer who worked for the Earl of Seaforth, and ended up being burnt at the stake by Lady Seaforth after she took exception to his predictions about her husband's philandering. But few ever reached those lofty heights. The ones who worked independently might help individuals with relationship problems or health issues – small-scale operations collecting pennies from here and there. The Bank then came up with the bright idea of finding the most talented seers from around the world and employing them. And so, the Pythia Project was born – named after the high priestess of the Temple of Apollo at Delphi. She was, in her day, the most revered and prestigious oracle among the Greeks, with great power and influence.

'Of those seers they brought in, your grandmother was by far the most talented,' Esfandiar says, looking into his teacup as though reading the leaves. 'She became their secret weapon, and from her insight they made uncanny moves on the markets, reaping gargantuan rewards. Indeed, so successful was the bank in this, they swallowed up a number of their competitors on their way to becoming the largest, most powerful bank in history, with interests spanning the entire globe.'

William Paterson once dreamt of making Scotland wealthy by colonizing Panama and establishing a free trade port there. That all went up in dust. But his vision continued in the RBS. Entire nations across the world were enslaved by its debts. The money flowed in freely and it seems Gran became incredibly wealthy.

'They knew she was the goose who laid the golden eggs and they threw money at her to keep her happy. It was important she wasn't poached by a competitor. We were young and living the life of Gatsby. It was all very decadent.'

'Gran? I can't believe it,' I say.

'Because in your head we're fossils,' Esfandiar says with a laugh. 'I wish you could have been to the parties she threw at Seton Castle in Longniddry. It was the famous architect Robert Gordon's final project in Scotland. Mary, Queen of Scots loved the place and your grandmother bought it from the Wemyss family, who'd fallen on hard times due to poor speculations on the stock market.'

Priya raises her eyebrows, and I'm thinking the same thing. A whole fucking castle? Decadent parties? That's not the grandmother who raised me. She wasn't exactly Ebenezer Scrooge but she was thrifty and not frivolous at all. There's a picture of her in the album holding a champagne flute and laughing in front of a castle, though. The whole thing's got me weirded out. Even if she'd lost huge chunks of dosh, she would have been okay if she'd squirrelled some away, surely? Did she blow it *all* like Patricia Kluge?

'What happened to the money?' I ask.

'It turns out messing with time in the future has unforeseen consequences.' The law of unintended shit happens. 'The Royal Bank of Scotland had an incredible run, and in so doing attracted more and more investors. What started off as an experimental project, dreamt of by some risk-taking middle manager, took over everything in the bank.

'The Pythia Project was a house of cards which rose higher and higher, creating imaginary wealth, heating up the market, until it became unsustainable. The highest returns are in speculative assets, and the balance sheet was filled with assets with no intrinsic value. They didn't create anything; they were peddling thin air.'

'As long as the money flowed in, and everyone got their bonus, Melsie and her colleagues kept it going.'

'Until there was a gust of wind and that was a catastrophe.'

'*The* Catastrophe,' says Cockburn.

The success of the Pythia Project sucked out funding from other areas of the economy, which is itself like a web. You can pluck out a couple of threads and it's fine, but when you finally hit the wrong one, it implodes. The stock market crashed. People lost their jobs, their livelihoods. Pensioners lost everything.

A great many were thrown out on the streets because they could no longer pay rent. It was like a financial nuclear meltdown. The pound became worthless overnight. Inflation skyrocketed. It was pure anarchy and mayhem on the streets of the United Kingdom. Everything fell apart at once, and the wheels of the economy ground to a screeching halt.

I remember the lessons from school about the Catastrophe. Viral videos of stockbrokers queuing like lemmings, leaping to their deaths from skyscrapers in the City of London. A run on the banks, with long lines of people sleeping at night outside them, only to be told there was no money when the doors opened in the morning. An all-pervading desperation and liquidity crunch squeezing global trade. The Royal Bank was the first giant domino to fall, taking with it huge swathes of the financial markets on every continent.

'It was the end of life as we knew it,' Esfandiar says. 'The free lunch was over.'

'Amidst that pain and suffering, hardworking people who'd done the right thing, gone to school, learnt a trade, saved, got a mortgage, and paid their taxes, were looking for answers,' Cockburn says. 'Whenever there's a crisis, prophets arise with ready answers. The separatists—'

'Independence movement,' says Esfandiar.

'Those who no longer saw the value of union with England and Wales emerged.'

I think back to my history lessons once more. The Union was always a product of Scotland's failure to gain a foothold in the empire-building game. The Spanish, Dutch, Portuguese, French and the English were so far ahead, reaping the benefits of slavery and plunder on a global scale. Scotland, the poorest nation in western Europe at the time, wanted in. But the Darien Scheme, the project to colonize Panama, was a catastrophic failure. It bankrupted the nation. The only solution was union with England. And when that happened wealth flowed in. The rest is history.

'Scotland wanted an empire, instead she got the Union. Without the fruits of empire, it was a flimsy arrangement,' says Cockburn.

'Like marrying up, only your partner goes broke,' Esfandiar says with a chuckle. 'You took the "for richer" part of the vows seriously, but never quite signed up to the "or for poorer" element.'

Between the two of them, they go on to describe the horrors of the age of the Catastrophe. Cockburn may have been young when it happened, but Esfandiar saw it all. People dying of starvation on the streets. Soup kitchens attacked by roving gangs. The gradual collapse of law and order. Amidst all this a rising nationalist sentiment. And so, to remind their subjects of the value of unity, the king and queen undertook a tour of the realm, seeking to reassure them that Britain would make it through this, as it had other crises in the past. But the whole country was falling apart, brick by brick, county by county, city by city.

'It ended in regicide, as you know. The king and queen murdered on the streets of Edinburgh by the separatists . . .'

The Catastrophe was a cascade of disastrous events in the United Kingdom. An unstoppable phenomenon, much like an avalanche. No one quite agrees on what exactly it was, or the precise mechanism, or even the timing entirely. The only thing everyone agrees on is that the RBS was the Bank That Broke Britain. And it seems Gran was at the centre of that.

'Your grandmother was a woman of conscience, but like us all, she'd lost her way in the pursuit of money.' Esfandiar bows his head and stops. 'It was all supposed to be harmless fun. As the world burnt down, we took refuge in her castle and drank expensive wines from her cellars, watching events unfold on our TV screens in relative safety. A few looters did try, but they stood no chance against three magicians . . . well two and a half, since we're counting me. It was pure chaos out there.'

I recall that Gran once told me the gifts of the ancestors were never meant for personal enrichment, but to help the community. Disaster inevitably comes when they're used for personal gain. I realize now she was speaking the truth of her own experience.

'I was just a kid, but I still remember the fear in the air,' Cockburn says. 'You heard the names of those who'd died daily. Some from starvation and a great many from being murdered. No one was safe.'

'It was dreadful,' Esfandiar says. 'I try not to think of those times. It makes me sad. And when I see what's happening in this city today, I confess I fear history is merely repeating itself.'

'Well, we've never recovered,' Cockburn adds.

Scotland went proper Mad Max from what I've read on it. Looting, raping, murdering. It was each man for himself. England fared no better, fighting amongst themselves for whatever they could get. It was the apocalypse brought live to you in your living room, in full technicolour.

The Catastrophe was televised.

The separatists took over Holyrood and declared independence for the People's Democratic Republic of Scotland. There was jubilation on the streets for what was supposed to be a new socialist Utopia. Who could resist when they promised food for all and blamed hoarding on the upper classes? Among them were savvy Scottish magicians, members of the Society of Sceptical Enquirers, who feared losing opportunities in a new dispensation. It must have felt like Britain was over.

'The rich and the aristocrats were fleeing left, right and centre. The Prince of Wales got on a plane with his family to New Zealand after his parents were murdered, fearing mobs in London would do the same to him. And in the chaos and confusion sown, one man stood up. A leviathan, the crown prince's younger brother. Do you understand now how we got here?'

There are those who put dates in an account and say the Catastrophe has been and gone. Then there are others who argue we are still in it, boiling away, only we've gotten used to living in hell. Amidst the raging chaos, the younger prince, who'd trained at Sandhurst, rallied his officers under his banner and declared martial law. With the army under his personal command, he restored order, first in England. He unified the various factions, including even the pensioners in Cornwall demanding independence after losing their savings, and gave them a common enemy and a common purpose. Once he had consolidated his position, the prince then marched his army north and declared war. Scotland was to pay for what it had done.

XXIV

And so the war began. This one dreadful act by a handful of thugs unified England in a way that hadn't happened since the Falklands War. The prince's army marched across the border, sweeping through villages and towns, before laying siege to Edinburgh and Glasgow simultaneously. It was never an even contest, and though our guys gave their all, defeat was inevitable. Hundreds of thousands more were lost needlessly.

'The prince was hailed as the protector of these isles. He had stayed when his brother ran. So he took the crown for himself,' Esfandiar says.

'Even though he's kept it ever since, his rule is not secure. There are those who still claim he isn't the legitimate heir, and he's always been wary his elder brother might try to rally the Scots from abroad, as Bonnie Prince Charlie once did.'

I recall something Gran told me, that history was a series of concentric circles – the same events happening over and over, with a new cast and different costumes. In the eighteenth century, the Young Pretender, Charles Edward Stuart, was the grandson of James VII and a claimant to the thrones of England, Scotland and Ireland. He had been born in Rome, at the exiled Stuart court, and dreamt of restoring the Stuart monarchy under his father James Francis Edward Stuart, known as the Old Pretender. The Catholic Stuarts had been deposed when James VII (II in England) had his arse handed to him for religious reasons. Something about imposing papist stuff and that malarkey. Anyhows, in 1745 Bonnie Prince Charlie made an expedition back home to kick off a rebellion. Well, let's just say it ended rather poorly the following year, with tons of people dead.

'The king keeps his boot on Scotland's neck in case his brother tries to stir things up here,' Cockburn says. 'This is the reason Ian has been very keen to keep Scottish magic out of a confrontation with England again. We are in a precarious position.'

'All that because of the Royal Bank of Scotland,' Priya says. She's been very quiet and looks tired after last night's adventures.

Esfandiar continues. 'Your grandmother Melsie took it very badly. I tried to argue with her, to tell her that she wasn't the one responsible. It was everyone in the Bank and the Society collectively who'd set off this chain of events. "I'm supposed to be a great seer but I failed to foresee the Catastrophe," she once said to me.'

In the last photographs in the album, Gran is much older and weary-looking. She dresses more conservatively, in dark colours, and doesn't smile or pose in the pictures as she used to. The body language between her and her friends has changed too. I look at a photo taken in front of the red sandstone building of the King's Theatre on Leven Street. Callander and Esfandiar are side by side, staring into the camera, but she has a distant look, her attention on something to the right, out of shot.

'She blamed herself for all the suffering she saw in the city. When I walked with her, she'd empty her pockets, give up her brooches, and on one occasion her shoes, returning home with nothing. But that was just a drop in the ocean of need. There were so many suffering at the time,' Esfandiar says. His tone is becoming more and more melancholic. 'Others in the banking industry didn't feel the same way. They'd squirrelled what they could away and felt entitled to it – that they'd earned it. As they saw it, they need only ride things out and it would be business as usual again soon. But Melsie had a conscience – an undesirable trait for the masters of the universe.'

He explains how Gran gave away all the money she had left. Investments in bullion and land that had insulated her from the worst of the shock. She donated to charities and started volunteering in soup kitchens, places she would hear people's stories and see their suffering first hand.

'She was struggling with her gift at the time too. It was as if her powers had waned. Once she told me, "Esfandiar, you cannot master time. It plays you like a puppet." That was when she began knitting like a madwoman. Where before she could *see*, now she needed an artefact – wool and needles – to divine.'

In time she'd gotten rid of everything, the last vestiges of her former wealth, and started a modest life in a little property in Forrester, which is where we first lived, until Gramps gambled the house away. It's difficult to take all this in. Can it really be my gran he's talking about? Much of it sounds like someone else altogether, but there are hints of her in there.

My hands tremble, the shock reeling through me at learning who Gran was. The secrets she kept from me.

I find a picture of her wearing an apron and serving food on the last page of the album.

'Can I have this one?' I ask.

'Of course you can. I would like you to have the whole album. It's too painful for me to look at now anyway,' he says.

I take the photo and put it in my jacket pocket, near my heart. Then I excuse myself and go look for the toilet. To the right in the hallway, just up ahead of the stairs, is where I find it. I lock the door, put the toilet seat down, and sit. The wave comes over me and I start to cry. Every moment I wasted not being with Gran. Every unkind word I said when I was moody or just being a dick. Every second I took her for granted. I cry because I didn't see the real her. I didn't know the weight she was carrying. When she tried to teach me her magic, I threw it in her face and said if it was so cool, then why were we so poor? She was right there with me all the time. Never got angry. Never got resentful. And she always loved me. Oh lord, how I miss her so.

My tears are the flood I wish would carry me back to her.

When the wave passes, I'm still. I get off the toilet and go over to the sink, where I wash my face and dry off with the towel hanging on the rack. I check myself out in the mirror, trying to see if I can find something of Gran in my face, but there's nothing. My eyes are red, little blood vessels streaked across the whites. Not much I can do about that. I take a deep breath and do the exercises Dr Checkland taught me. It's hard to do them right now, to stay present, but she said it would be like that sometimes. The important thing is to do it anyway.

I'm feeling fragile but a little more composed when I walk back into the drawing room. Callander's returned and taken my place next to his husband. The old gaffer's now dressed in one of his tweed suits with a white shirt on, though he's not wearing a tie today. I could sit next to Cockburn, but I prefer to stand.

'I didn't murder my grandmother, and that you would even think so says a lot more about you than it does about me,' I say. I'm done with this magician's way of speaking with forked tongues. Rather shoot from the hip.

'So I've been told,' Callander says, picking up the knitting needles and the half of the Fairy Flag we rescued. 'And I am very sorry for everything you've been through. I am sorry for your loss.'

'You made a fine speech at her funeral,' I say.

'I only said what my heart told me to. You have no idea what that woman meant to me and Esfandiar.' He goes silent for a while, as though he's searching for words. 'She warned me of what was to come, with a split in the Society and of a danger even greater than the Catastrophe, but I still hoped against the odds that she would be wrong, since her gift had waned and she was rather vague.'

'Doesn't matter now, we managed to stop it,' I say.

'We beat Wedderburn and his lot. Took the Fairy Flag, well, half of it, and Ropa's gran's knitting needles from right under their noses last night. They wanted to bring the first secretary, Henry Dundas, back, but they've failed,' says Priya and not without some pride.

'Then we owe you a great debt of gratitude, young ladies,' Sir Ian says.

Even Cockburn is forced to nod in agreement. She seems relieved the worst is past. I'm not going to be petty and throw anything in her face, but she's been a bitch before. And now I need DI Balfour off my case, so I can move on with my life and see my little sister. To hug her, as I should have been able to at the funeral . . . *Don't worry, Fenella, I haven't forgotten you either.* There'll be a reckoning for everything that's happened.

'You will ensure they're punished for what they did to Gran? All of them?' I say.

Callander nods. 'I would like you to return to the General Discoveries Directorate. Your grandmother used to work with me after she left the Bank, but that's a story for another time. Come back and work with us,' he says.

'We would be delighted to ensure you have the benefit of a full apprenticeship this time,' Cockburn says, sounding so earnest I'm taken aback. Only a few hours ago she was threatening me with prison.

'How about it, Ropa Moyo?'

One door closes and all that jazz. Funny, this used to be everything I wanted. To be a member of the Society meant the world to me. Now it seems like a rather small prize, a token, given all I've lost. Used to be I was chasing cheddar all the time and would have snatched at something like this. Money is the ultimate magic. Where does it come from? What gives it its power? It's just an illusion and I'm no longer so in awe of it. Now I realize the best people in my life have been folks from the slum, like Gary and Marie, or criminals from Camelot like Rob and Cameron. Those are people I can deal with.

'I'll think about it,' I say. 'Unlock your car and give me my fox back, Frances, I want to go home.'

And that's all there is to it. I'll go home to our caravan and sleep on Gran's bunk tonight wearing an old T-shirt of hers.

'Wait,' says Callander. 'There're guests of ours in the Old Coach House whom I am sure you'd love to see.'

'I'm not much in the mood,' I reply.

'Indulge me. Esfandiar dear, please could you go and call them.'

I'm low-key seething 'cause I have to stay and play the politeness thing. It's bullshit after everything, but Priya subtly gestures it's okay with her hand, and I go over to the wall to check out the Paolozzi hanging there. It's a collage of some old magazines: a car, a female model selling god knows what, with Goofy, an open fridge with milk in it, and some random stuff. It looks pretty, like a really smart preschooler made it.

I'm waiting a while, until Esfandiar finally returns with Calista Featherstone.

'Hello there,' she says and smiles.

Before I can answer Izwi walks through the door after her and my heart leaps with joy. I run over to her and smother her in a great big hug. *Thank you, thank you, thank you.* And when I feel her arms around me, the floodgates open again. She pats me a few times, and I must be squeezing too tight because I feel her squirm.

'Sorry,' I say, loosening my grip a bit. 'I'm just so, so happy to see you.'

I pull back and hold her by the shoulders. Can't believe she's actually here.

'Gran's dead,' she says to me.

'I know, sweetheart. But it's okay. She's in a better place now. And I know she's looking down on us, because she loves us very much. You especially. She used to talk about you all the time when you were at school.'

'She sent me messages,' Izwi says.

'That's good. Because we'll always have a piece of her in here.' I point my finger at my heart, and then point and tap her wee heart too. She holds my hand and smiles, but there's a thin film of tears in her eyes. Her chin wobbles and the corners of her lips turn downwards. She's grown so much in the little time she's been away at school. I could hardly see it at the funeral, surrounded by people as she was.

'I tried calling you, but you didn't pick up. I was so scared and you ignored my messages, Ropa.'

'Sorry, sis. I lost my phone. I'll give you my new number, okay? I would never, ever, ever abandon you,' I say. I wipe the solitary tear running down Izwi's cheek. And then she nods. She reaches into her jacket pocket and pulls out a playing card.

'I can show you some magic,' she says, sounding a smidge posher than I remember.

'Not in the house, Izwi,' Ms Featherstone quickly says. Then she turns to me. 'We've had a few accidents at school. I've had to spend a fortune fixing a hole someone put through the roof of my gymnasium. But a few mishaps here and there aside, your sister is doing very well. Your grandmother would be proud. I know she was of you both.'

'Thanks.'

With my little sister here, all the anger and frustration in my heart melts away. Yes, I still grieve, but I'm not alone. She's young and will forget things, but I swear I'll always be there to remind her of Gran.

The intercom goes off and Esfandiar, who's only just taken his seat, gets up again. Ms Featherstone goes over to one of the free wooden chairs and sits down. I notice she doesn't choose to sit near Cockburn either, but I'm past being petty now. Izwi's hair needs doing, it's grown pretty unruly. Nothing a bit of shea butter won't fix. I wonder how long I have with her. I really should style it before she goes back to school. *Stop, Ropa.* Okay, there'll be time for that later.

Izwi's already in full flow telling me about school and her new friends. I recall how desperately she didn't want to go when Callander first proposed it, but now it seems she loves the place. I find out who the bedwetters are in her boarding house – vital information. Then she's telling me about her favourite teacher. Apparently the pink jam slices on Fridays are amazing, and if you carry Mrs Drysdale's books, you might get a second slice, but not every time. It's a lot of information all at once and I'm enjoying listening to her little adventures, a needed distraction, when Esfandiar comes back looking pale.

'It appears we have an unexpected visitor,' he says, sounding anxious.

He's fidgety, pretty much wringing his hands, as Jomo Maige enters the room carrying a small silver tray with a black glove and a letter on it.

'Jomo!' Izwi calls out, throwing her arms wide open, and she makes to run to him but I pull her back, keeping her beside me.

T. L. HUCHU

'Hello, Izwi. Good to see you again,' Jomo says quietly. 'I've missed—'

'Don't you dare, man,' I say.

He sniffs and turns away from me, holding his chin up. He's dressed in the black robes of his cult. Seems like he's permanently swapped the Library ones for these now.

'Think very carefully about what you're doing,' Priya growls.

'Sir Ian Callander, I have been sent with an invitation for you,' Jomo says, ignoring her. 'May I give you this?'

He walks over to the coffee table and moves the teas to one side, before placing his tray directly in front of Callander. The gaffer seems unconcerned and doesn't give him the pleasure of a reaction. He holds out his hand and the letter floats up to him. Then the envelope tears itself open and falls to the ground. It's as though he won't demean himself by touching it. The letter within is written on vintage linen rag paper. It unfolds itself and hovers a foot or so from Callander's face.

He reads the letter and scoffs.

'What is it?' Esfandiar enquires.

'It appears I have been invited to a duel for my position by Henry Dundas, First Viscount Mieville and the First Secretary of the Society of Sceptical Enquirers. They propose it take place at midnight atop Calton Hill.'

Calista Featherstone stands abruptly, knocking her chair back.

'This is an outrage,' she declares. 'Young man, you're treading on very thin ice.'

'I await the pleasure of your response, Sir Ian,' says Jomo, ignoring her, arrogant and unconcerned by a threat from one

350

of the four heads of the schools of Scottish magic. I wonder what lies have filled his head for him to behave so brazenly.

But most importantly, how can Dundas challenge Callander when he's not of this world?

'This is a trick,' Priya says. 'We stopped them bringing Dundas back.'

'The first Viscount Mieville *has* returned and he also demands that the half of the Fairy Flag you stole be restored to him.'

'Jomo Maige, it is for your father's sake you are not a pile of ash on my carpet right now,' Sir Ian Callander says, and the letter bursts into flames mid-air. Jomo swallows hard. 'You will leave and never dare set foot on my property again.'

Jomo starts shaking, a bead of sweat rolling down his temple. The bravado is gone. He looks as I know him to be – a scared little boy, desperately trying to be the big man.

'Midnight, Sir Ian,' he squeaks, before turning heel and half running out of the house.

Callander sits impassive, deep in thought. Priya mouths *what the fuck?* to me, but I don't have any answers. This is unbelievable. I was there. When I took Sophie away, retrieved the knitting needles and half the flag, I broke the spell . . . didn't I? That cracking sound – it seemed to be the spell breaking. Or was it actually the invisible barrier, which prevented a certain spirit from coming into our world, shattering? No, that's not possible.

'What do we do?' Esfandiar asks. 'Even if he has returned, no one is permitted to challenge for the secretaryship outside of the Conference. Those are the rules.'

'It appears they are rewriting them. I have no choice. They are holding Dr Maige hostage. The letter states they will deliver his head to me on a silver tray after midnight if I decline this invitation.'

'Surely that's not possible!'

'Have no fear, Esfandiar. I've made the necessary preparations to counter anything they might do. This is why I met with Lord Samarasinghe earlier to iron out our differences. He is, despite appearances, a reasonable man. In exchange for greater cooperation between Scottish and English magic, he has agreed to stand with us should we be threatened. We will not be subsumed as we might have feared, but are moving towards an alliance of equals.'

'You cannot trust that man,' I say.

'I don't know the exact nature of your dealings with the Sorcerer Royal, but he is a formidable practitioner. He has given his word as an English gentleman, and I take him on it. With Lord Samarasinghe and the might of the Royal Society, we can put an end to this madness once and for all.'

XXV

Callander's decision has us shook right now. Poor Esfandiar is pacing around the room, utterly distraught. I want to reassure him, but don't know what to say. Even Priya, who's normally gung-ho, is sat quietly in her chair, face glum like she's at a funeral or something. Yep, we've found ourselves in a nippler. I would be wrong if I didn't at least tell the gaffer what I thought.

'It's dangerous to meet on their terms. They have the edge. I'd rather be the one setting the stage than walking into their trap,' I say.

'This is why we will take certain precautions. Esfandiar dear, you will take this half of the Fairy Flag to Aberdeen and the safety of Calista's school. If anything goes wrong, it will be secure there,' says Callander.

'I won't leave you,' says Esfandiar.

'You are also to take Melsie's granddaughter Izwi with you. Keep her safe. Yours is the most important task tonight,' says Callander, and I see what he's doing. By asking Esfandiar to take Izwi, he's made it impossible for him to refuse. The poet's not a fighter, and he would only get in the way. 'In the meantime, I will rally the magicians loyal to us so we can go out in force.'

This whole thing feels off to me, but I don't have another plan. Me and Priya apparently bollocksed this thing up, though I can't see how yet. Still, getting Izwi to safety and away from the violence in this city is a gift I'll take any day of the week in the present circumstances. And Callander is a great battle-ship. I must have faith in his abilities now. He defeated Wedderburn at Dunvegan, and he can do so again. He has to.

'I'll be taking Pudgy and Pattie with me too. Promise you will join us soon,' Esfandiar says.

'I'll be on my way to Aberdeen by tomorrow. Pack your things and hurry. The rest of you, ready yourselves.'

'I wish we could get Fergus Cattermole on this with us, but he's currently in Ireland at a conference,' says Ms Featherstone.

Professor Cattermole is the head of the Lord Kelvin Institute, and she's right, we could have used him tonight. I guess we'll have to wait and see who else Callander brings on board. Unfortunately, most of the Scottish magicians I know are pretty craven and unwilling to put their own necks on the line, regard-less of the cause.

I give Izwi another hug and promise I'll see her again soon, before Esfandiar takes her away. She grumbles, not wanting to go, but she does anyway. I guess the discipline of the Doric School's paying off. Priya asks to speak with me in private and we leave, heading for the dining room across the hall. There's a round table set under a chandelier in the middle of the room. I shut the door, a sinking feeling in my gut. We were so near, yet so far.

'How you feeling?' Priya asks.

'Like crap. You?'

'Bricking it,' she replies. 'I have to do this, I'm a member of the Society, but you don't, Ropa. You should go to Aberdeen and look after Izwi. She'll be left with no one if something happens to you tonight. I'm your friend and I love you. Please, now this is your turn to walk away, Ropa.'

I pull out one of the dining chairs and sit on it. It would be great to turn my back on this, to say it's not my fight, but these tossers murdered my grandmother. And I can't let Priya go there without me either. It works both ways. We just need a plan to make it through, but I'm coming up blank. Again, the only option we have is Callander's proposal.

'You're not going to leave, are you? Well, I had to try. Anyways, I need to check my chair and equipment to make sure it's kosher, ready for whatever happens tonight,' says Priya.

It doesn't matter whether you think everything's in there, you have to double check, and then triple check it. Once shit hits the fan, everything has to be on point.

'They'll need me tonight. I'm the one who can cast out the foul souls of those who are not in the light. And I'm going to send Dundas straight back to hell.'

'Promise me you'll be careful,' says Priya.

'You should have stuck with healing. Doing my old job's made you heedful, Ms Kapoor. That's an improvement.' I laugh and Priya catches a laughing fit too. They can take a lot from us, but they'll never take away our laughter.

When that's done a heavy silence descends. Callander's secretaryship is a very powerful position. He calls the shots and decides the future of Scottish magic, which is why this position is such a prize. If Dundas takes it over, then he'll be in charge and change everything – chasing goals which could only lead to more catastrophic consequences. Maybe that's why Lord Samarasinghe's decided to help us. He realizes that should the position go to anyone else, he might find himself squared up against a practitioner even less amenable to his schemes. That wouldn't please his master at all. Dundas was a powerful man in the eighteenth and early nineteenth centuries, so what if he has designs not just on Scotland but on England too? He can't have come back from the dead just because he missed the wonderful weather and haggis.

'Whatever happens out there tonight, I've got your back,' I say.

'Likewise, man.'

We fist-bump and she goes back to checking the kit under her wheelchair, which is bulkier than usual. This is one of those moments you want time to slow down but instead it speeds up on you. My anxiety's through the roof right now. Wedderburn always has a trick up his sleeve, and we've been bested thrice by my count. But you don't go to battle with doubt in your heart. Again, I've got to place my faith in Callander's plan.

'We're going to win this,' I say, psyching myself up.

'Amen, sister.' Priya finishes her checks and we return to the others.

I ride alongside Callander in his two-seater with River on my lap, the city lights going by in a blur. The vroom of his engine's the sort of power we need tonight. We're in a convoy, with Cockburn, Priya and Ms Featherstone bringing up the rear.

There's a travellers' horse-drawn carriage headed into Murrayfield, which I find odd. But Rob did say the Travelling Folk were in town, so whatever.

Callander's proper pensive, knuckles white as he grips the steering wheel tight. We're on Corstorphine Road, headed towards the city centre. I check out the gigantic Murrayfield Stadium where Scotland plays rugby. Normal rugby, not the magical sort. I snuck in there once as a kid with Jomo. We got caught, but they let us stay to watch the match anyway. The shops on either side of the road are shuttered. Remains to be seen whether or not those shutters will be torn off by tomorrow morning.

I do a double take as we have to slow down and go around some penguins waddling in the middle of the road – kind of random. Something's swinging in the trees up ahead too.

'Are those baboons?' I ask.

'I believe they are drills, closely related to the baboon,' Callander replies calmly.

And then we spot a lion with a glorious mane walking down the side of the road.

'Good God, someone must have freed the animals in the zoo!' Callander says, now with alarm, as though it's only just registered.

Edinburgh Zoo's only up the road. It's proper weird driving past all the liberated animals, who all seem to be headed into town. Like, I'm not for keeping animals in cages and all that jazz, but having Sumatran tigers and giraffes roaming free in the city isn't a great idea. And who knows where the zookeepers are at the moment, given the state of the city? The kangaroos hopping about are cute, though I worry they must be cold so far from home.

'What do we do?' I ask.

'We stick to our mission, Ropa. This is someone else's responsibility. Ours is the greater task that lies ahead,' Callander replies.

Reckon I'd rather take my chances with the wild animals, given his gloomy tone. We drive through Haymarket, where the cash machine near the station's been pulled out of the wall. There's debris everywhere on the streets, and a barricade's been erected on Dalry Road. I don't know whether it's to keep the looters out, or the police away.

'I was disappointed when you left after the events at Dunvegan Castle, Ropa. It's a pity I was never able to tell you what a fantastic job I thought you'd done. All the things that went wrong there were faults of my own oversight,' Callander says. 'You were one hell of a discoverer.'

'Water under the bridge,' I reply, shifting uncomfortably on my seat.

'I've placed responsibilities on you far beyond your years and I am sorry for that. As you have seen, the Society is broken. I needed fresh blood, someone with a different perspective, who doesn't have the old loyalties and prejudices. But I didn't do enough to shield you from the rough-and-tumble of our game,' he says.

'That's the problem. To you magicians it's all a game. To us in the slums it's our lives you're playing with.'

'I know.'

Still, the gaffer's one rich guy I like; they can't all be bad. The city's deserted tonight. The occasional group of police trot by on horseback, or drive around in riot vans. They don't stop us. In a car like this, with a man like Callander, it's obvious we're the folks they are supposed to protect. That and the property on Princes Street, whose shuttered shops don't seem to have suffered any of the devastation I saw in the Old Town. The straight streets of the New Town offer a disadvantage to the rioters. They can be kettled in and controlled more easily. Perhaps this was the whole point of the so-called rationalism of the design: it made people easier to control, unlike the Old Town, which was built to the texture of their irrational emotions.

A lone boatman's out on the loch tonight fishing.

The castle looms large in the night, bright spotlights shining on it, a not-so-subtle reminder of the king's power.

'You're not such a bad boss, you know?' I say.

'Very kind of you, Ms Moyo,' he replies.

On second thought, I actually could work for Callander again, for the right wage. After we're done tonight, I'll tell him I want the same terms he's given Priya. Might end up being the three of us in the General Discoveries Directorate – that'd be alright.

Thanks to Wedderburn's meddling with barriers and the everyThere, there are so many ghosts hanging about on the streets of the city. Old, misshapen ghouls, the ones who have no business with the living anymore, since everyone they knew should be dead by now. We drive past the National Gallery and the Scott Monument. The old writer sat within it seems to be scribbling a new history, one very much as dramatic as in his old novels.

I give River a wee rub behind the ears. She likes that.

'You've told me about Gran. I need to know more about my father too,' I say.

'He was a formidable man whose talents we've not seen since. I promise you that when tonight is done, I will tell you all about it.'

'You should have told me all this before.'

'I know,' he replies.

I want him to come out with it, but we have a situation on our hands right now. We hit the east end of Princes Street at the junction, with the Balmoral on the right hiding the sunken train station, and Registry House on the left, recording all the property the rich have in this city. I close my eyes for a good while as Callander waits for the traffic lights to change. There's a strange, yet familiar odour hanging in the air – something mulchy and rotting.

'I've never seen the city packed with ghosts like this. If it continues, they'll outnumber the living,' I say.

'We'll rectify those extranatural breaches once we settle this matter,' says Callander. 'Once I defeat Dundas and his people, your role will be to cast him out to the Other Place, a realm he cannot return from. Can you do that for us tonight?'

'Piece of cake,' I reply.

I try not to look at the spectres. I don't want them to realize I can see them. The ghost I got rid of at Arniston House, the one tormenting Sophie, fought harder than anything I'd anticipated. Tonight I'll have to do a better job, but I have a feeling it won't be at all easy.

The full moon hangs low atop Calton Hill, peeking through the broken clouds. A loud motorcycle pulls up to our left. The rider, in a leather jacket and tartan, pulls up his visor and gives us the thumbs up. It's our very own Dalziel of the MacDonalds of Sleet. He shouts something but I don't catch it because of how loud his Harley-Davidson is. The light turns green and he takes off ahead of us.

I'm buoyed by his presence. I've seen the Highland magicians fight before. They might be a wee bit uncouth, but they're tough as nails compared to the ones from this city. And as we go past the junction, I see Lord Samarasinghe's carriage coming down North Bridge, driven by his loyal coachman Briggs. The light must be red on his side, but he cuts in right behind us anyway as we approach Regents Road. Now that I consider the options in front of us, roping in Lord Samarasinghe was a masterstroke by Callander, and it simultaneously does away with the age-old frictions which have accumulated. I reckon even Bryson Blackwood would be proud of the gaffer.

When we pass by the Scottish Government offices, we take a left off the wee roundabout in front of the Old Royal High School. This road takes us up Calton Hill. I'm feeling more confident now. There's no way Wedderburn's lot can match the artillery we've got – we have the upper hand, and they'll soon find they've overplayed theirs.

The road up is narrow, with the face of the hill on one side and a fleur-de-lis-topped fence on the other. We reach the summit in no time, and see the pillars of the entrance to the Library under the brilliant moonlight. It's very still and peaceful up here, despite Dalziel's noisy bike. He stops just ahead of us, turns off his engine and climbs down.

'We are here, Ms Moyo,' Callander says.

I open my door and River leaps out, then I grab my backpack and follow her. The air up here smells like we're in a stagnant swamp. I shut the door and there is Briggs beside us, opening up for the Sorcerer Royal. Lord Samarasinghe emerges in his peaked cap, with his cape flowing around his shoulders, tiger's-head cane in his hand. He sees me and gasps with surprise, then claps his hands once and rushes over to me, a smile fixed upon his face. He stops a few feet away, casts his arms wide open, and exclaims: 'Ropa Moyo, still swimming against the current, nose above the waterline. I never doubted you for a second. Well done.'

'No thanks to you,' I reply sharpish.

'Oh, don't be a sourpuss now. We're all friends, and you have had the best of both English magic and the Scottish variety. I knew you'd make it. That is why you are my favourite, in the parlance of these parts, *wee lassie.*'

I roll my eyes and walk off before I'm tempted to punch the Sorcerer Royal in the nose.

There's a group of men and women standing on the free ground on the north side of the hill, in front of the observatory. They are all facing the Forth, almost as if they're tourists enjoying the view running all the way to Fife. The only one among them who deigns to look at us is Dr Maige, whose robes flow about in the wind. As we continue our ascent, I see Dalziel has halted next to a body lying in the middle of the road. It's that of an old man in a bellhop outfit, one of the quadruplets who guard the Library under Calton Hill.

Callander frowns and I can tell he's fuming.

'Cowards. We'll have their heads on pikes before this night is done,' Dalziel MacDonald says. He kneels down and closes the old man's eyes.

I feel River by my side, sticking close. And then Priya pulls up, looking proper serious like never before. Cockburn and Ms Featherstone arrive too, their expressions just as grim as the rest of us as we follow Callander onto the grass and towards the party of magicians up ahead. I check our flanks in case we might be ambushed, but the summit of the hill's pretty bare, so we'd know if anyone else was entering the fray.

Only Wedderburn turns to face us, forcing Dr Maige to do the same. He keeps his hand at the back of his prisoner's neck, and the head librarian's hands are bound together using the cincture rope of his own belt.

'Sir Ian, I am delighted you have accepted our master's invitation. It is a pleasure to see you again, old friend,' says Wedderburn. He turns to the Sorcerer Royal and bows low and long. 'The great and mighty Lord Samarasinghe, how good of you to join us.'

Samarasinghe regards him coolly and does not return his solicitous greeting. Wedderburn doesn't understand that the Sorcerer Royal dislikes flattery and respects only strength. The former rector of the Edinburgh School recovers quickly and scans our group. The spider is already drawing his web and I wait to see where the strands might stick.

'Avery MacDonald, this is your father speaking. How dare you embarrass us like this. And you, Fenella MacLeod, your clan and mine might have our differences, but no MacLeod in this age has ever stooped lower than you. Because of your shameful actions, your father lies raving in a mental hospital. He's no friend of mine, but I don't take any joy in his sorry state. You broke his heart and his mind both,' Dalziel MacDonald says. There's anger in his voice.

'Do not speak so harshly to the children. They have chosen duty to the nation over filial obligation. This is a brave thing,' says Wedderburn.

The last time that was cool was during Mao's Cultural Revolution.

'It's beautiful, isn't it? This sight I have not seen with mine own eyes in centuries. How changed is the Port of Leith. Where are the splendid fields? What became of . . .' This observation comes from a short figure with uneven shoulders, the left much lower than the right, who wears a navy blue loden cape. He has a tricorne hat on his head and a strange bearing – one so fragile it seems that the wind might blow him over. If I hadn't known who would be here, I would have demanded the name of this entity addressing us. His voice sounds dry and raspy, like the brittle pages of an ancient book being flipped. He remains still, admiring the view, even though all the rest of them have now turned to face us. The hubris oozing from them is proper winding me up.

All of Wedderburn's gang is here, except for Nathair Walsh and Lewis Wharncliffe. I wonder why they aren't. Maybe they're being held in reserve to spring up on us unexpectedly.

Doesn't matter, we'll take them however they come. I'd like nothing more than to tear Fenella MacLeod's face off. Jomo I would spank with my belt. I wouldn't give him the honour of hitting him like a man. I wanna kick all their faces in.

'We would rather not break any more eggs than we have to for this omelette,' Hutchinson says. 'Our intention is to save Scottish magic, and you are all talented men and women who will help us build anew.'

'What my esteemed colleague is saying is you need not die tonight, Sir Ian. Swear an oath to the first secretary, as we all have, and you will reap the rewards in this life and the next.'

'If he employs vipers like you, then he is not a man worth following,' Callander replies.

A flash of anger passes across Wedderburn's face, but his quick scowl is soon replaced by an even demeanour. The man in the tricorne hat finally turns slowly, pivoting on the spot as though his feet aren't moving.

'Mother of God,' Dalziel says.

The thing in the hat resembles only the shape of a man. Elements are assembled together as though Victor Frankenstein had run out of parts halfway through his project. The hands sticking out of the coat sleeves are dried-up and mummified. Though it wears a white shirt, this seems to be hanging off a collection of ribs rather than anything substantial. There's no neck, and the head sits directly atop the torso. For a face, it has the basic outline of one, with a shrivelled parchment of skin, flappy lips, two holes where there should be a nose, and slits where the eyes should sit. It's been knitted together using the magic of Gran's knitting needles. This is what a book returned to life looks like. It's enough to put me off reading altogether.

Behind those eye-slits a red vapour is visible – the soul which crossed over from another realm. I sense a feral hunger coming from it, and I should be scared, but with these top magicians around me I feel confident. Lord Samarasinghe appears more curious than cautious. Callander's stoic as always. Featherstone also appears unmoved. If they had meant to frighten us into submission, this has failed.

'I thank you for your services to the Society of Sceptical Enquirers, young Callander. You've done your ancestors proud. But I return to retake my seat,' Dundas says through those flappy lips.

'I am afraid that is not how we do things these days,' Callander replies.

'Then we must duel. It is the victors who write the rules. There seems to be so much of the old ways Scotland has forgotten. I've heard the cries of my people piercing the astral realm, begging for someone to come back and restore the glories of old. It's a shame I'll have to start by vanquishing a promising young magician like you.'

'The rules don't allow for that. You must wait until the biennial conference, sir.'

'So, the librarian is of no use to us. Kill him,' Dundas says.

'No, wait,' Dr Maige says, quivering. He begins to babble. 'The rules are archaic, and they were not designed to factor in a former secretary being brought back from the dead. Technically this is an interesting position to be in, and so the rules must be reinterpreted to cater for this unexpected event.'

I always thought Dr Maige to be straight as a thirty-centimetre rule. He claimed his role was to interpret the guidelines by which the Society operated as a dispassionate neutral. Yet now, with his own skin in the game, he is suddenly willing to be flexible in his interpretation of the rules. Typical.

'That will not happen. Surrender or we will lay all of you underneath the winter grass. You cannot hope to beat the two heads of magic on these isles,' Callander says in a grave tone. 'Lord Samarasinghe stands firmly with us, and behind him the might of the Royal Society of Sorcery and the Advancement of the Mystic Arts.'

Lord Samarasinghe clears his throat noisily and I know once he speaks this cult will have no choice but to fold.

'Well, Sir Ian, I did promise to stand with you, and here I am *standing* with you on this hill in the freezing cold. I've kept my word. But as far as I can see, this is a matter for Scottish magic. I am aware you have long valued your independence, so I shall defer and step aside. Let no one say the English go about interfering in the affairs of their fellow nations. Ladies and gentlemen, I bid you all goodnight.'

The Sorcerer Royal abruptly turns heel and begins to walk back to his carriage, leaving us dumbfounded. I know he's a man of unpredictable moods and I keep half expecting him to turn back, laugh, and say it was all a big joke. Surely he can't leave us like this? It's not as though the crown is served any better by having this Dundas zombie running about town. But Lord S keeps on walking and never looks back. Hung us out to dry like this morning's laundry. It's then I truly understand his nature. He was the same when I asked him for help. Lord Samarasinghe respects strength, and Callander asking him for aid was a sign of weakness. The Sorcerer Royal is a predator, and can't help but bite when he smells blood. I still don't understand why he would risk allowing Dundas to take control, though. What's in it for his sovereign?

'Can't trust the bloody English,' Dalziel MacDonald says, and spits on the ground.

As if to give a final insult, Briggs tips his hat and gives a wee bow right after he shuts the carriage door. We've just been well shafted.

Don't panic, Ropa. We're still looking good, our side's still formidable. It's better if we handle our problems in-house anyway. Callander's calm as ever, but when I look at the others I can see they're reeling from the blow. There's what could pass for a smile on Dundas's face and his soul glows redder than ever.

'We will forgive anyone who joins us and swears an oath of allegiance. You need not waste your lives tonight. There is no honour in preventing the march of progress,' Wedderburn says.

We all stay very still but there's a tension building, a static in the air that will discharge any moment. I'm reaching into my pocket for my katty 'cause we're coming to the precipice.

'Wait,' Cockburn says.

'Frances, don't you dare,' Calista Featherstone says.

'I'm sorry. Sir Ian, it's been an immense privilege working with you . . . but I can't waste my life fighting a lost cause. Maybe it is time the Society went back to its roots.'

And with that Frances Cockburn breaks the line and begins to walk towards the enemy. Fuckety fuck. She moves stiffly, almost robotically, as though compelled. I'm no fan of Cockburn, but for all her flaws, I always thought she was loyal to the gaffer. And never did we need her more than tonight. Wedderburn holds out his hands halfway between triumph and a warm embrace. The glee on their side is obvious. Now

I see the strain begin to show on Callander's face at last. Samarasinghe was always going to be fifty-fifty, but he could never have expected Cockburn to defect. It's the ones closest to you who hurt you the most. The field has tilted drastically against us. We are totally screwed in every single orifice and even in places where we don't have any holes.

XXVI

We need to bail and regroup. So long as Callander's still the nominal head of Scottish magic, we can rally again. There's no need to throw it all away on this field. That's what my head's telling me as the Dundas cult eagerly embrace Cockburn into their ranks. I wonder if this is how soldiers feel when they're on a suicide mission, knowing their orders are about to get them all killed. This isn't the time for ego.

'We can take these spineless cocksuckers,' Dalziel says. 'Every one of us is worth two of them.'

Wedderburn's phone beeps. He retrieves it, checks something, and laughs.

'It seems tonight is not your night, Sir Ian. Nathair Walsh and Lewis Wharncliffe have just reported that your husband has been abducted by the Travelling Folk.'

So, they'd sent the two lads after Esfandiar while we were here distracted? They probably hoped to get the flag and knitting needles back. But now the Travelling Folk have taken Esfandiar instead, which presumably means Izwi's been abducted by them too. I hope she's okay. This is all going bad. I need to go after her, but if I break ranks here then that'd be a disaster as well. I'm damned no matter what I choose.

All I want to do is hold Priya's hand, but we can't show weakness. Not now. Yep, I'm shitting myself. I just hope those wankers don't see my shaky hands. Fear is natural, though – it's what you do with it that determines whether you're brave or not. Everything rests on Callander now. He looks visibly pale. He's breathing hard and the mist of it in the cold air rises to the sky. His husband and my sister have been taken, but if I know Callander as I think I do, then the decision is already made for us. When he commands us to fight, I intend to lay everything on the line.

Calista Featherstone rolls her neck and flexes, ready for battle.

'Kill them all,' Dundas commands.

'Wait,' Callander says.

'Do you yield, sir?' Wedderburn asks.

'You invited me here to duel and I have accepted your invitation. A duel is an affair between two men, though I don't quite know if you qualify as a man anymore, Henry Dundas. Ms Featherstone will be my second. Let us settle this matter once and for all,' Callander says.

'It's too late for that,' Wedderburn says, pressing their advantage.

Dundas interrupts. 'Silence, young man. I've seen the decay of this age, the dismantling of the mores we laid down carefully to guide you in your conduct. I am more than a man, Sir Ian, and a god is bound by his word.' The words flow from his lips precise and legible, like the text of a book. He infuses each one of them with meaning as hard as stone. 'I offered you a duel and you have taken me up on it. So be it.'

371

'But you are not yet strong enough. We did not complete the process,' Wedderburn protests.

'One more word out of you,' says Dundas, holding up a desiccated finger. 'Who will have the honour of being my second?'

The cultists all clamour to please their newfound god. For the stupid thing called honour, we might have a fighting chance, and it seems we did do some damage at least by nabbing Sophie, the needles and the flag. All Callander has to do is kill a man who's already dead. Easy peasy. The only person who seems disappointed by this outcome is Dalziel MacDonald, who I'm pretty certain wants to kick his kid's arse. But there's something more important at stake.

I'm surprised when Jomo takes the centre, nominating himself as the Library's representative in the duel to oversee proceedings. If Oedipus ever had a little brother, it's my ex-best friend. Did they promise him the Library when they take over? I even find it amusing when he calls the seconds to him. He's the picture of a toddler stumbling around comically in his dad's too large wellies.

Calista Featherstone meets Viscount Mieville in the centre, while Jomo repeats the words his father once recited to me, when I seconded Callander for his duel with Wedderburn. There's way too much at stake tonight for him to pick me. In fact, I'm relieved. I'll happily stand in the terraces and watch. The negotiations are perfunctory, neither side is backing down tonight, but having seen Callander demolish Wedderburn, I can be confident he'll beat this grotesque book that's come to life. He is Scotland's great battleship, and gauging by the concern written on Wedderburn's face, Dundas has miscalculated. This ain't the eighteenth century.

Viscount Mieville returns to his ancestor, explaining the rules and the outcome of the parley. Henry Dundas places his hands on the viscount's face. Mieville tries to take a step back, but is held fast.

'You let your daughter escape us and so I am not fed properly for the task I am about to undertake. I shall therefore need your strength, my dear boy.'

'No, no, no,' says the viscount, straining to break free. But Fenella and Hutchinson immediately move in to restrain him, taking hold of his arms. Both of them have scratches on their faces from their encounter with Mrs Guthrie's bushes last night.

'But I did everything you asked of me,' he sobs. 'This is not fair.'

'Rest easy knowing you have played your part in my great work. The world only needs one Viscount Mieville at a time.'

There's the sound of cracking, almost as if every single bone in the viscount's body has been snapped at the same time. He flops back unnaturally, yet still the ancestor holds onto his face, drawing some kind of luminescent essence from his body. It seems to be extracted through the power of his excruciating screams. Unlike the essence taken from Sophie, this looks like the viscount's own soul is being sucked out and devoured by Dundas. The more he consumes, the fuller his form becomes. He begins to grow in stature too, just as the viscount shrinks, until his body flops to the floor like a jellyfish. Loose limbs and a misshapen head are the only things left vaguely resembling anything human. He has been reduced to a bag of flesh.

Henry Dundas stands taller, his figure more substantial, and where his legs had sort of hovered in the air like a spook, his feet are now firmly planted on the ground. He is still hideous to behold, though – definitely something extranatural and not of this world.

'Thank you for your sacrifice,' he tells the remains of his descendant, before walking onto the field.

Callander seems unperturbed, and has a deep frown of concentration on his face. He takes his place ten paces away from Dundas. The wind is cold and brutal on this winter's night as the two size one another up.

'Begin,' says Jomo.

Callander incants a black Zeusean thunderbolt and hurls it at Dundas. It lands true, with a formidable crack, forcing Dundas back a foot or two. The Black Lord gives a mocking laugh. There's a blast of heat that flows towards us, the result of an outstanding entropic shift. Such a lightning bolt would have dropped any ordinary man, but on Dundas it merely singes his white shirt, revealing the bones beneath. Callander isn't done, though, and he moves swiftly, already incanting a soliton and landing yet another blow. The temperature around us rises. There's an acrid chemical scent in the air. Callander dances around, creating angles of attack like a boxer who won't stay still. He launches a black thermosphere towards Dundas, who waves his hand, redirecting it into the air harmlessly. Still Callander drives forward, zig-zagging, changing angles and incanting at an incredible rate. It's as though Scotland's great battleship has opened all her gunports at once.

Dundas moves, but he doesn't have the dexterity Callander

has. He blocks a levitated rock thrown his way, and staggers further back, while Callander presses his advantage. I delight in seeing this ghoul, who would be a god, so roundly outmatched. Even his corner seems alarmed by the way things are going.

Callander reshapes the air itself and launches it as dark daggers aimed directly for Dundas's heart. The ghoul parries but several get through, cutting into his fine jacket and clothes, embedding into his old bones and soul. He grunts when hit and is driven back again. And when he tries to ward off the barrage, it's not enough to halt Callander's relentless attack. There's an unrestrained fury in the gaffer I've never seen before. The air around us heats up even more, as though we're in a steel mill and the reek of it burns the nose and throat. This is magic doing work.

'You are both skilled and formidable, young man. I con-gratulate you,' says Dundas, calmly stepping out of the way of a soliton and pausing.

I sense the subtle beginnings of an entropic shift, the building of a great force, as Dundas holds out his hand to receive Callander's thermosphere. This is about the size of a basketball, which Dundas intercepts then holds in the air, infusing it with his own magic. It pulsates like a star about to go supernova. The black sparks of Callander's casting become merged with a blue-white tinge, and it appears to be a violation of the laws of physics as the thermosphere shrinks to half its original size, yet possesses even greater energy. It diminishes further, until it's about the size of a small coin, and Dundas casually tosses it back towards Callander.

The ghoul turns away and goes back to enjoying the view once more.

This disc moves so slowly it appears harmless, save for a roar in the air, as though from a nearby jet engine.

Callander waves his hands, casting a heat sink which the thermosphere meets. But it doesn't slow down, and neither does the heat dissipate. Instead, it burns brightly through Callander's shield, continuing on its course. He responds with a thunderbolt to disrupt it, and where the two meet a sonic boom explodes, sending a wave of air that knocks us back.

Try as Callander may to hold off the flame, it carries on, slowly, relentlessly. Next, he tries gathering moisture from the atmosphere in a Poseidon manoeuvre, engulfing the flame in a water bubble to douse it, but it only burns brighter and causes the water to boil and steam.

Calista Featherstone opens her mouth in alarm, but she cannot interfere. Callander attempts to redirect the fire with a precise Aeolian hurricane, but it meets the hurricane winds he casts as though they were the breath of a toddler blowing out birthday candles.

'Move,' I shout, but it's too late, the spell finally hits him and his left arm bursts into flames.

Callander screams in agony, tearing off his coat and throwing it to the ground. But the flames on his flesh continue regardless, sizzling until they reach bone. I smell it burn. Priya cups her hands to her mouth. On the other side of the field, Wedderburn smiles broadly.

Callander falls onto his left knee, groaning in pain, his left arm ruined from wrist to shoulder. He's breathing in rapid, short, sharp breaths. And there's a look of confusion on his face. He tries to get up but just falls back to his knees again.

'Do you yield, young man?' Dundas asks.

'Ne-ver,' Callander replies in agony.

'I will give you a noble death. You deserve that much at least.'

Fuck their stupid rules, I'm a ghostalker. I won't let them kill Callander tonight, not on this hill. Now's the time to cheat. I pull my dagger out and break into a run, headed for Henry Dundas.

'No, Ropa!' Priya calls out.

'There are rules,' Jomo shouts.

I'm not playing their game anymore. I run past Callander, who is muttering to himself, my breath hot in the smoke-filled atmosphere. Dundas remains serenely enjoying the view with his back turned to me. Tonight, I'll be the one to cast him out to the Other Place, never to return. I channel all my Authority into this one act, this one shot, as I leap into the air, dagger ready to stab. Dundas turns swift as a whirlwind and catches my wrists.

I flail, dangling in the air, but he has me. The skin on my wrists burns and my dagger clatters to the ground.

'Ah, the little dead girl, we've met before, haven't we?' he says, looking at me through those slits he has for eyes. I'm defiant. No ghost has bested me yet. His arrogance will be his undoing.

'Henry Dundas, first Viscount Mieville, this is no longer your realm. You have no business here. I will not bargain with you, I will not negotiate, nor make any offers. By my Authority, I bind you, I cut off your tether to this world, and I cast you out to the Other Place, to the realm of no return, in which the gnashing of teeth is the only sound you will hear for all eternity. I cast you out.'

Dundas laughs mockingly and his cult joins him. Then he stops suddenly and turns menacing, his soul glowing beneath the dead flesh he wears for skin.

'No, dead girl. It is I who casts *you* out.'

'Eat my vag, Dundas. You can't—'

He throws me up and as I come back down, he strikes me hard in the chest. I'm driven backwards . . . I'm falling . . . My body crashes to the ground just in front of my old mentor Callander. But I keep flying back, my soul disconnected from my body. I can't feel the connection I had to it before. I can't feel anything. No heat or cold, the wind, I don't feel. No, no . . . I need to get back into my body. I try to swim towards it, but there's a strong force pulling me away.

This can't be happening.

Think, Ropa. Don't panic. You've been in the astral plane before. Focus.

I keep trying to push back, but the force dragging me away's too strong.

Priya rushes towards me, with River running right after her. She manoeuvres her wheelchair around Callander who is still prone and muttering. In one swift motion, without slowing down, she picks up my body and pulls it onto her lap.

'Stop her,' Dundas says.

Wedderburn lobs a golden thermosphere at her, but she veers west, running away from them. Avery casts a soliton which hits the back of her chair, just accelerating her further.

Her wheelchair bumps around on the uneven grass, gaining momentum. She veers left and then right, dodging all the missiles cast at her. Everything's going to shit. Fenella and Avery give chase, running on either side of Hume's Walk, the footpath circling the hill, in an attempt to cut Priya off.

I hold on as best I can, resisting the force pulling at me, but it's like swimming against a riptide. This has never happened before.

The wheels on Priya's chair clatter noisily as she tumbles down onto the path. My body flops lifelessly on her lap and River gives chase. She glances left and sees Fenella covering ground quickly, then checks right to see Avery sprinting to cut her off. But Priya keeps heading straight ahead, and her chair vaults over the edge where the hills drops precariously down a steep slope. Priya flies high into the air, tracing an arc.

She yells, 'ANEMOI.'

A trail of fabric and rope shoots out from underneath Priya's chair as it begins to drop to the ground. Gran's parachute spreads open in front of her, dragging the tilted chair back up into the sky. The wheelchair swings dangerously before Priya regains control. She flies towards Leith, then turns sharply across the face of the moon and heads towards the city to use the buildings as cover from the volley of thermospheres being thrown at her. River gives chase, running down the hill, but the flying wheelchair is too fast for her to catch.

Up and away Priya goes, still clutching my untethered body, fleeing our disastrous rout. I can only hover helplessly – even if I try calling out, she won't hear me.

Callander glances out, seeing her figure in the distance.

'Calista, take Dr Maige and go. I will hold them all here,' he says through gritted teeth.

'No,' Ms Featherstone says.

'Move, Calista,' says Dalziel, who is already running away towards his motorcycle.

Ms Featherstone glides at such a speed she's a blur of red, using the Hermes spell. She picks up Dr Maige, who is frozen in shock from the events. Wedderburn reaches for the librarian but is now blocked from getting to him. Hutchinson attempts to hit Ms Featherstone and Dr Maige with a fireball too, but it crashes against an invisible barrier. Callander has worked a spell, trapping himself and the Dundas cult inside a Newton Barrier, an impassable spell that returns any force cast against it. Just as he did around Dunvegan Castle. But he trembles. Beads of moisture on his face, a glazed look in his eyes, the strain of the defeat now evident.

'You can't hold me, Sir Ian,' Dundas says. 'Even Death herself couldn't hold me. Tell me, if I kill you now, will this remarkable spell of yours sustain?'

Even Wedderburn is moved. He takes a hesitant step forward from his gang, tilts his head, and regards his old friend Callander with pity and compassion. He holds out his arms, tears in his eyes.

'Please, Callander, don't be a fool. Yield now. It's over, my friend,' Wedderburn begs, his voice quivering. 'This is for the greater good. Give us a chance to show you the new, better world we will build.'

Callander looks up to the heavens, his expression turning peaceful despite his ruined hand, and he whispers, 'Esfandiar.'

Then he raises his good right hand high into the sky. There's a titanic entropic shift that washes from him into the fabric of Calton Hill. Lightning pours out of his fingers. Callander closes his eyes and bows his head. Suddenly there's a deafening explosion, a thousand bombs going off at once. Edinburgh quakes from the Old Town to the New, Holyrood to Leith, the buildings shaking. Nelson's Monument topples onto its side, and the pillars of Edinburgh's Shame tumble onto the ground.

And then, with an almighty bang, Calton Hill cracks. The ground opens up beneath their feet, it's hollow after all, and everything crumbles into the deep pit that's formed. Plumes of dust and debris burst out into the air, a carpet of it then settling over the city. The Library of the Dead is gone, swallowed by the earth, and with it Callander, Henry Dundas and all those of his cult.

I watch the devastation aghast. This isn't how we planned it; this can't be how it ends. But I'm no longer of this world and I am dragged into the abyss.

Fuck. Me.

About the Author

T. L. HUCHU has been published previously (as Tendai Huchu) in the adult market, but the Edinburgh Nights series is his genre fiction debut. His previous books (*The Hairdresser of Harare* and *The Maestro, the Magistrate & the Mathematician*) have been translated into multiple languages, and his short fiction has won awards. Huchu grew up in Zimbabwe but has lived in Edinburgh for most of his adult life.

Twitter: @TendaiHuchu
Instagram: @tendaihuchu